Love Letter in Cuneiform

Love Letter in Cuneiform

TOMÁŠ ZMEŠKAL

TRANSLATED FROM THE CZECH
BY ALEX ZUCKER

YALE UNIVERSITY PRESS ■ NEW HAVEN & LONDON

A MARGELLOS
WORLD REPUBLIC OF LETTERS BOOK

The Margellos World Republic of Letters is dedicated to making literary works from around the globe available in English through translation. It brings to the English-speaking world the work of leading poets, novelists, essayists, philosophers, and playwrights from Europe, Latin America, Africa, Asia, and the Middle East to stimulate international discourse and creative exchange.

Yale University Press books may be purchased in quantity for educational, business, or promotional use. For information, please e-mail sales.press@yale.edu (U.S. office) or sales@yaleup.co.uk (U.K. office).

Set in Electra and Nobel types by Tseng Information Systems, Inc. Printed in the United States of America.

Library of Congress Control Number: 2015942199
ISBN 978-0-300-18697-0 (cloth : alk. paper)

A catalogue record for this book is available from the British Library.

This paper meets the requirements of ANSI/NISO Z39.48-1992 (Permanence of Paper).

10 9 8 7 6 5 4 3 2 1

The lion, violent and sudden, expresses the present; the wolf, which drags away its victims, is the image of the past, robbing us of memories; the dog, fawning on its master, suggests to us the future, which ceaselessly beguiles us with hope.
—Macrobius

The essential business of language is to assert or deny facts.
—Bertrand Russell

CONTENTS

Love Letter in Cuneiform

THE WEDDING

Before Alice woke up, she had a dream that she was soaring or gliding. Any such comparison is of course too cheap to express the floating sensation she had. For a while she forgot herself. Then suddenly her heart reminded her, stopping short in the midst of its crow-like flight. She herself, though, kept to the hummingbird's path of her thoughts, until finally she took a deep breath and said it: *Tuesday.* At that moment it was all she could think of, subsumed in it, being it. Her day had arrived and she had begun to get used to the scent.

Between inhale and exhale, between holding her breath and the sparkling celebrations of pain in her lower belly, between the inertia of sun-basking to a copper tone and oozing tears of sweat quickly soaking into the bedclothes, two spots appeared before her eyes. She had to force herself to inhale. With some concern. It wasn't clear if the two dancing spots behind her firmly shut eyelids were caused by the contraction of her eye muscles and their pressure on her retina, or whether they might be viewed as something else . . . metaphysical, perhaps. After brief deliberation Alice decided for the latter. She completed the cycle of inhalation and exhalation, but no longer trusting herself enough to move, she lay motionless in bed, the spots circling before her still-closed eyes. One was the past, the other the present. It wasn't obvious which was which, but either way she felt that this was the most present, most perfect, and certainly most sweet-smelling day she had ever experienced. Suddenly she realized: Yes, of course — it was the smell! If she hadn't been in bed, her head would have reeled. The smell! It was the smell that woke her up. If not for that, she might have assumed it was the music drifting in from the next room. Alice involuntarily shuddered, drawing a sharp breath. Her lungs took in more air than she intended, and more than she was sure she could hold. She shuddered in fear, but the action kept on repeating, like she was drowning, taking water into her lungs. She ceased to perceive past and present, having forgotten which spot meant what and which one was which. As she opened her eyes, she was vaguely aware of a soothing tickling on the soles of her feet. Her eyes opened and her larynx released a sob. Then came an explosion, an eruption, a detonation, a sunny breeze, an avalanche, a downpour, a cloudburst, a landslide, in short . . . tears. Around her, around her bed, all around, in every direction, there were roses scattered everywhere. Every shade, color, scent. From the deepest black-red to the rosiest bright pink, from a brownish dark yellow to the gayest butterfly gold. They were all around, serving as her comforter, blanket, veil. Surrounding her, embracing her, refusing to let her go. And beyond them, beyond the land of the roses, by the door and on the windowsills, were lilies and chrysanthemums. The whole room smelled delicious. There were flowers everywhere she looked and roses everywhere she could reach. Today was Tuesday. Her wedding day.

She could hear music from the room next door. That meant her father was already up. One, he was nervous, which was why he was listening to music so early in the morning. Two, to try to relax he was listening to his favorite, Haydn, even though it meant he risked scratching the record, since his hands always shook in the morning, and three, she couldn't hear him humming along, which meant he was eating breakfast. Alice looked around and sat up in bed. The roses lay all around her, tickling the soles of her feet. And they were all fresh. How come I didn't hear my sweetheart and why did he let me just go on sleeping? she wondered. She walked out of the bedroom, down the hall, and into the kitchen.

"Where is he?" she asked her father. He sat in the kitchen, looking out the window.

"Where is he?" Alice asked again.

"Sitting, or more likely taking a nap, in the living room," her father replied. She went into the living room and found him there, half sitting, half reclining.

"Maximilian!" she cried, and before he could open his eyes, she realized that over the past few months her vocabulary had been reduced to interjections, euphemisms, and possessive pronouns, in particular *mine, yours, our,* and *ours,* all of them predominantly with verbs in the future tense. Or at least that was her father's observation. Maximilian smiled without opening his eyes. Despite believing herself immune to his smile after all these months, and even though he couldn't see, she returned his smile. Only after that came the hug.

"Maximilian!" she cried again. "Maximilian!"

Maximilian, name of a monstrance. Maximilian, name of the sun. An emperor's name. The name of a solar monstrance in a religious procession. A name with glints and rays of light shooting off in every direction. Depending on her mood and the condition of her vocal cords, depending on her weariness, energy, and joy, his name took on a different color, shine, and sparkle every time she pronounced it. It was a Loretan name. Lustrous, that is, as a polished diamond from Antwerp. Radiant, that is, loving. Golden, that is, all-embracing. It was Loretan, that is, every time it was spoken, one of the jewels in the monstrance twinkled with opulence and exaltedness, like gold and precious stones. He held her tight, eyes shut.

"Maximilian," she voiced his name again.

"I don't like to say it," her father spoke up from the next room. "Not only don't I like to say it, I only rarely think it . . . but before your mother comes, you have one last unforgettable chance to have breakfast with me, as chastely unmarried individuals, that is . . . So shall I put water on for coffee for the two of you as well?" After waiting a moment with no response, he shifted his weight on the chair, turning to the door several times to see how much of Haydn's sonata was still left on the record. He wanted to avoid having to listen to the next one, by Beethoven, who in his opinion had been grossly over-rated for more than a hundred and forty years. And on what basis? Alice's father wondered. "Ode to Joy"? If there was anything that distinguished the piece, besides the fact that it was used to mark the end of the Prague Spring classical music festival every year, it was its total lack of humor. How typically German, he thought. An ode to joy lacking humor.

"No intentional humor, that is," he said aloud. "Things, people, and ideas with pompous titles and a total lack of humor have always made careers."

"What's that, Dad? What did you say?" Alice asked, walking into the room.

"Lacking humor, I said. But that's not important now. If you don't mind, when the record's over would you two have some breakfast with me? I mean . . . that is . . . before your mother gets back."

"Well, maybe. I don't know," said Alice. "Let me ask Max." Meanwhile her father got up and went into the bedroom to turn off the record player, but didn't get there in time to keep the Beethoven sonata from beginning. Carefully lifting the needle from the record, he declared: "Even Schnabel can't save it. It demonstrates an alarming lack of talent and an exaggerated tendency to pathos on the part of the Bonn native."

"Who's Schnabel?" Alice asked from the kitchen.

"A very interesting pianist, who will be all too soon forgotten in this progressive era of ours."

"I see," Alice said. She dashed back to the living room. "Want to have breakfast with my dad?"

"It's up to you, Ali," said Maximilian. "Totally up to you."

"Well, all right then," Alice decided. Meanwhile, her father continued his train of thought to himself: Although Haydn is witty. God, is he ever. Even more so than Mozart. But is Haydn—German, or Austrian? That's the question. I wonder if it is nationality? I suppose not, that's probably nonsense. I don't even laugh at my own jokes anymore, he concluded. He slid the record carefully back into its sleeve and went to put the water on for coffee.

As Maximilian and Alice sat down at the kitchen table, Maximilian hoped his father-in-law-to-be wouldn't knock over the coffee and spill it across the table. He was always surprised that Alice's father had a clean dish towel prepared in advance to wipe everything up.

He was getting used to the fact that his future father-in-law spilled almost everything. Alice's father—like the stubborn remains of her parents' marriage—had long since ceased to be of any significant interest to him.

"Where did you get all those roses? Where are they from?" Alice asked.

"It's a secret," Maximilian said.

"Come on, tell me, where are they from?" she insisted.

"It's top secret," he said.

"The smell woke me up," Alice said.

"That's what I was hoping," Maximilian said. He laughed and gave her a light kiss on the neck.

"Alice said you were in Germany for a few days. What were you doing there?" Alice's father asked.

"I went to see my uncle," Maximilian said.

"Well, how was it? Anything good to report from the other side of the border?"

"Nothing special, really," Maximilian said. "My uncle wanted to show me the renovations he'd done on his house, but about two days before I came, he broke his leg, so I just went and saw him in the hospital. But I still felt like the poor relative."

"Mm-hm," Alice's father nodded.

"But," Alice chimed in, "Max said the train was delayed."

"That's right," Maximilian said. "In fact two trains were delayed."

"So the trains in Germany are delayed," Alice's father nodded, adding after a pause: "That would correspond to my observation."

"Which one is that?" Maximilian asked.

"Oh no, once Dad starts in like that, you know it's going to be pessimistic," said Alice.

"Well, after careful observation, I reached the conclusion that not only is the acting chaplain at our church not exceptionally intelligent, but in fact he's downright average."

"Not everyone can be Einstein, Dad," Alice objected.

"Of course not, for God's sake. I'm a fairly ordinary average man myself, and not ashamed to say so, but he's a member of the Society of Jesus, which is to say a Jesuit, and now don't get mad, Ali, but show me a Jesuit of average intelligence and I'll show you a dumb Jesuit. It's embarrassing and unacceptable. Think about it," Alice's father said, turning to Maximilian and counting off on his fingers.

"One, a dumb Jesuit. Two, the trains in Germany don't run on time. The next thing you know, the English will overthrow the Queen and declare a republic. There's something amiss in Europe, I'm telling you. Something amiss."

There was the sound of a key in the lock from the entryway, then the door opening.

"It's Mom," said Alice to Maximilian, running her fingers through his hair. "No, wait, there's somebody with her." She stood and walked to the entryway. There was a sound of shuffling feet and two voices, a woman's and a man's.

"Ahhhh, that would be the doctor," Alice's father said in Maximilian's direction. Maximilian just smiled politely. He had no idea what Alice's father was talking about. "And Květa," Alice's father added, standing from his chair.

Alice entered the kitchen with a man slightly younger than her father. He had his left arm around Alice's waist and was whispering something in her ear.

"Howdy, Doc. I knew it would be you," Alice's father said, shaking hands with the man. "This is Maximilian," he said. Maximilian stood and offered the man his hand.

"Antonín Lukavský," the man introduced himself.

"Also known as," Alice chimed in, "Uncle Tonda, alias Dottore. He's not actually my uncle. But he's a good friend of my father's."

"It's true. I am all those things," said the man.

"Max," said Maximilian.

Alice's mother entered the kitchen.

"Hi, Květa," Alice's father said.

"Hi, Josef," Alice's mother replied.

Antonín and Alice stood together side by side, watching Alice's parents.

"What were you doing?" Alice's mother asked.

"Waiting for you, what else would I be doing?"

"What was that you were listening to?" Alice's mother asked, looking around the room.

"Beethoven, I think," Maximilian said. "Wasn't it?"

"No, definitely not. I just didn't get there in time to take it off. I was listening to Haydn, Josef Haydn!"

"I just hope you didn't scratch it, playing it in the morning like that. You know how your hands always shake in the morning," Alice's mother said.

"By the way, you aren't related to the Esterházys, are you, Maximilian?"

"No," said Maximilian. "They go much farther back than we do, all the way to 1238. By the time they were princes, we were still grooms, at best."

"You see that?" Alice's mother said. "You see?"

"See what?" Alice said.

"The dish towels. He spilled again. You're going to scratch those records, Josef!"

"So what? They're his records," Alice said.

"You don't have to wash them, so don't worry about it," Alice's father said to her mother. "You know Haydn is buried there, don't you, Maximilian?"

"Where?"

"On the grounds of their estate. Wait now, what was it called . . ."

"He's going to scratch the records and act annoyed, and the main thing is he'll regret it," said Květa, appealing to Alice and Antonín. Antonín was doing his best to look anywhere but at her.

"I'm telling you, don't worry what I do with my records, and there's no need to concern yourself with whether I'm annoyed or not, since I don't live with you anymore and I don't intend to ever again! Now if you don't mind, Květa, stop worrying. Yes? Please? I'm asking you politely!"

"Oh," said Květa, "I didn't realize. I thought you were moving back in in the fall, after you finished repairing the cottage?"

"No, I'm not," Alice's father said, giving a shrug.

"Well, I'm sorry to hear that."

"I'm sure you are."

"So where did they bury him?" Antonín asked.

"Who?"

"Haydn."

As Antonín tried to steer the conversation elsewhere, Alice took her mother's hand and tugged her to the bedroom door.

"My God, that's gorgeous, Ali. It's gorgeous. All those flowers. And the smell! It's gorgeous. It smells wonderful." Her mother sat down on the bed. "Those are lilies, right? What are those, over there? And where did you get hold of flowers like that in March anyway?"

"Beats me," said Alice. "I have no idea. He won't tell me, says it's a secret. And once he says that, I'm not getting anything out of him. I'll keep working on him, though, and in a week or two he might let it slip."

"Now that's what I call love. But what *are* those flowers there called?"

"Which ones?" Alice said, trying not to prick herself as she gathered up roses from the rug. When she turned around, her mother was crying. Alice went and sat down next to her, carefully laying an armful of roses on the pillow, and wrapped her arms around her mother, huddled in tears on the bed.

"You knew, didn't you?"

"No, I really didn't."

"Oh, come on, Ali . . ."

"I didn't know, but I had a feeling."

Her mother's tears slowly subsided. "It smells so wonderful," she said after a while. "At least you're happy. At least my little girl is happy."

"Aren't I supposed to be the one crying on my wedding day?" Alice said.

Her mother nodded. "They may have taken away everything his family owned, but they still have their manners. So many roses, it's unbelievable." After another moment's pause she said: "So he really didn't tell you?"

Alice gave a noncommittal shrug. "Come give me a hand. We'll put them in water, 'kay?"

Meanwhile a few more people arrived. Two of Alice's friends, the best man, and another uncle and aunt, this time from Maximilian's side. Alice changed into her wedding outfit and came out to greet them. A blue dress, a light blue blouse, and a hat with a veil. A white dress would have seemed out of place in those times of hope and progress.

After coffee, cookies, quick introductions, and a few sentences about the weather, the wedding party and their guests piled into their two cars, plus the one they had borrowed, and set off on the short drive to a small town outside of Prague. Alice's father and mother each rode in a different car. A half hour later they came to a stop on the town square. On one side stood a small castle with faded sgraffiti and a priest sitting out on the bench in front.

Maximilian approached him, the two men exchanged greetings, and Maximilian introduced the guests, one by one. The priest shook everybody's hand, then led them through the streets to a church where the sexton was changing the papers posted in the display case next to the main door. Holding the papers rolled up and tucked in his underarm, he too shook hands with everyone. He unlocked the door, waited for everyone to file inside, and was just about to lock the door behind him again when a group of tourists appeared.

The sexton tried to explain that they were closed, even though normally the church closed on Mondays and today was Tuesday, so it should have been open. The most energetic tourist of the bunch had on breeches and a bright blue rain jacket. He was arguing so loudly the priest, briefly reviewing the sequence of the ceremony one last time, could hear him all the way in the sacristy. Abruptly, without finishing the sentence he had begun, he muttered something that sounded like "pardon me" and dashed out of the church to confront the tourist whom he had identified as the one whose voice he had heard.

The tourist, stunned to find himself face to face with the priest, fell silent. The priest looked him right in the eye. "The church is closed today for a special event. Any other questions, young man?"

The startled tourist looked around at his companions, but they just stood there closemouthed, watching him. "We wouldn't interrupt. We just wanted to take a look at the frescoes."

The priest put his fist to his mouth and cleared his throat. "If you can change into formal wear in the next five minutes, I will wait for you. Otherwise I'm afraid not. Do you have formal wear with you?"

"Formal wear?" the tourist asked.

"Formal wear," the priest repeated.

The tourist looked down at his clothes, then at his friends behind him. "I don't know."

"I'm afraid you don't," the priest said. "Do I presume correctly?"

"Pardon me?" the tourist said.

"I suspect you have no clothes other than the loudly colored ones I now see before me."

"Well yeah, that's all we've got. We just came for the day."

"So my fears are confirmed. Well then, seeing as you have no formal wear, I regret to inform you that due to the special event taking place in just a few minutes, I cannot allow you into the church. You are of course welcome to come back and tour our house of worship some other time."

"So you're not going to let us in, huh?"

"You presume correctly, young man. Nevertheless it has been a pleasure to make your acquaintance," said the priest. He spoke firmly but without a trace of irony.

The tourist turned around, and as he walked away, the sexton locked the main door. The ceremony could begin.

The priest gave the bride and groom a long speech whose recurring central theme seemed to be that the woman represents the body of the family, while the man is its head. Listening to his sermon, Dr. Lukavský, the family friend, wondered how much experience the priest had had with women, while Alice's mother, Květa, hoped her eyes weren't too puffy from crying. She was also glad the light in the church wasn't too bright, so the shadows were soft and nobody could really see her eyes. Toward the end of his speech the priest noted that in 1716 the groom's ancestor Jindřich had been elevated to the rank of count by the Holy Roman Emperor Charles VI, and that shortly after, his son, Mikuláš, had purchased the local castle and added not only a chapel but this church. The priest said that although aristocratic titles were no longer recognized, having been abolished by the Czechoslovak state under its first president, Tomáš Masaryk, it wasn't against the law to mention the days when not only titles and good manners were recognized but God's word as interpreted by the Holy Apostolic Catholic Church. He spoke about the unity of the throne and the altar, an involuntary smile spreading across his face during the boldest passages of his long-prepared speech.

Alice and Maximilian exchanged rings and kisses, and signed a document confirming that the state of matrimony was primarily a contractual arrangement, which at that moment was of course the last thing on the newlyweds' minds. After the ceremony, the priest invited the wedding party into the sacristy. Now, whether they liked it or not, Alice and Maximilian were on their own in the world. They answered everyone's questions, chatting about the declining quality of sacramental wine under the communist regime. Alice joked and laughed with her friends, while Maximilian drank a toast with a bottle of slivovice, which, as usual on occasions like these, somebody suddenly seemed to pull out of nowhere, but through it all, the metallic lace of their new situation slowly began to envelop them, closing in on them, fragment by fragment. Slit by slit the lacework net descended on them, enveloping them, protecting them, sealing them off.

As the state didn't legally recognize religious weddings, the bride and groom still had one more ceremony awaiting them. They had to make the trip back to Prague for a civil service as well. Along the way, Antonín thought some more about the sermon the priest had given. It seemed inappropriate in the emancipated era of the late 1960s, which believed itself to be, at least in *substantial* matters such as these, better than the ones that had come before. The time the priest's speech took up hadn't been useless. The objectionable nature of its content had been pushed just far enough that the moment when the bride and groom slid the rings on each other's fingers was more than merely a fleeting moment of fluttering bliss. The rolling back of the veil, the kisses and the signatures, had been a reward for that stagnant mass of intolerant interludes from which the sermon had been compressed like an obstructive obelisk.

Finally Antonín couldn't resist, and since he was sitting in the same car as the newlyweds and Alice's father, who was driving, he asked what they had thought of the sermon. Maximilian said he agreed with Antonín, adding in a slightly apologetic tone that he knew the priest had been preparing his speech for a long time and was very much hoping they would like it. What Alice said surprised him, though.

"What, did you think that he was going to defend the hippies and LSD? He's a priest, isn't he? What did you expect?"

"That's right, Toník, he's a priest," Alice's father said. "That's the way it's supposed to be. That's the way it should be."

When they got back to Prague, they still had an hour before they had to leave again for the civil ceremony, since the hall where it was taking place wasn't far away and nobody took it as seriously as the first one. Alice, Maximilian, and Květa brought out open-face sandwiches and wine and pastries, and the guests spread out around the apartment to relax.

A stocky man in a white coat and a flat brown cap drooping over his sweaty forehead rang the doorbell insistently. Next to him stood a shorter blond-haired man of medium build with a clean white apron over his light-colored pants and a white baker's hat on his head. The groom's witness was standing nearest the door, so he let them in. The taller man bent down to him and asked if he could have a word with Dr. Lukavský. The witness shrugged, saying that he didn't know anyone there and had already forgotten the names of everyone he'd been introduced to, but if they waited he would go find Maximilian and ask him. Maximilian found the doctor, aka Alice's uncle Antonín, and he came to the door. The taller man, in the flat cap, bent down and whispered in his ear. The doctor gave them a smile and gestured for them to come in. The three of them wound their way through the guests and went to see Alice's father.

"Josef, it's here," said Antonín.

"What's here?" said Alice's father.

"The surprise, like I told you."

"Oh, right, right. So you want the room for the cake, is that it?"

"Quiet," Antonín chided him. "It's a surprise."

"Of course. Well, put it in there in my old room. It's all cleaned up in there, and there's even a table."

They walked into the room. There was a dark wooden table with a folded newspaper on top, open to a half-finished crossword, plus a pair of glasses and a ballpoint pen. The man in the apron looked it over, removed the newspaper, the glasses, and the pen, took a tape measure out of his pocket, and measured the table while the other men looked on.

"Just under three feet by five feet," the man in the apron said disapprovingly.

"Not big enough?" the doctor asked.

"I said very clearly: I need five and three-quarters feet by six and a half feet. I was very clear!" the man in the apron said in an irritated tone.

"Well, we can expand it," said Alice's father. He looked at the doctor. "I thought you said it was going to be a cake?"

"Well, is it a cake, or isn't it?" the doctor asked, turning to the man in the apron.

"Of course, brother," said the man in the apron, who had already begun trying to figure out how to expand the table. The doctor gave him another questioning look, but the man in the apron ignored it and went about opening up the table's folded wings.

"It doesn't get used much, you know," Alice's father said to the man in the apron. "That's why it's stiff." He began helping to unfold the other parts of the table.

"That will fit. Yes, that will fit just fine," the man in the apron said, measuring the table with the additional panels installed.

"Now, I would just request," he said, looking around, "that nobody enter this room for the next thirty minutes."

Alice's father looked at the doctor, who looked at the man in the apron and said: "I think . . . that can be arranged. Don't you, Josef?"

"Yes," Alice's father said. For the next few minutes, as the man in the apron settled into the room, the taller, stocky man in the white coat, together with the doctor, proceeded to bring in boxes of various sizes. Each time they knocked, he cracked open the door and they handed him one or more boxes. When they were done, they stood in front of the door to make sure nobody walked in by accident. After exactly twenty-nine minutes, the door opened and the doctor, the man with the flat brown cap, and Alice's father were let inside. They entered the room and looked at the table. A marzipan palace towered on top of it, five feet tall.

The man in the apron was a pastry chef, that was now sufficiently clear, and what stood on the table was a combination of a Gothic cathedral, a castle, and a palace with multiple courtyards.

"Now that I didn't expect, Mr. Svoboda," the doctor said.

"Brother doctor," the pastry chef said, "a wedding, as well as a wedding cake, should only be once in a lifetime. May the bride and groom and their guests enjoy it."

After a moment's pause he added: "I hope, eh-hehm . . . that is, um, I think . . . I would appreciate it if I could say a few words to the newlyweds." He cleared his throat. "If it's possible, that is." He looked around the room at the others. The doctor looked at Alice's father, who couldn't tear his eyes away from the marzipan creation.

"Do you think that would be possible, Josef?" Antonín asked, but Alice's father didn't notice, just walking around the table, shaking his head, mumbling, "I've never seen anything like it" over and over and smiling to himself. Instead of answering the doctor, he turned to the pastry chef and asked, "What about the figures? Are the figures edible too?"

"Naturally!" said the pastry chef, sounding offended. "Everything you see before you is edible."

"That is incredible," Alice's father mumbled. "Truly incredible. It's a work of art."

"Naturally," the pastry chef said.

"Josef, do you think Mr. Svoboda here could say a few words to the bride and groom and their guests?" the doctor repeated his question.

"Oh, of course, of course," Alice's father said. "Just a minute. I'll bring them in."

The room gradually filled up. For everybody to fit, they had to stand in a circle around the table with the marzipan castle on it. Everybody went silent the moment they walked through the door. The conversation stopped dead and outside the church bells started ringing the hour, but nobody could concentrate enough to count the number of rings. Once the room was full, Alice's father looked around at everyone and said:

"Dear Alice and Maximilian, what you see before you is a gift from your Uncle Toník, and I believe he would like to say a few words. As for myself, the gentleman here who made the cake told me that even those little tiny minipeople are edible."

"So, dear Alice and Maximilian, honored guests," the doctor took the floor. "This is my wedding gift to you, and I must say, it's even bigger and more beautiful than I had expected. It wasn't so long ago that I gave Alice her vaccination for . . . for . . ."

"Tetanus, Uncle. Tetanus," Alice called out.

"That's right, tetanus," the doctor said. "You see, I still remember." He paused to look around the room. "But I'm not going to bore you with family stories, I just wanted to say that when I gave Alice the shot, she was so scared she crawled into a cabinet full of papers and I couldn't get her out. She made such a mess in there it took me a week afterwards to sort them all out. It wasn't that long ago, so I have to congratulate both of you now on this happy day, which I hope you will always look back on in those moments when not everything in life is going the way you'd like it to. So, once again, I wish you all the best, and I'd also like to thank the pastry chef, Mr. Svoboda, who actually gave me the idea of giving the newlyweds a cake. It really is a work of art, and it's much bigger than I expected, and now its creator, the pastry maestro himself, Mr. Svoboda, would like to say a few words to you about it. And don't be surprised if he calls you brother or sister. Mr. Svoboda?"

The pastry chef stepped in front of his marzipan creation, took a bow, slowly pulled from his pocket a piece of paper folded several times, and proceeded to read in a shaky voice.

"Honored bride, honored groom, honorable doctor, honored and dear guests, honorable investigator, dear brothers and sisters: Rarely do I receive an order that I am as happy to fill as this order from the respected Dr. Lukavský, who I hope I may declare as my friend. Despite that I have never met you personally, sister bride and brother groom, or perhaps for that very reason, I have taken the liberty of expressing in my creation the symbolic and universal qualities of the state of matrimony."

The pastry chef bowed again and turned so he had one side to his audience and one side to his creation.

"As you have surely noticed, the palace has three stories. The top one symbolizes heaven. This is why the saints, God, angels, and other special supernatural beings are located there, and as you see, it is rendered all in white, using marzipan with whipped-cream decoration. This is the so-called superterrestrial realm, which is beyond and above us. Perhaps someday all of us will reach it. Now if you please, notice that each layer opens so you can see inside."

The pastry chef looked around at everyone and lifted the castle roof so they could see the tiny figures inside, who seemed to be engaged in conversation with one another.

"The next level, the earthling level, is ours. Here we have a stylized bride and groom and wedding party, and as you see, the color is gray, which was of course created using a coffee mixture. This is the earthling sphere, as I already stated, yes, and finally we have the last layer, or ground floor, which is hell. As you see, it is dark brown, made out of chocolate, and if you please, chocolate lovers should direct their attention here. Through the windows you can see devils, satans, and a dragon or two, symbolizing the underground, the underworld, or hell. I especially recommend this level. I just finished the chocolate crème this morning using my own recipe," said Mr. Svoboda, looking up from the piece of paper his speech was written on.

"Looking at it from behind here, it reminds me of something else, too," Dr. Lukavský spoke up. The pastry chef bowed again. "Yes, very observant of you, brother doctor, very observant. I would expect nothing less, after all. After all, I'd expect nothing less."

"So am I right or aren't I?" the doctor insisted. "It reminds me of something, but I don't know what."

"I would expect nothing less. The brother doctor is a very observant being," the pastry chef replied. "Personally I think he's already here on the top level. I really do think so, right at the top. His soul is so full of compassion, mmm . . . compassion. I know his weakness, though, and I believe he prefers chocolate to whipped cream, which is on the ground floor in the devil's lair, so he'll have to descend into the underworld, mmm . . . But to answer the brother doctor's question, those of you who are more perceptive may have noticed that the frontal portion is, if I may say so, inspired by the Church of St. Ignatius, on Charles Square, and the decoration and inspiration for the saints continues in the same spirit. Of course, and this is unexpected, the main portion, the main portion, if you please, the one you were drawing attention to, brother doctor, is the unfinished cathedral in Prague, if you please, the one left unfinished by Václav, I'm not sure whether the Third or the Fourth, which has been standing now unfinished for several hundred years in the garden behind Jungmann Square. You know the one. This cathedral is standing there now, and I hope you will all find it delicious. Also I would like to point out that this entire combined cathedral, palace, and castle of cake is constructed sequentially, so as you see, it can be disassembled. Right here next to it I've placed a stack of takeout boxes, and each box holds exactly one piece of cake. So, if you please, no slicing! Really, no slicing, or the whole structure could collapse. No need to slice, just disassemble it. Dis-as-sem-ble! Sister bride, brother groom, I wish you all the best," the pastry chef concluded his speech, giving a bow.

As everyone applauded, Alice stepped up and gave him a kiss on the cheek. The pastry chef seemed surprised. "It's up to you, sister bride, which level you'll end up on. It's all up to you."

"Oh, come on," Alice said. "It's up to both of us, me and Max."

"Why, of course, that's what I meant, that's what I meant," the pastry chef said.

Then Alice threw her arms around the doctor's neck and the guests proceeded to circle the cake, peering through the windows, examining the saints set in the recesses of the facade, and breathing in the delicious smell of cocoa, coffee, and coconut. Meanwhile the pastry chef and his assistant said their good-byes and Maximilian and Alice went with Dr. Lukavský to walk them back outside to the street. The pastry chef and his assistant climbed into the ambulance that was parked in front of the building and drove off.

After they left, Alice turned to Antonín. "Well, that was a surprise."

"What?" the doctor said. "The pastry chef, or the cake?"

"Both," Maximilian chimed in, holding Alice's hand.

"Well, he's with us, actually," the doctor said. "A very interesting patient. I can tell you more about him sometime, if you're really interested." He looked at Alice and added: "I'll tell you more about him once I know more myself."

Meanwhile Alice's father gathered the guests together and they walked over to the wedding hall. The marriage officiant came out to welcome them in a black suit with a gold-plated chain around his neck. He explained who should stand where, and said they would get under way in a few minutes. They had ordered the smaller of the two rooms, but still, more than half the seats were empty.

"Well, you're a cozy little wedding, aren't you?" the marriage officiant remarked.

"If all my relatives were here, sir," Maximilian replied, "from the line that was elevated to the status of count in 1716 by Emperor Charles VI, after being confirmed as noble in 1578, we wouldn't fit into the biggest room in Prague."

"I see," the officiant said drily. His smile had disappeared.

"Thank God our socialist republic has ensured equality for us all, sir. Thank God."

"Uh-oh," Alice whispered to her father. "This isn't getting off to a good start."

"What's wrong?" her father asked.

"Max is giving that communist a lecture on aristocracy."

"Ah, the class struggle in practice," Antonín pitched in.

"Right, but we need his rubber stamp," Alice said, frowning.

"I've got nothing against the republic," she heard Max say. "It just bothers me that the state emblem violates all the most basic rules of heraldry."

"Rules of what?" the officiant asked.

"Heraldry," Maximilian repeated. "The system for creating coats of arms, state emblems, and family crests."

"So how does our state emblem violate this heraldry or whatever it's called?"

"It's a commonly known fact that the Czech lion can't have the Slovak emblem on its breast, since the center of a coat of arms is always reserved for the emblem of the ruling dynasty."

"Ruling dynasty?"

"Yes, ruling dynasty."

"Pardon me, sir, but we don't have a ruling dynasty. We have a government of the people, in case you hadn't noticed."

"Of course, that's the point."

"What's the point?"

"Since we don't have a ruling dynasty, the state emblem should be divided in halves or quarters, so the Slovak and Czech parts can be equal."

Alice's mother was observing the exchange from the corner of the room. When she realized what they were talking about, she rolled her eyes and walked over to Josef. She tugged on his sleeve and gestured with her eyes to step away so she could have a word with him.

"What's going on here, Josef?"

"Nothing. Just a lively debate."

"A lively debate? You realize your daughter is here to get married, don't you?"

"Yeah, so what do you want me to do?"

"Put a stop to it somehow, so they don't get in a fight."

"And how do you propose I do that?"

"I don't know!"

"What should I tell them?"

"Anything, it doesn't matter . . . Oh, Josef!" Květa turned around and stomped her heels against the floor, interrupting Maximilian and the officiant.

"Gentlemen, can we get started? A wedding is a big event, and the bride and all the rest of us are very nervous. Aren't you nervous, sir? What about you, Maximilian? I think the bride is about to faint at any moment. By the way, sir, I'm—"

"The mother of the bride."

"You have an excellent memory, sir. How do you remember it all, with so many new people coming in every day? I can't even remember the day-to-day things anymore, but of course I'm getting old."

"I don't believe it, madam," the marriage officiant objected. Květa grasped him gently by the elbow and led him away from the table with the refreshments.

Gradually the rest of the wedding party and the guests fell into line and entered the ceremonial hall to the sound of music from a cassette tape player. The officiant took his position behind the ceremonial table, his official medallion with the botched state emblem hanging from a gold-plated chain around his neck. There was still some nervousness in the air, and the officiant seemed to put more emphasis on the words having to do with socialism in his speech to the newlyweds. Maximilian and Alice exchanged rings a second time, kissed each other a second time, and signed the marriage agreement a second time. After them the witnesses did the same, and with that the ceremony was completed.

As they said their good-byes, the marriage officiant stepped up to Maximilian. "That was good with that state emblem stuff. Really great."

"Why?" Maximilian asked. "What do you mean?"

"Well, as it happens I was born in Banská Bystrica and I'm a Slovak."

Everybody went back home, the bride and groom changed their clothes, the men loosened their ties, and Květa sat down next to her husband on the couch in the living room. Once most of the guests were gathered together, Maximilian clinked a glass with a spoon and thanked everyone on behalf of himself and his wife for keeping the news of the wedding to themselves, ensuring that it would be an intimate affair. Then Alice stood up and invited them all to dinner in a nearby restaurant. Next, her aunt Anna got up and with tears in her eyes began to reminisce about Alice's childhood and adolescence. She had just launched into a story when Antonín suddenly interrupted to request that everyone raise their glass in honor of Maximilian's parents, who hadn't lived long enough to see him wed. Alice's aunt tried to regain control after the toast, but in the meantime the guests had lost interest in her story and, ignoring her, broke up into small clusters of conversation.

"Why didn't you do something, Josef?" Květa asked her husband. "Back at the ceremony, why didn't you do something when you knew he was a communist?"

"What does it matter now? Nothing happened."

"But it could have. You just stood there like a road sign."

"I couldn't even make out half of what they were saying."

"Then I guess you'd better turn up the volume on your hearing aid."

"I did have it turned up."

"You also have to make sure the batteries are fresh."

"Alice gets them for me. I even have a backup supply."

"So you really couldn't hear?"

"Yes, I heard some of it."

"All right then. Did you talk about it with Tonda?"

"Tonda's a psychiatrist, not a neurologist or an ear doctor."

"I know, but I'm sure he could find someone. He must have connections."

"It's just old age, Květa. Connections are no help with that."

"Oh, please. So you don't want to move back in then . . . Josef?"

Josef turned and looked into her deep green eyes. "I can't, Květa. Not yet."

"But why didn't you say something? I was already getting everything ready so you could have a room for yourself."

Josef laid a hand on Květa's shoulder, got up from the couch, and walked out of the room. Slowly the guests began to make their way to the restaurant, and at eight o'clock on the dot, after a few more toasts, dinner was served. There weren't more than twelve or fifteen people. The room emptied out by about ten o'clock. It was a Tuesday and people had to go to work the next day. That was the reason most of the guests gave when they left, even though they said they wished they could stay with the newlyweds longer. The last person still there with them was Alice's father. He settled the bill and the three of them headed back to the apartment. When they came to the entrance of their building, Maximilian and Alice said good-night to her father and announced that they were going to take a walk before they called it a night.

"Your wedding day only comes once, and in any case you have the keys. The church ceremony was very nice. That was a good idea, great idea. So is everything else all right?"

"Absolutely, Mr. Černý," Maximilian said.

"Absolutely? That's good to hear. How about you, Ali?"

"I'm glad you liked it, Dad."

"It was very nice."

"Yeah. It was worth it, Dad."

"So why wouldn't he let in that poor tourist?" Alice's father asked. Maximilian shrugged.

"And how did you all come to know that priest, anyway? I wanted to ask him, you know, but I felt embarrassed for some reason."

"It didn't take much convincing. He was the one who buried my father. He was happy to do it. Actually, it was kind of his idea. I was going to invite him to the wedding and he offered to do it himself."

"I see," said Alice's father. "Well, I think I'll go lie down now, and don't forget: There's plenty of food in there. They put the best stuff in the little fridge and forgot all about it, so don't forget to eat it. Even tonight if you want. I'll have my little machine turned off, so even the devil couldn't wake me. Just unlock it and take whatever you like."

"Don't worry. You go lie down, Dad," Alice said, giving her father a kiss on the cheek. He shook Maximilian's hand, turned, went inside, and the newlyweds went for a stroll. They walked down a couple of streets and through the park, but soon they got cold and decided to go back. Alice's father was already asleep.

Alice tried to stay awake while Maximilian was brushing his teeth in the bathroom, just long enough to say good-night and . . . I never would have guessed . . . being happy could . . . make . . . me . . . so . . . be-ing . . . hap-py . . . could . . . be . . . so . . . ti-red . . .

2

THE PASTRY CHEF

The police car driver waved lazily to the guard, who grazed his ash-colored hair with his index finger in an abbreviated hint of the usual symbolic greeting, and since the sun was out, instead of pushing the button that would connect the cables, sending an electrical current to the motor that raised the gate, he, the gatehouse guard, lifted himself from his chair. It was nice out, after all, the sun was shining, and he could use a stretch. He stepped out onto the concrete sidewalk lined with flower beds, twisted to reach back into the gatehouse from outside, and pressed the button. It was Friday and the clock above his head showed the time as exactly five forty-three A.M. The policeman's lazy wave and the guard's lazy salute would have made even the swans from the lake of the same name proud. The lazy gesture of the policeman behind the wheel represented a highly stylized expression of weariness from the night shift, a slight inconsiderateness, and at the same time an authoritative democratic-mindedness, which was nevertheless distinct from egalitarianism. For his part, the guard's precisely timed gesture in response demonstrated a moderate respect for the authority of the police car driver, who was bringing *them*—yes, *them*, since as everyone knows, the gatehouse guard is also part of the therapeutic process—not a *patient*, as in the past, but a *client*, as they were now called. A substantial part of the guard's choreography was his casual rocking at the knees—by the way, the guard had turned seventy just last year and had been doing this job for a good few years now and seen a thing or two in his life—and a substantial part of the guard's casual rocking at the knees was his nearly undetectable, incalculable, millisecond-long dwelling on his heels, which made it clear who was in charge here. And of course at the end came the trump card: he didn't remain in his cozy booth, looking out at the world from inside; he came out of it, though without so much as a glance at the policeman, an officer of the SNB, or National Security Corps, sitting behind the wheel; he just lazily twisted sideways and pressed the button from outside the booth, causing the foreign-made electric motor to raise the gate. Naturally the guard didn't give it a second thought, just as Paganini didn't think twice about how to perform vibrato in concert, it was automatic, the product of a lifetime of virtuoso experience. That's just the way it's done, boy, I don't care if you're bringing in a major from the parachute team. This hopping in and out of the guard booth in the morning mist is a double-guaranteed trump card, or a joker, if you like. It shows who's running the show here at the main gate at five forty-four on a Friday morning, friend!

And so the foreign-made electric motor proceeded to raise the gate at the main entrance to the psychiatric treatment center, its well-oiled sound carrying through the morning mist almost—elegantly. It faintly reminded the guard of his neighbors' well-fed angora cat, who as far as he could tell did nothing but eat, drink milk, sleep, and purr. The pampered bitch didn't do a damn thing else all day. The police car entered the hospital complex, the gatehouse guard rocked up on his heels one last time, and now at last the day could successfully begin.

The car pulled up to a pink-colored pavilion. The officer stepped out of the car, slammed the door shut, turned and looked at his two colleagues seated in the rear with a small man between them, then turned back to the building, walked up to the front door, and rang the bell. He waited a while, shifting his weight from one foot to the other. It was obvious from the way he moved that his concentration was slipping away. There was the sound of footsteps, then a man in a white coat and cotton pants opened the door, releasing a blast of sharp-smelling institutional air into the balmy morning breeze. It entered the policeman's nostrils without anyone bothering to ask whether he liked it or not, evoking memories of long hospital corridors. Corridors with walls divided by a stripe of oil paint running horizontally at eye level. The washable walls, tiled floors, and green and yellow paint always gave the officer a headache. He'd never given it too much thought, but the smell of that useless, cheap disinfectant interrupted his train of thought and put him on edge. If he could have, he would have sealed up his respiratory openings like an animal from some imaginary planet, or strapped on an oxygen tank like a deep-sea diver, so he could walk down the long green-and-yellow corridors without having to breathe that dishonest air. For now, though, the policeman just shared with the man in the white coat the facts that constitute the empire of the institutional universe. He informed the hospital attendant standing before him of the irrefutable facts, the facts of the arrival of the detained citizen, the facts substantiating the existence of one detained living body, three persons of authority, and one automobile. These definitions and descriptions lent his brief discourse the flavor of a meeting of medieval negotiators from a long extinct empire, who, unexpectedly and inconveniently, under dispensation from some imperial or divine authority unknown to them, are to transmit and see to the implementation of Kepler's laws of planetary motion, which neither of them understood very well, or which they both understood only *approximately*. And yet, without anyone's asking, it is their responsibility to see to it. It is their responsibility to see to the conjoining of two unconnected empires in accordance with laws they neither know nor understand. It is their responsibility to see to the transmission of a peculiar gift, a curious avian wedding ritual involving neither dancing nor praying. And meanwhile both of the pragmatic old fellows, even as they discuss the details of the instructions, are far away in their minds.

The two men stepped through the door and from outside heard the sound of the door locking. The orderly, leading the police officer, walked in front. After a few yards they stopped at another door, which the man in the white coat unlocked. He let the policeman in, then walked through the door himself and shut and locked it from the other side. The policeman had been here several times now and was always glad that he had not only his uniform but also his gun. His gun with seven rounds in the magazine, albeit with the safety on and resting in its holster, well maintained and well loved, giving him a true feeling of power that from time to time he contentedly felt spreading through his soul. True power, not papers and rubber stamps, not the filling out of forms, not attending training and learning new regulations and legal amendments by heart, but his well-maintained and well-loved gun, that was true power. If his superiors had known more of the world of his ideas and, God forbid, his private thoughts and feelings, they would surely have had reason for concern. He knew something fundamental, though. He knew that true power, whether the medics locked or unlocked the door, was slumbering in the holster hanging from the belt of his uniform, and that this true power of his had the number seven. The number of bullets in the magazine was the sum of his power. Then he reminded himself that his commanding officer had already negotiated everything in advance and impressed upon him the need to speak to the doctor briefly and clearly. Which the policeman had fully intended to do. However, at the last minute something had changed, and before they left the police station someone called from the hospital telling them not to come to the admissions unit but straight here, to the pink pavilion. Somebody somewhere had suddenly remembered that they had the detained man's medical card, so they had come here and the policeman was here now. On the one hand this procedure always surprised the officer, and on the other he found it tiresome, but at the same time it also made him feel his work had meaning. He had long been aware that it wasn't just catching criminals or maintaining order or some abstract idea of law. Increasingly, he found himself performing clerical duties, and he wasn't sure it was right. He was irritated by the lack of clarity, which nobody was dealing with. The two men came to another locked door, which was almost in the middle of the long corridor. The man escorting the policeman knocked and waited. There was no answer and after a while he gave the policeman an apologetic look. When he knocked a second time, the door opened. On the other side stood another man in a white coat and white pants, a doctor. He opened the door wide, told the orderly he could leave, and showed the policeman to a chair. The policeman sat down, nodded thank you to the doctor, unbuttoned the chest pocket on his uniform, and took out a small notepad. The doctor offered him coffee and a cigarette, but the policeman declined both. Although he had assumed he would just hand over the detainee to the doctor, the matter turned out to be more complicated than he had thought. The deputy chief at the precinct station had explained the case in detail over the phone to one of the doctors here, but as of this moment that doctor was nowhere to be found. Watching and listening to several phone conversations in which one of the doctors tried and failed to find the other one, the policeman realized that he would have no choice but to try to explain the whole thing himself. He wasn't happy about it, since that meant complications, but for the time being he sat indifferently, gripping his notepad in his hand and looking out a large, wide, barred window at the tree branches swaying outside. He couldn't hear the wind. He could just see the movement of the leaves and the branches, with the asphalt road behind them.

When Mrs. Marhoul, the neighbor of the later detained pastry chef Mr. Svoboda, called the precinct station, according to the police record it was two thirty-three A.M. Seeing as she was more than seventy years old and there was nothing unusual about her phone call, nobody paid it much attention. Mrs. Marhoul was an elderly widow who lived with a small pinscher, and the entryway of her apartment looked like a small country museum. There were two display cases of mineral specimens and one with polished flasks of various colors. A few pictures and drawings hung on the walls, showing views of Prague from different perspectives, and an unfinished drawing of a railroad station under construction that looked somewhat out of place. Mrs. Marhoul welcomed the officers in, but didn't invite them into the living room or the kitchen, instead sternly informing them that they had arrived more than twenty minutes later than their colleague on the phone had promised. The two officers felt cramped between the display cases. First because her dog kept walking around them sniffing at them, and second because the cases seemed fragile, shaky, and liable to smash into a thousand tiny pieces at any moment. It was complicated to avoid the pinscher, what with the display cases on three sides and Mrs. Marhoul on the fourth. Then the old lady decided to give them a lesson in mineral collections and the geological bedrock of Prague and its surroundings. Originally the officers had thought she was just being polite, but by the time they realized what was happening, they were up to their necks in an explanation of tectonic plates, fractures, and bedrock. It wasn't easy interrupting her lecture, but the more experienced of the two men awkwardly managed to turn the subject back to the reason for her call. She wasn't pleased, but she concluded her talk, saying that, as they could see, these specimens, which her husband had collected, and the pictures, which he had painted, demonstrated that the city and its surroundings were unrivaled. Unrivaled! She repeated the word several times with her index finger raised in the air. Unrivaled. Meanwhile the mineral specimens glowed phosphorescently through the glass of the display cases. Each piece rested on a lace doily, with its Czech and Latin names written on a now barely legible card. Before the police had a chance to ask, she informed them that the reason the framed drawing of the unfinished railroad station was hanging on the wall was because her deceased husband hadn't had a chance to finish it. When it seemed like she was on the verge of describing the last few months of his life in the hospital and the pulmonary sanitarium, the more experienced officer ordered her to lock her dog in the room next door or they would leave. That provoked the reaction he hoped for. The old lady was insulted by his lack of manners or respect for old age and finally got to the point. When she spoke about her husband's death, there was no longer even a hint of emotion; any feelings of pain or sadness had long since faded away. The seventy-year-old woman's account was more like a lecture on national history than an ordinary description. Her desire to hold up her former marriage for admiration was too great, though it was the matter of least interest to the two officers. It had never even crossed her mind to call herself a widow, she was just the temporarily abandoned wife of an irresponsible husband, who in his declining years had suddenly had the bad manners to pass away. She still blamed him for it and was building up a store of condemnations, which someday he deserved to hear.

At approximately one o'clock in the morning from the next-door apartment there was the sound of a scream, maybe even a struggle, followed by sudden silence. When one of the officers asked in a skeptical tone how the old lady could have heard it, he received an admonishing look and a lecture to the effect that not all elderly people were as incapable as the young generation thought and that they weren't demented either, or even just plain deaf. That forced the officer to apologize, which Mrs. Marhoul took advantage of to instruct them to take a good look at the shiny black stone, adding that silver was also mined in the vicinity of Prague in the Middle Ages. The policemen, having no appetite for any further commentary, interrupted to offer thanks, stepped back out in the hallway, and rang and knocked a while on the door of the neighbor's apartment. That calmed the old lady down and improved her mood, and afterward she wouldn't even admit to having had any objections to the young generation. Everything had gone as she expected, as she had hoped. She stood peering out from the doorway a while, but when nobody came to answer the door for the two policemen, the less experienced one told her they would have to search the building and the garden one more time, so she should lock the door just in case anyone dangerous might still be nearby. That made her happy, and she did as she was requested.

The officers searched the entire building but didn't find anyone. As they were going through the garden, however, they discovered some shards of broken glass from the window of the apartment the widow had told them about. They were aiming the cones of light from their electric lamps into the bushes along the garden wall when suddenly they heard the sound of uneven wheezing, like the compression and expansion of bellows in some human or animal organ, maybe even the tearing of a lung. Then a scream sliced the night air, from the canopy of the darkening clouds right down to the ground. A cry, a wheezing, a disembowelment. What surprised the policemen the most was that the cry was requesting their presence. Yes, it wanted them. It was asking for help, begging to be rescued, screaming for them not to leave him alone, not alone with him. Screeching and howling. The policemen switched off the safeties on their weapons and aimed the beams of their flashlights at the bushes where the voice was coming from. They could hear the voice running out of breath, it wouldn't be long before it broke. The beams of their lights intersected as the officers advanced toward the source of the uproar, in the bushes along the wall, looking back every moment or two, just in case there was somebody else around. Finally they pulled back the last branch of the thicket to find a man huddled in a dirty brown coat.

"Police," said the more experienced officer. "What's all the racket about?"

"Police?" said the man. "Really? Well, you do have the uniforms." That was all he managed to get out before he fainted. Meanwhile, several lights had gone on in the windows of the building overlooking the garden.

As they untangled the man from the bushes, the officers realized that he had a broken leg. They tried to examine it, but the man had wedged himself in so firmly between the wall and the bushes that it was difficult to extract him. When they finally managed to do so, the more experienced of the two switched on his transmitter, reported that they had found a wounded man, and requested an ambulance and instructions. The ambulance and another police car arrived almost simultaneously. Given the suspiciousness of the wounded individual and the broken window on the second floor next to Mrs. Marhoul's apartment, they decided to do one more search of the building, the garden, and the vicinity. One of the officers rode with the man to the hospital, in case they needed to write up a report of the incident and take a statement from him.

"The double break in his leg could be the result of an unfortunate fall from the second floor," the doctor told the policeman, who had spent all evening bored in an office at the precinct station and was pissed off that they had stuck him here, in surgery, to keep his eye on a guy who couldn't run away anyway. He couldn't have cared less about the description of a double fracture, and after the doctor had repeated it to him twice, he realized there was nothing else wrong with the suspect and made a mental note to himself: leg broken in two places—not going anywhere! Once the detainee had been examined, the officer entered the room. The man with the broken leg was lying in bed with several large pillows under his head. A smile spread across his face on seeing the officer. There were two other male patients in the room, one of whom kept trying to roll over in bed and the other whose otherwise peaceful breathing was interrupted by an occasional snore.

"I'll tell you everything," the man said to the officer. "Thank you so much, really. Have you caught him yet? He must be out there somewhere." The policeman shook his head, pulled up a chair to the bed, and sat down.

The smiling man in bed was named Karel Souček. He was a thief and had confessed to trying to rob the apartment on the second floor. He had accessed the pastry shop by way of a side street, walked through it, and jimmied the door that led up to the second-floor apartment belonging to the pastry chef and his wife. The thief also stated that he had caused minimal damage, as he had jimmied only one lock; the skeleton keys he had worked on the other doors. In the course of his conversation with the officer who took his statement, he emphasized several times that he had never met the owner of the apartment, one Marek Svoboda, pastry chef. The thief asked whether the policeman could lend him a typewriter, they must have one in the hospital somewhere, and who else would need it at this time of night—or was it morning by now? Just give him a typewriter and he'd tell the officer everything, a complete confession, get it off his chest. He said he didn't want to have anything to do with that nut. Never seen him in his life. Been in jail twice before, so he's what you'd call a repeat offender, but just stealing, nothing worse than that. All the officer had to do was write up a preliminary report, he didn't expect a confession, nobody had even reported a theft yet. But he couldn't fail to notice that despite the occasional smile he kept flashing so bizarrely, the thief seemed nervous. So the officer told him they would wait till morning to take the rest of his statement, since otherwise it would disturb the two sleeping patients. The thief agreed that he had a point but still suggested the officer at least take down some notes so he would have something to sign and later on he could prove that he had cooperated from the start of the investigation, right from the very start, he emphasized, again, several times.

Karel Souček had gained entrance to the pastry shop from a side street called Hlavsa. There were only three buildings on Hlavsa Street, the rest of it consisting of a six-foot-high wall around the garden of the building he had broken into. There too, according to his statement, he'd had to jimmy the door; that was the property damage he'd caused. He had walked through the pastry shop, sampled two or three cakes, but didn't find any money in the cash register. But that didn't surprise him, he had figured on that. He found the door leading to the second-floor apartment and opened it with a skeleton key. He walked up the stairs, and as he was looking around the apartment, Mr. Svoboda had surprised him coming out of the kitchen. At first the thief had been startled, but then to his amazement the pastry chef said hello, walked past him, went to the toilet, and took a leak without even closing the door. Then he went into the bathroom, carefully washed his hands, walked past him again, nodding hello, and went back to the kitchen. The thief was stunned, and being concerned, as he said, that something wasn't quite right, he followed Mr. Svoboda into the kitchen, afraid he was going to call the police. While the thief was weighing what he should do, the pastry chef came out a third time and asked whether he had eaten anything yet and whether he would like a snack. He apologized that ever since his wife had been gone all he had around was cheese; he hadn't had a chance to buy any salami or anything else for breakfast. The thief said this had surprised him so much he asked the pastry chef how come he wasn't afraid of him.

"Why should I be afraid of you?" the pastry chef had replied. "We are all brothers in suffering, you the thief, me the pastry chef. The sun shines on all alike."

"But the sun isn't shining now. It's nighttime," the thief managed to say.

"You're right there, brother," the pastry chef said. "It's nighttime in my soul, too." Pausing a moment, he added: "Help yourself, brother. Take whatever you need, or whatever you think you need." Then he just asked the thief to leave the radio in the living room, since listening to the misfortunes of the world helped him concentrate. And he needed to concentrate to be able to do his work. So the thief took some money and a few small items, but he was still nervous, seeing that nothing like this had ever happened to him before. He decided the pastry chef must be a wacko, so he'd just take what he came for and get lost. That's what he should have done, he should have hit him over the head and made a run for it. Then he wouldn't be lying here in the hospital with his leg broken in two places and all these other problems.

"What other problems?" the policeman asked.

"That's just it," the thief replied.

Before he left, he took all the money that was there, but as he was walking down to the ground floor he had a feeling there was something wrong about the whole thing, so he decided to go back and take another look around. He tried the door to the kitchen, the one room he hadn't been in yet, opening it as quietly as he could, but the pastry chef heard the hinges squeak and, back turned toward the door, bent over the table, where he was busy working on something, he said to the thief, "Come in, brother. Come into my workshop, where the vanity of the world is echoed and reflected. Come into my shell, my sanctuary. Come in, let me embrace you before your departure."

The thief had no idea what the pastry chef was talking about or why he wanted to hug him, and he definitely didn't know why he was calling the kitchen a workshop and a shell.

"I think I'll go now," he said, scanning the room with the quick, precise, experienced gaze of a thief. At first he thought he didn't fully grasp what he was seeing. There were human body parts spread all over the kitchen. Hands, feet, breasts . . . As he opened his mouth to gasp for breath, the pastry chef slowly turned toward him, still sitting in his chair, holding a woman's head in his hand.

"This used to be my wife, brother," he said. "She isn't here anymore, so I have to re-create her. That way at least the memory of her will still remain. You see?" As the thief suddenly realized what was going on, the pastry chef stood from the chair, the woman's head in his hand, and started walking toward him. Oh my God! the thief screamed in his head. Oh my God! No! He wanted to run but couldn't move, as if his heel, his Achilles tendon, had sprouted roots that were anchoring him to the ground. He couldn't take his eyes off the ghastly sight of the kitchen morgue.

Until finally, when the pastry chef was almost right on top of him, he screamed: "Stop where you are, dammit! Not one step closer!"

"Why not, dear brother?" the pastry chef asked. The thief couldn't even think anymore. Edging backward as the pastry chef came closer, he suddenly spun around and ran through the nearest door, spotting a window that overlooked the garden, a way out of that gloomy apartment of horrors. Imagining he could feel the pastry chef's breath on his neck, although in reality it was just his hairs standing up in fright, he shielded his head with his hands and leaped out the window, shattering the glass, flying . . . down.

A fierce pain in his leg brought him back to consciousness. For a moment the pain yanked his instinct for self-preservation out of the drawer of his consciousness. But then his fear of the madman returned and the thief realized he was now in the garden, bordered by a wall at least six feet high, at a great disadvantage, with his unworthy life about to come to an end. He realized that he should repent. Being a nonbeliever, an atheist, he didn't know the word *penance*, but my God, he now knew its measure. As best he could—atheistically, unbelievingly, hopelessly—ending his wretched, accursed, unhappy life with some semblance of prayer or godless appeal for the resurrection of his soul. He remembered a movie about a revolution he had seen recently in which the condemned men were executed by a firing squad. Arms thrown wide, singing a song, racked by bullets. He was sure a terrible death awaited him, maybe torture, which was why his soul now had to prepare, it was the only thing certain, there was no doubt in his mind. He had no weapon, and the moment he tried to stand, the pain was so great he nearly lost consciousness. So he slowly, gradually, crawled over to the wall, where at least he couldn't be seen.

He had to drag his leg behind him, making an effort not to cry out in pain. He tried but he knew that his wheezing resounded in every direction. He wouldn't be anywhere in sight when that monster came to do to him what he had done to his wife! He had to be prepared, he knew it. He didn't know exactly how, but he knew he had to be ready.

The officer who had overheard the thief's confession was both dismayed and pleased. It was horrible, sure, but it could also mean a substantial bonus, or maybe . . . just maybe . . . even a promotion. He got up from the chair, mindlessly ordered the thief not to leave the room, and went out to the hallway. There he grabbed the hand of the first nurse who walked by, pulled her into the room, instructed her to stay there and keep an eye on the injured man, and notified his commanding officer by telephone.

Another police car pulled up to the building, and the officers energetically leaped out. They surrounded the house and garden and secured all the openings through which the suspect might escape. In contrast to the original squad's investigation of a disturbance of the peace, the mood was completely different now. The deputy chief of the precinct was also present, having already woken the chief, his immediate superior, who had instructed him to secure the area, detain the suspect or suspects, and file a report with the Criminal Investigation Department afterward. Time marched onward before that could happen. In an hour it would start getting light. The police found the address they were looking for, turned off their safeties, one covering the other, and quietly stepped into the side entrance of the pastry shop. Quietly they searched it, two members of the squad remaining on the ground floor while the rest of the team crept up the stairs. The door was locked. After a moment of uneasiness they decided to force it open. On the second attempt they were successful. Several policemen rushed in and flashlights shining and pistols in hand proceeded to search the apartment. The apartment was quiet. All of the rooms were quiet, except in the living room, where a voice on the radio was discussing the nuances of international politics. After a moment's hesitation the policeman standing nearest the receiver switched it off. The house and its occupants were still asleep. The doors had been either fully or partially open in all the rooms they had searched so far. The only room with the door closed, a wafer-thin light emanating from under the threshold, was the kitchen. Two officers, safeties off, took up positions on either side of the door. The first policeman, who stood on the right, opened the door and the two policemen from the left rushed into the room, shouting, "Hands up and nothing will happen to you!" In an instant the pastry chef was flat on the ground. His hands were twisted behind his back and he was put in handcuffs. Nobody else was in the room. As the police led him away to the squad car, which drove him straight to the police station, the officers charged with securing the building until the CSI arrived began searching through everything they found in the kitchen. The thief was right: There was a woman's head on the kitchen table. A pair of breasts rested on top of the refrigerator, and part of the sole of a foot was on a small shelf over the stove. But when they turned on the lights, they got a surprise. They looked at each other, stunned. "Can you believe it, guys?" one of them said. "It's all made out of marzipan."

He was right. Only under the harsh light of the kitchen bulb did it become clear that the mess of human arms, breasts, feet, and head had all been perfectly sculpted from marzipan and other ingredients. The realism of even the tiniest detail was stunning, some of them even said terrifying. For instance, the hairs on the left arm were created from tinted caramel fibers. There was a birthmark on the forearm, and the ankle of the left leg had a little lizard tattooed on it and a strip with Indian motifs. The most remarkable thing of all, though, was the woman's head. It was wrapped in a scarf with thick black hair poking out from underneath. Her lips were curled into a smile and her eyes looked straight at you. Shining and alive, the only thing they didn't do was blink. The officers walked awkwardly around the kitchen, unsure what procedure to use in this situation. Just then, the deputy chief of the local precinct walked into the room.

"Good god," he said as he opened the door and stopped in his tracks. "So it's true. We've got a maniac here." Then he noticed the three faces looking at him and caught sight of the fourth member of the crew, who hadn't yet noticed his arrival and was absorbed in licking a human hand.

"You must be out of your mind," crowed the deputy chief. "You're suspended effective immediately." At which point the officers standing in the middle of the kitchen snapped back to their senses and started explaining to the deputy chief that what he saw was just an illusion. He wasn't seeing what he saw; he only thought he saw what he was seeing. We don't see; we expect, thereby filling our lives with undue disappointment; in short, it's all just one great big confection. Given this explanation, after a thorough search of the apartment failed to unearth anything out of the ordinary, apart from the lock the thief pried open, the presence of the police was left groundless and unjustifiable. Inhabitant of the apartment detained, thief in hospital, theft unreported, dead body absent.

"So what do we do now?" one of the officers asked. "There isn't anything here, so there's really nothing we can do."

That thought had occurred to the deputy chief a while ago, but he was hoping either they would turn something up or the chief himself would put in an appearance. He reached a decision.

"I want everything photographed. Call off CSI or we'll be the laughingstock of the precinct. Secure the premises temporarily and clear the hell out." As he left, he peeked into the kitchen for one last look at the marzipan breasts, the tattooed ankle, and especially the woman's head, the pupils of her eyes fixed on whoever happened to step through the door.

"That is one fine-looking woman," he said. But even before the last word was out of his mouth, he knew he shouldn't have said it. It was somehow . . . inappropriate. The whole thing was inappropriate somehow.

The pastry chef's name was Marek Svoboda. Medium build, average height, hair vague in color, manners unremarkable if pleasant. The kind of man who was difficult to remember. This indefinable fuzziness, however, disappeared the moment he spoke. For one thing, he didn't act naturally, the precinct chief observed. Anyone else in his place would have been intimidated at first, and then angry. Anyone else, after the police broke into his apartment, slammed him to the ground, handcuffed him, and locked him in a preliminary detention cell, would have wanted a lawyer, asked to file a complaint, demanded a written or verbal apology. Not him. He just smiled when they removed the handcuffs and said he didn't hold it against his brother policemen. They were all just brothers in suffering, he said. Calling them brother wasn't a violation or an offense, or anything else they could keep him in custody for. Nevertheless, the precinct chief knew the pastry chef wasn't normal, and there was something fishy about it. When he asked him why he had decided to make a woman out of candy, he said because his wife had left. When he asked why he hadn't reported his wife as missing, he said he didn't miss her because she had left with someone or left him for someone else. When he asked whether he could see her farewell letter, the pastry chef just sighed and said he couldn't because he had eaten it. When he asked him why he had eaten it, the pastry chef said he wanted to have at least part of his wife inside him. When asked whether he had killed her and wanted to admit to it, the pastry chef just grinned and said he hadn't killed his wife, he loved her, and asked the chief whether he had committed any crime that he should confess to. And that was the problem the chief of the precinct was now trying to solve. The man was definitely not all right. His wife had either left him for her lover or run away with him, but either way she was missing. He was making a version of her out of marzipan and calling everyone brother. None of which was a violation or a criminal offense. But then the chief got an idea. There was a law that said that a person who was a danger to himself could—even against his will—be committed to an insane asylum. Usually it was applied in cases of suicide, but why not this weirdo?

When the doctor heard the story of pastry chef Marek Svoboda, as reconstructed for him from the notebook of the policeman who had brought him to the psychiatric hospital, he wasn't pleased in the least. Peculiar behavior wasn't enough to have a man institutionalized against his will. Certainly, he said, the officer could understand that. If it were, they'd have to lock up half the people in the city. It didn't appear to be mental illness so much as what's known as a borderline case, somewhere in between a disorder and harmless eccentricity. The policeman was unhappy. They didn't have anything on the guy, which meant not only they'd have to let him go, but also they'd have to apologize, and of course he was the one who'd failed to get him into the nuthouse. The conversation wasn't moving in a promising direction. As the doctor rummaged around in a drawer, trying to find the intake forms, the officer, grasping at one last chance, interrupted him.

"Pardon me, Doctor," he began, "but the chief told me the person he spoke to said Mr. Svoboda had been here for treatment before. Is that true?"

"Yes, it is," the doctor replied.

"And what was he in for?" the officer asked.

"That's confidential," the doctor said. "I'm sure you understand that I can't tell you."

"All right." The policeman decided to try a different tack. "Could you go ahead and take a look at him anyway? He really is acting strange."

The doctor slid shut the drawer he had been searching in vain for the intake forms, and nodded. It was starting to get light.

Pastry chef Marek Svoboda sat in a chair across from the doctor looking calm and focused.

"Hello, Mr. Svoboda, or should I say good morning?" the doctor said. "I'm Doctor Lukavský. It seems you had a busy night."

The pastry chef gazed back at him, but didn't seem inclined to respond.

"Well, Mr. Svoboda, the police think your behavior isn't entirely typical and that I should evaluate you in light of what happened last night. What do you think about that?"

The pastry chef didn't answer, staring at the branches swaying outside the window. He seemed to be mulling it over.

"Do you think the police have the right?"

The pastry chef smiled faintly and stared straight at the doctor. "My name isn't Svoboda."

"Pardon me," the doctor said. "I must have missed something. It says here: Marek Svoboda. Profession: pastry chef."

"That was my name," the pastry chef said. "That's what it used to be."

"Aha," the doctor said. "Then what is your name now? So I'll have my records straight."

"My name is Jesus Socrates Amenhotep Hitler, dear brother," the pastry chef said.

"All right," the doctor said, writing down the full name on a sheet of unlined paper where he was taking notes. He was going to need those patient intake forms after all. Looking at his watch and concluding the head nurse might be there by now, he stood, opened the door to the hallway, and called to a passing orderly. "Excuse me, could you bring me some forms from the nurse's office? Three-one-fives, thanks."

The policeman, sitting on a bench next to the office, thought to himself, There we go. Now we can get rid of this guy without any scandal.

3

AFTER THE WEDDING—
FIRST MEETING WITH FATHER

After the wedding, Maximilian moved in with Alice and her parents. Meanwhile, her father repaired the cottage and they all watched captivated as he sawed beams, hammered nails, and mended the roof with precise, crystal-clear movements, movements that splintered apart into thousands of mirrored fragments, transforming his precision into a blurry silent slow-motion film the moment he climbed down from the roof and put away his tools in the meticulously organized wooden cupboard. As soon as he stopped work on the cottage, his hands began to shake like the leaves on an autumn tree, quivering before they break away from the branch and begin their waltzing descent to earth. The newlyweds had been planning their honeymoon for the end of summer, but in August Russian tanks came rolling into the country, leading them, like so many others, to consider leaving Czechoslovakia for good. It was their first fight. Maximilian wanted to leave, but Alice couldn't imagine leaving behind the country where she had been born, never to return. No longer being able to see their garden, their flower beds, the proud radishes, tomatoes, and tulips at their cottage? Giving birth to their child in another country? Obviously a child born in Germany, England, or Canada would be German, English, or Canadian, not that that in itself would matter, but she would never be able to fully understand her son or daughter. Added to that was the fact that all the tanks and demonstrations against the invasion left her cold and indifferent. First she discovered that her occasional rheumatic pain had settled down. Then she felt better every day than she had the one before. And finally she discovered that she was expecting. One day, as she was putting jars of preserves away in the kitchen cabinet, she opened one of them, sank her index finger in and scooped out a thick, yellowy, fragrant chunk of apricot. Maximilian, spotting her as he passed through the room, opened the sideboard, took out a teaspoon, and handed it to her. But she just shook her head with Olympian detachment. Little by little Alice began to understand something she had never noticed before. Every beginning, the true beginning of anything with nothing preceding it, is a little like birth, just as every ending is a little death. Feelings like those deserved the rank of cliché, she thought, a distinction of honor earned in combat on the battlefields of the body and mind. Ordinary experience, of the sort nearly everyone has, endlessly repeats until it loses all its uniqueness, and that was exactly what she was feeling. She saw the desire for originality as utterly absurd and alarmingly useless. The only thing that mattered, whether the baby was a boy or a girl, was that it be healthy. Paging through a disreputable oversized magazine with its weekly ration of curiosities from India, the latest advances in technology from the United States, and dispatches on hunters in Siberia savoring the meat of a thousand-year-old frozen woolly mammoth, tucked between a new recipe for mutton and modern fashion trends in Milan, Alice discovered an article on medieval paintings. Two of the illustrations depicted prideful saints and the third, the Virgin Mary at the Annunciation. Printed in color around the Madonna's head was a halo in a shape that reminded Alice of a bubble. Yes, a bubble, Alice thought. You could even say a bubble of God's grace. That was what Alice felt: the bubble of pregnancy was also a bubble of God's grace. The worst thing about it was that she didn't even feel guilty anymore for not feeling guilty. Their country was occupied, there were tanks in the streets. Her husband wanted to emigrate, her mother and father were sad and timid, and after a few weeks of quick anger they had quickly and timidly grown old. But it made absolutely, positively no difference at all to her, since she was expecting a child.

When Alice looked at the picture with the angel announcing to Mary that she was to be the Mother of God, it was immediately obvious to her that whatever weary, hunched medieval painter had created the image, he must have inquired of his beloved medieval wives, his lovers and the mothers of his children, what God's grace actually was, and apparently he had been well informed, since how else could someone like him—a mere man—have drawn that rapturous bubble of God's grace which she herself had felt. Alice knew nothing about the accounts of the medieval mystics; she knew nothing about their ecstasies, about radiant darkness and their mystical inability to distinguish between themselves and God's glory stretching into the infinite universe. Maximilian noticed the change this *expecting* had caused in her, and being a mere man he tried merely to understand. Yet Alice didn't know how to tell him. How to explain the state of pregnancy to someone she loved absolutely and with no reservations, how to explain something to him that he could never experience. She ran up against the barrier of language, the stone chasm suddenly stretching between them from top to bottom. And then, all of a sudden one day, right after waking up, it hit her: "Bliss, Maximilian. Carrying our child is bliss. I think that's what it was like when people still believed in heaven. Though actually . . . it's probably much better!" It was nine months in a bubble of God, and Alice wished it would never end. So when Maximilian handed her a medium-sized teaspoon as her index finger bore a mass of pungent orange-colored apricot jam to her mouth, she just cast an unconcerned look at his astonished face and with indifferent delight let the fragrant matter dissolve first on her tongue, then in her mouth, before letting its sweet taste with a touch of tart soak into her palate and swallowing, or, to be more precise, letting it slide gently and with visible pleasure down her throat. Maximilian stood before her, hand outstretched in a gesture of unneeded assistance. He stood watching his alluring wife, sitting there over her morning coffee not caring one iota what anyone thought of her, what anyone felt, just absolutely content with herself and her life. After swallowing the jam, she licked off her index finger with relish, making a sound with her mouth that could be classified either as satisfaction, pleasure, or a crude, somewhat apathetic smack. Maximilian was suddenly at a loss as to how to interpret the sound, or how it should be interpreted.

"So I guess you don't want the spoon, huh?" he said when she was done. And in the time it took Alice to raise her eyes, he added, "How come?"

She replied: "I want to savor it with all my senses." If later Maximilian had thought back on his life with Alice, if he had ever taken the time to consider their relationship, he would have arrived here, at this swallowing of the jam with a piercing smack that he didn't understand, the moment in which Alice began to be lost to him. Snug inside the opium bubble of sweetness that was her pregnant existence, Alice gradually ceased to be a lover and became permanently and irrevocably a mother. The state of fatherhood certainly couldn't compare, and that was the reality Maximilian feared. Like Alice, he didn't hide his feelings much, and when he shared how he felt with his friend Honza, a design engineer of transistor radios and portable reel-to-reel tape players, a Christian, a father of firm morals and four children, his friend told him:

"You know, Max, every woman who gets pregnant and has a child is like a diode. I know it sounds strange, but I specialize in low-voltage electrotechnology, and there's no better way for me to explain." Maximilian didn't know what the function of a diode was, so he asked his friend what he meant by this odd analogy.

"A diode conducts current in only one direction, and once a woman has a child she's never the same again. From then on, you'll always come second for her," Honza said. "It's normal, it's fine. Get used to it, Max! The sooner you do, the sooner you'll be able to take it easy." Maximilian was so exhausted by his friend's lengthy electro-ethical analogy that he gave up on even trying to understand, though he sensed that what he didn't grasp would make loving it all the more difficult.

When the boy was born, for Alice it was an unpleasant awakening from nine long months of bliss. Suddenly she began to worry about the things Maximilian had been worrying about for months.

She had terrifying dreams, a desire to leave her country forever, and was surprised at the most inconvenient moments by sudden bouts of prolonged arthritic pain. She wanted to leave, run away with her child and husband, and hide somewhere where there would be peace and quiet and no Russian soldiers. The problem was that when everybody had been trying to persuade her of that while she was pregnant, she persuaded them of the opposite, and nobody had the will or the energy left to do it anymore. The child was named Kryštof, and a few months after he was born, Alice got the urge to have another. It wasn't a child she wanted; it was the state of pregnancy she missed. Her uncle Antonín the doctor, after sending her for a few tests and examinations, told her something about hormones and the levels of some substance or other in the blood, but it sounded too scholarly and too Latin to actually explain anything.

Alice was born in 1950, a few months before her father was arrested, convicted, and sent to prison. Alice didn't remember any of it; she knew the whole thing only from the stories and recollections of her relatives. Her mother went to visit him every month. Sometimes Alice went with her, but they wouldn't let her inside anyway, so she stayed with her aunt in the neighboring town. Then one day, after ten years, her father showed up at home. Alice knew him from stories and photographs. She received letters from him, which her mother read to her until she learned to read and could read them for herself. Although she did her best to hide it, her mother wasn't glad to get his letters. Most of the time she cried and Alice knew it, even though her mother tried not to let her see. And then one day, after her tenth birthday had passed, they let her father out. Alice was looking forward to it. They were all looking forward, and they were all nervous and happy. When they first locked him up, her mother made the rounds of the offices, then various relatives and acquaintances increasingly visited them, together with her mother reading through heaps of papers, which they then filled out and which they discussed in a language Alice didn't understand. Then one day her mother said she had a big surprise for her: her father would be coming home in two weeks. They were letting him out after ten years, instead of thirteen as the original sentence had called for, and he would be living with them again. Alice didn't really understand when her mother said her father was coming back home, since as far as Alice remembered he had never lived with them. For her it couldn't be a return since she had never seen him leave. Her father was due home from prison on a Thursday. The two weeks with her mother till then were unbearable. Alice couldn't figure out what was wrong. If nothing else she was glad her dad was coming home, since they hadn't been allowed to talk much about his being in prison. All Alice knew was that, as her uncle Antonín put it, her father was a brave man who had stood up to injustice, and that was why they had put him in jail. This regime, Uncle Antonín went on, were all just a bunch of criminals, you couldn't expect anything good from them. Alice didn't really understand what a regime was, but she figured it must be someone important like the school inspector, who not only her teacher Mrs. Svobodová feared, but even the principal of the school, Mrs. Krausová, and that was something. Alice also knew there were things she could talk about only at home, not at school or in shops or on the street. She was looking forward to her daddy coming home, even if her mother was constantly washing, tidying, rearranging things, and dusting. One day Alice overheard her asking Antonín whether or not she should repaint. He convinced her she shouldn't, saying:

"Take it easy, Květuš. When Josef comes home, he can repaint. You can do it together if you want." At which her mother, as usual, broke down in tears. Why her mother was crying over painting the apartment, Alice truly could not conceive.

Her uncle Antonín also brought pills that her mother sometimes took, which made her calmer, but still, every now and then, for instance when they were standing in line at the bakery, all of a sudden tears would start rolling down her mother's face, and when Alice tugged on her sleeve either her mother refused to talk or she would just say the bakery didn't have such and such a dessert, like Sacher torte, which her daddy loved. Everything connected with her father was sad, so slowly but surely Alice stopped loving him, because every time she remembered him her mother cried and it wasn't really clear at all why. The apartment was tidied, the windows washed, flowers replanted, her mother even checked Alice's toys at least four times. It had gotten to be too much to take, so Alice spent as much time as she could at her friend Tereza's. Her mother left her over there sometimes, since Tereza's grandfather was also in prison, though a different one than her dad. There was a picture of him in their living room: a big powerful man with a big belly, a large mustache, and a gaze that pierced to the bone. He had one hand tucked in the pocket of his waistcoat with a watch chain hanging out of it, and Tereza's grandmother always said he was a good man and didn't deserve it. Alice didn't believe her, though, since in the photograph he looked really strict and unfriendly. And besides, his belly was so big and looked just as strict as his mustache and his implacable gaze.

On Tuesday, Tereza went over to Alice's in the afternoon so they could do homework together. The past few weeks Alice's mother had been buying all sorts of things they'd never had at home before: lipsticks, combs, compacts, even a few little bottles of perfume. Alice and Tereza tried them all. They had permission from Alice's mother, though they were instructed to be very careful with everything, as it cost a lot of money. When the doorbell rang, they were sure it was going to be their neighbor Mrs. Poláčková, either asking to borrow flour, eggs, milk, yeast, or something else, or asking for the flour, eggs, milk, yeast, or something else to be returned. The two girls looked at each other and grinned.

"Poláčková?" Tereza said.

Alice grinned again. "I don't suppose you have any yeast, sweetie?" she said, then went to answer the door. She looked out the peephole but didn't see anyone. It wasn't Poláčková then. Poláčková always stood so you could see her through the peephole. Alice turned and went back to Tereza.

"Who was it?" asked Tereza.

"Nobody," said Alice. "There's nobody there, and if there's nobody there, we can't open the door for them."

After a moment, the doorbell rang again. The two girls got up and went to the door to look.

"Somebody's there," said Tereza. "Take a look." Alice looked and saw a man standing with his back to the door, holding a bag in his hand. The girls looked at each other again and Alice opened the door to find her father standing there. She recognized it was him right away because there were photos of him all over their apartment, most of all in her mother's room. But he was much, much skinnier than in the photographs.

"Hello, Alice," he said.

Alice stood holding the door handle. "Hello, sir."

"I'm your daddy, Alice," the man said.

"I know, sir," said Alice.

"May I come in?" her father asked.

"Yes, Mr. Daddy," Alice said, glancing uncertainly at Tereza. Tereza stood in the corner of the entryway, silently taking it all in. Alice's father stepped into the entryway and saw her. "You must be Tereza, right?"

"Yes, sir," answered Tereza. Then after a moment's hesitation she asked: "Are you Alice's daddy?"

"Yes, I am," he said.

"OK," said Tereza. The man closed the door behind him, bent over, picked Alice up in his arms, and lifted her to the ceiling. Alice didn't know what to do, but whenever Uncle Antonín, Aunt Šárka, or Uncle Bedřich picked her up like that, she would wrap her arms around their neck. So now she did the same. The man began to laugh, which Alice liked, but he was also making her face wet, which she didn't like so much, since she and Tereza had just been trying on a new, glorious-smelling pink face powder. She pulled away, trying to sneak a look at him as he held her high above the ground. After a while he set her back down, pulled a large handkerchief from his pocket, and blew his nose. That got Alice's attention, since neither she nor her mother ever used a handkerchief that big. She knew there were others like it ironed, folded, and stacked in her mother's closet, with the rest of her father's things. Those handkerchiefs were reserved for use on scraped knees or fingers cut while chopping onions or carrots; you didn't blow your nose in them. Afterward they went in with the dirty laundry, to be boiled, ironed, and folded in stacks in the closet in her mother's room. Alice turned and ran off to her mother's room. She opened the closet, took two huge, freshly ironed handkerchiefs from the stack, still smelling of detergent, returned with them to her father in the entryway, and deposited them in his hand. Her father gave them a quick glance, no longer smiling, then all of a sudden he stared Alice straight in the eye so hard it made her shudder. If she had been eating, she was sure she would have choked. The look in his eyes was so stern, she didn't even dare breathe. She decided later she'd have to talk it over with Tereza. After all, he shouldn't look at her like that, such an odd, stern look, when she hadn't done anything. Then the man raised his eyes from her, looked around the entryway, and ran his hands through her hair. Alice knew grown-ups did that when they wanted to be nice to a child and didn't know what to say. Meanwhile Tereza put on her shoes, bowed to her father, told Alice good-bye, and went home. She didn't know exactly why but she felt superfluous.

Alice's father went into the kitchen, opened the cupboard, took out a large earthenware mug from the second row that nobody else ever used, and unerringly reached for the shelf where the big can of coffee was stored. He knows his way around, Alice thought. My dad. He knows his way around here. At home, here in my kitchen.

She had been so excited, so scared, so angry at him, and now she had no idea what to do with this big, tall man. So she just stood there, looking up at him, him looking down at her—he was a lot taller than her mom—until it got a little uncomfortable and started to make her dizzy.

"Where's Mommy?" he asked once he'd made himself coffee. He sat down at the table and looked at his daughter.

"Running errands," Alice said. "Also, she told me you weren't coming till Thursday." They sat in the kitchen a while. Then she showed him around the apartment. Not much had changed in ten years. He was surprised at how formal she was with him compared to the way she'd been in their letters, and he marveled at what a big girl he had for a daughter. In the last photo he'd seen of her, she was barely six months old. Alice, on the other hand, marveled at the fact that in spite of his height he didn't run into anything, deftly steering clear of the lamps in the kitchen and the living room, and at the way sometimes when he ran his hand through her hair, his palm was so dry the calluses caught on her hair. She also noticed his skin caught on the fabric of her blouse when he stroked her arms and shoulders, and she was a little worried he might tear it. His hands were so hard they were like a grater, and they definitely needed a manicure, or at least a proper greasing with some really oily cream, the kind her mom and Aunt Šárka used, but she didn't dare say so out loud. She would have told anyone else, but he was her father, and that was totally different. Neither of them afterward would remember how long she spent showing him the living room, kitchen, and entryway, or how many times she repeated the names of her three dolls, which evaporated from his head as quickly as she said them. Alice noticed that he did some strange things, like sitting down on the ground a few times, on the floor in the bedroom, for instance, and leaning against the bed, which everyone knew you shouldn't do. The ground isn't for sitting on, even if there's a carpet on it. You sit in a chair or an armchair. You can play on the ground, but only when you're little, not like her. Alice didn't know how to tell him, though, since he was so big and she was still a little afraid of him. And then, all of a sudden, the next thing she knew it was evening and he was sitting in the dark on the ground, where you never sit, leaning against the bed and she was sitting on his knees, and it was nice, and even though she was always a little bit scared in a room that was dark, she wasn't afraid here now, though on the other hand she was a little bit scared of the tall skinny man, so it also wasn't nice. Then all of a sudden she heard keys jangling at the door, and all of a sudden she felt his heart pounding loudly, right through his shirt and his jacket, and all of a sudden he squeezed her so hard it hurt, gripping her by both wrists, and he got that odd look again, looking toward the door that led to the kitchen, left slightly ajar. Abruptly he stood up and without saying a word took her into his arms, still clutching her a little more tightly than he needed to, and Alice began to thrash a bit, feeling like a trout caught in a net. He cracked open the door to the kitchen another inch and Alice could hear her mother in the entryway, taking off her shoes and changing into her slippers, wondering out loud where Alice was and whether Tereza had already left. Then she turned and saw the two of them standing in the doorway. Him, her husband, holding her daughter, and she bent down one more time, out of habit, to adjust the straps on her house shoes, and then went to him, saying only, "Josef, Josef . . ." not finishing the sentence the way you're supposed to, the way she always did when she was admonishing her daughter. And she came to them and stroked Alice's hair and put her face next to his, and Alice had a feeling her mom was going to start crying again, which made her uncomfortable, but surprisingly she didn't cry, she just held her husband by the shoulders and hugged her, and Alice noticed that her father's heart, which just a few moments ago had been beating as fast as a herd of gazelles, which she once saw in a zoo, was beating slowly now, almost deliberately, but then again she could feel the warm thin little trickle pulsing in her mother's hand, driving the blood to her fingers, which clutched her and stroked her, and the trickle kept changing, growing stronger, then settling down, then roaring like a storm. And then her dad stood her on the ground, and somehow it became clear it was dinnertime now, so she went to sit in her chair and he sat down across from her and her mom started making a cheese spread, and he looked at her, devoting as much time to his wife as to his daughter, and her mom just came over every now and then and stroked her hair, and his too, the way you do to little kids, but some- times—almost as if she didn't want anyone to see—she would also quick as a wink, inconspicuously stroke his hands, which were rest- ing on the table and were much bigger than her mom's. So they had something to eat, and since her mom hadn't been counting on her dad to arrive until two days later, she didn't have any food prepared, she'd reserved it all in the shops for the next day so it would be fresh, and so they had cheese spread with chives, and even though Alice normally didn't like the way it tasted, today it didn't matter because, frankly, she barely even realized what she was eating. She was too busy looking at her dad and at her mom, who looked totally different than Alice had ever seen her before. When they were done, they went to sit in the living room and her mom showed her dad two LPs that it was obvious he really liked because he got a wrinkle slanting across his forehead, and it looked a little bit like a frown, but later she found out that was just the way it looked, but actually it meant he was extremely happy. On the cover of one of the records there were some men in suits that made them look like penguins dressed up for a dinner party, as her dad later said, looking very serious but giving her a quick wink on the side so no one noticed except her, which made her smile, and on the cover of the other record was the head of a man with really curly hair and funny little glasses, and also a piano all painted in gold. Then her dad asked her mom to put on the record with the man in the funny glasses.

"I haven't heard that one in years, Květuška."

"Now you'll be able to listen to it twice a day if you want, Josífek."

Alice didn't like that her mom called him Josífek, so she walked up to them, looked at her mom, and said to them both: "That's my daddy, and his name isn't Josífek."

Alice's father looked at her again with that look, only this time she didn't shudder, since she'd already experienced it once before, and she was brave, and he sat her on his lap and said: "Mommy, Alice is right."

And she was glad he sat her on his lap, because the music coming out of the record with the man in the funny glasses on it was making her really sad, even though she also thought it sounded beautiful and inspiring, it was making her sadder and sadder. And after that all she remembered was two great big strong hands lofting her through the air and carrying her to her bed and laying her down, and two smaller hands taking off her dress and pulling her nightgown on over her head, and how she liked the feeling of lofting through the air, and even though her uncle Oldřich sometimes carried her like that, these were her daddy's hands, and that was something totally different, and just before she fell asleep she thought she'd better ask her mommy what kind of cream to buy for her daddy's hands, since the one her mommy had was too flowery, and he might not like that since he smelled more of tobacco, and she smelled that too as she fell asleep, even though her mommy didn't like tobacco and anyone who smoked had to go out on the balcony, but her daddy didn't have to go out on the balcony, she was sure of that, and that was all she remembered of that day.

The next morning when Alice woke up and looked at the clock, it was already past eight thirty. Startled, she clutched the comforter to her chest, until she realized she could hear her mommy and daddy talking in the kitchen and her mommy was laughing. She couldn't remember her laughing like that before. At the same time Alice thought it was strange her mommy hadn't woken her as usual. She sat up in bed, dropped her legs to the floor, and ran into the kitchen. Her mommy sat next to her daddy, her chair pushed up right next to his, holding his hand. They both smiled when they saw her, but didn't say anything. Alice awkwardly stopped in her tracks, realizing again how late it was. She should have been in school a long time ago. Her mommy looked at her and made a face she normally only made when the two of them were alone at home. Her mommy was in a really good mood.

"Overslept, did we, Ali?" Alice just nodded a few times. She still didn't know what to say.

"That's all right, sweetheart. You don't have to go to school for the rest of the week. I've already talked to your teacher about it."

"Now give me a kiss," her daddy said. Alice ran first to him, then turned to her mommy, and carefully gave them each a kiss.

4

A VISION OF HITLER

Dr. Lukavský didn't have time for the patient right away, so he filled out the forms and admitted him to the unit, but that was it. The patient brought in by the police, pastry chef Marek Svoboda, who called not only the doctor but everyone else, including the patients and orderlies, *brother* or *sister*, appeared calm and collected. There was no need to establish a diagnosis yet, the doctor still had time. The man, who introduced himself as Jesus Socrates Amenhotep Hitler though his parents had named him Marek Svoboda, was in the right place, the doctor concluded.

That afternoon he had Mr. Svoboda brought in and asked whether he could explain his new name. The pastry chef fixed his gaze on the doctor.

"I'm not sure you would understand my explanation, brother doctor."

"First of all," the doctor said, "I'd like you to call me just ordinary normal Dr. Lukavský."

"But, brother doctor, doesn't it comfort you to know that we're all equal under the sun?" the pastry chef said.

"Mr. Svoboda, please," the doctor said. Mr. Svoboda paused and the doctor tried again.

"Could you tell me why you changed your name, Mr. Svoboda?"

"Yes, brother doctor, I could," said the pastry chef. "But first I would ask a brotherly favor, if you could open the window and let some of little brother wind in for us." The doctor jotted down a note unrelated to Mr. Svoboda in the file open in front of him, laid his pen on the table, stood up, and opened the window a crack. The sound of the wind in the branches of the broad, leafy trees that lined the main road of the hospital complex penetrated the room. The pastry chef stood up, walked to the window, and stared out through the bars.

"How far is it from here to the capital, brother doctor?"

"You mean to Prague?" asked the doctor.

"Yes, brother, I mean precisely that," said the pastry chef.

"About two and a half hours by car," said Dr. Lukavský.

"You see, brother, two and a half hours by car, that's a great distance, and we humans are even more distant from one another than that."

"What do you mean?" the doctor asked.

"I knew you wouldn't understand," the pastry chef said.

"Do you mean the distance in human relationships?"

"I've hooked one and now I'm reeling her in," the pastry chef replied.

"Mr. Svoboda, what's going on with your wife?" the doctor asked.

"Dear brother doctor, my sister wife left me and all that remains of her is a letter good-bye."

"Why did she leave you, Mr. Svoboda?"

"She found herself a noble lover, brother doctor," the pastry chef replied.

"Do you have that letter, Mr. Svoboda?"

"Dear brother doctor, I ate it," the pastry chef replied.

"Oh, I see," the doctor said.

"Oh, I see," the pastry chef repeated. "Now she's let go and is floating away."

"Pardon me?" the doctor said. "I'm not sure I understand."

"Oh, brother doctor, brother doctor. I must reprimand you, for I sense a fraction of impatience in your voice."

"You're right, Mr. Svoboda. I am impatient. I have a long shift ahead of me and there are some things I'd like to find out about you." The pastry chef, still standing at the barred window, ran his hands over his face, as if wiping off a layer of dust, walked back to the table, and sat back down in the chair facing the doctor.

"Why do you call yourself Jesus Socrates Amenhotep Hitler, Mr. Svoboda?"

"I've had visions, brother. I've had visions."

"Visions?"

"Yes, brother. Visions."

"What sort of visions?"

"Woeful, brother, woeful."

"I'm not sure I understand you, Mr. Svoboda. Could you help me a little, please?"

"I'm doing what I can, brother doctor. With all my strength . . . with all the strength I can muster."

"And what are these visions about, brother—I mean, Mr. Svoboda?"

"By all means call me brother, my dear brother doctor," the pastry chef said with obvious delight. "After all, as you know, here under the sun, the moon and the various comets, we are all equal . . ."

"Of course we're all equal," the doctor said, smiling. "It says so in the constitution," he added after a pause.

"Ah, how inappropriate, brother doctor. How inappropriate," the pastry chef said.

"What is inappropriate, Mr. Svoboda?" asked the doctor.

"Inappropriate is inappropriate—that is inappropriate. Being ironic, sarcastic, and quoting a scrap of paper instead of an insight into the human soul, brother."

"Oh, I see," the doctor said. "I see," he repeated. "I apologize if I offended you."

"Brother doctor, a long road awaits you, a long road. The only ones we can offend are ourselves, not another or a third or fifth or seventh or eleventh or thirteenth or seventeenth . . ."

"I see, Mr. Svoboda. So tell me about the visions," the doctor said with recognizably greater emphasis. The pastry chef clasped his hands in front of his face, as if about to pray.

"Each of my names was revealed to me in a vision."

"Why don't you tell me about that last name of yours, Hitler."

"It was a cruel vision, brother doctor. Long and cruel . . . but mostly cruel."

"We have time, Mr. Svoboda. Today I'm on the night shift as well."

"You're on the night shift, brother, and yet you are beneath neither the stars nor the clouds. How sad, brother, how sad. How shabby and sad your life is. Do you realize that, brother?"

"Certainly," the doctor said, clearing his throat. "Certainly, yes, but why don't you tell me something about your vision, Mr. Svoboda? Do you think you could do that?" The pastry chef visibly pondered the question, clasping and unclasping his fingers several times.

"Even wild animals are kinder to each other than people are, remember that, and unfortunately and sadly, I'm no different, so at least I try to be kind to myself." He paused a moment, then added: "I'll tell you my vision, but only on one condition, brother doctor. One condition."

"I can't promise you anything, Mr. Svoboda," the doctor said cautiously. "But what condition is that?"

"It's an absolute condition, actually . . . yes, yes, absolute," the pastry chef said. "Either you meet it, or you won't find out a thing, brother doctor."

"Look now, Mr. Svoboda. I don't think you can impose any conditions. After all, I'm not putting any on you."

"Aren't bars conditions, little brother?" the pastry chef said.

"Mr. Svoboda. Now, you know—"

"My condition is . . . absolute and isn't open to discussion," the pastry chef interrupted. "If you want to hear the vision, the image of my truth, may the universe be blamed, which is the same thing as praised, you mustn't interrupt me. Otherwise, you just won't find out. Which will neither benefit nor harm the cosmos. But don't try to bargain with me! Even I deserve as much pitiful respect from your white coat, which needs a washing. I wouldn't even dare roll dough in such a coat. Ugh, ugh, ugh!"

"I certainly don't intend to interrupt you," the doctor said, somewhat taken aback. He realized he was making an effort not to look at his coat. "You could have told me that to begin with," he added in an insulted tone.

"You just need to listen, doctor. You just need to listen, brother," the pastry chef said sternly.

"Go ahead, Mr. Svoboda. Go right ahead, and I won't interrupt. After all, I'm very interested in what you have to say."

"You promise?" the pastry chef said.

"Of course," the doctor replied.

"You won't interrupt even once?"

"I promise," said the doctor.

"All right then. Then listen closely, brother doctor," the pastry chef said, and he folded his hands in front of his face again as if to pray.

"I was asleep. I was sound asleep, calm and content, my wife had just had her birthday. We celebrated it the way she wanted, with just a couple of friends. Afterwards, that night, we made love and fell asleep in each other's arms. When I woke up, my head hurt so bad I thought it was going to burst. I got up out of bed, but just then another wave of pain came over me. What they call a migraine, I suppose. Staggering from the pain, I crashed into the table next to the bed with my right shin. I heard a sleepy woman's voice say, 'Honey, not again?' The pain was so bad that all I could see was constellations and galaxies of painful, piercing lights. Then someone gently took my hand and spoke to me. It was the same voice as before, only now it was whispering. Then two hands wrapped around my waist and gently sat me back down on the bed. Someone put a glass in my hand. I understood that I was supposed to drink, so I drank. It tasted like mango juice. I drank it, thinking it was strange it tasted like mango, which I love but I'd never tasted before. The hands that sat me down on the bed lifted the leg I had banged, rested it on the bed, and proceeded to wash the wound. Then I felt the hands fasten a bandage to my shin. 'Just lie down, honey,' the voice said again. 'You'll feel better in a while.' But I got up and said no, I had to go to the bathroom. So the two arms lifted me back up a little and I realized I should get up, and blindly, since I still couldn't open my eyes, I followed them. I entered a room, groping my way to the toilet bowl by memory, and sat down. I relieved myself, then remained sitting there on the toilet. As gradually the pain began to recede, I dared to open my eyes a crack. I was sitting in a bathroom. The sun was coming up outside the one large window and I had no idea where I was. I didn't know this place. I leaned against the wall, breathing slow and deep. I glanced at my shin and saw the bandage on the spot where I had bumped myself. The pain had let up, so I stood, wrapped a towel around my naked hips, and stepped out of the bathroom. There was a woman sitting in the hall. As I opened the door she lifted her head, and judging from the look in her eyes I gathered that she loved me. She asked if I was all right and I nodded. I didn't know who she was, I just assumed I loved her too. I suspected it, but I wasn't sure. She stood up next to me and again asked how I was, then escorted me back to bed. I sat down, feeling the pain subside and waiting to see what the woman would do. She didn't do anything special, just laid down beside me. Then she looked at me and said: 'Back again?' I wasn't sure what she meant, so I just shrugged. 'Back again?' she repeated. 'You've got a migraine, don't you?' I nodded my head a couple of times, since it seemed like the most reasonable thing to do at the moment. 'It's just the wind coming in off the desert from the northeast,' she said. 'Thanks, Martha,' I said, and it wasn't until I said her name that I realized I knew it. It was like climbing onto a bike and discovering you know how to ride even though you never learned. 'Let's just hope you feel well enough to go into the city tomorrow.'

"'The city?' I said.

"'Yes, Albert, the city. For those new bulbs you ordered. They called yesterday to say they'd come in, and asked if they should deliver them.'

"'Right, the lilies,' I said automatically. As the corners of her mouth lifted, her face finally began to look a little familiar, and when she said, 'Yes, honey, the lilies. That must be one hell of a migraine. You really do look awful,' I said it would be fine, and operating from memory I picked up my wallet, keys, and driver's license from the bedside table that I had banged my shin against. I looked at my license and there it was: Albert Hegel. That was me: Albert Hegel, gardener and amateur botanist. I went outside and walked around the flower beds, taking in the elegant shapes of the lilies blooming. Extending around the vast building, half residential, half warehouse, was a heavyweight pipe for irrigating the soil. So I guess I already finished it, I thought. I finished and now I just have to install the standby pump. I was a gardener and an amateur botanist, an expert on the cultivation of new species of lilies and orchids. That's what the pipe is for, I realized. Doing something like that on the edge of the desert wasn't easy, but I had inherited the land, which meant it was free. Martha was my wife and the next morning we were supposed to go into the city.

"The trip took about three hours. The desert—as always—was gorgeous. When we got to town we went to the garden center, where they had several boxes of lily bulbs packed and ready for me. The boxes were specially adapted to maintain the correct level of moisture in the loam where the bulbs were embedded, though once we got them home I knew I would have to soak them in an antifungal solution. The owner, who also worked as a salesman, called me by my first name. His name was Stephen and I called him Steve. I sensed a certain degree of admiration for me at the nursery, but it wasn't clear why. Martha looked at me the same way as they did—with obvious respect—and it plainly made her happy. As we drove back, she said something to the effect that they saw me as a superman. 'Why is that?' I asked, puzzled. 'Well, no one else has ever succeeded in cultivating new species of lilies and orchids in the desert. As if you didn't know,' she said, wrinkling her forehead. Of course I knew, but I still wasn't feeling entirely myself. While I was at the nursery, Martha went to the supermarket, the hairdresser's, the post office, and rented about twenty videos.

"'Why so many?' I asked on the way back.

"'Well, when do you think we're going to get into town again?' she said.

"'Usually we make it about once every three weeks,' I said.

"'That's right, every three weeks,' she said. I suddenly realized the drive didn't take three and a half hours, but much longer. I just hadn't noticed because I had slept most of the way while she drove. We got home late that evening. Martha went straight into the shower and I carried the crates of bulbs into a room where, one by one, I washed them off and deposited them in a long tank, which I filled with anti-fungal solution. It took me till nighttime. That night we met in the kitchen and it dawned on me that this was probably one of our common routines. There were some letters on top of the fridge, along with some bank statements, advertising flyers, a few magazines, and an envelope with a university letterhead on it. I opened that one first. It was a polite letter from an officer in the admissions department informing me, allegedly with sadness, that due to the high volume of applicants they couldn't accept me. I paced around the kitchen a while, then went outside, made a couple of housekeeping notes on some of the plants, and then got angry. Martha was rearranging boxes of food in the freezer when I walked in, but seeing me she stopped, sat down at the table, and waited to see what I was going to do or say. I didn't know what to do or say. I was just enraged.

"'Be careful you don't hit your shin again, honey.' That was all she said. Nobody before or since has ever addressed me with that strange word, *honey*. She seemed to know I had been rejected. 'I really had my hopes up for you,' she said after a minute, 'but maybe it's time for you to let it go. It's devastating you. This is the fifth time they've turned you down.'

"'No, the sixth,' I corrected her. 'The first was before we knew each other.'

"'You know how much I want it for you, but it's devastating you to get these rejections, and it devastates me that you're devastated.' I had nothing to say to that. We had strictly budgeted the movies Martha rented to make them last till our next trip into town, but that night we went through at least four and I drank almost two bottles of Jamaican rum. The next day I didn't wake up till afternoon and didn't feel like talking at all. A week went by like that.

"On Monday a buyer from one of the companies I worked for

occasionally, a man by the name of Winter, was supposed to stop by. I don't know what possessed him to drive all the way out to the edge of the desert to see me, but he came. As I welcomed him, it became clear that he had brought along his nephew, who was eager to see my flower beds. I showed them whatever they wanted. As they were leaving, his nephew asked, 'So is there any building going on around here, Mr. Hegel?' It felt funny, him calling me mister. He couldn't have been more than ten years younger than me, maybe sixteen or seventeen. 'I don't think anyone's building anything around here,' I said. 'We would know if they were, don't you think, Martha?' 'No, of course not. We would know,' she repeated. But the young man insisted. I didn't think about what he'd said for some time after that, but several weeks later it came back to me. A few months earlier I had finally finished my artificial irrigation project. It cost me all my savings, all my earnings, and Martha lent me all her savings as well, and it turned out it actually worked. Now we just had to live extremely modestly for the next four and a half years or so, as we slowly paid off our debt, but I was sure we would earn a return on our investment. I was grateful to Martha for going in on it with me and for the fact that she liked it here too.

"Without wind, there is no desert. The desert and the wind are like brothers by blood. One settled, the other a drifter who pops in from time to time with a sack full of gifts from all the wonderful places he's visited to make up for his bad conscience. The desert is deserted and lonely, and acquires her knowledge of the outside world via the wind. The gifts the wind brings with him are small, microscopic particles of earth. Particles of earth that erode soil and rock. Particles of earth so small that even a slight breeze is enough to keep them airborne, like clouds or airships. Gravity doesn't apply to them. They remain in the air forever, suspended like souls in purgatory till they ascend to paradise or plummet into hell. They are weightless and free of commitments, traveling light, catching a lift on the air currents, elbowing through whirlwinds, creeping along, saltating from one to another, clambering from there to a third. A grain of sand measures roughly a fifth of a millimeter in diameter and scatters in the wind like fog or dust. Usually the wind lifts a particle of sand and carries it only an inch or two over the dunes at a speed half or a third as fast as the wind itself. After a while the grain of sand crashes into another, which then takes off, and the whole thing repeats all over again. About a quarter of all the grains of sand in the desert shift back and forth this way, depending on the speed and direction of the wind. The process is known as aeolian transport, and if you can understand it, you have at least a chance of also understanding the infinity of time. Every desert is like a gigantic hourglass with the sand trickling from dune to dune, back and forth, up and down. Do I need to tell you how much I love the desert? I was seven or eight years old, living with my parents at the edge of the desert, as I do now, when I got a new encyclopedia for my birthday. In it I learned that deserts are not only on Earth, but on Mars and other planets too, which so captivated and delighted me that I ran straight to my father with the news. I could tell he was happy I was happy, but I don't think he understood why. The important thing for me was that there was something connecting the Earth and Mars. I imagined the two planets as connected hourglasses. Later on, I actually imagined us living on Mars, surrounded by red sandstorms. What boy wouldn't want to see that? And now I lived in the desert. The closest significant landmark to our house was Mount St. Aloysius, which rose to a height of 3,560 feet. That was where Martha and I lived, that was where I had my house, that was where I irrigated my flower beds.

"Once I had finished the last part of my irrigation system, my work was more or less done. I had invested money in the pumps, drilling several new wells, and all that was left to do was some occasional maintenance. I was very proud of my artificially irrigated flower beds, seeing that no one had ever tried it before. The flowers did better than ever, which meant greater yields and faster repayments on my debt. Then one day, having nothing better to do, I got it into my head to go look at that place in the desert that Winter's nephew had mentioned. I wanted Martha to come along, but she said she didn't have time. No time? Us? I had the feeling she was just making excuses, and when one day after breakfast I decided to drive out there, Martha said she would come along after all. We set out early. When you live in the desert, you have to leave early in the morning so you don't get caught out in the midday sun. We drove for several hours, and when we reached our destination, I saw a long barbed-wire fence stretching into the distance. Beyond it was a dirt road leading to a group of large buildings. We came to a small building at the entrance to the fenced-in lot that looked like a gatehouse. We pulled up in front of the gate, I honked the horn a few times and got out. Martha stayed in the car. She seemed a little tired and there were beads of sweat on her forehead even though we had the air conditioning turned all the way up. After a little while, two men came out. One stood at the gate while the other gave me a hesitant glance. They both had on some kind of uniform.

"'Hello,' I greeted the man who stopped in front of me. 'I'm your neighbor. My wife and I live about three hours from here.' I offered my hand. He looked right through me and my outstretched hand.

"'You have entered a military installation without authorization. Please vacate the premises immediately!' His rudeness caught me by surprise. I turned to Martha in the car, but she just sat there looking out from behind a pair of large, impenetrable sunglasses.

"'You must be mistaken,' I said. 'I know the local maps in some detail, and this land is state-owned, not military, as you say.'

"'Please vacate this military installation immediately, or I will have you placed under arrest,' said the man in the uniform. Now I was outraged.

"'This is a free country and you aren't going to tell me what I can or can't do. I know my rights as a citizen, and—'

"The man in uniform interrupted: 'You are on a military installation here, in the middle of the desert, Mr. Hegel, and everyone on the grounds falls under the jurisdiction of the military police. It is within my authority to arrest you on the spot.'

"'Arrest?' I repeated in disbelief.

"'Yes, sir, arrest. Now, please vacate this military installation immediately!'

"'But this isn't a military installation . . . ,' I started in again. The man pulled a small, official-looking notebook from his breast pocket, opened it, and began to read:

"'You have trespassed on a military installation and remained on it without authorization despite repeated warnings. It is within the authority of the military police to place you under arrest in accordance with the powers granted us in accordance with applicable laws, in particular the Law on the Protection of Military Installations, Military Property and . . .'

I didn't wait for the rest. I turned around, walked back to our car, climbed in, slammed the door, started the engine, and turned the car onto the road heading the other direction.

"Martha looked at me. 'What a nice way to start the week.'

"Still filled with rage, I looked at her and said: 'Don't try to tell me this is a military installation. I studied every single map of this area in detail when I was trying to find alternative water sources for the flower beds, and there was nothing like a military installation anywhere!'

"'Oh, I know, honey. After all, you've lived here since you were a child,' Martha said. 'But you see for yourself the barbed wire, the soldiers, the gate. So why argue?' The trip back felt like it took forever. About halfway through we switched drivers, and there was one thing I couldn't get out of my head. I could have sworn that at one point the guard called me by name. He definitely said *Mr. Hegel.* I kept replaying the situation over and over, but I couldn't figure it out. Before we got home, I mentioned it to Martha. I told her one of the guards or soldiers, or whatever they were, had called me by name. She said that was impossible, since we'd never been there before. 'Right,' I said. 'I thought the same thing, but he definitely said my name.'

"'That's impossible,' she repeated. 'There's just no way. You must have heard wrong.'

"The next day I went to do something in the garage and noticed the jeep we had driven had a scratch on the fender from when Martha had pulled into the garage. For the next few days, nothing out of the ordinary happened, but when Steve called from the garden center I told him the story.

"'File a complaint on the bastards. Is the army out of their fuckin' minds? They set up a base in the middle of the desert and we don't have any rights? You better complain. God only knows what they're doing there!' When I mentioned it to Martha at dinner, I couldn't help notice it made her nervous. I let it pass, pretending I didn't notice, but after six years of living together it's hard to hide anything perfectly, including feelings. I had the feeling Martha knew something she wasn't saying. It was a funny feeling, not believing her. I thought it would turn out to be something hilarious, some kind of joke. That night, just as I was nearly asleep, Martha went to the kitchen for something. I was going to call to her to bring me something to drink, but then I heard her close the kitchen door and made myself get up. I was just about to open the door when I realized she was talking to someone on the phone. But that wasn't what made me stop so much as the tone in her voice. Whoever it was, she was speaking to them in a nervous whisper. I stood listening with my hand on the door handle. What she was saying didn't make any sense:

"'Absolutely. Oh, absolutely. You shouldn't have done that. Mm, I don't think so. You don't understand. He wants to make a big stink. Yes, his friend told him he should complain. Of course it's a mess! Of course! I don't know. That could give the whole thing away. That's all I know. Oh, sure. Sure.' I opened the door and walked into the room. All of a sudden her voice shifted from a nervous whisper to a quiet, even-tempered tone, and the topic of conversation took a sudden turn as well.

"'It's too late now. Right. I'll call back tomorrow. I'll give him the message.' She hung up the phone and turned to me: 'My brother says hi, honey.' I nodded, opened the fridge, grabbed a box of juice, and headed back to the bedroom. I had no idea what was going on, but I knew Martha was lying to me. I tried to fall asleep. Just as I could tell what she was thinking and feeling, she could tell for me too. I was confused. Instead of sleeping, I lay there wondering what she had been talking about. She mentioned me and a complaint, which could have been either about my failed attempt to get into university again, or the military installation surrounded by barbed wire that wasn't on any map. The next morning I went out to the garage, and as soon as I saw the scrape on the fender, things started coming together. First, Martha had tried to dissuade me from driving out to the buildings Winter's nephew had told us about, which belonged to the military. Second, the whole time we were there, she didn't set foot out of the car and what I had interpreted as fatigue might actually have been nervousness. I was amazed it hadn't occurred to me sooner. Next, she'd scraped the jeep entering the garage right after I told her the guard had called me by name, even though we'd never been there before. Again, nerves. And finally, the phone call.

"The next morning, I got up before sunrise. Quietly, so as not to wake Martha. I looked at her a few times. Her hair, her permanently dry skin. I came this close to reaching out to touch her and give her a kiss, the way I usually do. Love can lead to ill-considered actions. I stopped myself, not wanting to wake her. I was in for an adventure. Ever since I completed the irrigation system, I'd been a little bored, feeling like there was nothing to do. Once I got dressed, I realized that everything was going according to plan. Most adventures, if I remembered correctly, got under way at dawn. I took some food and a few boxes of juice from the fridge. I filled a plastic canister with drinking water. Finally, I loaded everything into the car and quietly pushed it out of the garage. I didn't want to start the engine, since it might have woken Martha. I had left a note on the kitchen table saying I went into town to pick something up from Steve. Which was true and I did. What I didn't do, which I wrote in the second part of the note, was stay the night at his place, in fact just the opposite. I intended to get inside the military installation and find out what was going on. After about ten minutes of pushing the car, I started the engine, climbed in, and set out on my way. A few long hours later I pulled into town. I stopped by Steve's, then went to see a movie, and from there I walked to the town library to copy the latest edition of the state map. Just as I'd thought: It showed nothing on the site where the military installation was located. I asked the librarian if it was possible there might be something that wasn't shown on the map. After giving it a moment's thought he said it was, and recommended I go to town hall, since they were likely to have the most recent changes entered on their maps. On my way to town hall I realized that the fencing around the installation, as well as the buildings I'd seen in the distance on either side of the road from the gatehouse, as well as the gatehouse itself, weren't new structures. Well preserved, yes, but not new. The whole thing must have been there a good few years now. When I got to town hall, the man at the information desk sent me up to the third floor. I sat down on a bench in the hallway and waited my turn. When they called me in, I explained to the lady which location I was interested in, and she told me straight out there was nothing new there, but she would check. After a while she came back with a large cadastral map. Just as I expected, there was nothing indicated on the site. I paid the fee for the copy, and before I left I asked her how a military installation would be marked on the map.

"'In yellow,' she said. 'It would be marked in yellow. But it would also be indicated in the legend.' I asked again if there was any military land in our district. The answer was: no! I guess it was obvious what I was thinking, since without my even asking the lady went on to say that there were very specific laws and rules covering these things and they weren't required to let me in. What they did there was their business. But everything had to be registered, that was the same all over the country, the laws were very strict on that. I went away satisfied, though at the same time a bit disappointed. I'd been looking forward to an adventure, but having learned there wasn't actually supposed to be anything there, and having possession of the document to prove it, the risk involved in my operation had greatly diminished. I had proof in my bag that those soldiers had no business being there. I stopped by Steve's one more time that afternoon and told him what I had found out. He shook his head and said it didn't sound right to him. He also promised that if Martha called he would make something up, so she wouldn't get worried. I could tell he was concerned, since he asked if everything was all right between us, meaning me and Martha. I said yes, but I didn't know how to explain the feeling I had that she was hiding something from me, so I didn't go into it.

"I left town that afternoon with a rough outline of the military compound drawn in pencil on the map. My plan was to come at it from behind, climb over the barbed wire, and enter one of the buildings. Everything went boringly according to plan. I turned off the road home, just as I had marked on the map, and reached the spot about a half hour after sunset. I was a few miles away from the barbed-wire fence. I drove all the way around the site, so none of the soldiers would see me, till I came to the opposite end of the barbed wire, where I had been with Martha before. I took out my equipment and double-checked it all again. Gloves and a heavy blanket to drape over the barbed wire. A rope, two flashlights, large and small knives in sheathes. Two pairs of shoelaces. Just in case! Two large thermoses of coffee. A camera. Two extra rolls of film. Clean underwear. Three pairs of socks. First-aid kit. I felt like I had everything an averagely competent botanist could need for an expedition like mine. I scoped it all out with binoculars. The perimeter was shaped like a large rectangle, with five elongated structures in the middle. They all looked the same. One of them had a square yellow sign on the corner with the letter *H*. Near one of the other buildings was some sort of electronic device. The only things I could make out, though, were two helicopters and a couple of antennas. A few men in uniform walked from one block to another while I watched through the binoculars.

"It got dark an hour after sunset. I put everything in a backpack, except for the flashlight and blanket, which I carried in my hands, and set out. When I got to the fence I crouched down, seeing a couple of people walking again from one building to another. The fence was more than ten feet high and topped with barbed wire. It took me two tries to drape the blanket over it. Then I pulled on my gloves and started to climb. It was harder than I expected. Even with the blanket, I ripped my pants on one of the barbs when I swung over the top. It looked easier in the movies. I realized I hadn't practiced, or done any training at all. I jumped down and tried to pull the blanket off, so it wouldn't be seen and attract any unwanted attention. In the process I sliced open the skin on my forearm through my shirt, on a wire I hadn't noticed before. I took a bottle of disinfectant and a rectangular bandage out of my backpack on the ground. I unscrewed the bottle, poured disinfectant over the wound, screwed the cap back on, put the bottle back in the pack, and applied the bandage. Adventure in full swing, I concluded. Even had my first injury. At first I was going to leave the blanket, but then I decided to take it with me. As I sat there trying to stuff it into my backpack, I heard a metal sound. Startled, I pressed myself flat to the ground. A set of floodlights, which I hadn't noticed till then, began coming on. I was sitting right underneath one of them. If anyone came out right now, I would be totally exposed. The lamps were mounted on the fence at intervals of about sixty yards. I noticed more lights, slowly beginning to shine in the darkness, attached to the faint outlines of buildings in the distance. They were about three hundred yards away. I took off toward them at a sprint. About halfway there I heard voices and dropped to the ground, trying not to breathe. The tension was starting to give me a headache. The voices traveled to the other side of the building. Then came the sound of a door closing and then silence. I got back up and ran to the nearest building. Creeping slowly around it, I noticed the buildings were arranged in a U-shape. I turned a corner and grabbed hold of a door handle. Locked. I tried the next one. The same. I moved on to another building. It had windows made of frosted glass so you couldn't see in. Finally one of the doors swung open. I stepped inside and found myself in a hallway lined with doors on either side. All of them had an upper panel of clear, transparent glass. The lights were on in the two offices at the far end of the hallway. I tried the handle of the room nearest me. Locked. I moved down the hallway, trying every door. Finally, one of them opened. I went in and sat down on the ground so I couldn't be seen from outside. I looked around the office. Two desks and a couple of electronic gadgets. On the other side of the office were some monitors with their screens turned away from me. From the hum and the glow, it was obvious they were on. Still hunched down, I crept across the room so I could get a look. At first I couldn't really tell what I was looking at. Two of the five monitors had no signal, their screens showing just a grainy gray. The other three had what looked like feeds from a few different rooms, captured on security cameras. There was something odd about them. I looked one more time more closely. The first monitor, then the next . . . then again.

"I'd never seen my house before in black-and-white. At first I didn't understand, and when it finally hit me, I was so startled I almost stood up. It couldn't be. What I was looking at was my own home: my bedroom, my living room, my study. That's impossible, I thought. The pillows on the sofa in the living room looked unfamiliar on the black-and-white screen, since in reality they were green. But I could tell it was them from the pattern. That was my bookcase, too. A monograph on the town of Assisi I had been paging through yesterday and forgot to put back on the shelf was right where I remembered seeing it this morning. Panic. There had to be some explanation for this, it was impossible. Laughter. It's impossible because it's unconstitutional. Paranoia. I'm a lousy, bungling adventurer and it's too much for my brain to deal with it, so it's throwing hallucinations at me! No, this isn't possible, this is spying and that's illegal. How come? Panic again. Pounding heart, sweaty hands, dry throat. How come?

"I started opening drawers. Nothing out of the ordinary. The usual office stuff: staplers, erasers, pencils, pens. Some notepads. I crawled over to a long file cabinet and opened a drawer. Folders and binders. I opened one. Information about me. Another. The same. Paranoid visions squeezing my brain. No, it's too much. Everything about me was in there. The first one had photos of me, the second one copies of my report cards from school. From first grade on. The files fell out of my hands. I was too weak to pick them up. I pulled another file out at random: copies of my scholarly articles on peonies and lilies. I didn't get it. I opened another: descriptions and drawings to the tiniest detail of toys I played with as a child. I couldn't take anymore. The air conditioning was turned off and I urgently needed to get outside into the air. I stumbled into the hallway. I didn't care anymore whether anyone saw me or not. What was it all, anyway? I needed fresh air. I opened the door to the building, stepped outside, and realized I was shaking. I sat down on the ground in front of the door and stayed there like that.

"The door I had stumbled out of, which I now sat with my back to, suddenly opened and the conversation approaching me stopped. Three men in uniform surrounded me. I felt like I should do something, so with some effort I raised my head and looked up at them. As my eyes met theirs, one of them gave a surprised whistle. Another one said:

"'Ah, so Mr. Hegel has paid us a visit.' He turned to the one who had whistled and said: 'Go make the announcement: Directive Fourteen, Article Eight.' As the soldier ran off with the order, his superior turned to me:

"'So, what shall we do with you, Mr. Hegel? What shall we do? We were expecting you to come visit, yes, indeed, but not so soon.' I just looked at the officer, trying to think what to say, but before I could come up with a response, the door burst open again, and two soldiers came running out, headed for one of the helicopters. They opened the cockpit, climbed in, and I was engulfed in the roar of the propeller. Dust and grit filled my eyes. A moment later, they lifted off, soaring up and out of sight.

"'You have a lot of explaining to do,' I said, as the helicopter receded into the distance. 'And I mean a lot.' The officer nodded, helped me to my feet, and the other soldier, standing behind me, handed me my backpack, which I had dropped.

"'Just don't start in with the constitution,' the officer said. 'We have an exemption.'

"'Exemption?' I asked. 'Who do you think you are?'

"'How much have you actually seen, Mr. Hegel?' asked the officer, holding open the door to the block that I had just left a few moments before. 'How much do you actually know?' No way, I thought. I'm not going to fall for that stupid trick. 'At this point we're required to tell you everything. Under Directive Fourteen, your operation today means our experiment has concluded.'

"'Experiment?' I said. 'What are you talking about? Do you realize how many laws you've broken?' The officer didn't respond, indicating with his hand which way I should go. When we came to the end of the hallway, he opened the door to his office.

"'Have a seat, please. What would you like to drink: coffee, tea, beer, wine, mineral water? Whatever you want.'

"'What I want is for you to explain this to me,' I said.

"'I understand,' the officer nodded. 'I understand and that is precisely why I have initiated procedures under Directive Fourteen.'

"'Man, I don't know what the hell you're talking about, and I couldn't care less.'

"'Mr. Hegel,' the officer said, 'I would ask you to hold out for another,' he looked at his watch, 'twenty-three minutes at least. Directive Fourteen means that the project's Crisis Committee will convene within half an hour and explain the whole thing to you. I myself am not a member, and although I did undergo training concerning this matter, I am not authorized to tell you anything else. Once again I would ask you to wait, as the team of specialists who worked on the experiment can explain everything in less than thirty minutes. Meanwhile may I offer you some refreshments and suggest that I call a doctor to examine the surface wounds you suffered, I would assume, from climbing over the fence?'

I shrugged and the officer cast a look at the other soldier, who nodded and walked out, leaving me and the officer alone. The two of us sat there with the air conditioning on full blast. The soldier returned with a tray of drinks, trailed by a man with a briefcase in hand. He placed the briefcase on the table and opened it. He glanced at the bandage on my arm. He ripped it off, disinfected the scratch again, and reapplied it. From the way he moved I got the impression he was a little squeamish about touching me. I decided I was just nervous.

"'I need to make a call,' I said. The officer nodded:

"'And to whom would you like to place your call, Mr. Hegel?'

"'My wife,' I said. He nodded again.

"'She will be here in,' he glanced at his watch, 'seventeen minutes.' I shook my head to indicate I didn't understand.

"'That helicopter you saw take off was for her,' the officer said.

'She's also a member of the Crisis Committee.' What kind of bullshit is this, I thought. I decided to have a drink and let things run their course. Then I heard a helicopter and a few moments later a man of about sixty with a bald spot appeared on the other side of the glass-paneled door. While he adjusted the knot of his tie with one hand, with the other he knocked on the door. He entered and said:

"'Good evening, Mr. Hegel. I'm the director of the project.'

"'What project?' I asked. 'What are you doing here anyway?'

"'Follow me, please, to the conference room,' he said. After a brief pause, he repeated himself, this time somewhat more somberly: 'If you would, follow me.' I stood from my chair and followed him out. We exited the office and walked to the door leading out of the building. The director went first, holding the door with a nervous grin, as if to express his condolences. I stepped out into the yard. Everything looked different now from the way it had when I climbed the fence. The whole area was illuminated by spotlights, which I hadn't noticed before. I saw my car parked in an alley between two of the buildings. It gave me a good feeling. The last time I had felt that way was when my mom caught me smoking. I was fourteen, but I felt like an adult and she didn't know what to say. She wanted to be strict, but I could see in her eyes that she felt like laughing. As far as she was concerned I was a grown-up, so she respected me, in accordance with that belief, by saying nothing. Again the director held the door open for me as we entered another building. There was carpeting on the floor. Inside, a soldier stood flanking either side of the doorway. We continued on until we came to a big upholstered door. Two more soldiers stood there, one of whom opened the door. I felt his eyes follow me as I walked past. I did a quick scan of my pants and shirt, but all the buttons were in place. Maybe I'm sweating too much, I thought. My armpits were completely soaked. The director held the door for me, as before, and we entered the room.

"A set of conference tables was arranged in a semicircle on the left side of the room, with six or seven people seated behind them. I saw Martha and ran toward her. She sat huddled at one of the tables in a T-shirt, pants, and bathrobe. They must have woken her up, I thought. Before I could reach her, though, two hands took hold of me from either side, lifted me up, and slammed me down on the ground before I could say a word. The director came over and, standing above me, gave an awkward shrug:

"'I forgot to mention it, Mr. Hegel, but you aren't allowed to talk to Martha.'

"'What do you mean?' I said angrily as the two soldiers who had thrown me to the ground now lifted me to my feet. He just shook his head. On the other side of the room there were two tables. At the far one sat the doctor, the only person I already knew. The soldiers shoved me toward the table next to the doctor.

"'Who the fuck do you think you are?' I said. Now I was out of control. 'What do you think you're doing to me and my wife? You fucking bastards. What do you think you're doing?' I screamed.

"'In fact, Mr. Hegel, Martha is not your wife,' the director said. 'Martha is also a member of the experiment.' I sat down at the table. The doctor stood from his table and walked over to mine. While the director spoke in hushed tones with the members of the committee on the other side of the room, the doctor said to me:

"'Mr. Hegel, what you're about to hear now may be upsetting to you. You may even find it shocking. In fact,' he said with an unpleasant grin, 'it would be astonishing if what you learned here today *didn't* cause you shock. If you'd like, I can offer you a calming injection, or at least a mild sedative. It won't hinder your cognitive capabilities in any way.'

"'Go fuck yourself,' I said. 'Either that or just sit down and leave me alone.' The doctor walked back to his table and, addressing himself to the director, Martha, and the other committee members, loudly declared:

"'You may begin,' then took a seat. He rotated his chair so he could continue to observe me, which made me uncomfortable. On the other side of the room, the director rose to his feet.

"'Ladies and gentlemen, I apologize for having to call you together today so hastily, but as it happened, Mr. Albert Hegel here paid us a visit today. He came in his car, which he parked not far from our institute. He climbed the fence and intruded into Block F, where he discovered and most likely read a variety of materials. Under Directive Fourteen, in this situation the experiment concludes and we are required to explain it to Mr. Hegel in its entirety, as the directive states, with respect to his civil rights. As you recall, last week we heard a summary of the situation from Dr. Wagner and Martha here.' When he said her name, I winced. 'We did of course anticipate some activity on the part of Mr. Hegel, but it came sooner than we were able to foresee. Even in science one can't think of everything,' the director said, pausing for an apologetic grin. This guy really knows what he's doing. Guess he's done his share of speeches, I thought. 'I'd like to ask Dr. Wagner to begin,' the director said, bowing to a woman of about forty-five seated to his left, directly next to Martha. She rose from her chair to speak.

"'Mr. Hegel, what you are about to hear may surprise you. But understand that this experiment and its purpose are perfectly legitimate from a legal point of view, as the research it relates to is considered so important that we were granted an exemption to your civil rights and liberties. Our study concerns the identification and detection of evil. As you no doubt know, since we insisted on unprecedentedly high standards for your education, World War II ended in Europe some time ago. I won't waste time on the details. Suffice it to say that, since then, many scientists, historians, and politicians, as well as the general public, have been interested in the question of to what extent the origin, development, and conclusion of this terrible chapter in history was influenced by the central figure of the German Third Reich, namely, Chancellor Adolf Hitler. Concentration camps, eugenics, untold suffering, et cetera. In short, this lies at the core of a question to which no one has ever been able to find an answer, since Hitler committed suicide in the closing days of World War II. No one had a chance to confront him with the horrors he inflicted, as they did the other members of his monstrous regime in the trials at Nuremberg. Today we have the luxury of being further removed in time, so we can see that the trials were not perfect and left some questions unanswered. Hitler's absence dealt a heavy blow to the investigation of evil. Then, more than fifty years ago, his remains were rediscovered and secretly deposited for safekeeping at our institute, devoted to the research of evil in all its forms. The project's mastermind was Professor Robert Fischer, who, regrettably, did not live to see its inauguration. His chief contribution consisted of the idea that individuals who wreak evil should be re-created and placed in other historical and family conditions from the ones in which they were raised, so that we can evaluate their development, behavior, and actions at close hand, which would allow us to reach a conclusion as to whether evil is hereditary, or whether all of society contributes to its existence. Scientific debate thus far has been divided between those who claim the entire Second World War was caused by a lunatic, versus those who maintain it was the result of a long-term process, dating as far back as ancient Sparta. On one side of the debate are those who argue that the decisive factor is education, while others insist on the primacy of inheritance, with Fischer's principle of testability held as absolutely fundamental to both camps. The problem is, no one succeeded in carrying out the so-called Fischer experiment during Fischer's lifetime. More than thirty years ago, however, we were finally able to develop a technology sufficiently reliable for the production of one hundred percent, shall we say, doubles using the remainders of tissue from the deceased. The words *original* and *copy* truly cease to make sense at this point. In short, as by now you have probably guessed, you are identical with the individual named Adolf Hitler. In honor of Professor Fischer's idea, you were even given a name whose initials are the same as your predecessor's. The surname *Hegel* was proposed by a group of scholars who upheld the view that the roots of Nazism could already be clearly detected in the philosophical writings of Georg Wilhelm Friedrich Hegel. Their methods were somewhat unseemly, but nonetheless they succeeded. Your name therefore does not, as you have assumed up to now, come from your ancestors, or your forefathers from Europe. Dr. Réti and Dr. Duchamp are in charge of the philosophical aspect of the matter.'

"Panic attack, pounding in my temples, heart in my throat. I looked at Martha, who they wouldn't let me near, but her gaze was fixed about ten feet in front of the table where she sat, her eyes resting firmly on the carpet. She didn't look at me once the entire time. Suddenly the doctor was standing at my side, syringe in hand. I shook my head. He remained there a moment, then sat back down. I tried to snap out of it, but no luck. From what they said, my whole life had been run by somebody else. I asked them. One of them said yes.

"'All right,' I said, 'then how come I have blond hair and I'm six feet, one and a half inches tall? That's not what Hitler looked like, if I remember correctly from the pictures in our textbooks.' The director chuckled unpleasantly:

"'Mr. Hegel . . . Albert . . . there were some genetic variations that we didn't want to influence, so we left them alone. The fact that you look physically—and I emphasize, only physically—different from Adolf Hitler, doesn't mean that you aren't him. It's a common question from laypeople.'

"'So I am him, even if I don't look like him?'

"'Yes, exactly,' said Dr. Wagner.

"'May I speak with Martha?' I asked.

"'Of course,' said someone I didn't know.

"'And who are you?' I asked.

"'Oh, I'm sorry. I forgot to introduce myself. I'm Dr. Réti.'

"'All right,' I said. 'Can I talk to her then?'

"'Please, be my guest,' Réti replied.

"'Actually I wanted to speak with her in private.'

"'Oh, I see. I'm afraid you aren't allowed to speak with her in private.'

"'Why not?' I asked.

"'Because the experiment is over now.'

"'But I want to talk to her,' I said. 'I want to talk to her right now.'

"'I'm afraid that isn't possible,' Réti said.

There was a moment of silence. Then a man in a wrinkled jacket with no tie stood up. 'My name is Sommer, Dr. Sommer. This international project consisted of controlling all the factors that could be controlled once you were cloned. We recorded everything, and all or most of the things and people you have come into contact with have been involved in some way in our project. As you might suspect, the members of our committee, and the experiment as a whole, have relatively close ties with the Office for the Protection of the Constitution, Freedom, and Democracy. Which means we also often benefit from their expertise.'

"'What does that mean?' I asked.

"'That means that within the framework of the experiment we had to find a way to keep you in partial isolation, which is why you inherited land out here on the edge of the desert. Had you lived in a city, the urban influences, in addition to the impossibility of controlling your encounters with individuals, would have made evaluation of the project unfeasible. For our purposes, it was absolutely essential that you be in at least partial isolation.'

"'And what about Martha?' I asked.

"'Ehm-er,' the man said, clearing his throat. He shifted his weight several times, cleared his throat again, unscrewed the cap on the bottle of mineral water in front of him, screwed it back on without pouring any into his glass, and said, 'Naturally, all of us here feel a certain sympathy for you. We aren't insensitive people, or monsters, in spite of our using the . . . how shall we put it . . . unorthodox procedures of the Office for the Protection of the Constitution, Freedom, and Democracy.'

"'So, what about Martha?' I asked again.

"'Martha is a valuable collaborator of ours, having undergone not only a strenuous competition but an equally strenuous program of education and physical training.' My throat went bone dry.

"'What do you mean, collaborator?' I asked.

"'Well, she kept the hidden cameras in operation, wrote a detailed report every week, kept us advised on unforeseeable issues . . . and so on.'

"'What sort of issues?' I asked.

"'Hmm . . . well, for example, your efforts to study botany. It took no small effort on our part to sway the results of the entrance exams so you wouldn't be accepted. Several times. Once, even in spite of our efforts, you nearly got in. When it came to your thirst for education, we had to leverage every bit of influence we had. People began to ask questions. And although she wasn't successful, Martha also tried to sway you on that . . . hmm . . . errh . . . to avoid any damage to the experiment.'

Martha was still staring about ten feet in front of the table where she sat.

"'So why can't I talk to her alone?' I said.

"'That would be against rule number six, Mr. Hegel,' the director interjected. 'Rule six prohibits it.'

"'I don't give a shit about your rules,' I said.

"'We really do sympathize, Mr. Hegel, but unfortunately we can't comply with your request,' said the director. 'I know it's frustrating, but please try to accept it.'

"'Just to finish what I was saying,' Réti went on. 'Everything around you has been monitored since you were born. You were placed in a standard and specifically modified average environment. Your father and mother were also part of the project. However, your mother had to withdraw prematurely, as a result of her forming too strong an emotional bond with you.'

"'So my mom isn't dead?' I said.

"'No, of course not. She was a member of the experiment.'

"'And I can't see her either, huh?'

"'No, I'm afraid that, again, this is strictly a rule six situation. I'm sorry. As for the rest . . . all of your books, videos, any electronic media you listened to, all that was monitored. Who you met with, your journals, your feelings, intimate relations with Martha, all of it. The things you were attached to as a child—toys, books, postcards, souvenirs, even the smallest items were recorded and evaluated by a team of experts on an ongoing basis.'

"'You're a bunch of maniacs,' I screamed.

"'Mr. Hegel, no one expects you to understand a project intended to elucidate the essence of evil. With all due respect, it isn't as though you're an expert.' Réti paused, and suddenly the director announced:

"'Let's have a half-hour break.'

"Everyone, including Martha, got up and walked out of the room, leaving me alone with the doctor and the guards. I'd had enough.

"'I want to go home,' I said. The doctor answered, but I wasn't listening anymore. I rose to my feet, feeling tired, unbelievably tired, tired all the way to my core, in the innermost part of my body. I was tired and wanted to go home. The doctor walked out and a few minutes later returned with some papers, which he shoved into my hand. I took them without looking. He offered to fly me home in the helicopter. I refused, so he said if I wanted, we could drive home in my jeep instead. I nodded. It was the longest trip home of my life. One of the soldiers drove, with another military vehicle behind us. In the car the doctor told me the cameras had been disconnected and removed from my house. I asked him why I should believe him. He said it was all there in the documents he had given me, which I was supposed to sign. I refused and he didn't insist. After they drove me home and parked my jeep in front of the garage, I looked at the fender again, the one Martha had scraped when she was parking it after our trip out to the military base. I decided to ask the doctor whether Stephen, the owner of the garden center, was also one of them.

"'I don't think so,' he said. 'Definitely not. You can find everything there in those documents.' The doctor and the driver got in the car that had followed us and drove away. I went inside. Hallway. Kitchen. Living room. Bedroom. Not a trace of Martha's things anywhere. They had cleaned it all out. Completely. I took a beer from the fridge and set it on the table. Then I took out two bottles of mineral water and drank them one after the other. I put the beer back in the fridge. I didn't want to be drunk. I walked around the house and the flower beds. The irrigation was working. I just made a slight adjustment, then went into the bedroom. I looked under the pillows. Her things weren't there either. No nightgown. No handkerchief. They had been thorough. Didn't miss a thing. I fell asleep and woke up around six in the morning. I thought the whole thing had been a nightmare and I could tell Martha about it. I was even looking forward to it, until then I realized she wasn't lying next to me.

She wasn't outside or in the living room. She was gone. Terror: sheer, pure, snow-white. On the table in the living room I found the folder of documents I had dreamed about. They were there. I went into the storeroom, took out some things left behind by my parents, who actually weren't my parents. I had to search through a few boxes before I found what I was looking for: my old textbooks. I pulled out the one on history and flipped to the section on World War II. I felt a tingling in my left index finger. I don't know why. I went to wash up. Then I went into the room where I stored my seeds, fertilizers, and chemicals. I took some of the chemicals with me into the kitchen and made a cocktail out of them, adding in a little bourbon and vodka. It tasted awful. I made about a pint of the stuff and drank every drop. Then I lay down on the bed and lost consciousness. The last thing that went through my mind was that Socrates must have died something like this, or at least that's what they wrote in one of those textbooks.

"And so I died, brother doctor, I died. I lost all consciousness. And all of a sudden I see a helicopter appear, landing right on one of my flower beds, like they didn't care one bit that I had my peonies there. And they don't. Kind of pisses me off, but what can I do, I'm dead, right, Doc? But you be quiet, don't say a thing. And I see them carrying my body out of the house, totally dead, and putting my body in the helicopter. And then I see it in the morgue, open wide, like swinging doors thrown wide open. I see my heart and lungs and stomach, and they're taking samples. Too bad I'm not made of glass, I think, then they wouldn't have to whittle away at me with their scalpels. So they stick everything in all these devices, I have no idea what they're for, and then I read: 'Results: The genetic material of the stem cells extracted for testing from the body of Mr. Albert Hegel is not identical with the genetic material of Adolf Hitler; on the contrary, there are clear and convincing indications that he is a Slav of Russian origin,' and so on and so forth . . . and at the end they write: 'Our conclusion is as follows: Mr. Albert Hegel is in actuality a clone of Russian soldier Alexander Ivanovich Babel, entrusted with the collection of Hitler's remains as part of the first unit to enter Berlin after the fall of Hitler's regime. There was undoubtedly genetic contamination of the material, most likely a hair or flake of dandruff from Alexander Ivanovich. Therefore we declare the material, along with the entire experiment, to be totally useless. Mr. Hegel was a genetic duplicate of Mr. Alexander Ivanovich Babel.' And so on, brother doctor, and so on. And the world cruelly goes on spinning without so much as a blush. And at the very end of the report, 'P.S.: *Experiment must be repeated. Evil must be defeated.*' Without so much as a blush, brother, without a single blush!"

5

VOLUNTARY QUESTIONING

Mr. Černý sat on a wooden bench in a long narrow hallway. The bench was painted glossy brown. It was three P.M., but no one had called his name yet. A few people stood down the hallway. His summons was for two thirty. He sat and waited. It was an October afternoon, and sounds drifted in through the dusty windowpanes from the street outside. Mr. Černý stood up, stretched, and straightened the knot on his tie. There was nothing on his mind that he was aware of. His head felt totally empty. Totally empty and totally quiet. Another few minutes went by. He stiffly ran a finger along his tie again. He stopped and stood a while, tilting his head slightly to the side, then turned, stopped, and stood again. Rooted to the spot. Then he knocked on the door. On it was a metal plaque with the number eighteen. It was quiet a moment, then he heard footsteps. The door opened and a girl appeared.

"Hello," said Mr. Černý.

"Hello," said the girl. The sound of a tram could be heard amid the silence in the hall.

"What can I do for you?" the girl asked.

"I have a summons," said Mr. Černý. "A summons," he said again, pulling a twice-folded sheet of paper from an envelope. The girl took the paper from him, turned it upside down, and took a long look at it. She shifted her weight from one heel to the other, then said without raising her eyes: "They aren't here anymore. They moved to the building next door." She folded the paper and handed it back to him. "It's an invitation, not a summons."

"Oh," he said, "that's good, but how do I get there?" The girl looked over his left shoulder out the window into the street and past it into the park on the other side.

"Go two flights down," she said. "Just two, though! Not all the way or you won't be able to get there. Two flights! Then stand facing the staircase . . . the big ones. The main stairs. With Masaryk in front. A statue of Masaryk. Turn your back to Masaryk, so the main stairs are in front of you, and go right. Walk down the hall. Make two turns: first right, then left, till you come to the stairs. Go down them and you'll be in the building next door." She paused a moment. "Well, that's it," she said.

"Thank you," said Mr. Černý, and he turned to walk away.

"Wait a minute, sir!" she called after him. "Wait. The door number." The sound of her heels echoed through the hall as she returned to her office, then a moment later came back out. "131B," she said.

"Thank you," said Mr. Černý.

"This is building A," she added. "That's building B."

"Thank you," he said again.

"Good-bye," the girl said.

"Good-bye," said Mr. Černý.

On his way from building A to building B he had to turn back several times. Twice he stood in front of the Masaryk statue and twice he turned his back to it. On his third try he finally made it. He found door 131B, knocked, and turned the handle. Sitting in the room was a man of about thirty in glasses. He removed them and looked up at Mr. Černý.

"I'm engineer Černý," he said, introducing himself.

"Hello, sir. I'm Lieutenant Havránek," the man said, glancing briskly at his watch.

"I was delayed," said Mr. Černý.

"No problem, sir. No problem at all. Ever since we moved, nobody can find us. Let me guess: You waited and waited, and when nobody called you, you went to ask what was going on. Am I right?"

"Mm-hm," Mr. Černý said. "Exactly."

"I'm sorry I didn't write to you with our new office number, but I didn't have a chance. I apologize."

"Should I come back some other time then?" Mr. Černý asked.

"No, if you have time, we can look at it right now. Please, come in and have a seat."

"How late do you work?" said Mr. Černý.

"Don't worry about that," said the lieutenant. "And please, sit down," he repeated. He stared at the papers on his desk a moment. "Would you like some coffee? It's all we have right now. You know, with the move. You can imagine."

"No," said Mr. Černý.

"Coffee?"

"No, thank you," Mr. Černý said, after a moment adding: "I can't imagine. The move."

"Oh, don't bother," said the lieutenant. "You sent us a request for an inquiry, or rather investigation, into Mr. Jánský."

"Yes."

"Fine, but before we begin, it would be best if you could tell me a little something about yourself."

"What do you need to know?"

"Well, for example, where you met him. When was the first time you saw him. That sort of thing." The lieutenant smiled encouragingly.

"You might as well ask me to tell you my whole life," said Mr. Černý. "It's all right there in your papers."

"There are a lot of them missing, you know," said the lieutenant, wagging his head. "A lot," he repeated, again wagging his head. "I'm guessing you're retired now, sir?"

"What has that got to do with it?"

"Nothing, but are you?"

"Yes," said Mr. Černý.

"Then whenever you're ready, we can begin," the lieutenant said, smiling again.

"What don't you have there in those papers?" Mr. Černý asked.

"We've got a thing or two, but according to the law as it stands, I'm not allowed to tell you what I know from the files and what I don't."

"Why not? I don't understand."

"Not many people do. In fact very few people understand, especially since this is the third law we've had on it now, and God knows how many amendments."

"What does that mean?" asked Mr. Černý.

"That means if you had come six months ago, I could have told you everything, but now I can't tell you anything."

"But I wrote to you more than nine months ago, and in your reply you said you wouldn't be able to get to it for six months."

"Quite right, Mr. Černý. Quite right."

"So why didn't you do it while you still could?"

"The office is under different leadership now, Mr. Černý. Completely different leadership, as you know."

"I don't care what kind of leadership it has."

"I know what you mean, sir. I know what you mean, and I know it isn't easy to understand. I can't even properly explain it myself. I understand and I know you're upset that it's taking so long. But as an employee of this office I have to proceed strictly according to the law. You understand."

"But then why didn't you call me right away?"

"Sir, I wasn't working in this office yet six months ago. And neither was my boss, and neither was his."

"So what am I supposed to do then?" Mr. Černý asked.

"Well, you could tell me how you actually met this Mr. Jánský."

"What for? I was locked up and convicted."

"That's true, but you didn't have your record expunged in the sixties."

"I applied for it to be expunged."

"I realize that, Mr. Černý, but . . ."

"They didn't grant it because the Russians invaded. You should know that."

"I do know that, sir, and I know how unpleasant this must be for you, but—"

"If you know it, then why are you asking me?"

"Even what little I know I can't tell you."

"But six months ago you could have. Yes?"

"Yes. Six months ago I could have, but not now. Now the law has changed, as I said."

"And . . . ?"

"You see, if I told you what I know, I'd be breaking the law. Not the previous one, but the current one. And since the accusations you make are serious enough to land Mr. Jánský in court, I have to proceed strictly according to the law. Do you understand?"

"Not really."

"If I didn't proceed strictly according to the law and the case were to go to court, his attorney could prove that I violated legal procedure. And as a result the whole case could be dismissed. Do you understand me now, sir? I'm on your side, and so is this office, but we all have to proceed according to the law. Strictly by the law."

"And what if the law changes again?" asked Mr. Černý. The lieutenant shrugged.

"Then we'll have to proceed according to that. Strictly by the law in place at the time we do it." Mr. Černý tilted his head as though he were thinking, but didn't say anything. The lieutenant observed him in silence, then after a moment said:

"I forgot to mention, sir, that you should feel free to smoke if you want. I don't mind at all." Mr. Černý returned his head to an upright position.

"I didn't realize that you were on my side, as you put it." The lieutenant nodded. "But if you're on my side, then why didn't you do something about it yourselves?"

"We often get that question," said the lieutenant. "You know, we can't—we can open a case on our own initiative, but only on the basis of requests brought by a citizen. And now that you've lodged a request for the investigation of Mr. Jánský, we can get involved in the case."

"Involved?"

"Yes, involved," said the lieutenant. The door opened and a heavyset woman of about forty with bleach-blond hair walked into the room.

"Hello, Lukáš, how's it going? Oh, hello," the woman said, turning to Mr. Černý. "How's it going?" She set her purse and briefcase on the floor and took off her coat. She hung her coat on the coatrack and smoothed out her jacket, picked up her purse and briefcase from the floor, walked to the desk facing the lieutenant's, and sat down in the chair. She placed her briefcase on the desk, opened it, and pulled out several sheaves of paper, which she placed on the desk. She shut her briefcase, set it on the floor, and started hunting around for something in the drawers of her desk.

"Everything's going well, Helena. Everything's just fine," said the lieutenant.

"That's not true, sir. Not true at all," said Mr. Černý. "Nothing is fine!"

"Well now," said the blonde, giving the lieutenant a look. The lieutenant put on his glasses without bothering to reply.

"Mr. Černý here sent us a three fourteen," he said.

"A three fourteen, hmm?" said the blonde. "And would that be an A, or a B?"

"Well, I'd say more like a B," said the lieutenant.

"Hmm, all right, B," said the blonde.

"What do you mean 'B,' and what is that number you said?" Mr. Černý asked.

"Well, if it's a B, it has to be handled very carefully. You can't even leave the gentleman alone here in the office . . ."

"Certainly, I'm well aware, but the situation hasn't presented itself," said the lieutenant.

"What situation?" asked Mr. Černý.

"Well, the situation has yet to present itself," the lieutenant replied.

"And what situation would that be?" asked Mr. Černý.

"If, for instance, the lieutenant here needed to take care of something in the office next door, say, or go to the bathroom, then you would have to leave the office," said the blonde.

"You think I might steal something?" said Mr. Černý. "You think everyone's a thief, or what?"

"Sir, there's no reason to take it so personally . . ."

"Pardon me, but how else am I supposed to take it?"

"It's just a regulation to make sure you don't accidentally look at the file."

"The file?"

"Yes, the file," said the blonde.

"But it's my file," said Mr. Černý.

"That may be," said the blonde, "but orders are orders and we're required by law to respect them."

"Mr. Černý isn't pleased that the whole thing has to be initiated all over again," the lieutenant told the blonde.

"I don't want to initiate anything. I don't even know what it is, and I don't intend to sit here and tell you my life story. When you get to be my age you might understand."

"We do understand, sir, but the law and the courts aren't going to."

"Do you realize how old I am?"

"It makes no difference, sir. The law applies equally to everyone."

"I already explained to Mr. Černý that we're on his side."

"Yes, we are," said the blonde. "Not only that, but we're here for your sake!"

"I forgot. Mrs. Nováková here is my director," said the lieutenant. The blonde bowed to Mr. Černý. "Major Nováková."

"Right," said the lieutenant with a shrug and a raise of the eyebrows.

"There may be an option here," the blonde said, stepping toward the window. She tested the soil in one of the flowerpots on the sill with her fingers, then folded her arms on her chest.

"You did a beautiful job taking care of my flowers. Really beautiful. I don't have to worry anymore when I go away on business trips."

"What option would that be?" asked the lieutenant.

"Well, the gentleman here could write a statement for us."

"What kind of statement?" asked Mr. Černý.

"Well, instead of us dragging you in here, you could write down for us everything you think is important to the case," the blonde said, turning from the window to Mr. Černý.

"I'm sorry, but I still don't understand," said Mr. Černý.

"Well, we need information from you to use as the basis for initiating an inquiry, and what we have we can't let you look at, since by law you aren't allowed to see it. So what we need is something like a biography from you."

"Biography?" said Mr. Černý.

"Actually, it would be your biography, except at the top we would call it a statement. As far as the contents, though, it would be your biography. Is that it?" the lieutenant asked, fixing his eyes on the blonde.

"Exactly," said the blonde.

"All right, but what should be in it?" asked Mr. Černý.

"The best would be to put in everything you think might be useful," said the blonde.

"Yes, that would be best," said the lieutenant. "We can always cut something out afterwards, or make a summary, but the best would be to have as much as possible."

"All right then," said Mr. Černý. "And once I'm done?"

"Once you're done, give us a call and either you can bring it in or send it to us. We'll take a look and then let you know where we can take it from there."

"It'll take me a while to write."

"The most important thing is for it to be typed," said the lieutenant.

"Right, that's very important," said the blonde.

"Typed?"

"Yes, typed, so we can copy it afterwards. If we don't have to transcribe it, it will save us a lot of work."

Mr. Černý thought a while. "I used to have a typewriter at home. It should be there somewhere still."

"That's good," said the blonde.

"So we're agreed," said the lieutenant. "Once you have it written up, give me a call. I'll read it through and we'll take it from there."

Mr. Černý rose from his seat together with the lieutenant, who gave him a brief, energetic handshake. The blonde, still at the window, nodded good-bye.

The old man stepped out into the long narrow hallway and noticed the dust particles floating in the streams of autumn sun, a few of them here and there drifting into the shade, where they became invisible, ceasing to exist. The laws of attraction didn't seem to apply to them.

Back in the office, the blonde gazed affectionately at her flowers. "I'll probably have to replant this one next week. And the geraniums are just running wild," she said.

"I had no idea we could do it that way," said the lieutenant.

"Yeah, well, as long as the bio is written and submitted to us as a statement, it gives us authority to act on the basis of that."

"That never occurred to me," said the lieutenant.

"Yeah, Vašek's done it like that a few times down in Budějovice."

"I had no idea."

"But it won't do us any good anyway."

"No? Why not?"

"Because the poor old guy will probably die before he finishes it. Even if he does make it all the way to the end and doesn't go out of his mind from reliving all the horrors, they're still planning at least three more revisions to the law."

"And that'll affect this too?"

"Well, not directly, but indirectly it's going to mean even if he does go ahead with it, the whole thing'll be a wash."

"Shouldn't we tell him?"

"Once the amendments go through, sure, but it hasn't happened yet."

"But it might."

"Yes, it might, and it probably will, but it hasn't happened yet."

"So what do we do?"

"Let grandpa have a few more months of hope. Keep taking care of my flowers like this, Lukáš, and I'll put you in for a promotion."

"A bonus would do," said the lieutenant.

"After a watering like this, a bonus is practically in the bag."

"So what about grandpa?" said the lieutenant.

"Well, if it's looking totally hopeless, we could put his name in for a medal."

"We could do that?" asked the lieutenant.

"Not officially, of course," said the blonde. "But unofficially it could be arranged."

"How so?" asked the lieutenant.

"It all depends on the situation, my dear Lukáš. Maybe we can't help him, but a medal doesn't cost anyone anything, and if there's an appropriate occasion, we'll see. From the looks of it," said the blonde, taking another look at the flowerpots, "I think I'm going to have to buy some peat."

6

APPLIED DANTE AND A THEORY OF LANGUAGE

Dr. Antonín Lukavský arrived at work a half hour early that day. It was genuine, authentic prespring. He walked through the main gate of the park surrounding the institute and greeted one of the two apathetic guards. Then, realizing what time it was, he decided to go and sit a while by the small artificial lake, which was still only partially filled. He sat down on a bench, rummaged around a while in a big gym bag, and finally pulled out a thick book whose cover suggested that it was a technical publication. It had been a few years now since the Soviet-led invasion of August 1968, and technical publications were increasingly hard to come by. He reached into his pants pocket, pulled out his cigarettes, opened the book, lit up a smoke, and began to read. Behind him stood a tall bush that would burst forth with flowers over the course of the coming weeks, giving off a scent that was practically narcotic. For now, though, it was just a bush. The garden's layout, with its forking paths unexpectedly dividing and uniting, ensured perfect privacy. There were just two spots that offered a view of nearly the entire park. Every now and then Antonín thought about suggesting they put in plants around each pavilion having some association with the illnesses treated inside. As he lit his second cigarette, he heard two voices engaged in discussion behind him. He ignored them for a while, but eventually his concentration lapsed and he began to eavesdrop in spite of himself.

"But they don't get it at all, Marek," said the first voice.

"No, Václav, they certainly don't," said the second voice, higher and shriller.

"They don't get the meaning of the myth or the assistant," said Václav.

"Or the assistant," Marek repeated.

"Although actually . . . the myth *is* the assistant, isn't it?" said Václav.

"Absolutely, brother. We're in agreement there. Full agreement, not the slightest debate."

"And yet they don't understand," Václav said.

"Of course the question posed in that way is neither substantiated nor explicated. Though of course," Marek gave a shrill laugh, "what do they truly understand, right?"

"What do they understand?" Václav repeated in his lower voice.

"It's neither posed nor substantiated nor explicated, am I right?"

"Of course, things are constantly coming into being," said Václav. "Danger and delight, no one is forgiven anything, or absolved of anything, either. Danger and delight just keep on wrapping themselves in new sheets, and no one is forgiven even so much as a cent."

"You're right about that, little brother. Not a penny," Marek said.

Suddenly realizing that the second, higher voice belonged to his patient Marek the pastry chef, Dr. Lukavský perked up his ears.

"So what would you do, friend, if you had to write a myth? What would it be about?"

"I think the best . . . hm . . . I think it's best when they're about a country or a person. Don't you?"

"No. Listen, friend. You're not paying attention. Pull yourself together. Sharpen up and stop eating so much of that French herb. I can't stand the smell."

"All I smell is cigarettes."

"Cigarettes? Please. The whole park stinks of French seasoning."

"I promise it won't happen again."

"The answer is hidden, as always, in what you were saying. As always, the most enigmatic problems are best hidden in broad daylight."

"In what?"

"Broad daylight," Václav repeated. "That means out in the open, in other words staring you right in the face. A myth shouldn't be either/or, but both/and."

"Both/and?" Marek said.

"Yes. Both about a country and about a person."

"So there you go."

"Exactly."

Dr. Lukavský heard a loud belch, immediately followed by a yawn. Then a third voice breathlessly joined in:

"I just woke up at the edge of a pool of water where I was walking along the bottom and rushing toward the surface. You see, surfacing equals waking up. One is always equal only to one. As long as it isn't divided by zero, that is. Then I woke up and overheard the two of you. But the main thing I wanted to say is, Stop eating so much garlic, František. I can't stand it. And we're out in the open."

"That's what I keep telling him," Václav said. "It stinks up the whole place, and besides, who knows what side effects it has?"

"Side effects?" the pastry chef said. "What side effects?"

"Who knows?" said Václav. "Maybe revolution."

"Revolution?" the pastry chef said. "As a side effect of eating garlic, or as you call it, the French herb? Alias the culinary weed?"

"The influence of digestion on political and philosophical thought has without doubt yet to be adequately explored," Václav said. "I'm giving you both an assignment for tomorrow. Consider carefully which dishes would best represent the following three slogans."

"I'm going to have to write this down," the third voice said.

"First, Liberté, Egalité, Fraternité. Second, God Save the Queen. And third, Truth Prevails!"

"The last one's easy, brother Václav. Wild boar with cowberries," the pastry chef said.

"Why wild boar and why cowberries?" Václav asked.

"I was soaking wet when I trudged over here. In my dream I overslept a little and had a little swim. It was quite the rude awakening when I sloshed up to shore. As to your question concerning myths, I must say, years ago I outlined this very problem in a letter to my friend Scaliger, vicar general of the imperial government in Vicenza and Verona."

"If you don't mind, Duarte, get to the point, or we'll all catch cold out here," Václav said.

"Fine," said Duarte. "You today are partial to illusions of equality, but we never suffered such illusions for a moment. What I wrote to him back then may be of use to you."

"Maybe," Václav replied in a menacing voice. "Yet every work has multiple meanings, multiple uses. To put it candidly and straightforwardly, every work, and therefore every life, no matter how small or trivial, is polysemous."

"What does that mean?" the pastry chef said.

"That means," Duarte went on, "that every work has more than one interpretation. The first is literary: from the Latin *litera*, meaning 'letter,' meaning literally literal. The others are allegorical, moral, and anagogical."

"You're going to have to stick it out in the woods on your own, you prick! Or my name isn't František!" the pastry chef cried. It looked as if he was going to pounce on Duarte any minute. Dr. Lukavský got a little nervous, wondering whether he should intervene in the discussion, when all of a sudden he heard:

"What are you talking about?" said Václav. "You're Marek, remember?"

"Oh, right," Marek said, calm returning to his voice. "My apologies, friends, but long foreign words make me crazy."

"Don't worry about it," said Duarte. "That's why we're here, right? So we can be under rigorous medical supervision. But perhaps I might explain by way of example, for example," he said, unconsciously smacking his lips. "For example, take the example of Psalm 114, which tells us: 'When Israel went out of Egypt, the house of Jacob from a people of strange language, Judah was *his* sanctuary, and Israel *his* dominion.' That's how it goes, yes, yes . . ." He smacked his lips drily again, then went on: "So just to plod along here, dissecting the words alone, what these words lined up like swallows on a wire actually tell us is that the sons of Israel walked out of Egypt under Moses' leadership."

"There were no telegraph wires back then, Duarte. What are you babbling?" Marek said.

"He's right," Václav chimed in. "There were no telegraph wires back then."

"But there were swallows," Duarte snapped back. He went on: "Meanwhile, allegorically, Psalm 114 speaks to us of redemption. Our redemption and ours alone, friends. Redemption through Christ our Lord. As for its moral meaning, well, even in this immoral land of ours and the area adjoining it, the moral meaning is a turning away of the soul from poverty and depressing sorrow toward a state of grace. As for the anagogical meaning, it signifies a liberation of the soul from the slavery of transgression into eternal glory and freedom. But please—I emphasize: please—this is not to be confused with *liberté*. All of these things may be called allegorical, seeing as they are neither literal nor historical. As I have just demonstrated, the obvious conclusion is that the material, the subject matter, must be twofold, double, or dual. In order for both meanings to apply."

"If I understand you correctly," Václav said, "it's a little bit like an alternating-current generator. Only that has three phases, so it would be triple."

"It might have something to do with the Holy Trinity, although in the interest of prudence I would just as soon avoid that for the moment," Duarte said. "In principle, however, you're most likely right."

"If I understand all this correctly, the meaning of a myth ought to be Earth," Václav said.

"Precisely, precisely," Duarte cheered. "In our case, an Earth that has been raped. Although when we look around us, it certainly seems to enjoy it. And Earth has been allegorized as a raped woman since time immemorial."

"Don't you think that's kind of a stereotype?" said Václav.

"Absolutely, absolutely, but there's nothing I can do about it, and besides, I was hoping to have a little chat with you now about three-phase electric power and the threefold nature of God."

"Brothers, I'm dying for a cigarette so badly I can taste it," the pastry chef said.

"I can taste it too," said Václav, standing up from the bench. Suddenly Dr. Lukavský realized they were talking about him. He put his book back in the gym bag, cleared his throat, stood up, threw the bag over his shoulder, and stepped around the bush.

"Hello, Marek," he said.

"This is my brother doctor, friends," said the pastry chef. "And these are my friends, doctor. This is Václav," he said, pointing to a brown-skinned African man of average height eyeing the doctor suspiciously. "And this is Duarte," he gestured toward his dumpier companion, who stood a half head shorter.

Duarte gave the doctor a kindly nod. "Greetings, Dottore. I'm Duarte. Duarte Alighieri, also known to my friends as Dante!"

The doctor gave them each a cigarette and offered Duarte a light. The African stuck his in his breast pocket and went on carefully watching the doctor.

"Well, I'm going to have to be on my way," said Dr. Lukavský.

"We didn't even notice you, brother doctor," said the pastry chef. "It must be the white smock."

"But I'm not wearing my smock."

"Exactly, that's what I mean," the pastry chef said.

"I was just on my way to work," the doctor said.

"Happy consultations," said the African.

The doctor gave them all a quick glance and headed off for his office.

That day at lunch in the cafeteria, he sat down at a table with his colleague from the pavilion next door and told him about the conversation he had overheard.

"That one, the black man—actually he's mulatto—his name is Václav and he's been with us a month now. Knotty case. And the other one, that's Dante."

"Dante?" asked Antonín.

"Dante," said his colleague.

"So how did that mulatto man end up with a Czech name, especially one as Czech as Václav?"

"He doesn't talk much to anyone. Always reading and writing. Reads all sorts of things, I've noticed. The file he came in with said he knew Czech remarkably well for a black man."

"I thought you said he was born here?"

"He was, but some people think no matter who a Czech mixes with, there's no way their children can learn Czech."

"Even if they were born here?"

"Even if they were born here."

"And what do you think?"

"I don't think anything. I don't want to get in trouble."

"Isn't that kind of strange?" asked Antonín.

"Some people say it clearly proves that people of mixed background can never learn to speak proper Czech, even if they were born here. Never mind blacks."

"Even if they were born here?"

"Even if they were born here. By the way, this is a revolutionary new theory."

"Really? I didn't think that kind of thing existed anymore. Theories of race and whatnot."

"Don't even say the word *race*. Are you crazy? I hope no one heard us," Antonín's colleague said, glancing furtively around the room.

"Fine," said Antonín. "I won't say the word *race*. But I thought theories like that went out with World War II."

"World War II?" said Antonín's colleague. "Now don't get angry, Tonda, but you always were naïve. World War II?" Antonín's colleague said again, rolling his eyes to emphasize his utter dismay at the backwardness of the Czechoslovak universe and the adjoining regions.

"So what's the story with that Václav fellow? What is he doing here?" Dr. Lukavský asked.

"I asked the same thing, but he didn't want to tell us too much.

He just said he was writing something for fun and he'd appreciate it if we left him alone. Said he enjoys writing, even if he doesn't know Czech that well. From which I deduced he probably knows about that theory."

"I see," said Antonín. "Well, let me know if anything new develops. I think he's friends with one of my patients."

"Will do. Assuming, that is, I'm lucky enough that he decides to talk to me." Antonín's colleague straightened the dishes on his plastic tray, stood up, said good-bye, and carried his dirty dishes to the corner of the cafeteria, where he placed the tray on a small table designated for that purpose.

7

PERSONAL STATEMENT AKA BIOGRAPHY
(NINETEEN NINETIES)

Dear Lieutenant,

I was born November 24, 1915, which means I am now more than seventy years old. Before I come to a description of my education, origins, and other information that most of the authorities have required of me during my life in this country, however, I would like to make a few basic points. As you know, I am a retired engineer. As a result, expressing myself verbally does not come naturally to me. Nevertheless, the reason I am writing to you is as follows: I would like to request that your office investigate the activities of Mr. Jánský and submit to me a report on this investigation. It is my belief that any person who tortures another person is committing a misdeed, which is to say a crime, regardless of when and where it takes place. It is therefore my belief that in torturing me Mr. Jánský committed a punishable offense. I would like to stress, however, that it is not his physical punishment I seek; I am not asking that he spend time in prison. Provided my memory is correct, his birthday falls on March 23rd, which means he is a few months older even than me. Having been granted the good fortune to live to this age, I no longer demand either retribution or revenge; nonetheless, your investigation still matters to me. It matters because of my wife, Květa. What you know or do not know is not clear to me. Following the kind advice of you and your colleague, in the following pages I shall attempt to express and impart whatever I can to enable you to commence — or initiate, as you say — your investigation.

The reason for my approaching your office is personal. I feel this is my last chance to make my marriage whole again. I do not know what you have in your files, but the fact remains that my fate, and that of my wife, was, and I am afraid still is, connected in some way or other with the fate or—if you will—the life of Mr. Hynek Jánský.

Hynek and I made each other's acquaintance in high school, at the so-called *reálná škola*, for natural sciences, and that marked the beginning of a long-lasting friendship. Some time later, I went off to study civil engineering at the Technical University in Prague while he went to law school at Charles University. The two of us went on weekend trips with friends. We went to pubs, concerts, soccer matches. And then, one day, on our way to some hill or other, a group of girls joined in with us, and one of them was Květa. I admit, she didn't appeal to me at first sight. I didn't much like her name—Flower!—or her figure, but she had a nice voice. Both she and her name struck me as so . . . vulgar. And when I found out in the fall that her favorite flower was dahlias, it didn't surprise me at all; I had never been fond of them either. I was young, Lieutenant. I was young and I thought love meant loving only roses or hyacinths, and when it came to girls, only Kateřinas or Maries or Barbaras. Certainly not any Květas, Lieutenant, definitely not! And then gradually I realized I was missing something. Yes, I was missing the girl with the ordinary name. Of course I didn't know it. I wasn't aware of anything. I wasn't aware of love. I was just missing something, I was lonely. All of a sudden I felt more alone than ever before. And whenever somebody mentioned they had seen her somewhere, my heart, which back then was strong as a rock, would flutter up into the air before settling back down to earth. And then too, to my surprise, I began to get jealous. I was jealous of everyone who spent time with her while I had to study. I didn't feel flames of passion. I didn't feel like I couldn't live without her. I didn't feel the agony of a barren planet floating through the empty universe. Nothing like that. But when I asked her to marry me, I thought she would say yes right away, and when she said she needed a week to think it over, I was confused. Instead of going home and attending my lectures the next day, I walked the city for two days, and the third day I fell asleep on a bench in Letná Park in the afternoon. I wanted to talk it over with someone. I was thinking maybe Hynek, but I had a feeling he wanted to court her, too, so I kept it to myself. A few days later we saw each other, and I eagerly asked if she'd made up her mind, and she said yes! She didn't have to say anything, actually, since I could already tell by the tone in her voice. It wasn't until years later, before the birth of our daughter, Alice, that I asked her why she had taken a week to make up her mind. She said she thought I was acting too confident. "Me, confident?" I said. "Yes, you," Květa said. "How so? In what way?" "You acted like . . . like it was the only solution." "For me there was no other solution," I said. "Was there for you?" "Not really," she said, "but I wanted to shake you up, at least a little. I was so in love with you and you didn't even notice." "But I asked you to marry me," I said. "You did," Květa said, "but not until after almost everyone else had already done it and I had chased them all away, waiting for you." Suddenly I realized why Hynek had been avoiding me. "Did Hynek ask you too?" I asked. "About three times," Květa said. "In fact, he was really mad at me for a while. I didn't tell him I was waiting for you, but he always was sharper than you when it came to those things. Maybe that's why I chose you. I mean, apart from the minor detail that I was head over heels in love." That's what my wife, Květa, told me, Lieutenant. That's what she told me back then. And I realized: I hadn't just chosen and fallen in love; I had also been chosen and loved. It hit me, that moment, in prison. The feeling, the feeling of Květa's love, it was so obvious: her love for me. It was like a little Christmas in the middle of the Siberian tundra.

I'm a technical man, Lieutenant. An engineer. I feel my feelings, but I don't analyze them, and there are certain things, including emotions, that I'm just not wired for, as they say these days. Back in my day, they taught us that love should be romantic, so when real love came along, I almost missed it. I wasn't wired for it. I know that now, and it's all right. At my age, you're only embarrassed by your physical shortcomings, which may be unattractive but are more awkward than anything else. I've always been relatively proud of the fact that I don't let my feelings drag me around like some of my friends and colleagues do. Every now and then, of course, I get flooded with waves of emotion, positive and negative alike. But the vast majority of the time I keep them under control. Whenever I've found it difficult to cope with my feelings, I've thrown myself into my work or devoted myself to my family. That's what I've tried to do, all my life. Needless to say, our youth was an eventful one, some have referred to it as revolutionary, and as far as my field is concerned, it was definitely revolutionary. When I began my studies and I was learning how to perform static calculations, I used a slide rule. A slide rule operates on the basis of relationships, a system of distances, scales, and corrected errors. Its invention and perfection were the product of sophisticated thinking about the problem of numbers and scales. Then came calculators, and now computers. Like every old man, Lieutenant, I feel closest to the things I learned in my youth. I remember thirty years ago, sometime back in the sixties, Květa read me an article about some Eastern religion or philosophy. The author was trying to explain the concept of total and complete peace of mind—I think I would say peace of brain. The whole article was about how not to assail your mind with thoughts burdened by feelings and moods. When she finished reading it and we talked about it after dinner, I told her, That's exactly what I do. They wrote about mandalas, which, if I remember correctly, are a sort of circular symbol, and about reciting prayers, and about rosaries with a hundred and eight beads that you slip between your fingers in between breathing in and out, and about freeing the mind. The peace they described was something I always felt whenever I worked. I liked work, I liked calculating. I liked the feeling of holding a slide rule in my hands, and even though eventually I was forced to use calculators, I never got used to them. Numerical series were my rosary beads. The sliding movement of the cursor along the scales, that was what freed my mind. Calculations and computations of sums, those were the prayers I recited. Even as later on the calculators they gave me got better and better, I always kept a few slide rules in the third drawer down on the right. The drawer was locked. Needless to say. I didn't want anyone to see my pet slide rules and think that I was against the times. I wanted to be with the times, I just didn't quite understand it all. So I said as much to Květa, without giving it too much thought, and she opened wide her big green eyes and looked at me and said: "So that's why you stay at work so late all the time? You really love it, don't you, Josef?" I don't remember anymore what I said, but whatever it was, it didn't make much sense.

One of the signs of old age, Lieutenant, at least in my case, is that your brain ceases to be rational. More and more I'm subject to my emotions and moods, and worst of all, once I enter down the path of one of those mental processes, which are still for the most part new to me, I never know when or where it will end. It's a journey into terra incognita, and even though in any unfamiliar terrain there are always makeshift landmarks you can use to help determine your spatial coordinates, at my age, with my old man's emotions, I'm afraid it just isn't possible. Instead, it feels more like a desert, where any orientation point, any system of triangulation, is constantly changing and therefore can't be used to map your position. Although the fact is that even the Sahara Desert is nearly ninety percent rock, which most people don't realize, and therefore even my second comparison above would seem to be unfounded. It seems to me that just as there is no universally accepted method for measuring the magnitude of pain or love, I lack a suitable and properly calibrated instrument with which to measure my feelings.

Assistant Lecturer Horský taught us at university, and sometimes he would also tell us stories about his travels in Syria and other parts of the Middle East. He had been there as a young man with Professor Hrozný, the scientist who deciphered the language of the Hittites. He told us about how they made him responsible for technical oversight of the project: surveying existing conditions, producing a basic mapping of territories, drawing site plans, and also collecting beetles. Really! He was an engineer who collected beetles. He said that was the hardest and most demanding part, since he didn't like beetles, but the head of the beetle division at the National Museum had asked him to do it, since the museum didn't have any beetles from those parts yet. Frankly, I wasn't too interested in Assistant Lecturer Horský's adventures in Turkey and Syria. But then one day, as he was ending his lecture, he veered off again into the Turkey of his youth with the words: "The date November 24, 1915, will be forever—remember, forever!—engraved in the history of Czechoslovak and world science," and I woke from the state of half-sleep in which I spent most of my afternoon lectures. Here allow me a small detour to say that up until my imprisonment, I had always passed the hour between two and three P.M. engaged in a light afternoon nap. Unfortunately, this regular habit of mine came to an end the day I was imprisoned. As I stated above, I am still incapable of falling asleep in the afternoon to this day, even in the most favorable environment. The truth is I fear I might have unpleasant dreams related to those ten years I spent behind bars. But back to Assistant Lecturer Horský. Occasionally his lectures happened to fall precisely from two to three P.M., in which case I was obliged to forgo my afternoon nap, although I would doze all the way through the lecture. But all of a sudden the date he mentioned, November 24, 1915, woke me up. That was the day I was born. "What happened that day?" I asked, incongruously torn from my slumber. Assistant Lecturer Horský gave me a suspicious look and said in a voice laden with irony: "Apparently you have been absent more than once, Mr. Černý, or you would know that was the day of Professor Hrozný's immortal lecture at the German Oriental Society in which he solved the riddle of the history of the Hittite state, culture, and literature—all of this, if you please, gentlemen, through his decipherment of a language previously unknown, albeit written in cuneiform script, which at that point was known. A deed worthy of a genius, gentlemen, and it is our privilege to be able to walk the same streets of Prague as Professor Hrozný." It was the same date. The date of his lecture was the date of my birth. A few days later I told Květa and she was even more intrigued than I was. "Don't you think it's interesting?" she asked. "I do, but it's just a coincidence," I said. "All right, but what did he actually discover?" "He didn't discover anything, he deciphered it," I said. "What?" Květa asked. "A language, a language nobody knew." "You can do that?" "I suppose so. If he did it, that means you can." Květa couldn't get it out of her head. She was so obsessed she went to the library and took out a book on ancient cultures and languages. It gave the same date as Assistant Lecturer Horský had told us: November 24, 1915. My date of birth. The day I was born was the same day Professor Hrozný showed the world a new language. It's no mean feat, deciphering a three thousand–year–old language, I'm telling you, Lieutenant. And this wasn't the Latin alphabet, this was in cuneiform. Hittite was the oldest Indo-European language preserved in written form. Truly an accomplishment. The history of the Hittite people. Their gods, their laws, their lives. Weddings and funerals, rewards and punishments, battles and wars, won and lost . . . Language is the key to all these things, but what good is it when their empire died out twelve hundred years before the birth of Jesus Christ?

Cuneiform? The first time I saw those odd wedge-shaped marks, they looked to me like waterfowl tracks. Like footprints of birds with webbed feet. Much smaller, though. Like some sort of aquatic sparrows. The characters of cuneiform script were made using a cut reed as a stylus and pressing it into moist clay. The marks it makes are wedge-shaped, hence the name *cuneiform*—from *cuneus*, "wedge," and *forma*, "shape." The script is said to have originated in Mesopotamia with the Sumerians, but it was adapted for use by many different languages, much like the Latin alphabet today. Whenever you aren't sure about something and it happened a long time ago in the Middle East, just chalk it up to the Sumerians! Of course that's just an old man's inappropriate comment, Lieutenant, don't pay it any mind. They say the Hittite documents written in cuneiform script represent the oldest Indo-European language. And for your information, Lieutenant, the Hittites inhabited the area covered by present-day Turkey and Syria, known in my youth as Anatolia.

So really the only reason for my interest in the whole thing was that Květa was intrigued by the fact that my birthday was the same day as Professor Hrozný's famous lecture on deciphering the Hittite language. She had a better imagination than I did, she always has, and over time I learned not to oppose her using logical arguments and facts. It was easy, I didn't even have to try that hard. You know, when she let loose her fantasy—or actually I should say fantasies, since she was overflowing with them—it was truly a beautiful thing.

You could see the expression on her face change as she imagined what the people back then would have thought if they had known that someone would still be interested in them three thousand years after their death. Did it ever even occur to them the way it does to us? Did they talk about it when they were raising their children? Going into battle? Celebrating weddings? It may not seem too original to you, Lieutenant. I realize a lot of people have thoughts like these in certain situations, when they visit a museum, say, or tour a historical site. But when Květa talked about it, her eyes would get big as saucers one minute, then shrink to slits the next, and sometimes she would close them completely. I must say, I find it obnoxious when a person closes their eyes while talking to someone else. Few things irritate me more than lack of manners. But when Květa shut her eyes for a few seconds, Lieutenant, that was something entirely different, because the instant she reopened them, they were that much greener, that much bigger, that much deeper. I admit sometimes I didn't grasp her conclusions and deductions, but I didn't interrupt, even when her conclusions violated the simple logic of causality, a cornerstone of any objective argument. I was happy just to look at her, just to be able to watch. Initially I didn't get it. It was like a spreading disease, a gradual surrendering of my own abilities, just to listen to her, just to watch, to look at her, be with her. Yes, the more she spoke about those things the more I loved her. Plain and simple, I loved my wife. There was nothing original whatsoever about my feelings. They were completely banal.

And then one day it occurred to me—all important things occur to people one day, or at least that's what they always write—that there were still languages that hadn't been deciphered. Professor Hrozný had done it; maybe I could, too. I still remember what she said when I told her. "That would be fabulous, Josef. That would be absolutely, positively fabulous." We had just been swimming in the pool at Žluté lázně, and maybe it was the way her hair was blowing in the wind that made what she said seem so attractive. Maybe I wanted to impress her. Yes, I wanted to impress her. I wanted to be with her, in the realm of her imagination with her hair blowing in the wind. And unlikely as it may sound, I must admit some limitations on my part as well. It had never crossed my mind before that there might be languages that hadn't been deciphered. Even with a star like Professor Hrozný there in front of us the whole time, even with all the newspapers reporting his latest discoveries in the Middle East, even with all that going on, right in broad daylight, so to speak, it had never dawned on me personally. Květa and I had been once or twice to public lectures by our famous professor. I sat beside her, looking at her, and as we were walking home I realized I had no idea what the lecture had been about. All I knew was it was the closest I had ever been to being jealous. The professor had had her undivided attention for forty minutes. As we walked home, she was in a wonderful mood, cheerful and sweet, laughing the entire way. I couldn't concentrate at all. And that's when it came to me: I would try to decipher a language! Květa and I could do it together. Needless to say, as soon as I had this bold idea, my very next thought was that I was indulging in dangerous fantasy. Nevertheless, I was intrigued by the idea. It was childish in the same way as wanting to walk through ancient catacombs, or trying to discover treasure on a deserted island. Today I can see, even if I was unable to admit it at the time, that I felt a bit like Abbé Faria and the Count of Monte Cristo crossed with Heinrich Schliemann, the discoverer of Troy. I beg you not to judge me too harshly, Lieutenant. All I wanted was to impress a woman, a feeling that was new to me. I had never had much of an imagination before, so the idea excited me. Without mentioning it to Květa, then, I attempted to find out how one went about deciphering an unknown language. I knew nothing about it, but my sense was it had nothing to do with static calculations, a subject I had always mastered with flying colors. Eventually, by way of a few subtle questions, I learned that cracking a language would impress Květa even more than I had initially thought. I still had a memory of the photo I had seen in a biography of Heinrich Schliemann. He was wearing a black suit and his wife, Sophia, stood beside him, adorned in jewelry thousands of years old, which they had discovered together. I wanted to give Květa something, something extraordinary, stupendous. Something entirely beyond my capabilities and strength. Foolish, obviously; how could it be otherwise? It is foolish to try to express affection and love.

I got started. The first thing I learned was that everyone who ever deciphered anything was a brilliant linguist. I was neither brilliant nor a linguist. All of them were proficient in their own mother tongues. I was proficient in mine. All of them were proficient in the languages of Europe's great powers: unfortunate German, elegant French, and imprecise English, as well as the dead languages Latin and Greek; some also knew the languages of the Old Testament. The stupidity of my endeavor was gradually revealed to me. Nevertheless I didn't give up. After all, I knew from the start it wouldn't be easy. The most important thing is a system, I told myself. A system and accurate, logical thinking. Somehow I neglected to pay attention to what they said between the lines about brilliance and intuition. I had a new hobby. Having a hobby was in itself a new and fascinating experience. Unfortunately, history intruded on our lives as it had on the lives of the ancient Hittites. The times we lived in were all too interesting: a brief, frantic two-year run of democracy after the war, followed by a communist putsch. I was allowed to work a while still and then I was arrested. The reason is irrelevant now. What does it matter when my marriage to the only woman I ever loved is ruined? I don't harbor much hope that anything can be repaired in my case, at my age. I would just like us to be able to forgive each other. Or rather, for me to be able to forgive, since after all, I can't speak for her. I would like to be free of the bitterness that eats at my heart. I would like to forgive. And now forgive an old man for taking up your time with his blather. If you are losing time, I am losing my mind. I loved her alone, which is probably seen as something of a material defect nowadays. I come from a different time, though, a time that is on its way out. In fact, it is nearly dead and gone. I could still afford the luxury of not choosing from one of the other options.

I was arrested, taken away, and when they brought me to the interrogation room and sat me down, there was Hynek sitting across from me. Hynek Jánský, my dearest friend, my tennis partner. A polished attorney at law. First he tried to convince me to sign something, then he begged, then he swore up and down, and then he practically started crying: "Josef, dear Josef, my friend, if you don't do what I ask, there are others who will come after me. And they will be like wild animals. That's how they are, believe me. I know them and they will kill you. You won't survive even one session, Josef. We both know that. Even the bravest hero couldn't stand up to them, and you and me, we're no heroes. We're just ordinary men, tennis partners." And he was right. I never have been a hero. But at first I didn't sign. I hadn't yet realized that it wasn't just about me. It all happened so fast, it hadn't hit me yet. The arrest happened so suddenly I had trouble getting my bearings. And he was right, the ones who came after him really were like wild animals. What he neglected to tell me was that they were at his command. Little by little, I saw my friend Hynek change before my eyes into Ullikummi. Ullikummi, a giant made of stone, was also deaf and blind. His father, the Hurrian god Kumarbi, made him that way so he wouldn't be susceptible to beauty or compassion. If you want to know more, by the way, you can read the Kumarbi cycle of myths. But at any rate, Kumarbi was the father of all the Hittite gods, until he was dethroned as ruler, for reasons that are beside the point now. In order to regain his throne, he fathered several monsters, including Ullikummi, whom he spawned by having intercourse with a rock. Once he was born, Kumarbi deposited his hell-spawn on the shoulder of the god Upelluri, who stood in the netherworld holding up the earth and sky, kind of like our Atlas. Nothing could move Upelluri. He was oblivious to everything. He noticed nothing even when heaven and earth were separated and cut apart from each other with a copper saw. A deed that shook the universe. A deed that made worlds wonder whether they would crumble into atoms. A deed that caused the gods to stop breathing and their hearts to pause in flight. And because Upelluri alias Atlas felt none of this, Lieutenant, Kumarbi placed his spawn, the stone monster Ullikummi, on Upelluri's shoulder. And indeed, Upelluri felt no pain until Ullikummi started to grow. After fifteen days the stone giant towered all the way up to the sky, and the god of the sun noticed him, and then all the other gods saw he was there and were seized with panic and dismay. They called for the storm god, but even he didn't dare do anything, and so his sister Ishtar, who was possessed of many womanly charms, decided she would enchant the stone giant. Kumarbi, however, had counted on this, which was why he begat his son from a rock, creating Ullikummi deaf, blind, and devoid of feeling. The storm god set in motion a sort of general mobilization, calling up thunderbolts, gale winds, hailstones, and his two sacred bulls, but good fortune was not on his side, Lieutenant. Teshub the storm god and his seventy godly allies lost the battle. Ullikummi continued to grow, threatening the storm god's palace itself, a place where all dreaded to set foot. It was forbidden even to mention, and its master could be spoken of only in riddles, never by name, lest its owner be summoned. Ullikummi was threatening the palace of the storm god, his shadow covering more and more of the land as he grew. The sun god had to change his path for fear of Ullikummi, leading whole landscapes to perish for lack of sunshine. The lack of sun caused hunger, misery, and death, but the gods were even more fearful than the people, because they had more to lose and Ullikummi was growing without end. The gods, yes, the very gods themselves were at a loss, and so they had no choice but to seek the advice of Ea, god of wisdom. Nowadays they would call in a consulting firm for an assessment, but different country, different customs, as they say, Lieutenant. Now, when the god of wisdom realized that Ullikummi was growing on the shoulder of Upelluri, he consulted the ancient annals for guidance and learned that he had to cut Ullikummi off, detach him from Upelluri, using the same tool that had once been used to cut apart heaven and earth. This all happened in Hittite myth in Mesopotamia thousands of years ago, and the name of the deaf, blind, and unfeeling stone giant, Ullikummi, sounded so harmless to me, so onomatopoetic, so innocent, just like the name of my erstwhile friend and tennis partner, Hynek—an outstanding amateur tennis player who I later found out had denounced tennis as a bourgeois sport and played it only in secret—a friend of mine and my family's, my friend Ullikummi. And then all of a sudden my friend Ullikummi explained to me that I was just a harmless fool, a regular idiot, if I couldn't see that this wasn't at all about me, but part of a master plan of tyranny and revenge by one set of people against another. It was under way even as we spoke, and my role in it was negligible. He said that if I didn't sign the statement they had prepared for me and learn it by heart, it would only take one call for them to bring in my wife as well, and who was going to take care of my little daughter then? He spoke with his back facing me. It was springtime and we could see a cherry tree blossoming in the yard out the window. But I knew, I could feel, that he was savoring the effect of his words on me and the fear that they evoked. He knew he just had to mention two names, just a casual comment—Oh, say, by the way, how are Květa and your dear daughter Alice?—and I would do whatever he wanted, whatever they wanted me to. Anything. I still couldn't believe my senses. Which for that matter by that point were considerably damaged. By then I could hear in only one ear anyway, because when they fire a gun off next to your ear, it's not just the pain and the pulsing of blood and the earthquake that shatters your body, from your spine to your muscles and spilling into your capillaries . . . by then I just couldn't believe that what I was hearing was the voice of my friend Hynek proposing blackmail to me. I didn't know and I couldn't understand, because no one had bothered to tell me that at some point along the way he had changed into Ullikummi. Into a blind stone giant who had come to destroy me, and keep on destroying me, blind and deaf and heartless, with no concept of love or beauty, let alone compassion or friendship.

And so they locked me up. I was locked up for ten years. Alice was only a few months old when they put me away, and I'm sorry for those ten years. I'm sorry I didn't see her grow up. When I came home, she was almost eleven and headed full steam for adulthood. And though I tried, I never could make up for those years. When I came home, I was a stranger to her.

But even before then, before I completely gave up on everything, at those moments when I still had some barely quantifiable fraction of hope, I tried to hold on to my dream and at least learn a little bit, as much as I was capable of, about the cultures of antiquity. By the time I came home from jail, Professor Hrozný was dead. I knew he had been trying to decipher another script, called Linear B. From what I heard, he had failed or come up short, but before they released me from prison, an English architect named Ventris deciphered it, in 1956. He was an architect, I was a structural engineer. We were practically colleagues. All that I found out only after my return to freedom. Outside our country, time passed quickly; inside, it had come to a standstill. More out of habit than anything else, as a sort of luxury hobby, every now and then I go to the library and borrow some books on antiquity. I circled around it for a long time, but then it struck me it would be good to learn another language, one that people actually spoke. So I gave it a try, starting with French. I took it slow and steady, and I admit I wasn't much good. I got the grammar, even the exceptions, and the pronunciation, too, but whenever I studied the vocabulary I would slip into a black hole and get caught up in unwanted memories. The moment I closed my eyes so I could concentrate on the words, I would find myself back at the interrogation, in the dark, sitting on a metal chair with a scarf over my eyes, caked in the blood running down my face, just barely breathing.

After a while I gave up. I couldn't keep going back to the worst moments of my life. Throughout all my studies I had been able to learn difficult things by closing my eyes and watching them appear in front of me like a series of wide-angle color pictures. I couldn't do that anymore. I had no choice but to surrender my youthful dreams, and all I had left was my shabby attempt to win back the love of my wife.

Dear Lieutenant, I'm not entirely sure this statement or biography of mine will be of any use. In any case, I hope it is, and I am fully at your service.

Respectfully,
Ing. Josef Černý
(structural engineer, retired)

8

FIRST VISION OF IMMORTALITY: PERSIA

Dr. Antonín Lukavský wasn't entirely satisfied with pastry chef Marek Svoboda's explanation as to why he had adopted Hitler as one of his chosen names. Needless to say, the patient exhibited clear paranoid tendencies in relation to women and to human society in general. On top of that, there was the notion of scientific progress put to monstrous ends, which existed solely in the patient's imagination. Technically it wasn't feasible, nor clearly would it be at any point in the future. The one thing that was clear in all of this was the patient's predilection for fantastic stories. Dr. Lukavský also considered whether the patient might have some reason to simulate a psychological disorder, but he could find no apparent motive. There had been a change on the unit, however. The arrival of the pastry chef had led to a sharp increase in the quality of the otherwise mediocre fare. He had very quickly introduced himself to the hospital cooks, and the food not only smelled good now but was also unusually tasty, and Antonín couldn't help noticing that the patients, the staff, even he himself, had begun to look forward to meals. As for Svoboda himself, however, after a few weeks it was clear he didn't need to remain on the unit, and he was released under the condition that he visit Antonín in his office once a month. The two of them talked about everything imaginable, and Antonín actually enjoyed their conversations. He found Svoboda's directness refreshing. More than once they ended up in a dispute about the meaning of medicine.

"What is the point of it anyway?" Svoboda asked.

"Health!" said Dr. Lukavský.

"And once the causes of every disease are discovered and they are all cured?"

"That's an abstract problem. I'm not concerned. It won't happen in my lifetime."

"And what comes after that?" asked Marek. "After that, its true nature will be exposed, which is the desire for immortality. I'm almost certain, brother," he said firmly. "I've had two visions on this topic, two visions on immortality. Today I'll tell you the one that took place far from here and in the past. Next Thursday I'll be passing by and I can tell you the other one, which transpired here, but in the future."

He began as follows: "We were traversing the mountains. My wife and I, my younger brother, a few relatives, and a team of porters, helpers, and servants. I could no longer tell whether we were refugees or merchants. For that matter, the difference between them didn't seem so great. We were surrounded by high mountains. I said we were traversing the mountains, but what I should have said was we were trying to avoid them. Traversing the mountains doesn't mean traversing *over* the mountains. We attempted, craftily, like clever snakes, to slip through gorges and passes, bribe guards, pay guides, avoid customs. We were attempting to elude our natural fate, we were attempting something daring: to survive. We sold a variety of goods, smuggled a variety of goods, bought and sold everything there was to buy and sell, and even then we had only enough to shield our nakedness. We headed for Persia, evading one army after another along the way. By early spring I hoped to be in Tabriz, where I had arranged some business the previous year. This year we set out a little sooner, but spring had changed from a blossoming maiden into an old woman, her face covered in smallpox. Winter wasn't going away. In fact, just the opposite.

"On the twelfth day of our journey, I noticed my wife was looking more agonized than before and it took all the effort she had just to stay on her horse. At first I attributed it to her women's problems, which surely God, in his omnipotence, had inflicted on them as punishment for the suffering they caused men, but then I heard the cough racking her chest with a cracking sound like kindling. The light in her eyes had dimmed, her blue-black hair had lost its shine, and I began to worry whether I would be able to fend off Azrael, the archangel of death. I hadn't slept a wink in days, and after a week of her falling asleep with her head on my lap, listening to the parched sound of her breathing every night, I decided that we would return home. But I made my decision too late. Yet another accursed army belonging to yet another accursed power, this time from blasted Europe, was driving yet another wave of dying refugees before it like a swarm of insects. The way north back home was impossible now, for God, whose sight causes the stars to rise and fall, had dealt us another blow: Again the barbarians sought to seize control of our passes, our mountains, our minerals, the wealth of our land and what lies beneath it, and I wished to God, whose name is eternal, that he might deal them the same injustice as he had dealt us. My younger brother tried to get hold of a doctor and wise man recommended to us by my friend the rug merchant, but when we came to the designated location, we found the whole village empty and marked with the sign of fire. I walked through one, two, three burned homes and ordered everyone back on their horses, even though my people had a whole day's march behind them and I had to bring them into line with a few cracks of the whip. I ordered them not to waste time burying the bodies of the dead, lest we share their fate, and to load their rifles. If anyone wanted our lives, they would have to pay the price. I could no longer bear to look at my wife, so I rode to the head of my people and ordered my brother to keep his eyes on her and let me know when she was at her end and the angel of death was in sight. At midday we came upon a few other traders. They were happy to join our ranks, and as I didn't know the way too well I was glad to have them. When it was time for prayer, my brother came to me and said sadly that my wife's life was hanging by a single silk thread of hope, and the fibers were quickly unraveling. One of the traders who had joined us overheard and told me his father was a doctor. He said he'd picked up a thing or two from him and asked if he could examine my wife. So I took him to her and saw my wife for the first time in two days. She was more beautiful than ever and she was dying. I left the trader to tend to her, and went off with my brother to pray to God, whose mercy knows no bounds. I prayed and asked for advice. What to do? We were in unfamiliar territory, murderous barbarians to the north, thousands of refugees to the northeast, Tabriz many miles away, and if we strayed from the road, either the fanatic European barbarians would get us or somebody else. Before I had finished my second series of prayers, the man who had examined my wife came to me and said that if we didn't come down from the mountains to allow her a chance to heal, she would die within a week. If I wanted to save her, I had to descend into a valley immediately. And since God, who weeps over our deeds, had seen fit to punish me with stubborn and unrelenting love for my suffering wife, I made up my mind on the spot. I took counsel with a few of the other merchants, who knew the area, and was told that there was a valley just a few hours' rough ride away; we could make it before nightfall. I silently thanked God, who knows even the most secret intentions of our hearts, and immediately gave the order to change route. We were somewhere between Armenia and Persia. I sent my best rider out ahead on my best horse as an advance guard, instructed my brother to guard my wife like the apple of his eye, and we began our descent. The way was poorly marked, strewn with rocks, and hadn't been used in years. The only regular traffic it saw was the mountain stream that flowed down it every year in spring. As we made our way along the trail, unwinding before us like a ball of snakes, I was afraid one of our animals was going to break its neck. In the event, the animals were more fortunate than one of my servants, who tripped and went tumbling down the incline. A few hours later we passed his body at the foot of the mountains. Another of the servants tried to take advantage of the speed of our descent to quietly slip away with his horse and a few of the other animals. He climbed off his horse and took out his dagger, pretending to pry loose a stone lodged in the horse's hoof. It was too old a trick to fool me, and besides, the last time I had spoken to him, he kept his eyes fixed on the buttons of my doublet, and only God, in his infinite mercy, could have mercy on a man I didn't trust. So I waited around the next bend, and when he didn't appear I went after him. I spotted him driving the animals back up the mountain and gave a yell, but he didn't respond. The bullet from my rifle sent his unworthy soul back to God, the all-watchful father.

"Before sunset we reached the valley, and the first village was in sight. Judging from the houses, it looked to be a settlement of about two hundred souls. It was divided down the middle by a narrow river with a bridge arching across it, whose pillars were adorned with decorations of an exquisiteness I had never seen before except in Baghdad as a child, when I went there on my first business trip with my father. But my main concern was to find a doctor. In fact there were two in the village. At first neither of them would agree to see her, explaining that we were foreigners and according to their custom they weren't permitted to visit foreigners after sunset. When I offered them money, one of them accepted and went off to treat my wife. The other just shrugged and started back to his home. Wanting to be sure my wife would live, however, I proceeded to break a few of his ribs to make him understand that I wasn't about to leave my most precious flower in the hands of a single village healer. After changing her dressings, brewing her a tea of medicinal herbs, and rubbing her down with ointment, they realized that all their friends and loved ones were imprisoned in two rooms at the local inn, which I had occupied with my men. I told them in no uncertain terms that if my wife died, she would not die alone. That was all I had to explain, and I doubled my guard in the evening.

"The next morning, awaking from dreams in which I tried first to persuade and then to bribe Azrael, the archangel of death, with several years of my life in exchange for the life of my wife, I went for a walk and spied one of the healers bathing my wife's shawl in the river under the bridge. I was infuriated. Only my brother kept me from beating him to death. That was their treatment? I was enraged! Pleading and wailing, the healers' families tried to convince me that the water under the bridge had healing properties. I didn't really believe it until the next day, when the skin on the healer's face was once again fresh as a newborn's, bearing no trace of my fists or my boots.

"Before I went to sleep that night, I quietly entered the room where my wife lay sick. I prayed for her, truly at my wit's end as to what I might promise God in return for her life. I had already offered mine long ago, but it seemed that was too little. I reflected on it a while, then went for a walk at the foot of the mountains and checked up on my guards. The next morning I waited outside my wife's door for her to wake up, and when I heard her softly singing her favorite song, I walked in and saw that she had been restored to health. Her hair sparkled, her skin glowed the way it used to, and as I quietly surprised her with a hug and a kiss, I saw the shine had come back to her eyes, almost too bold and as ever before with a tinge of vanity, thank God, whose power is invincible. I paid the healers and set their families free. They bowed their heads to the ground, having never seen so much money before, since they were even poorer than us. A few hours later they came back, saying they didn't want to keep it all. So I told them to give it to those worse off than them, and they walked away with a lighter step, fully satisfied.

"I stayed in the village a few more days with my people and goods, wanting to be entirely certain my wife was cured, then we set out from the village across the bridge to one of the roads stretching south through the nearest pass. We set off at dawn with no one around for miles except the innkeeper's son, whom we had hired as a guide to lead us to the pass. As we were crossing the bridge, the horses got spooked and reared up in panic. Seeing that my wife was in danger of being thrown by the dapple gray, I leaped down from my horse and scooped her up amid the crush of people, four-legged beasts, and goods. As she gazed at me in gratitude, one of the horses swung its rump around and knocked me off the bridge into the water. I was lucky. If he had kicked me, I wouldn't have come out of it alive. The river was shallow under the bridge, so I waded out, climbed back in the saddle, and we went along our way. In a few hours I was dry. But I couldn't fail to notice that our guide's behavior had changed. He looked deeply alarmed when he saw me fall in the river. 'I'm right here next to you, friend,' I told him. 'Nothing wrong with me. Just a little dip in your healing waters, that's all.' The glummer he looked, the harder I laughed. The expression on his face even lifted the corners of my wife's mouth in a smile. He asked if my whole body had gotten wet. I said yes. He asked if my head had gone under as well. Again I answered yes. 'Then God have mercy on you,' he said. 'How come?' I asked. 'The water of four streams flows into this river,' he said. 'Scholars say this river is the last remainder of the Garden of Eden, which according to the holy books was located here on our lands near the border of Armenia. And that means,' the voice of the innkeeper's son rose to a tone of desperation, 'that the water of this river causes immortality. As a result of the world's corruption, its power has been diminished, but if you immerse your whole body in it, it is said you cannot evade immortality.' I tried to correct him, pointing out that we talk about evading an enemy's sword, or a deadly illness, or a bullet, but not immortality. 'God, have mercy on him, for he knows not the power of your deeds,' said our guide. He lowered his eyes to the dusty road and the first spring flowers breaking through the patches of melting snow, and didn't lift them again. 'Superstitions,' said my brother. 'Nothing but the superstitions of backward folk who have no idea there are wars raging and governments falling all around them every day. All they've got is their old, uncultivated minds.' He laughed so hard he almost fell off his horse. Superstitions . . . I laughed along with him. We reached the pass, bribed the guards, and crossed over the border. We were in Persia now. The path to Tabriz was wide open.

"I bought a house in Tabriz, my wife bore me several children, I founded a business, and my brother and I sold goods all over Persia, Turkey, and Armenia. It felt like my family had finally begun to flourish. Then one day, on the outskirts of Baghdad, we were negotiating the price of turmeric with another buyer, when he began regaling me and my brother with criticism. Finally he said, 'Your older brother is the one who should be running your business, not you.' I just laughed in his face, but the next day at the market I looked in one of the mirrors they had on display for sale and froze. My brother's hair was streaked with silver, but not mine. His hair was thinning, but not mine. Every day my brother's skin was creased with a new set of wrinkles, while mine remained the same. In horror I mounted my horse, which by the time I reached home had been run ragged, like all the others before it. I opened the door, knocked over the servant, and dashed with a trembling heart up to my wife's room, seized her in my arms and carried her out to the balcony to count her wrinkles in the full midday light. She laughed aloud but then began to choke on her laughter, baffled by the meaning of my behavior. The number of wrinkles on her face had increased since our last journey, since her illness and the births of our children. She had lines that hadn't been there the year before, laugh lines and lines of worry, lines of surprise and amazement, lines from determined prayer, from gritting her teeth while making love and from naughty gossip and women's talk. I took the biggest mirror we had in the house and held it up to my face. Again I froze, transfixed in horror, then I smashed it to pieces. My face hadn't changed over the past few autumns. All the scars I had acquired were fully healed. I could no longer even find them. The number of wrinkles on my face was still the same. Now I realized what had happened: I had become immortal, I was cursed. Doomed to see the death of the one dearest to me, my beloved wife. Doomed to see her change into an old woman and deprived of the chance to repose beside her in my old age. Doomed to see my brother, my children, my friends and enemies, transformed into a host of shadows led away by the archangel Azrael, while I alone remained the same, unchanged, cursed. May God, whose majesty knows no bounds, forgive me my pride and suffer me to wash away my sins. May God, who is eternal, grant me to see the end of my days.

"One sleepless night, in a fit of grief and soul-wrenching sobs, I confided my terrible secret to my wife, and God, whose loving embrace is beyond enduring, rewarded me with a heavy, dreamless sleep. The next day on opening my eyes I saw that my wife had spent the night awake. I guessed that she had been protecting my slumber, driving away the spirits of darkness and summoning legions of angels to help with our sorrowful fate. The next day before sunup she grasped me by the hand and took me out to see her uncle, her father's oldest brother, who lived on the city's outskirts. We told him our story. He listened carefully, sipping tea, his diminutive eyes receding into the cracked lattice of his shriveled skin. With his docile movements and deep wrinkles, he reminded me of an African elephant. When we had finished our story, he gazed at me somberly and said: 'My son, you have offended Azrael too many times. Your arrogance seems to know no bounds.' I rose from my seat at the insult, and only respect for his age stopped me from unleashing a string of curses at his expense, the mildest of which would have been to declare that he had the soul of a mangy stray mutt. The old man looked at me askance and softly laughed. Then he asked me to hand him a few books and some scrolls of paper from the shelves. He said he hadn't been able to reach them in ages but hadn't needed them for years. Opening the books and unrolling the lengthy scrolls of paper and parchment covered in foreign scripts, he began to read through them, losing all interest in us.

"The sun was just coming out, and for the first time that day my wife smiled, saying that was how he had always been. In most of her memories he was engrossed in books, and in order to keep his children from disturbing him, he had learned to make the most delectable sugar cakes anywhere in the region. As long as they didn't disturb him, they could play quietly in his room and afterward they would get sweets. But if they weren't quiet, they got them anyway, since he was their uncle and didn't have the heart to tell them no. He never did find it within him to get married, and for that matter what woman would have wanted a man like him, who cared only for his books and lived off of the charity and respect of others? But all of the children loved him. After many hours of sitting in his meager dwelling, fetching water, loafing about, and driving away unpleasant thoughts like mosquitoes, as evening fell and I decided to turn on the lamps, all of a sudden my wife's uncle stood up and snapped shut one of the books. He looked at me and said: 'Your problem has been more hinted at than identified and described by scholars, but I can explain what happened. According to holy scripture, the Garden of Eden was in fact originally located in Armenia. What the villagers told you is probably true. As you may know, our religion, as well as the religion of the barbarians, even the religion of those Christian dogs, dreams of a paradise where our souls will be freed from the cave of darkness and ignorance; where we will come face to face with

God, whose glory shall extend unto eternity. Even that ancient and peculiar religion which does not recognize God, whose founder's vision was likely inspired by divine spark in a deer park in India, has a shrine in the region you described to me. It never occurred to me before that there might be some truth to these legends.' Then my wife's uncle spoke about the various types of angels, and gates from one heaven to another. About paradise, which can be entered only by him who is adequately prepared. He showed me our holy scriptures, as well as those of the pagans and the barbarians. He demonstrated the connection between what had happened to me and the verses of several prophets, including the barbarians' as well as ours. He demonstrated not only connections but contradictions, which were restored to a divine harmony uniting things that were, in my pitiful, uneducated, sickly opinion, incompatible, like an abandoned withering flower in the marketplace, the first encounter of lovers, and the foresight of saints. I listened to it all carefully, stunned and dismayed by his vision and scholarship, but I couldn't fathom how it was related to my shabby fate. I couldn't see where my own kismet fit in all of this. My spirit flagged and hopelessness weighed upon my bowed back. Just then my wife entered the library with our dinner. Her uncle, standing with his gaze fixed on the garden, was explaining something to me about Raziel the archangel, God's closest servant, separated from his Lord by nothing but a screen. Without so much as moving his head, he answered my wife, who hadn't said a word: 'But of course, little one, I know. Forgive your conceited old uncle, who is just drunk on his own eloquence. Now then,' he said, turning to me, 'what do you understand best? Tell me what you understand best, and I will try to advise you and my little one.' I didn't know what to say. I was going to say I understood trade, but before I could open my mouth, he nodded. I was going to say in recent years the new rifles were selling best, but before I could even get the words out, he shook his head disapprovingly. Then I said: 'I'm the finest spice dealer in the region. I buy and sell aniseed, star anise, tarragon, galanga, cardamom, bay leaf, turmeric and coriander, nutmeg and walnuts. I sell sumac and saffron, ginger and hyssop. I love the smell of spices as much as I love the jingle of money they bring me.' 'What do you get,' my wife's uncle asked, 'when you mix hot paprika, white pepper, a touch of fenugreek, turmeric, coriander, and cardamom?' I laughed out loud: 'Everyone knows that's the basic mix of spices for curry,' I said. 'That's right,' he nodded, 'and you have too much hot paprika and choleric pepper in your disposition. You're hot-tempered, to put it mildly, and you've crossed paths with Azrael, the archangel of death, several times in your life. You probably even did so in his domain, in the territory that used to be the Garden of Eden. That time when you killed the servant who was trying to rob you, did you feel remorse?' His question was clear, as was my answer. 'Of course not,' I said. 'How else could I do business, how else could I look after everything, how else could I clothe my family? How else?' The old man looked at my wife and shrugged his shoulders. 'Too much fire, little one. Too much fire. When you rode down into the valley by way of the trail that resembled a viper's nest, which no doubt you will be surprised to know is described in a book I once bought in Medina,' the old man went on, 'you crossed the former border of paradise, the land where the Garden of Eden was once located, and when you killed your servant, that brought on the curse you now bear. The angel of death took his revenge by soaking you in the water of im-mortality. Which shows a certain sense of humor on his part, I must say,' my wife's uncle said. I had no idea what he was talking about, but for once I decided not to interrupt. After a brief pause, he went on. 'Your only chance now is complete repentance.' 'What does that mean?' I asked. 'It means you never take another person's life again. It means you put your hot-temperedness at the service of those who are powerless, whom God has given the gift of suffering.' 'You mean that I should become a poor man and a beggar?' I asked, raising my voice. 'It won't help you to see things in opposites,' he replied. 'Help him, if it's not too late, little one,' he said to my wife, with an expres-sion on his face that made it clear that we should leave.

"A few days later I sent my brother to see the old man and ask what he had meant by his words and what I should do. I wanted him to explain everything in plain and simple terms. I was just an ordinary businessman, not a scholar like him. The answer came back: 'Give up the things you love most.' After a few days of denial, rage, and considerable annoyance, I sent my best, most spirited stallion to the director of the city orphanage to sell to help pay for the children's food and clothes. He sold it at the market for a large loss; I was seized with such rage when I found out that I went straight over to see him. As I stepped into the room where he sat hunched over the orphanage's hopeless accounts, ready to upbraid him for losing at least a third of the thoroughbred's actual worth, we were suddenly interrupted by two children, a boy and his sister whose scarf he had taken and refused to give back. For some reason I had the feeling I knew them from somewhere. The girl begged her brother at first, then tried to take it back by force. But he was at least a head taller, and standing on his tiptoes he waved the scarf above his head, well out of her reach. The director chided them both, snatched the faded scarf from the boy, returned it to his sister, pushed them out the door into the yard, and turned to me: 'Do you know those children? Years ago supposedly their oldest brother rode with you on a trade expedition. They say he died somewhere in the mountains. Their parents passed away prematurely, and they didn't have anyone else except their older brother, who did what he could to provide for them, but he died on your expedition through the mountains, leaving them orphans.' My head suddenly started to spin, and when I came to on the bench, the director was gripping me by the shoulders. Those children were the brother and sister of my servant, the one who had tried to rob me and whom I had shot without hesitation. The director was talking to me, but I couldn't hear a word he said, I just saw his mouth moving and the puzzled look in his eyes. I came back to my senses only when he held a cup of tea to my lips. I walked out and the next day I donated funds for him to expand the shelter. Another few days later, I went back to the director and inquired as to whether it might be possible for me to adopt these children, the brother and sister of the man I had killed. His face lit up and he said clearly the gossip he had heard about me was wrong. It wasn't true my soul was as hard as stone. When I saw the way his feelings were reflected on his face, with every flicker of his soul visible, I was amazed he hadn't sold the thoroughbred for even less. I had the children officially declared as my own, and since they were older than the ones my wife had given birth to, they were assured by law of receiving the largest share of my property in the event that Azrael changed his mind and decided to let me die some-day. Later, my wife told me there had been nights when I cried out in my sleep, screaming words she had never heard me speak, such as *guilt* and *shame*, and begging for *forgiveness*. I still remember some of those dreams, as harsh as God's justice, whose care crushes us as we crush olives in a wooden press to make oil. A few months later, I heard one of my assistants in the carpet warehouse say to another: 'Our master has really gone downhill the past few weeks. He got old all of a sudden.' They never did find out why I gave them a week off and paid the dowry of one of their daughters.

"That day I went back to see my wife's uncle. But the house was abandoned and the old man was gone. The neighbors said he had gone off to buy sacred manuscripts near the border with Arme-nia. When I told my wife, she said she went to cook and clean for him every now and then, and that he had left a letter for us with the neighbors. The calligraphy was more beautiful than any I have ever seen since. In it, my wife's uncle, who still addressed her as 'my little one,' wished us both a good life and said that he had heard my fate, like a river, had returned to its original course. Then, as is the wont of old people, he spent forever reminiscing about the days when he was young and my wife and the other children played in his room. The days when he was still full of pride and daring enough to draw back the curtain concealing God's intentions. But now, he said, he understood that our fate was even for him an invitation to step into the unknown.

"As testified to by this story of mine, I too recently found my-self remembering moments in my youth, which is something only old and sick people do. That's me now, old and sick, just waiting for Azrael to escort me on my way. I suspect his visit will coincide with the ripening of the olives, and I hope there will be time still for me to complete this year's harvest."

Dr. Lukavský had taken down a few notes while listening to the story, and the next day he went to the library and compared a few different versions of the stories from *The Thousand and One Nights*. He began with the table of contents. Then he looked in the index. Finally, he looked through the story titles, and even read some of them. But he couldn't find the pastry chef's story anywhere. After more than an hour he realized he had to give up the search since it was time for his afternoon appointments. I must have overlooked it, he concluded. It must be from here. But amid the crush of other work, he was unable to devote any further attention to verifying the sources of the pastry chef's lively imagination.

9
EROTIC GAMES

When they took Josef away on suspicion of subversion, Alice was exactly three months and four days old. Květa didn't know what to do or where to go, she just had a feeling she had to do something, and fast. It felt as if speed was the most important thing, as if charging recklessly forward, like spring shoots bursting forth from the earth, offered some sort of hope. She took the baby and went to her mother's. But the moment Květa saw her mother standing there, old and uncomprehending, she realized that it wasn't only Josef she had to worry about, but her mother as well. Changing her granddaughter's diapers, she began to look settled and peaceful again. Květa explained to her that three men had shown up at their door, ordering Josef to collect his identification papers and come with them. They wouldn't even let her touch him, and when she disobeyed and tried to hug him good-bye, one of the men stepped in between them and put his hands firmly on his hips. It was the first time Květa had ever encountered fear. Her arguments, pleas, and explanations fell on deaf ears. Making the whole thing even harder was that it wasn't at all clear what to argue against, what to plead, or what to explain. All her efforts seemed to be completely ineffective. They took him away, just like that. She was surprised at how calm and restrained her husband was. Almost as if he wanted to go, to be with them. As if there were some kind of secret bond between them. As if . . . And then they took him away. And he was out of her sight. She ran down the stairs with them, in spite of his quick and unexpectedly firm shake of the head to signal his disapproval, as though he knew something she didn't. But then when she got to the front door of the building, she heard her child scream, and the sound of her daughter's vocal cords stamped her heart or soul or brain with resolute sobriety. Her daughter's cry was a cry of pain and, now also, longing for Josef. Longing like a guest, bold, brash, and sober, who has registered, pulled out his credentials and slapped them down on the reception counter, the trump in a game lost in advance, and doesn't mind in the slightest that the previous guest hasn't packed yet, left, and returned the keys, isn't put off one bit that the sheets haven't been changed. Longing just soberly and matter-of-factly watched as the three men led Josef away, knowing he was to replace Josef and stand in for him. Her daughter's cry made Květa run back up the stairs, lift her into her arms, and part the curtains so she could see out the window to where the car with her husband was parked. But they were all gone. Afterward, her mother tried to reassure her, saying it had been five years since the war now, things had finally settled down, they were all Czechs after all, nothing could happen as long as a person was honest and decent and hardworking, what could they possibly do to him?

Once her daughter had fallen asleep, Květa left the building without saying good-bye. It wasn't until she was out on the sidewalk that she realized she had no idea where to go to look for Josef. She walked the city till nightfall. With no destination, no companion, no reason. As the streetlights came on, she suddenly looked up and saw the statue of St. Wenceslas, surrounded by four saints. Looming behind them was the edifice of the National Museum, filled with fossils, stuffed birds, and rocks, and the skeleton of a whale. Květa stood there on Wenceslas Square, gazing up at the patron saint of the Czech lands with the giant gilded stone box behind him, its contents plundered and snatched from nature. Then she heard a newsboy and realized he was offering her a paper. She took it, paid, and put her wallet back in her purse. When she heard his voice assailing her again, she decided to ignore him, quickly turning off into Krakovská Street and entering a shopping arcade. Suddenly somebody put a hand on her shoulder. She turned and saw an elderly woman. "Miss . . . miss, your newspaper. Your paper."

"Ma'am," Květa said. "It's ma'am, not miss. Ma'am."

"You dropped your paper," the woman said, handing it to Květa. Květa nodded thanks. The newsboy's voice was out of range now. She unfolded the paper. The front-page story was on the latest census. The headline said as of March 1, 1950, there were a total of 12,338,450 people in Czechoslovakia, of whom 8,896,133 lived in the Czech lands, comprising Bohemia, Moravia, and Czech Silesia. Květa walked silently through the arcade, her mind empty. She stepped out onto the sidewalk and looked at the numbers again. How could anyone figure that out? she thought. Such a big number. So many people. Too many to visit them all, she mused. I'm sure there's some office that does it. I wonder which of those numbers is me? And which ones are Josef and Alice? Eventually Květa decided the last three of the 8,896,133 residents must be them. Definitely, she thought. Those last three must be us, and there must be an office somewhere that does it.

After a few days, her mother came to visit. Before she even stepped in the door, she pressed a piece of paper into Květa's palm. On it, in big shaky grandmotherly letters, it said: Hynek Jánský, J.D. Below it was a street address and the name of some office she'd never heard of. "He'll definitely help us," her mother said, draping her coat on a hanger. "He'll definitely help us," she said again, walking into the kitchen. "He's always been partial to you," she added, before turning her attention to her grandchild.

Květa knew that Josef was being investigated for something he clearly couldn't have done. What could he be guilty of, when all he ever did was sit at home or in the office doing calculations? Besides, as he used to say, a structural engineer is the kind of expert the communists are going to need, because statics, my dear Květa, statics is part of the science of engineering. It's got nothing to do with politics. It's what keeps buildings from falling down, and bridges and dams and towers and factories, it's what keeps all of them standing. That's what he used to say, but now she wasn't so sure anymore, and it had occurred to her several times, no matter how hard she tried to suppress the thought, that even the impossible was possible, and Josef may have been mistaken, he may have made a grave miscalculation on that beautiful new-looking snow-white plastic slide rule of his. And now, as a result, Květa stood before Hynek Jánský, doctor of both laws, best buddy and friend. A skilled tennis player and, once upon a time, a member of the same tennis club as she and Josef. Hynek wore a smile and, as usual, a perfectly tailored pinstripe suit. A small vase of primroses stood on a table in the middle of the office, and a young man with documents under his arm rose from a small table in the corner of the room, probably a clerk. Hynek nodded to him and he left. After several days of trying to find her husband and failing, she had ended up at Hynek, which in that crazy time of confusion was probably the best thing that could have happened. "Květa, honey, come in, you don't have to stand over there by the door," he said, holding out his hand. His handshake was brief, firm, friendly, and dry, and he smelled of aftershave. After his clerk or secretary or whatever he was had closed the door and the spring in the lock clicked shut, he brought her hand to his mouth as if he were going to kiss it, as had been the custom prior to the war, but he didn't, because the communists had been in power for well over a year now, and any gesture as bourgeois as that would have been foolishly compromising, and yes, in fact dangerous. It would have been less risky to kiss her on the mouth than to kiss her in any overly sophisticated fashion.

She was still the same, yes, almost the same, Hynek noted. She may have put on a little weight since having her child. He gripped her hand the way he had learned to do at meetings when welcoming and parting with his political partners, matter-of-factly, without hesitation. His secretary-cum-clerk knew what to do next, rising, bowing first to him, the commissioner, then to the woman he'd never seen but the commissioner clearly knew, the woman with the deep green eyes. Eyes so green the secretary nearly gasped. Luckily he didn't have to say anything, so he was able to hide it. He bowed, closed the door behind him, and went off to jot down in his semiofficial diary that today Comrade Commissioner Dr. Hynek Jánský had received a visit from a woman of about twenty-eight. He hurriedly looked up her name in the visitors log at the reception, where the green-eyed brunette in a suspiciously elegant skirt suit had signed in as Květa Černá. In the next column she had put her date of birth and ID number, and the secretary was pleased to see he had guessed her age correctly.

Once they were alone, Hynek could no longer contain himself, lifting Květa's hand to his mouth, until he was nearly kissing it. In the end, however, he was constrained, almost against his will, by his ruthless self-control, the same quality that made him such a fearsome tennis opponent, his lips stopping precisely 1.45 inches short of her fingers in the lightest intimation of a kiss. He smiled, taking cognizance of the fact that Květa had indeed gained weight since having had her child. As he raised his eyes from her hand, he couldn't fail to register the undulation of her body, dominated by the peaks of her breasts, the whole package hidden beneath her dress like a landscape blanketed in snow.

He slid one chair away from the table, she sat down, and he pulled around another chair, directly across from hers, so it was at her side. Then he let her tell her story. Her husband was locked up, yes, he was in investigative detention, but the word *investigative* didn't mean anything. Uncle Josef Vissarionovich was on the throne in the Kremlin, and the phrase merely meant that Josef was locked up. Nothing more, nothing less. It didn't actually mean that anyone was investigating anything. It was just a humble, fawning expression of the geometry of power. Nothing more, nothing less. He said he would find out whatever he could about Josef. He didn't say his boys had already ridden roughshod over him. He said he would *try*, and he said he didn't want to get her hopes up. All this he said with a serious, sincere expression, brightened only by momentary flashes of happiness at the fact that he was seeing her again.

Looking back on it, he was glad she had rejected his offer of marriage before the war. He was constantly in meetings anyway, he wouldn't have had time for a family. The only thing that still irked him a little was the fact that she had turned him down for Josef. She'd waited for him, for Josef, to speak up and ask for her hand, while Hynek had offered to marry her a whole year before. It had been awkward. Yes, awkward. Hynek was honest, he didn't lie to her. He just . . . left some things out. Like the fact that his boys had given Josef a nice going-over. Not him! His boys. He also hadn't made the mistake of contacting her first. He just waited for her to find him on her own. He had always known what was going on with Květa. He'd kept track. But the other way around? For her, the whole thing had ended before the war. For her!

If at least it hadn't been his best friend, Josef, who never did understand women. Josef, his friend. His best friend, the klutz. If it had been anyone else but Josef, he could have stood the rejection.

As Květa walked away, she was glad Hynek hadn't taken advantage of the situation to invite her out for a drink or lunch or coffee, so they could reminisce about old times before the war. He appeared to be completely reconciled to the fact that she was the wife of another man. Once upon a time, after all, the three of them had been friends.

After Květa left, after he opened the door for her and she walked out of his office into the hallway and he shut it behind her again, Hynek spread his arms wide and threw himself against the yellowed wooden paneling, trying to embrace it, hold it, and then, quietly, so that no one on the other side could hear, he sank to his knees. Then, no longer entirely in control of himself, he began stroking the chair Květa had been sitting in a moment before, running his fingers lovingly over the vase she had held in her hands. Over and over he caressed it, working himself into a state of thorough intoxication, of boundless bliss. You see, Květa, honey, he smiled to himself, everything's going smoothly. Everything's going just fine, and this time it's going to be the way that I want it, sweetheart. This time it's going *my* way.

Nowadays people were being locked up like they were on a conveyor belt, one after the other. Assembly line production, which debuted in the United States with Henry Ford's introduction of the Model T automobile, had been greatly improved. Ford, a model capitalist and a master innovator, engineered the process to perfection, but the rainbow of pastels they painted the cars with dried too slowly, increasing production time, which made it more expensive, leading him to make the statement that capitalists adore with the same devotion that Zen Buddhists attach to the study of koans: "You can have your car painted any color you want, as long as it's black." Which goes to show that Henry attained a higher level of enlightenment than the disciples in the bamboo grove meditating on the sound of one hand clapping. The worshipers of capitalism bow down in amazement at Henry's masterful insights into cost analysis, business margins, markets, advertising, and undreamed of curves of expenditures and profit; they bow down in amazement like Christians at the recounting of the legend of St. Francis and his sermon to the birds, and then clumsily try to spin a lacy web of theology in which to snare their Christian God, the same way they once netted larks with which to flavor their delicate French and Italian pâtés. Graceful, confident, and fierce, the monumental evolution of the East European mind culminated in the assembly line production of mass trials. The investigation means nothing, it's all in the accusation. The spiritual tradition of torture, dating back to the dawn of Tsarist Russia, joined with classical German philosophy and the genius of Marxian analysis, meant the executions were already under way. The perpetual underestimation of small nations and their traditions. The perpetual underestimation of the Slavic element and its contribution to the building of a better world. All that energy and human ingenuity, all of it together combined to bring about the concentration camps and mass trials. So much unrecognized genius for the enrichment of the world.

Květa didn't hear anything from Hynek for a month. As she waited, her mind gradually absorbed the fact of totalitarian power. Finally, she decided to contact him herself, but Hynek said he didn't have time. Two weeks later he did. He told her there was going to be a trial; he told her Josef would be convicted for defending a man at his job and trying to shield him from justice. Josef had stood up for the former owner of a nationalized enterprise. Under the current circumstances that was sheer foolishness. Josef said the owner was a decent man. But how could that be when he was a capitalist! Hynek told her there was nothing he could do. Everyone investigated is convicted, that's how it works. The accusation is everything. Hynek was telling the truth and had no intention of hiding it. He had far-reaching plans for her, but not now, not yet. For now, she would blame him, she would break down, throw a fit. For now, he had to leave her be. Leave her exalted demeanor and gracefully carried neck to relax. Her mind and her body, because he, Hynek, had his own plans for her.

Hynek Jánský owed his successful career not to hard work or talent, but to the humble fact that he realized the most important thing of all was dull, boring, tiresome, if not outright dreary patience. It was an insight so banal it was almost frightening. Most people were proud, and almost everyone, including Květa, thought they were special, exceptional, unique. But he, Hynek Jánský, doctor of both laws, knew and was proud of the fact—as proud as if he had discovered some timeless law of nature—that he was exactly the same as everyone else. He was proud not to be unique or exceptional, proud to be patient and utterly conformist. He won his tennis matches by avoiding risk, playing from the baseline, no crushing overheads or clever lobs, not him. Instead he waited to capitalize on his opponent's errors, silently and sweatily chasing down every ball, for as long as his strength held up. His shots never skimmed the net or landed dangerously close to the line. He hit them three feet inside the court, and he was the one who won.

Květa's behavior would be entirely predictable, entirely unexceptional, the same as that of all the other wives of the convicted men. It made no sense to expect anything original or out of the ordinary, for the simple reason that it made no sense to expect the impossible.

First, then, in a few weeks, Květa would turn desperate. She and her beautiful face, with her filly's hips and her exalted stride, would fry in a hell of anxiety. At night, generally between two and four in the morning, she would wake and start sobbing, sobbing uncontrollably, until she understood that the thing she feared the most was in fact what was going to happen. She would swallow tears until her eyes dried out and the circles under her eyes smelled of sand, until her eyes were dry and bloodshot, like a mirage that refuses to disappear, like the neon signs that shine at night on every corner, and then she would see him everywhere, at every turn.

During that period, Hynek would avoid any contact with her. Perhaps a meeting or two in public, twenty or thirty minutes at most.

It was important to give her hope, but he had to be noncommittal, he couldn't compromise himself, and he definitely had to avoid getting into any situation where she threw her arms around his neck and started to sob. That would be foolish and asexual, reinforcing feelings of bonding and cohesion, in other words brotherly, which was the one direction he didn't want it to go in. He would wait until after the worst of the pain had passed, and the weariness and bottomless heartache began to settle in . . . and along with them, naturally, rage at the one who had been arrested, locked up, and tortured, rage at the convicted man himself. Yes, Květa would get angry at her dear husband, Josef.

That's the way it always is. People have always blamed the dead, the ones captured or killed, or failed to protect them. That's the way it always is, and that's the way it's always been. How long this phase will last is difficult to know. Once it ends, Květa will stop crying. She still won't sleep well and she'll feel guilty, but that's all. And when it happens, Hynek will be nearby. The next phase can be identified by the fact that her eyes are no longer red from crying all night and the circles beneath them are deeper. He'll be nearby when that happens. And then, a few months later, she'll finally come to terms with the fact that her husband is going to be locked up for many years. Gradually she will learn to accept it, she can settle down and stop *carrying on* and discover that it's possible to live just for her children and then . . . finally, at the very end . . . comes the first hesitant realization that she also needs to do something for herself from time to time. She discovers that she doesn't have to spend every waking moment thinking about the concentration camp where her husband is rotting away and will continue to rot away for the next thirteen years. Then, out of the blue, yes, all of a sudden she discovers that she's still a woman too.

This phase would last several months, although the individual stages of the process could be catalyzed or accelerated. It may have been irritating and unpleasant that it lasted as long as it did, but Hynek's patience had rarely betrayed him.

After a few months, Josef was convicted and sentenced to thirteen years in prison. He would be released in 1963. Květa had lost weight, her scalp had sprouted a few gray hairs, and the circles under her eyes were visible from a distance. Hynek said that although there was nothing he could do during the legal proceedings, he could help Josef once he was convicted by ensuring he was sent to a less harsh correctional camp, a less harsh concentration camp. By now Květa had come to terms with her fate and the crystalline logic of despotism. She was grateful to Hynek for helping Josef. Every now and then Hynek would turn up out of nowhere, sometimes with hard-to-find items. About a week after Alice's first birthday, he showed up at Květa's door with a carefully wrapped, delicious-smelling paper bag. When he opened it and took out the oranges, the scent flooded through the apartment like a river, in one spot hanging in the air like a lake, in another just a thin trickle, and in yet another cascading like a waterfall. Hynek's visits never lasted more than a half hour; sometimes Květa even wished he would stay longer. But he needed only a few minutes to plumb the depths of despair in her eyes. His rich experience had given him an infallible sense for distinguishing which level of personal hell the poor husbands and wives of the convicted were on at any given moment. When Květa came to Hynek's office after the verdict was pronounced, he wrote his address down for her in a few quick, precise strokes, whispered to her not to come to his office anymore, and to stop by his place if she wanted anything. She stopped by roughly one month later. By that time her mother, too, had gotten used to the fact that her daughter had lost her husband for the next thirteen years. The husband of one of her friends, a man of over seventy, had also been arrested. He had lost so much weight by the time of his trial that the only way she had been able to recognize him in court was by his mustache. Also his hair, which until recently had been brown, turned white. It was hard to believe the man the communist court rewarded with a sentence two years longer than Josef's, allowing him to celebrate his eightieth birthday in a uranium mine, would even manage to survive. The fact that neither man was a criminal was unimportant; the implacable geometry of power liquidated anyone defined as an enemy in the context of the class struggle.

Květa's mother felt her strength leaving her and sensed she wouldn't live to see Josef's return. She hadn't said anything to Květa yet, but with the wisdom of the old, the wisdom that comes from recognizing one's own weakness, she tried to spend as much time as she could with her granddaughter. Květa had reached the final stage of pain by that point, and was reconciled to her fate. The week before she went to see Hynek she bought herself a new skirt. Years later, probing her conscience, she still wasn't sure whether it had been a coincidence or whether the cunning voice of her subconscious had seized the opportunity.

It was early spring when she went to see him. Hynek brewed a cup of Brazilian coffee, which you couldn't find in ordinary stores, while Květa looked out at the blooming trees lining the embankment. She held her cup in both hands, enjoying the sensation of breathing in the bitter aroma as she stood staring out the window with the hot porcelain burning her hands. Hynek went to the kitchen for sugar, but on his way back he came to a stop in the doorway, surprised. Seeing the flirtatious smile on Květa's face as she gazed out at the tree blossoms, he knew his days of harsh self-discipline would soon be a distant memory. She took a sip of the coffee and rose from her chair to lean against the windowsill. The way her puffy skirt flowed over her hips, accentuating her buttocks, the way the color had returned to her face with the hesitant application of cheap powder, these things spoke volumes. Together with her thin blouse and the growing warmth of the spring day, all of this compelled Hynek to ask:

"What would you be willing to do to make things better for Josef, Květa?"

"Whatever it takes," she said, attaching no importance to his words. "Whatever it takes, of course."

"I'm serious," he said. "I'm being serious here." She glanced over her shoulder, then turned, blood rushing to her cheeks, and said in a faltering voice:

"You know I have no money, though. We barely get by as it is."

"Now you've insulted me," he said. "Now you've really insulted me. Of course that's not what I meant."

"For God's sake, I didn't think you wanted it for yourself," Květa said. "I just thought you might need it for a bribe . . ."

"What is it you value most about yourself?" Hynek asked.

"I don't know."

"What is it?"

"No, seriously. I don't know," she said.

"But you're willing to help him?" he asked again.

"Of course," she said.

"Listen, Květa. I can help him. I'm going to try. But there's one thing I want from you. I want you to give it some thought."

"Oh, please," Květa said. "I think about it constantly. It's all I think about."

"Not like that. That's not what I mean," Hynek said. "What I want is for you to understand for yourself what it is."

"What do you mean?"

"I want you to come see me next week so I can be sure that you've thought it over." Květa sat back in her chair in front of the empty cup, visibly upset. "Do you have any idea what they're doing to them?" Hynek asked.

"I think they deprive them of food and sleep, and sometimes they beat them."

"Yes, Květa, that's right. But why? Why is all this happening?"

"Because they want them to—"

"Because they want to break them. And to break someone, first you have to humiliate them," Hynek broke in. He paused a moment. "I want you to come see me next week and tell me what would be the worst thing for you—I repeat, for you—the thing that would humiliate you the most. Come and tell me, so at least I'll know I'm not getting involved for nothing."

As the two of them exchanged chilly good-byes, Hynek noted to himself that whenever she got offended, her neck got longer and her whole body seemed to stretch higher. Yes, she's even more beautiful when she's offended, he concluded. I'll definitely have to make her angry more often. The next day in his office, out of sight of his secretary, he arranged for Květa to receive a summons to appear at an ally's office, where she was told there was reason to believe that she wasn't taking adequate care of her child. How predictable: the next day she rang at his door. He assured her that he would do everything in his power to make sure Alice wasn't taken *into custody,* and then sent her home.

Hynek's unusual willingness was a comforting surprise. It reassured Alice that she could trust him. The next time she came over, she sat down and proceeded to tell him all of her worst fears. It was like opening up the city gates to the devil. Hynek was prepared for a long session. He listened attentively as Květa ran down the list, ranging from nightmare fantasies to everyday annoyances, waiting for her to come to the part about her body. After about forty minutes with scarcely an interruption from him, it finally came. Hynek listened as she mixed imagination and intimacy, like stinky cabbage with sweet roses. Interesting, but incongruous. As, flushed in the face, she revealed all her forbidden pains and secret sexual desires, Hynek finally interrupted, acting as if none of it interested him, to ask about something she had said at the beginning.

"You said you couldn't stand to be tied up or put in handcuffs. I actually have some right here. I can show you how they work," he said, and he gave her a brief demonstration. "Here are the two keys. You can take them home and try it. Just pretend. Take them with you, and next week when you come, you can put them on in front of me, first on your feet, then your hands. Just for the experience. Just so you can feel what it's like."

Little by little, with each weekly visit, they went farther and farther. It started with the handcuffs. It was odd at first, though at the same time there was something exciting about it. Květa wasn't sure if it was Hynek, his unusual requests, or she herself. She put the handcuffs on herself at home a few times, and the only thing she was afraid of was that she might lose the key. When she was at his place, she snapped the bigger set around her ankles and the smaller ones around her wrists. Next, Hynek hogtied her arms and legs together with rope and left her like that for about half an hour while he sipped red wine and smoked an American cigarette that he had saved especially for the occasion. After half an hour Květa asked him to untie her, saying she needed to pee. Hynek agreed, knowing she still had a long way to go. When she came out of the toilet, he gave her a hug. "There, you see, my scared little duckling. In reality it's nothing. It's only our fear that paralyzes us." Gradually, over the next few months, slowly but surely, they reached the point that Hynek had been aiming for all along. And one day he said: "Now bend over." Květa bent over, rolled up her summer skirt, and underneath it appeared her naked buttocks, hips, and bosom. From that point on, each time they met, new hidden pleasures were revealed, grounded in pain and the gratification of insatiable, unacknowledged desires. If Květa showed up even just a few minutes late, she had to kneel down in the entryway on all fours, and Hynek would plant as many blows on her back and behind as she was minutes late. Květa found herself so mercilessly drawn not only to him but to the pain he inflicted on her body and mind that she would intentionally wait in front of his building, increasing the number of blows she was to receive. Gradually she fell in love with Hynek and the pain he inflicted on her. After a few months, they both gave up pretending that Hynek was trying to help Josef; their affair itself was the bond that united them. The moment Květa closed the door, she ceased to be Květa, instead becoming a filly or mare, as Hynek liked to call her. The moment he spoke to her, her whole body tensed up, her neck stiffened, and she didn't know what would happen next. "My tame little filly," he would say. "She tried so hard to resist, but now she enjoys the taste of forbidden fruit. Don't you, my juicy little mare." She accepted his insults and humiliation with special pleasure, and it didn't occur to her until several months later to ask how he had done it. How he had transformed someone so proud and independent as her. "Pavlov," he replied. "Pavlov and his famous experiments on dogs. Simple, proven, works on everyone. The theory of conditioned reflexes. Never forget, my dear, my perfect knowledge of Russian. Man does not live by Ulyanov alone." Every so often, Květa would vow never to set foot inside Hynek's again. She even attempted it a few times. The first time it lasted three weeks, and he told her if she wanted to come back, he would have to teach her a lesson she was never going to forget. She nodded, stripped naked, and asked for some folded handkerchiefs to hold between her teeth.

Her neck, head, and face were the only parts he left untouched. Even in the scorching heat of summer, Květa wore long sleeves, dark stockings, and long skirts that blocked out the sun. She started locking herself in the bathroom so her mother wouldn't see the scars encircling her body like a chain mail shirt. When she tried to break off their relationship, weeping, gritting her teeth, and sobbing, she got what Hynek called a second object lesson. She didn't want to see him anymore, but she longed for the orgasms that came with his beatings. After she went back to him, her body was constantly on fire, burning like never before. He used a new method of beating, new types of instruments. It felt like her body had been whipped with a thousand stinging nettles. But the truth was that the overlapping orgasms they shared following her beatings were more powerful than ever. She loved her body and hated her soul to its depths. Yet the feeling of complete submission, along with the feeling that somebody actually cared about her, was so exceptional she couldn't break it off. Sometimes she would break down in tears out of the blue, when it was least appropriate. It was always the same moments, the ones when she would remember Josef and realize what had become of her. Of her: she knew she couldn't put the blame on anyone else. She rang the bell, the door opened, Hynek stepped aside to let her in. Her eyes were glued to the floor. On the right side of the hallway was a bookshelf that had belonged to the Germans who lived in the apartment before the war. Hynek glanced at his trusty Russian watch, engraved with an inscription from the minister of the interior in recognition of his successful liquidation of the enemies of socialism and peace, and said: "You're seventeen minutes late, bitch. Since that's an odd number, we'll multiply it by an even one. How about four. How much does that make?" "Sixty-eight," Květa said. "All right," Hynek said. "Now bend over!"

10

THE TORTURER

(1)

Before the first Russian tanks arrived in 1968, magazines and newspapers began to publish reports of the cruelty, ruthlessness, and abuse suffered by political prisoners in the fifties. According to the reports, one of the worst masterminds of these atrocities was a police commissioner named Jánský. Not only did he humiliate prisoners with beatings and coerce them into acts beyond the pale, but he also severely abused their relatives and friends, and those he identified as nearest and dearest to them. He used them against each other. Not only did he deprive men of their manhood in such a way that they could never again experience the pleasures of love with their wives, but he flooded their minds with doubts and false hopes, blackmailing them, tearing at their souls. Any man who entered his working quarters soon wished to be dead and burned to dust. The newspapers said investigations were needed, special commissions, trials for the torturers; but then the Russian tanks arrived, and once they were settled in on Wenceslas Square, nobody had the appetite to investigate anything anymore.

In 1964, Hynek Jánský was dismissed from his employment as investigator and his vague classification of commissioner-officer was abolished. It seemed there was no longer use for his science. There was even talk that he should be punished and given a taste of his own medicine. His superiors, however, succeeded in having him released rather than suspended. Had he been suspended, it might have affected his pension, and in general could have led to a whole range of inconveniences. Instead Dr. Jánský was released from his position and hired as assistant chief stock clerk in a small produce warehouse on the outskirts of Prague, where he was responsible for a staff of seven, a handful of forklifts, and maintaining the temperature of the frozen fruit and vegetables. All his years of expertise, his irreplaceable experience, lay fallow. His subordinates were negligent, and his only superior was a drunk who laced his morning tea with rum. But then came 1968, Russian tanks entered the country, and over the next few months Hynek received a series of visits at work, his old colleagues coming by to see how he was doing. He was ashamed he had nowhere to invite them except the neighborhood pub. They would sit and have coffee or goulash, and even though none of them ever came right out and said it, he knew his former bosses were checking up on him to see if he was still prepared. It went on like that for some time, until finally, around Christmas 1971, one day as usual he came to work and waiting outside the gate for him was a car with a driver, who handed him a sealed envelope. The moment he saw it, Hynek knew his days of hardship were over. It had been decided that every specialist was most useful doing the work he knew best. With shaking fingers Hynek tore open the envelope and pulled out a few sheets of paper. The most important one was his appointment as instructor at a newly founded academy. The driver, who had been watching him out of the corner of his eye, grinned. "An appointment, comrade? An appointment?"

"Yes," Jánský replied. "But . . . how did you know?"

"You aren't the first or the last . . . comrade," the driver said, offering a warm smile. "So, where to? Where can I drop you off? Or," he tipped his head toward the warehouse, "you want me to pop back inside for your things?"

"No, that's all right," Jánský said. "I can get them myself."

"Just remember," said the driver, still smiling, "always make sure to say good-bye to your coworkers. It might not be the last time you see them. You know the saying, comrade: Be nice to the people you meet on your way up, because you might meet them again on the way back down."

And so Dr. Hynek Jánský became an instructor. Quickly and

unexpectedly. His new workplace was on the opposite side of town from the warehouse of carrots, cucumbers, and other frozen vegetables. He had a vague feeling that the newly restored leaders were somehow ashamed of their new institution. In any case, however, it was a nice commute, especially in the spring. Every day he went to work, he walked from the tram stop past the low building of a nursery school, followed by a playground. After the playground he turned left and took a brisk nine-minute walk across a plot of land that had probably once been an orchard; now someone was trying against the odds to make a park out of it. At the intersection coming out of the park, Jánský headed left each day, and two and a half minutes later he stood before the expansive, welcoming building of the academy.

As an instructor, Dr. Jánský taught what was known as special techniques in nonpolice interrogation. His new institution in fact had nothing to do with the police. Odd as it seemed, no one asked who or what oversaw the academy, nor was anyone told. Jánský threw himself into his new work with gusto. His lectures analyzed the various types of pain, with every part of the human body described, depicted, and characterized in minute detail. He knew his way around nerve endings the way some travelers know their way around train stations, airports, and seaports. He knew every gateway, door, and pathway of pain, every pressure point, inside and out. His students, or, as the academy preferred to call them, trainees, were mostly men and hailed from vaguely named state institutions situated on the city's outskirts, in villas with no address on the door, so as not to attract any unwanted attention from mailmen or overzealous gas and electric meter readers. Their employers, their institutions, and for that matter they themselves, more or less, didn't exist. The fervor with which Dr. Jánský delivered his lectures at times overwhelmed even his rugged, experienced trainees, who wondered how one could bring oneself to butcher a human soul like that, never mind a body, imagining what it might be like to be on the other side, the wrong side, and fall into their instructor's hands. This wasn't just a few slaps or a punch, a fist and a few broken ribs, this was science. In all the years he worked at the academy, however, the one thing Jánský regretted was that, despite repeated urgings on his part, his findings, which his Russian colleagues developed and he expanded on with unusual diligence and skill, were never approved and published as a textbook or lecture notes. He didn't succeed, despite pushing for it up until he left the position for a well-deserved retirement in 1980. Thus his knowledge and understanding could be passed along only orally, through his lectures behind carefully closed doors. Like any good teacher he did his best to make the subject matter appealing to his pupils. He wanted them to be able to grasp it for themselves and to develop the knowledge and skills he taught them. He wanted his pupils to surpass him. Every year he began his first lecture by saying, "There are as many ways for our body to cause us pain as there are for it to bring us happiness and pleasure. That is the basis of our science, which we must always take as our starting point. But remember, dear friends, there are at least three times as many ways for a person being questioned to tell us what he knows, or what we want to hear." Here he stopped for a well-measured pause before adding: "Exercise One: Describe the ways in which your own body brings you pain and pleasure. We have twenty minutes remaining until the end of class. Please begin writing. I will collect and evaluate your work at the end of the hour."

(2)

In spring of 1968, a journalist came to visit engineer Josef Černý. He was the third one that year. A young man with about twenty-five years of life behind him. Eager as a puppy, he got straight to the point. But Josef had no interest in talking to anyone, and was disturbed that the journalist showed no interest in classical music, despite Josef's repeated attempts to change the subject. The young man wasn't interested in music, nor did he make any attempt to pretend to be, which in Josef's opinion would have been the polite thing to do, and besides, he got Josef's address from an organization Josef had never heard of. The young man also refused both coffee and tea. How can you have a proper conversation with a stranger without any coffee or tea? Josef asked himself. All the journalist wanted to hear about was Jánský, and he didn't seem to understand why Josef didn't want to talk about him. He just kept going on about justice and the rectification of old wrongs. What could a young man like him know about justice, Josef thought, absentmindedly shuffling the papers on his desk. Suddenly he surprised himself: "Are you in love?" he asked the young pup. The journalist nodded and blushed. His blushing led Josef to decide not to throw him out as he had the ones before him. None of them had been interested in classical music either, on top of which they had confused statics with statistics. Reasons enough, in Josef's view, not to trust someone or waste time on them. Seeing the journalist's red face, however, prompted him to change his mind and supply some cautious answers to his puppy dog–like questions. And so as Josef began to speak, the young man squinted his eyes and scrawled away in a notepad propped on his thigh. When Josef was done, the young man asked for a glass of water, drank it down in one long gulp, thanked him, and left. That was the last Josef ever heard of him. A few weeks later, Antonín stopped by with a newspaper article featuring several names, including Josef's. Some of what he'd told the journalist was in there. After dinner Josef brewed himself his usual evening weak cup of coffee and sat down to read the article. Among other things it said a commission had been formed to investigate the case, that it was about time, etc. Every single sentence contained the words *justice, punishment,* or *vindication.* At the end of the article was the address of an organization for victims to contact so that every case could be properly investigated. Josef was taken aback. He had never thought of himself as a victim. Not him. The idea of being a victim didn't fit with him or his profession. He had always viewed himself as having had an accident, an unpleasant political accident with lasting consequences, but the thought that he might be a victim had never crossed his mind. He sat down at his desk and opened the drawer with his round slide rule. It was his pride and joy, and he'd always found its special shape to be calming somehow. He redid the calculations that had come out fine the day before, but even after recalculating he still didn't feel like a victim. Yes, that commission must be up to something. The question was whether the lines of force of their intentions intersected at any point with the vector of his political accident. Even traffic accidents with lasting consequences had a logic of their own, he thought, but he still didn't feel like a victim, which actually made him feel bad. He decided to wait for his wife, who was out at the cottage, and when she got back he gave her the article and asked her what she thought. But Květa refused to comment. It was obvious to look at her that anything having to do with Josef's imprisonment made her extremely uncomfortable. So Josef deposited the article in his desk drawer, and there it stayed.

That year Květa decided the apartment needed painting. This time, for a change, Josef was looking forward to it, since he had his future son-in-law, Maximilian, to help him, and together with Květa and Alice, they readied the apartment for this irregularly occurring holiday, this quaint domestic ritual of beautification rooted in an era of fears about public and private hygiene among the urban population. Josef left the choice of color and pattern to Květa. The only place where he reserved the right to have a say was in the color of his study, where he also strongly advocated for the absence of any pattern. Once the decisions were made, the women were sent to the countryside, and Josef and Maximilian had the whole place to themselves. Compared with how long it had always taken him working with Květa, Josef was surprised at the speed with which he and Maximilian finished the job; instead of being done on Friday evening, as he'd expected, they were finished on Thursday morning. He still had one day of vacation left, and everything was already done, including the cleanup. Suddenly Josef found himself alone in the high-ceilinged apartment, with the fresh smell of chemical pigments coming off the walls and the tang of the city wafting in through the open windows. Slowly, with no particular goal in mind, Josef began going through the papers in his desk, and so it was that the article calling for justice and the settling of old grievances came into his hands once more.

It didn't take him long to decide. The speed of my decision, he thought, is directly proportional to the absence of my women. Forcefully folding the article into his briefcase and exiting the building, he purchased three rolls from the bakery downstairs and set out for the address listed at the end of the article. The official he found there, after a long-winded explanation of the commission's founding principles, informed Josef that they had had a file open on Dr. Jánský for some years now. He added that Dr. Jánský was now a stock clerk and worked somewhere on the outskirts of Prague. The information surprised Josef and somewhat dulled his determination. Nonetheless, he had made up his mind not to let the case go, so he requested they give him whatever information they had available. There wasn't much, but the official, who insisted on addressing Josef as Mr. Engineer, finally shared with him that he expected Dr. Jánský's entire dossier to go to court in a few months, and asked Josef whether he had any desire to testify in the case. Josef said he would give it some thought, the official handed him an official-looking piece of paper, and Josef put it in his briefcase and left. A few days later he decided that, although he wasn't too happy at the prospect, he was willing to testify, and sent the paper giving his consent back to the commission by registered mail. Then nothing happened for another few months. August 21, 1968, the Russian tanks arrived, the official from the commission emigrated to West Germany, Canada, then the United States, and eventually settled down in Argentina. The commission's files were lost amid the confusion, the commission itself was dissolved, and Hynek Jánský finally ceased to be concerned about his fate.

(3)

Every now and then, one of Hynek's former bosses would stop by the warehouse. They would go to the pub for a bowl of goulash or a cup of coffee and talk about the weather. The pleasant conversations affirmed their ongoing friendship. On one such visit a colleague of his, previously induced into early retirement and now back on active duty, brought him a bundle of old papers. It was raining out and the papers were drenched. He set them on the chair next to Hynek and tucked into his goulash, complaining about the weather. Once he was done eating, he wished Hynek happy reading, and before he left, he told him: "If I were you, I wouldn't put that in the recycling." Ever the joker, Hynek thought to himself with a faint smile. He was just grateful to still have friends he could rely on. When he got home, he cut through the rough strings with a pocket knife and the bundle of old papers unfurled before him like flowers of innocence. His whole life was there. His high school diploma, a copy of his college degree. Evaluations of him drafted by his coworkers. His entire career was in that bundle, including most of the materials and testimonies intended to serve as the basis for charges against him, assembled by the commission that wanted to take him to court. Hynek read through it all, sorting, taking notes, crossing things out. Some of the prisoners he had investigated he no longer remembered at all, others he had only a cursory recollection of, and then suddenly his eyes alighted on a carefully completed form in familiar handwriting. The numerals were so perfect they looked as though they had been stenciled. He recognized the distinctive *e*'s and *a*'s, as well as the signature at the end: Josef Černý, structural engineer.

Hynek felt—hurt. How could Josef do that? How could he denounce him? How was it possible? You couldn't even count on old friends anymore. Everyone nowadays, just like that commission, just like those journalists, was whining on about truth and justice when all they really wanted was revenge. It wasn't up to him and they knew it. Churchill and Stalin agreed between them who was going to live where, they drew the lines of influence, determining where the boundaries of empire began and ended. He just administered the geometry of power. Of all people, Josef, as a structural engineer, a stress analyst, should have understood that. How could he not, when he still lived with Květa, despite being nearly castrated? He filled out a form? He wants the truth? Let him have it. Let him enjoy it, let him feast on it, let him choke to death on the whole fucking thing. All's fair in love and war, he knew that! Total commitment is the only way to stand the test, not just in the Middle Kingdom or the Thousand-Year Reich, but in the realm of the heart. Total commitment is pure power with no equivocation. Pure and clear as the mountain air. Total power is total love. And that's why she was mine for ten years. For ten years her brain and her body were mine. Her thoughts and her soul. Her dark green eyes and the triangle between her thighs. Because in the total battle for her love, I won. And the winner never asks if the losers love him. The winner just wins and unreservedly destroys the slightest sign of reservations. Because, dear Josef, the winner is the man who wins. It was that simple. That straightforward. That clear. The winner overruns the trenches in love as well. The winner wins. That's why Květa was mine for so many long, beautiful years. That's why she came back to me: because love is control and the winner is the one who wins.

Later Hynek realized that, however fine his thoughts, he had let himself get carried away by them, and felt the need to do something practical. So he sat down at his typewriter and began to write. It was a wide-ranging letter, several pages in length, with some technical formulations that betrayed the author as someone who was employed in state administration and probably had some medical training. The style was precise and unambiguous. The writer provided an in-depth analysis of the relationship between Květa Černá, wife of engineer Josef Černý, and an investigator, professionally classified as officer-commissioner, by the name of Hynek Jánský, doctor of laws. The letter described when the relationship between Jánský and Černá had begun, how long it had lasted, and what it consisted of. Under the heading The Effectiveness of Pain, it went on to enumerate, in precise, clinical language, which methods of touching and striking the body of Květa Černá had been employed. The types of pain and types of pleasure. The reasons why she had returned again and again, even after her husband, Josef Černý, was released. The description was calm and unemotional. Dr. Jánský was satisfied; he was unequaled when it came to writing reports. After reading the letter through to himself, he was perturbed to discover he had nothing else he needed to bring to the post office. All his bills were paid, postcards sent. The next day he rode the tram to the main post office on Jindřišská Street and sent the letter by registered mail. When he filled out the form, under sender's name he put: Květa Černá. A crafty joke, he thought. And with that the matter was settled. Yes, he was still a bit of a demiurge or *spiritus agens*. Still a force to be reckoned with. The feeling warmed his heart.

(4)

Josef was at home alone when the doorbell rang. His wife and daughter had gone out shopping. "Again?" he said, with the infinite naïveté of a man who thinks that everything necessary for the wedding has been purchased. As if once all the things for the wedding had been bought, the preparations for it could be brought to a close once and for all, and they could devote themselves to something else. This time they said they were going to a department store on Wenceslas Square to buy some sort of ribbons. "Ribbons," Josef repeated. They already had some ribbons somewhere. What did they need any other ones for? As if they didn't know that colors were just electromagnetic waves anyway.

"Measurable. That's right, mea-sur-a-ble!" he repeated, raising his voice. Of course, it was no use trying to explain. He knew they would only laugh at him. In a good-natured way. "Spare us the technical details, Dad. Just tell us which color you like best," his daughter said, and then she and Květa would both conclude that his taste in color was questionable. As if he didn't know. Of course!

"Alice is more and more like Květa every day," he said. No doubt a lot of it was the wedding . . . but so many other things, too. Yes, and of course they had blossomed. Both of them. Undisputedly. There was no denying it. Both his wife and his daughter had blossomed. And entirely unexpectedly they had bought him a box of expensive, very expensive and very good, Cuban cigars. They told him he just had to save one, to light at the wedding dinner when he gave his speech as father of the bride. The cigars came in a wooden box of twelve. Well, now there were just ten, but the wedding was only two weeks away, so no need to worry they wouldn't last. He never had smoked that much. Just occasionally and by himself, so he could really savor the experience. The best was smoking while listening to something nice. Something he could savor. The best was with Antonín. Listening with him, even if they didn't say anything, that was the best. He knew how to appreciate it.

Studying the box of cigars, Josef decided to invite Antonín over.

He could bring some brandy. They could enjoy a couple of cigars and to go with them, what else, Dvořák's String Quartet in F Major. The Czech composer who wrote on the other side of the pond. Especially that third movement. Full of sunshine. Obviously American.

Before Josef could accept the letter from the mailman, he had to sign again, one line above, since the first time he signed by accident for the wrong delivery. His mind was still occupied with the third movement of Dvořák's quartet. For some reason he couldn't remember what the tempo was.

The melody, a melody like that of course is easy to remember, but the tempo, that's a different story. The tempo comes from God, as one conductor said. Josef held the letter up closer to his eyes and suddenly stopped humming. The sender was listed as Květa. It took him aback, and for a moment he was afraid something had happened to her. Yes, it was his wife's name on the back side of the envelope, but the handwriting wasn't hers, that was obvious at first glance. He took a long, dull, narrow knife from his desk that he used to open letters and slit open the envelope. He read standing up, just taking little half steps to the side every now and then. He would clear his throat, lift his foot, but then not follow through. When he finished reading, he realized his throat was dry, parched as sand.

Instantly two things were clear. First: Something had snapped like a spring on a clock tower. Something had ended. Second: His whole life he hadn't understood his wife a bit, not one single drop. After reading the letter he folded it back into the envelope and put it in his pocket. Was it true? If so, what else did he not know about? A railyard in his head with no switches. Once the dull, hazy feelings had passed, a single clear thought emerged: *However hazy your thinking, don't panic!* Whether or not it made much sense, Josef kept repeating it to himself over and over.

After a rapid succession of alternating various types of despair with feelings of rage and utter ruin, he suddenly became aware of the taste of salty cheese in his mouth. *Don't panic*, he shouted at himself several times, but it didn't help keep his head clear. What do you do in this situation, he wondered, when you find out you're a cuckold and your wife is a whore? It wasn't even that so much as who it was with. Of all people! Whoring herself to him! He swallowed the salty taste and found he had bitten through his lip. I'm starting to—yes. *However hazy your thinking, don't panic!* Maybe it was just the usual false accusation, the kind this country has such a tradition of, it's practically in our blood. Of course, first he had to carry out a survey of the terrain, determine the type of bedrock and the freezing depth, in order to know how deep to build the foundations, and then, assuming it was even possible, determine whether there was any evidence for the allegations in this slanderous denunciation. These thoughts circled in Josef's head, as well as a number of others, no matter how strenuously he tried to suppress them, along with anything that even remotely resembled a feeling. Emotions meant the death of his marriage, while thoughts gave it life—that much, unfortunately, was plain as day to him. Any feeling was like a dead fish trapped in a net of thoughts, pitifully and clumsily struggling to keep from tearing open. Suddenly his favorite room was tinged with blood. Looking out from under his eyelids, even his good, solid desk, abounding in stability, suddenly seemed to take the shape of an altar, on which sooner or later some anonymous goat would have its throat cut. Yes, his mind raced, yes, if the harsh reality is that all of it is true, then I am that goat, or some other animal sacrifice, and the blood covers the walls that are closing in on us. Unable to bear the thought of waiting, Josef's mind—not him, his mind—peevishly rushed to engage its technical capacity, trying to calculate how far the goat's/his blood might spray if he slit open his carotid artery at this very moment. Lacking a basic knowledge of physiology or medicine, his mind had to perform several fairly complex arithmetic operations, and several decisions had to be made regarding which formulas to use for the calculation. His lack of focus considerably complicated the process. The heart is a pump. Quarts of blood, reportedly four to six. Viscosity, internal friction of veins, arteries, capillaries. Fluid density. Pump force. Diameter of the opening. Yes, it wasn't actually that hard, and as his mind, not he, arrived at the final conclusion, he took a few steps back from his good, stable desk, feeling as if his throat had already been slit, the blood even now dousing the freshly painted walls. The bright idea of killing him or her also occurred to him, which calmed him down a little. But even before the thought subsided, he was certifiably sure he was incapable of murder; his own experience with it was irrefutable — unfortunately. I'm going out of my skull, he realized. My thoughts aren't even listening to me. All at once it was obvious he couldn't wait for Květa at home. He had to get out! He pulled the envelope from his pocket again. He opened the denunciation and read through it one more time, laid it on his desk, took the extra set of keys to the cottage in Lhotka from one of the drawers, and walked out the door.

(5)

Alice never did find out why the day they were finalizing the last details of her wedding dress and tracking down those irresistible honey-colored ribbons, her mother suddenly shut herself up in her father's study and started to cry. From the shape of her wrinkles Alice concluded it wasn't over the wedding. Josef had left the letter on his desk, and at first Květa ignored it. For tidiness' sake she preferred to just put it away and do a quick dusting. That was what she always did when she was anxious, and with Alice's wedding coming up she was anxious constantly. The fact that the letter had been sent by registered mail was obvious from the way the color stood out against the pleasing brown of the desk. To pick it up and read it wouldn't be that unusual, Květa decided in those few fractions of a second that divided her happy life from the feelings of devastation and frustration that awaited her in that moment. When she grasped what the letter said and the fact that Josef had already read it, she let out a sob. She didn't read it all the way to the end, there was no need, everything written in it was true. She took the letter, put it back in the envelope, went into the bathroom, tore it into little pieces, threw it in the toilet bowl, and flushed it down. She went back into the study, sat in the chair at her husband's desk, and looked through all the drawers, but except for a few slide rules and some books of engineering, math, and physics tables, she didn't find anything. She had always felt a certain pride at the fact that he understood those things. Even now the feeling was still there. She wasn't sobbing anymore, and she knew there was nothing left for her to do but wait for her husband. She had to just sit and wait.

Alice knew something was wrong. She wasn't alarmed that her father wasn't home, but the fact that her mother was sitting in his chair with swollen eyes augured something unpleasant. As far as Alice could remember, her mother had sat in her father's chair only on a few occasions, and it was always when she was angry at him. Now, though, it looked like she was afraid. "Just leave me here. I'm all right. I just need to sit here and wait for your dad." That was what she said when Alice went to look in on her. Smells like trouble, Alice thought, but she couldn't pay any more attention to her mother, since she was supposed to meet Max at the train station in half an hour, and as it was she wasn't sure if she would be on time. She gave her mother a kiss on the cheek. Her eyes were puffy, and she was trying to act as if nothing was wrong. Just in case, Alice did a quick scan of the room, but she didn't notice anything unusual. She put on her new heels and dashed off to meet Maximilian, pausing in the entryway to call out to her mother that she might stay the night with him, adding that he'd never seen these shoes before and she was curious if he'd even notice, since she was sure he'd seen more interesting shoes in Germany. And she was gone.

Josef came home that evening. The only light on in the apartment was the lamp on his desk. He walked in and saw Květa, sitting at his desk, moving the scale back and forth on one of his slide rules. She sat huddled in the chair, obviously afraid. He saw her fear and remembered he had left the letter on the desk.

"Květa? Květa, honey?" he said, looking her in the face.

"You were never supposed to find out, even though I did do it for your sake, too," Květa said. Despite having spent the past few hours composing and decomposing sentences in her head to arrive at what she was going to say, she knew it sounded unseemly.

"I'll be at the cottage, Květa. Tell Alice I'll be there, would you?" said Josef. He picked up the briefcase he took with him to work every day, and left. That night Květa couldn't sleep. At least it meant a temporary reprieve from the nightmares, though she could hear their wings flapping above her head, and in her waking moments she had visions of long forest clearings, separated from one another by pain and regret.

On hearing the key in the door and the rhythm of her daughter's ankles, she breathed a sigh of relief, faintly recalling the bizarre, unsettling dream she had had and feeling grateful to be awake. She dreamed that her husband had left her, that he had left her forever, and the pain she felt in the dream tore her in two. She woke feeling empty, then sighed with relief, looking forward to sharing the unusual dream with her husband. The feeling of relief didn't last long. Even before the sweat could bead on her brow, she realized it hadn't been a nightmare. When Alice came in with rolls, milk, and the morning paper, along with her father's keys, which she had found in the mailbox, and asked why they were in there, the walls of anxiety came crashing down and Květa began screaming, crying, and wailing. What she had viewed as a dream just a moment before was sheer reality. Alice tried to give her a hug, tried at least to keep her from falling out of the chair and hurting herself on the sharp edges of the furniture. But the force of Květa's grief was devastating, ravaging her heart and mind without letup. The moment her mother's cries quieted down, Alice brought her into the bedroom and gave Maximilian a call to let him know what was happening and ask him to come over. Alice couldn't stop hugging him once he finally got there, but neither of them knew what to do in a situation like that. At one point Květa pulled herself back together long enough to stagger over to the bedroom door and announce, "Your father left me. He left me, but don't you ever hold it against him. It's me he left, not you, sweetie." Then she went back into the bedroom and went on sobbing.

From then on, Josef lived at the cottage in Lhotka. When anyone asked, he told them he had decided to remodel it into a proper country house where he could spend his retirement, and he actually did start on some of the alterations. If they asked how Květa felt about it, he just didn't answer. He moved his things out of the apartment in Prague, making sure to choose a time when he wouldn't run into his wife, and eventually friends and people they knew stopped asking questions and got used to the fact that they lived apart. The fact that he had to spend two hours a day taking the train to work and back during the week was his problem, no one else's. At least that's what he told Alice when she asked him about it. After a while, even she got used to it.

11

SECOND VISION OF IMMORTALITY

Without anyone saying, uttering, or mentioning it, word spread, around the square and then around the city, that the device needed repairing. Only when this verdict reached us, wrapped in a veil of obscurity and uncertainty, did most people realize, to their painful embarrassment, that no one actually knew what purpose the device served. Even I was not entirely certain, despite that my great-grandfather made repairs to the device during the last remodeling of the city hall and its main tower. The situation reached the point where the city council, forced by no one knew exactly what—probably some vague sense of responsibility—decided to appropriate funds to repair the device. The news reached me from several sources until finally it came about that I was, shall we say, indirectly and reluctantly invited to assist in the repairs. The problem was that although we managed to dig up some of the old drawings and plans, along with a notebook containing all the mathematical calculations, deliberations on use of materials, and records of payments in a currency that no longer exists, even after a thorough study of all these documents and drawings it wasn't entirely clear to us what purpose the device in the tower had in fact originally served. The city officials and city council came up with the idea of holding a public competition. Casting a net, they called it, in the hope that it would turn up somebody who remembered what the device had been for. Yet at the same time they remained handcuffed by an undifferentiated mixture of humility, fear, and shame at our own ignorance. The device had been the pride of our ancestors, that much we knew. Generations ago, people traveled from all across the continent to look at it. Bunches of tourists clus-

tered in front of city hall with their oldfangled optical imaging appa-
ratuses, capturing visual likenesses of the exterior of the device. In
those days it wasn't yet possible to capture sound and image simultaneously, and even on the few occasions when they succeeded, everything came out flat. There was no common way to produce a natural
three-dimensional reproduction. Then people sat down and observed
the image on a flat screen from a distance, with no way to step into it
and take part in the action unfolding before them. Amazingly, they
didn't seem to find it boring. Vilém, a historian I came to know while
working on the reconstruction of the device, explained that people
in those days would look at the flat images in special books. Apparently, friends would get together, look through the books, and narrate
them as they went along. Usually the pictures showed their family
or friends and the places they had visited. A whole complicated etiquette developed around this custom, which today only a handful of
specialists understand. After long and cautious deliberations it was
finally decided that the device would be repaired, in spite of the fact
that its purpose remained unclear. Master architect Matthias Heinz
and I were selected as cochairmen of the Committee for the Restoration of the Device to oversee its reconstruction and, eventually, full
restoration. We were appointed by the city council, and I can honestly say that I believe our appointment was well received by all our
fellow citizens. We decided to begin by collecting all the documents
related to the device in a large room at city hall provided to us by the
city council. From today's standpoint, with the device in operation
again for so many years, it would be easy to laugh at our beginnings,
dismissing our efforts in hindsight with the cheap observation that
while we were gathering together the documents, none of us on the
committee, and I daresay, not one person in the city, thought to walk
up a few floors, cross the connecting bridge, and enter the tower to
see what the device actually looked like. Master Matthias had the
idea to reexamine the story from more than two hundred years ago,
which every little child in our city knows by heart. According to the
story, a prominent composer was invited here to attend the premiere
of a magical opera he had written for our beautiful city, and the splen-

did production met with a surprisingly enthusiastic reception. As a special honor, he was given a tour of the tower, including the device. Later, in his memoirs, the composer declared it to have been the most perfect, beautiful, and cruel thing he had ever seen in his life. As we now know, his *Cantata for the Device of Justice and Progress* became a kind of unofficial anthem of our city. The composer is of course Leopold XVI. Even in the accounts of his visit to the device, however, there is no clear explanation of what purpose it served. Either everyone at the time knew what it was for, or they were trying to cover up their ignorance.

After a studious analysis, the financial information unexpectedly turned out to be the most helpful to us. Reading through the balance sheets, one of our historians stumbled upon the astonishing fact that partial reconstruction of the device alone, performed by my great-grandfather a hundred and fifty years ago, cost far more than the rebuilding of the municipal sewers after the memorable seventeenth earthquake and the introduction of the extraplanetary network version 28.9 combined. This fact clearly demonstrated that the device in the tower was of irreplaceable value to our ancestors, and yet its meaning and purpose still eluded us. We were fumbling in the dark. Surprisingly, we weren't too bothered, although naturally, in the evening, when we would retire to one of our city's cozy little pubs, we were occasionally met with questions regarding the progress of repairs on the device. The information we had assembled thus far was inconsistent. In fact, each piece of information seemed to contradict all the others. Some accounts appeared to say the device offered the ability to display the human soul. Others claimed it could determine the true nature of an individual, a family, and, ultimately, even a whole city or society. In opposition to that were theories, perhaps best described as physical, that maintained that the whole device was originally designed by astronomers to gaze into the farthest depths of space and time. Other documents indicated that it had some function in determining the principles of justice, philosophy, law, and death. Some references suggested that at one point the device had been something like a living creature, actively involved in the running of the city. None of the sources were in agreement.

We decided to keep our visit to the device a secret and perform our inspection during a weeklong sporting event that typically absorbed the attention of most of the city's inhabitants. In the middle of the week would be a decisive friendly match between our team and the neighboring country. That afternoon was an ideal time for our visit.

We set out with our recording instruments, souls brimming with courage and hope, and ascended to the third floor of city hall. We walked down a long narrow corridor hung with hand-painted portraits of the town fathers, dating back even farther than the last reconstruction of the device. As we walked down the hallway, it suddenly occurred to me that my great-grandfather must have passed through here more than a hundred and fifty years ago. He too must have looked at this line of grim-faced men in dark suits. Just how old the paintings were was obvious from the fact that not one of them portrayed a woman. Yet the device, as we all knew, was even older still. When we reached the end of the corridor, we opened the door and walked down a short flight of stairs, which brought us to another door, leading to the tower. It goes without saying that we were uneasy. Master Matthias and his assistant opened a trunk they had brought with them and took out some heavy iron objects, with which they commenced to open the door. The rest of us were quite baffled by this complicated system, which looked to us something like a ballet or athletic performance. They kept turning and turning the iron objects, which gave out a series of loud groans. Just as we were beginning to wonder whether Master Matthias and his assistant had overestimated their strength, the door swung open. We stepped inside and found ourselves in a hall with a vaulted ceiling. Master Matthias touched my hand and pointed upward: "That," he said, "is a barrel vault." I stopped for a moment, uncertain how to reply. Under the stairs that led up to the tower was a statue on a stone pedestal, a figure of a man with a rooster's head and wings. His arms were outstretched, as if about to embrace us. His eyes were covered with tape. How prescient, I thought. People centuries ago had no conception of the possibilities of present-day genetic art, yet how accurate and far-reaching their vision was.

Subsequent research on the statue by the historian Eleanor at least partially revealed its meaning. She was the only one to notice that as we were leaving the tower the statue's arms and wings were in a different position than when we had entered, and she brought it to our attention. The same thing happened on the other days we visited. Sometimes the statue's lips were stretched into a smile, other times it wore an expression of disappointment, and at still others it was biting its lip with its wings wrapped around its body. As a thorough examination revealed the statue to be a solid bronze cast with no mechanism concealed within it, we took the statue's changes of position and expression to be one of the many mysteries of the device and everything related to it. Eleanor discovered in the archives a reference to the fact that the tower had once been known as the Cock's Tower and one of the earliest names for the device was the cock's works. Researchers disagreed on the name's origin, but the most convincing theory was that in the twilight of antiquity there had been a fortress on this site, a citadel called the Cock's Nest, and the name Cock's Tower had evolved from that. In this instance etymology, the science or art of words' origins, gropes for an explanation. In the past it was written *cockworks*—in other words, obviously, cock's works. Now at least we understood the importance of the man-cock statue: It was a symbol of the original Cock's Tower and cock's works, which our ancestors had placed there as a symbolic guardian. After further research Eleanor told us there was yet another name appearing several times in the same context that was perhaps even older than *cockworks*, which was *clock*. It meant nothing to any of us. The historical records were of no avail. The word *clock* is unknown today. Maybe there was a misinterpretation somewhere along the way, who knows? In any case, we decided not to use the word, as we couldn't safely say what it related to or what it was meant to describe. Just as we don't know what in fact the thing called a clock was supposed to have done. From all indications there was most likely an error in copying the word from one document to another, which led to the unusual and plainly mistaken name *clock*.

We switched on the lights and saw a few faded frescoes and some wooden benches along the walls. Past them was the staircase up to the tower. Master Matthias went first, followed by his assistant, and I went third. After several minutes of climbing, panting for breath, we arrived at another door. Master Matthias again applied his irons to the door, and we stepped into a large square hall occupying the entire floor space of the tower. We had reached our goal. Several tables stood pushed together in the middle of the room. Resting on top of them were wooden chests of various sizes, some painted with tableaux that were now quite cracked and worn, others inlaid with metal and various types of wood. There looked to be about sixty in all: roughly twenty large, five medium, and the rest small. Each chest had an opening for an iron, and after pausing a moment to catch their breath, Master Matthias and his assistant took out their irons and began opening all of the chests, one after the next. Inside the first was a set of iron gears wrapped in what looked like leather. The second contained mirrors; the next, drawings and books; and the next, particle accelerators and decelerators. We realized the device had been dismantled and placed in the chests for safekeeping. Once all of the chests had been opened, we gathered the contents together and catalogued everything. Two of the large trunks were full of books and papers, which we assumed were instructions for assembling the device. We couldn't be sure, however, since the writing on the diagrams and in most of the books was in a language formerly spoken by scholars, probably the Páli dialect. One of the small chests also contained notes written by my great-grandfather. I couldn't help but feel moved when my colleagues showed me. Some of the books and drawings were plagued with mold and falling apart, so it wasn't simply a matter of assembling the device; in fact we would have to partially re-create it. In the course of this process we hoped that its meaning would be revealed to us. Thankfully, Eleanor was able to reconstruct one of the texts that seemed to us to be central:

"The theory of vitalism, also known as the theory of life force, was suppressed and swept under the carpet roughly three centuries ago, yet new insights into human consciousness have recently been unified with the latest findings in the field known as quantum mechanics, an unexpected and sudden development with compelling implications for the field of theology or divinity. As teachings on God have gradually been unified with teachings on the origin of the universe, the study of human consciousness has been unified with the study of the human soul. Now these findings, taken together, have enabled us to build the device. A device whose power is immeasurable, a device that underpins and frames our existence as individuals, as well as the principles of state and empire. The anthropic principle, that is, the idea that we see the universe the way it is because if it were different we would not be here to observe it, has been successfully unified with the no-boundary condition, which explains the infinity of the universe by the fact that the universe has no boundary in imaginary time."

It took us several months to assemble the device. Meanwhile, the news that we were near putting it into operation spread throughout the city and its environs. Speculation of all sorts emerged. It was rumored that anyone who came within a certain proximity of the device felt a sensation of extraordinary pleasure. It was rumored that anyone who came within a certain distance experienced a feeling of incredible dread and suddenly grasped the meaning of the word only hazily explained in old encyclopedias under the heading *hell*. It was said that when one stood before the device, one could see not only one's own future but the future of several nearby galaxies. It was said that when one stood behind the device, one could see not only one's own past but the past of a large portion of the Milky Way. It was said that when one touched the device, one's mind merged with the minds of one's friends and enemies. Many things were said, and all that was said—whether fortunately or unfortunately—was true!

What we kept secret from all the authorities, however, was the main purpose of the device. It was revealed to us only little by little, bit by bit. Eleanor, our colleague from Aquitaine, a mixed land of

French and English, was the first to grasp an inkling of its secret. She shared her conjecture with Master Matthias, and ultimately he shared it with me. Initially she was uneasy when Master Matthias told her he had let me in on her thinking concerning the device. Then, when we all tried it ourselves and everything that had been said about it turned out to be true, Eleanor came forward with Master Matthias and his assistant, and through a series of lengthy and detailed calculations convinced us there was much more to the device than we dared to admit. Their explanation involved a theory of grand unification, which merged weak and strong electromagnetic interactions, refuting the theory even as they confirmed it, then continuing with a discussion of the singularity of the idea and the phenomenon in space-time, whereby the curvature of space-time increases exponentially with the infinite value of human emotions.

When they concluded, a long, doleful silence spread over the group. I suspect many, like me, failed to grasp the details of the calculations, or the transmutations of superlight and superheavy particles in relation to the shrinkage of spatiotemporal fields. Yes, few could grasp the details, but the gist of it was clear. Still, no one dared imagine that the device could address the fundamental problem. Could it truly be the instrument of such grace? The room was quiet, the only sound the breathing of those present.

Eleanor believed the device had far greater powers than any before we had tested. She believed it was essentially a doomsday device.

After a period of time which I am unable to estimate, gradually we awoke from our trance and it was clear there was an unspoken question: Who would be the first to test this enticing theory? We took a quick vote, and the majority of the Committee for the Restoration of the Device was divided between Master Matthias and Eleanor. Two or three members were incapable of casting a vote, experiencing such a profound sense of happiness that we chose not to disturb them. The fact that both candidates had received the same number of votes presented us with a seemingly impossible situation. Then all of a sudden Professor Alexander Pazdera, who up until then had been one of those off in his own world, absently smiling, declared clearly and distinctly: "Let whoever is oldest go first. They deserve it most." That hadn't occurred to any of us. No one had bothered to count their age since . . . centuries ago. Yet again, Alexander had demonstrated his uncommon depth of understanding. His proposal was accepted by the Committee, along with Master Matthias and our colleague Eleanor.

Master Matthias went and stood on one of the two foci of the ellipse that formed part of the device. Then the device was set in motion and Master Matthias disappeared before our eyes. We heard some noises that to me sounded like a snatch of a plaintive melody, although later someone said it was the sound of a soul leaving the body. I don't know, it seems to me that each of us heard something different. And then it happened. His body lay before us. Master Matthias was dead. We all wept with emotion and joy. Yes, I can say that it was the happiest day of my life.

It was the day we were finally rid of our accursed immortality. Our accursed, despicable immortality, which had been with us, like the plague, for so many hundreds of years, afflicting us the way the plague once afflicted our ancestors, back in the now nearly inscrutably dark age of the cathedrals. For thousands of years our accursed ancestors lived as parasites on life, having perfected their lives and in so doing ours as well—unfortunately, to the point that they achieved what they called *absolute valorization*. The word *immortality* was no longer in use by that time, no one would have understood it. Humankind had become immortal. For generations it was no longer possible to die of disease, injury, ill will, or suicide. Humankind had achieved absolute valorization, a goal it had staked out for itself in the dreadful gloom of ancient times. Thus did we become the monstrous descendants of monsters. And thus did we now finally cease to be immortal creatures and once again became mortal, which is to say human.

12

MAXIMILIAN

They gave their boy the name Kryštof, the mildest male name that Alice was willing to allow. In celebration of not only their love but the joining of their families, Maximilian had suggested he be named after one of his ancestors who had made their mark on history. The problem was most of the names were of Polish or German origin, and Alice didn't see any reason to complicate their son's life with a name that even his parents had difficulty pronouncing. So Kryštof is what stuck. To Maximilian the name sounded both moderately ponderously Baroque and at the same time sufficiently lofty, and so ultimately, after several groaningly polite arguments he conceded, reconciling himself to the name of Christ's carrier, one of the Fourteen Holy Helpers. Alice was upset that her father and mother had broken up for no apparent reason, but most of her attention was swallowed up by the child. Nor could it have escaped anyone's notice that despite his loud, boisterous nature, Maximilian had begun to act differently toward Alice. He had become a father, which filled him with joy but also brought back a vague, fuzzy drove of memories and feelings, regrouping and swarming, searching for their leader, like circling swallows weaving Persian motifs into the heavy carpets of memory. Flocks of memories, assumptions, and inklings were returning home. Remembering his parents, the buds of a kind of understanding began to ripen inside of Maximilian. His employment had ceased to be enjoyable and begun to make him tired, and he would wake up sometimes with his forehead coated in the pearly sweat of nightmarish dreams, whose content, however, he could not recall.

Maximilian was unhappy. He wasn't satisfied with himself, feeling more than ever before like a stranger in his own time. He had married Alice out of the deepest love for her, and she had already fulfilled part of the unwritten marriage agreement by bringing their son into their world, but what about him? What was expected of him? He wasn't sure, and he wasn't happy about the fact that he wasn't sure. He was as sleep-deprived as she was from getting up to feed the child, and the only thing that still provided him any remnant of self-esteem was the fact that every afternoon he would lock himself in his office, take the phone off the hook, sit down in the office's one armchair, and fall asleep.

The company Maximilian worked at manufactured souvenirs, and his vaguely defined job consisted of reviewing proposals for new products. He corrected any gross grammatical errors and ensured that the names of the towns and villages that ordered the souvenirs from them were spelled and engraved correctly. What he enjoyed most was the pins with city coats of arms. They were so cheap, though, he wondered how his work could ever be worth it to someone. Every now and then, for instance, he would point out that there was a difference between a belted and an unbelted fleur-de-lis, but nobody cared except him, no one else was interested, and eventually he realized it was better to be left alone in his office undisturbed, especially now, when he needed to catch up on his sleep. Thus his passable knowledge of the insignia of cities, institutions, and high church dignitaries, instilled in him by his father, a little-known local historian in his lifetime, lay fallow, nor was his patchy knowledge of history, also handed down from his father, of any practical use. What good did it do Maximilian, for instance, that he knew in detail the history and meaning of the papal bull *Inter gravissimas*, his father's favorite? To be precise, the bull, issued on February 24, 1582, prescribed a change in dates, designating that October 4 was to be followed by October 15 that year, which was of no help to Maximilian in dealing with the inner turmoil caused by his fatherhood. Under the bull, the new calendar was not introduced in the Czech lands until 1584, when January 6 was followed by January 17. All this to compensate for the inaccurate calculation of the length of the year in the Julian calendar by Caesar's astronomer Sosigenes in 46 BC. Over the course of several centuries the original one-minute difference had increased to enormous proportions, so the calendar had to be adjusted. Maximilian knew all of this, but it was useless now as he watched his wife in awe, realizing that her physicality since she had given birth both attracted and repelled him. How much in humans is animal, and how much in humans is human? The question unsettled him. The same way it did that he couldn't wait for his son to be old enough to talk about things that interested nobody else for miles around but him.

Whenever he thought about the successful birth of his son and his completely insignificant role in it, the role of every man, he plunged into an insecurity that gradually turned to irritation. Sometimes he would go pay a visit to Father František, who had performed their wedding ceremony and who, drawing from either the depths of the earth or his own soul, had created his own version of Catholicism, with which he sought to offer support to Maximilian, although in fact he had so far succeeded only in driving him away from the Church. In those godless days of communism, Father František believed that strictness of faith and rigor of the soul were what were needed to preserve tradition. It was now evident that the current pope had been mistaken in trying to bring the beauteous Christ to unbelievers cloaked in the garments of consumerism and an ill-defined freedom. Certainly life in Bohemia, the most atheistic nation the Earth still tolerated on its surface, had proven this to be true. The only result of the benevolent Father František's mercilessly long speeches was that Maximilian felt utterly and entirely alone. Alice's father had moved away to the cottage in Lhotka, and her mother had gone off to live with her distant aunt Anna, who was old and lonesome, and took an exceptional interest in the young family, though she sometimes mixed up Alice's and Maximilian's names with the names of other people, living and dead, a small oversight that did nothing to take away from her love. After Kryštof was born, Alice's father invited them to come stay with him at the cottage. "For the air," he said, proceeding to spew the names of chemicals and their values in various units. "They've measured it all in Prague," he said, "but it's secret, top secret, so don't tell anyone. Unless they do something about it," he added, "we're all going to croak like animals, either that or we're going to mutate into some totally different species." He never revealed the source of his information on the purity of the water, air, and food supply.

Every now and then they would go and visit him at the cottage. They were a strange family, Maximilian thought. Josef, Alice's father and the grandfather of their son, had suddenly up and moved out to the cottage just before their marriage, and came into Prague only on holidays, when he was sure he wouldn't run into his wife, Květa, Alice's mother and Kryštof's grandmother. Usually Alice spent most of her time at the cottage weeding the flower beds and doing her father's laundry. It took a while for Maximilian to realize that was probably the real reason for their visits. He would load his son in the carriage, wheeling him around Lhotka and the edges of the vast forest. When it was warm, he would plant himself on a bench under the trees outside the pub, sipping beer and rocking the baby in his carriage.

One afternoon the voices on the other side of the widespread chestnut tree he was sitting beneath were louder than usual. An older woman with gray hair tucked tightly under a scarf was quarreling with an old man.

"I saw them, Mr. Hořejší. I saw them with my own eyes."

"What did you see, Růženka? What?"

"The snakes. Huge monsters, thick as my thigh."

"Your thigh, hmm? And how many years ago?"

"It's been almost thirty years now," said another voice.

"Well, I'm telling you, Mr. Hořejší. There were two of them: two big snakes hanging out of the tree, and the bigger one was as thick around as my thigh."

"You still have nice legs, though. Give me a look, why don't you, huh?" the old man said, trying to lift the woman's skirt with his cane.

"Oh, give it a rest, Mr. Hořejší, will you? God knows where that cane has been."

Maximilian started paying closer attention.

"Well, apparently the things crawled out of that private zoo they had up there at the castle in town. See, when the Americans advanced, the Germans started shooting at them from the hill overlooking the river, and the greenhouses and the zoo and all that were on the other side, where the scrap metal place is now, so when the Americans threw a grenade or whatever it was back at the Germans, it hit the zoo and the animals escaped and scattered all over the woods. A year later my husband, rest his soul, said he saw a great big porcupine, and the priest from the next village, before they locked him up, said he saw monkeys. I'm telling you, that's what happened!"

"Růženka, please. People say all sorts of things. You know the saying: Talk is cheap!"

"Well, if you don't believe me, then don't ask." Suddenly the woman turned and marched straight up to Maximilian.

"You," she said. "Yes, you. You're a Černý, aren't you?"

"Yeah, I mean yes," Maximilian said. "He's my father-in-law."

"So ask Mr. Černý, the engineer, whether it's true. He saw them too. He saw them."

"What did he see?" Maximilian asked.

"Oh, forget it," she said, turning to the old man with the cane and a few other elderly men who had gathered around to listen. "That's 'cause you're not from around here. That's 'cause all of you came after forty-five."

"Now, Růženka, don't go dragging that into this," the man with the cane shouted.

"Ask Černý, he saw the monkeys running all over the woods after they escaped from the zoo. It was a regular menagerie! I'm telling you."

"Aaah, so what did you say your name was?" the man with the cane asked Maximilian.

"Maximilian."

"And the little fella's Kryštof, right?"

"Yeah, that's our son. But how did you know his name?"

"Everyone knows everything about everyone around here. But

make sure you ask that father-in-law of yours, the engineer. You ask if he saw them. If he saw those monkeys."

"All right," said Maximilian. "I'll ask."

The woman meanwhile waved good-bye to the man with the cane and walked off with a jug of beer.

"You tell me," said the man, striking his cane on the ground to emphasize each syllable. "You tell me how tropical animals like that could survive the cold. No, sir. They don't have any winter down there in Africa and Australia. Am I right? And what would they eat, besides?"

"Leaves, Mr. Hořejší! Leaves!" shouted the woman with the jug, who had stopped at the gate to the garden restaurant, hearing the man's remark.

Maximilian didn't get a chance to ask his father-in-law that day, but that night he had a dream about being lost in a zoo, so the next day he made a point of inquiring into the matter.

"I saw them. I saw several animals," said Maximilian's father-in-law. "The Germans were retreating, the Americans were advancing, and one or the other of them blew the place to smithereens and the animals escaped. That's war, you know? Until one winter after the war, I don't remember which year anymore, but it was bitter cold, and all the animals were dying. The priest that was serving there, Růžička or something, I think he was called, but originally he had a German name, he gave a really nice sermon about how it was like living in the Garden of Eden. Paradise and all that. Like we were in paradise and we didn't even realize it. He saw the animals, too. I think it was just before the coup, or was it after? I can't remember now. But I'll tell you more some other time."

Maximilian and Alice's marriage was not flourishing. Having a child did not cement their relationship and fill it with love and joy. Their genuine expectations were straight-out, absolutely, genuinely unfulfilled. After the birth, the last glimmers of Alice's upbeat spirits faded as the sweet hormones of her snuggly pregnancy drained out of her bloodstream, leaving nothing but the futile gray of dusty streets stretching out before her.

She felt a little better when she took their son and went to visit her father at the cottage, but as good as she felt being there, she felt worse seeing her father deteriorate without the care of her mother. Sometimes he would forget to cut his nails. Sometimes he would go several days without shaving, and sometimes he just plain forgot to eat. When she reminded him, he would get angry at himself, so after a while Alice stopped reminding him, since when he felt bad, he would fire back at her viciously, turning his guilty feelings back on her. Her parents vied with each other in their offers to take care of Kryštof, but the oddness of their breakup didn't add to Alice's peace of mind. They both made a show of listing all the ways in which it was their fault. And meanwhile Maximilian changed jobs so he could earn more money, but the more he earned, the less he was at home. When he came home at the end of the day, sometimes he was so tired he would fall asleep at the dinner table before he finished eating. When Kryštof was a year old, the whole family got together. It was the first time in more than a year her father and mother had seen each other, and her mother treated it like a military operation, preparing for weeks in advance. New clothes, new haircut, manicure, pedicure, new pumps but properly broken in, so they wouldn't pinch her feet and make her unpleasant or nasty toward Josef. It took her a whole week to choose a perfume, suitable both to her age and her objective. Friendly but not seductive. Friendly and therefore seductive, not like the rapid-acting scent of youth, but the relaxing scent of a late afternoon. Her mother devoted several months to her preparations, with the deliberate single-mindedness of an explorer setting out to conquer the North Pole. When her husband arrived in Prague from the cottage, however, she was completely disarmed. Dressed in an old sweater and with a two-day growth of stubble, his tall, thin frame was even more hunched than it had been the last time she saw him. He spent most of his time playing with Kryštof, and when he left he forgot to take the gift from his wife, tickets to a concert that she had been hoping to see with him. It had taken Květa several days of running around paying bribes to scrounge up two tickets for the young Canadian pianist whose performances of Bach's *Goldberg Variations* had become the stuff of legend. She'd had to bring out the heavy guns, and didn't have any more trumps left in her hand or in her heart. Alice was a proud mother, Maximilian was a proud father, and Kryštof was the center of their universe, but the difference between the way his grandparents looked was too great for anyone not to notice. When Josef went out to the balcony for a smoke, a handful of half-smoked butts fell out of his pocket. Alice quietly raged at him for wearing his old brown sweater when just the week before, on her last visit to the cottage, she had ironed his suit and two dress shirts and cleaned up his shoes. The cool, distant, secretly horrified look on her mother's face at seeing her husband again after a year spoke volumes, and the dominant atmosphere of Kryštof's birthday party was a direct reflection of the embarrassment everyone felt except for Josef and Kryštof. The grandfather crawled around the apartment after his grandson, neither one of them paying any attention to the rest of the guests. When the two of them got tired and little Kryštof began to drift off to sleep, his grandfather left to catch the train. His departure was rather abrupt. In fact, the only person he said good-bye to was Kryštof, but the boy was still too young to be able to tell anyone. When Květa left, a few minutes after him, she said to Alice: "You should've told me how he looks now, Ali. You should've told me! It wasn't nice of you not to warn me." And she walked out. Alice didn't bother to try anything else after that. She had enough on her hands with her own marriage. Putting her parents' relationship back together was beyond her. So she went on caring for her hastily aging father, and in the brief moments when her husband was at home she tried to enjoy him a little at least.

Increasingly, the sweetness of her first and only pregnancy was just a memory. Alice was now caught up in the murky flow of everyday life, submerged in the muck at the bottom, and the only thing that was clear was the aquarium window through which she observed her marriage. Maximilian was rarely at home. He fended off any questions with either silence or some implausible story. Once Kryštof turned three, Alice tried every now and then to broach the possibility of having another child, but whenever she did, she could be sure she wouldn't see her husband at all for the next few days. Then as a rule he would turn up at dawn stone drunk with his buddies, turning every trip to the toilet or bathroom into a strange game, the goal of which was not to step on any of the arms, legs, or bellies belonging to the heaving bodies whose breath flooded the apartment with alcoholic fumes. When Maximilian sobered up and Alice tried to talk to him, it would end up in a quarrel that never failed to include a bitter exchange about how little money they had. More and more, their conversations turned into rows and their arguments into obstinate misunderstandings, leaving behind a grubby desperation that smelled of carbolic acid, chloroform, and tincture of iodine. The mutual wounding increased to the point that any means to alleviate the pain was good as far as Maximilian was concerned, even if it did kill half his soul along with it. It wasn't a lack of caring on his part. Just the opposite, it was the growing realization of his own pathetic failure. His own failure flavored with sweat, pain, and a dash of blood. It was staggering to look into the void. He had all sorts of strange dreams. In one of them, the most absurd, he was an astronaut. Through most of the dream he was slowly and carefully putting on a spacesuit, before going out to repair the space station's outer shell. Then the line that secured him snapped and he floated off into space, drifting farther and farther away from the mothership and farther and farther away from Earth. In one version the space station had portholes; in another it didn't. But every time he had the dream, Maximilian knew his wife was inside, brewing him coffee or baking him an apple strudel just the way he liked it. She never made it to the window in time to see him float away. Obviously she couldn't actually brew coffee in zero gravity, but in the dream that didn't matter. Maximilian always woke from it with a lung-crushing anxiety. Another thing about it that bothered him was there was no weightlessness inside the station; it was just like on Earth. Contrary to the laws of nature, it was only outside that there was no gravity. Either way, Maximilian saw all his dreams as basically simple ones about his utter failure.

It was soon obvious to Maximilian that his marriage was slipping out from underneath him. He didn't know exactly what it was, but the continuous onslaughts of emotion and fatigue, combined with the perpetual lack of money, brought him to the point where he was willing to try something different. He made an effort to be more honest, not to be like his father. They were living in different times, after all. It was the seventies, time to harvest the ideas planted by the hardworking minds of the sixties, dreams of brotherhood, equality, love, and the harmony of the spheres — all of that made it to Czechoslovakia during the brief interlude when the Iron Curtain lifted. Maximilian wanted to liberate himself, not politically, but personally. After all, there were still Russian tanks and Russian soldiers in Czechoslovakia's barracks. He wanted to be free, even if sometimes it wasn't entirely clear what from. But one look at the magazines, with their in-depth reports on the most current psychological trends, and it was obvious to him that he needed to free himself from himself and his own prejudices. He didn't know what his main prejudices were, but once he grasped the general theory of human development, he also grasped that the devil of ignorance could hide inside any thought or feeling. He realized that if his life had any value, it was in understanding himself, and he hoped his efforts would also produce a turn for the better in his marriage. And so it was that there, on the strictly drawn boundary between the fertile fields of psychological theory, the idea of honesty was hatched. Honesty consisted of giving vent to his emotions. Letting go of self-control and giving vent to feelings, all feelings, since they alone contained the truth. That was the understanding Maximilian arrived at. In practice that meant drinking a bit more at parties, and when he came home late at night now, he got much angrier than before he had adopted the theory of honesty. When he and Alice had a dispute, sometimes he would hit the table. After a few months he started grabbing her painfully by the wrist, and not long after that he hit her. The first time, he seemed drunker to her than she'd ever seen him before. The second time, he was sober and he told her it was his anger and he needed to give it free rein. When he hit her the third time, her shoulder slammed into the wall and still she refused to be afraid of him. The bruises and fear didn't appear until later.

When Kryštof was four and a half, the doctor recommended that

Alice stop using contraception for a while. By that time Maximilian was sleeping more at his friends' than at home, and Alice didn't even want to hear how many lovers he had vying for his attention. And so it was several months, as a consequence of his sparse and irregular visits, as a consequence of their sporadic and irregular lovemaking, before Alice was sure she was pregnant. She knew it, though, even before she was sure. That feeling she hadn't experienced in five long years was back again. Even little Kryštof noticed something, despite spending more and more time with his grandfather, who often took him out to the countryside on weekends. Alice was back in a bubble of stupendous bliss. A bubble that was sweet and nourishing, and guaranteed absolute protection and security. Even if she broke up with Maximilian, it wouldn't matter: She would finally have two children, and that was what was important. She continued taking Kryštof out to the cottage, where his grandfather initiated him into the mysteries of numbers, geometry, and checkers, and every now and then, usually on Saturdays, Maximilian would show up for the evening, or an evening and a half. The arguments they waged were as fierce as trench warfare and as inevitable as the fact that their love was being transformed — into sulfur, charcoal, and saltpeter, from exhaustion and endless worry into hatred. It blew up just as quickly every time. All it took was a look, a sarcastic tone or well-chosen gesture, and the attack was on. First the accusations flew, then came the counterattack. And then Alice said:

"You can go to hell for all I care! I got what I want from you, which is Kryštof and the child I'm carrying right now! I can take care of them both myself. I wouldn't trust you with them for five minutes — they might grow up to be like you!"

It wasn't until after Maximilian hit her and she was on the floor, wiping the blood from her face, that it dawned on him what she had said.

"You're having a baby?" he asked.

"Yes," she said, "with you, darling. I'm having it with you."

"And who do you think's going to pay for it?" Maximilian snapped back. He grabbed her by the hair and started beating her.

Josef didn't have a clue about their nightly arguments. For one thing he slept on the next floor up, in the room with Kryštof, and for another he took his hearing aid out at night. When Kryštof had a bad dream, he would climb in bed with the old man and hold his hand. If it was really scary, he would tug on his grandpa's hand till he woke up. Josef would switch on the lamp he had on his nightstand and put in his hearing aid. There was no point in Kryštof trying to say anything until then. That was how it went this time too, only instead of telling his grandpa about his dreams, the boy put his finger to his mouth and said, "Listen, they're having a fight again." Josef could hear the voices of Maximilian and Alice from downstairs. He sat up in bed and slung his robe over his shoulders. "I'll go straighten them out, buddy. It'll be fine, not like last week," Josef said. He walked downstairs, and when he opened the door he saw his son-in-law gripping his daughter by the hair, flailing at her as he tried to drag her out from under the bench where she was curled up screaming. He hurled himself at Maximilian, but the length of his jump corresponded only to the strength of an old man, as opposed to the intentions of a father protecting his daughter. He tripped over a toppled chair and landed on the ground. As he got to his feet, Maximilian stood over him, drunkenly screaming at him to stay out of it.

Since Kryštof always whispered to him at night, Josef had his hearing aid set to the maximum, so when Maximilian roared at him it was so loud it hurt. In a spur-of-the-moment reaction of self-defense, Josef slapped him with all his weight behind it, staggering his son-in-law. Maximilian stopped screaming at Josef and punched him. In recollecting it to himself, Josef later classified the blow as a not-so-artful right hook. He tried to dodge it, but was too old and slow to avoid the incoming fist completely, though instead of taking it square on the chin, where it was aimed, he caught it on the left side of his jaw. As he fell to his right onto his back, he landed across another chair lying on the ground. He noticed it was there, but it happened too fast for him to avoid. As he hit the ground, he felt pain in his right forearm and ribs. The room was dead silent. Maximilian kicked something furiously and walked off. Josef felt the vibrations in the floorboards from the slam of the door outside, then silence. After a while he lifted himself and crawled along the ground on all fours until he found his hearing aid, which had fallen out of his ear. He put it back in, but didn't hear anything, so he pulled it out again, opened the battery cover, and saw the battery wasn't touching one of the contacts. He readjusted it, snapped the cover shut, put the hearing aid back in his ear, looked at his daughter, and heard her say, "I think my water burst, Dad! It burst! I think I'm bleeding."

The neighbor who drove them to the hospital had corduroy pants and a windbreaker on over his pajamas. Josef was wearing a torn robe, pajamas, and hiking boots. Kryštof was dressed as if he were going to school, and Alice was curled into a ball on the fold-down rear seat, bleeding from her genitals. The whole way the neighbor was saying indignantly: "That bastard, that bastard engineer, he could've killed you both. I say lock the sonuvabitch up." He also gave each of his passengers a ski cap with a pom-pom. "My heat's not working," he explained. "Take it, so you don't catch cold!"

The district hospital wasn't able to save Alice's child. The doctor held Josef's hand when he broke the news to him. Josef swore. The doctor took a closer look at him and said, "He did a pretty good job on you too. Why don't you come with me for some X-rays." "I can't go anywhere. I've got someone with me," Josef said, pointing to his grandson. "He can come with you," the doctor said. "Either way you need an X-ray." Kryštof walked through the hospital with his grandfather, who was found to have a bruised jaw, a broken left forearm, and two fractured ribs. As they applied the bandages and set Josef's arm in a cast, Kryštof began to cry. He wouldn't even play checkers with the pocket set that Josef found in the neighbor's car, and meanwhile his daughter had just miscarried a child he didn't even know was on the way. Josef asked if he could make a call to his wife in Prague. When Květa picked up the phone he said: "I think you'd better come. Alice had a miscarriage, I'm all beat up, and the little one's bawling. I hate to say it, but I think you're needed here."

13
K V Ě T A

(1)

I never could get used to that bed at my aunt Anna's. Even after all the years I slept in it, I still considered selling it or throwing it away. I tried to get it repaired when I moved in with my aunt, but the upholsterer I found through a classified ad was more interested in paying me compliments than in upholstering. He was several years younger than me, so naturally I was flattered. I thinned down some after Josef moved out, so I was finally at the right weight. Not that I was delusional, but at the time I was still hoping Josef might come back to me. Anyway, the bed was only halfway a bed. Originally it had been built as a daybed sofa, with a tall, cushioned backrest that curved around the right from behind, so it could support your head and part of your back. I felt comfortable and safe in it. When I didn't want to sleep, I could just load it up with pillows and burrow into them. I set up an old floor lamp behind it that Aunt Anna kept in the storeroom. There were just a few tears in the lampshade I needed to repair, and it hung over the chair like a miniature canopy. I tried a few bulbs of different voltage before I found one I could read to without being blinded.

Everything in the apartment was old. The furniture, the carpets, the lamps, the stove, but the oldest of all was my aunt. Before I moved in with her, this tall lady from health services with a funny hairdo was going to have her put into a retirement home. Aunt Anna had no children, so she was on her own, and I thought there was something odd about the authorities deciding to move her just when the neighbors started to take an interest in her apartment. I talked to her on the phone once or twice a month. I'd always ask if she needed anything and arrange for whatever she wanted, but the last few months, after Josef moved out, I spent most of my time sobbing and forgot all about her. It wasn't until I went to see her again, a while later, that I realized how far downhill she'd gone. Her neighbor Mrs. Martincová, who helped me take care of her, had broken her hip and had to go to the hospital, so my aunt was all alone. It had been nearly six months since the last time I saw her, and she was her usual gregarious self, so I didn't notice at first, but then she started calling me Libuše, Hanička, Karolína—everything but Květa. It was obvious the poor thing was confused. So instead of taking care of Josef, I took care of her. The first thing I did was spend two weeks doing laundry, wiping dust, and throwing away old, useless things. Then I washed the windows and doors. My aunt sat watching, calling me a different name depending on what I was doing. Once, covered in dust and dirt, I was dragging a rug out to the courtyard to beat it, and she looked up at me from her little table in the kitchen as I stood straddling the doorway with the rug over my shoulder, dressed in old clothes, dripping sweat, with a wicker swatter under my arm. She took off her glasses and shook her head, saying, "Now you must be Zorka." Then she shook her head again. "Shame the way you turned out. You ought to take better care of yourself." From then on, I noticed that she talked to me based on the way I was dressed—there was a method to it.

I came across several photo albums while I was cleaning, and in fact just that morning, when the phone rang, I had been lying on one of those big old leather albums in my sleep, with it digging into my ribs. It was still dark, and when I picked up the phone I heard Josef. His voice sounded like autumn. He told me what had happened to Alice and him and little Kryštof. I threw on the bare essentials and called a taxi from a phone booth to take me to the train station, since it didn't occur to me till I was already on my way. When I got there it finally hit me and I started shaking all over. As the whole thing dawned on me, I made a quick call to Toník, seeing as he was a doctor. Luckily he was just getting off his shift, so he came to pick me up in his car and we drove to the hospital together. On the way I told him one more time in detail what Josef had said over the phone. He handed me a thermos of coffee he hadn't finished while he was at work, told me to drink some, and stopped at a newsstand along the way for cigarettes.

As Toník parked the car at the hospital and we got out, I saw our neighbor Vašek smoking on the steps. He looked sad. That frightened me more than anything else. I still remembered him as a little boy. He was maybe three or four years older than Alice and had always been a jokester, so it was shocking to see how downhearted he looked. When we entered Alice's room, she was looking out the window while the two other patients ate breakfast in bed. There were two chairs by Alice's bed, one on either side, with Kryštof asleep in one of them. I sat down in the other one. Toník just stroked Alice's hair and went to look for the doctor on duty.

We got there late, I got there late, far too terribly late. I gave my little girl a hug and held Kryštof's hand, trying as hard as I could not to cry. It wasn't easy. We tried to be quiet when we came in, but Kryštof woke up anyway. "Hi, Grandma," he said. He noticed Josef wasn't there and added, "Grandpa must've gone to pee," then curled up under Alice's arm. Josef walked back into the room with Toník, said hello, and for a while I had the feeling he was actually happy to see me. We sat there until the nurse shooed us all out to the hallway, since the other two patients couldn't walk and it was time for pee-pee and poo-poo and general morning hygiene, and out in the hall Toník told us that the examining doctor said they had written up everything so it could be used as the basis for a police investigation. Meanwhile, Vašek had come in from outside to join us, and when he heard he said, "Lock him up, the piece of shit!" I was happy somebody said it. But at the same time I was baffled how things between them had gotten so out of hand. Then Vašek said he was sorry, he had to go to work, but he would be glad to give me a lift to the cottage. I said I would go there to pack some things for Kryštof and Josef and Alice, since they couldn't stay in the hospital and would have to come back to Prague with us. When Toník nodded, I knew it was all right for Josef to come and there wouldn't be any problems. Toník just thanked

Vašek and said he would take me himself. So we left Josef and Kryštof in the hospital with Alice and drove out to the cottage. I took only the bare necessities of clothing for them, and for Kryštof some crayons, jigsaw puzzles, and two construction sets, plus two matchbox cars and a little orange plastic tractor. For Josef I took a coat, dress shoes, trousers, an umbrella, and his briefcase. Afterwards I thought better of it and gave the briefcase to Toník, since Josef always grumbled whenever I so much as touched his briefcase. If I remembered correctly, it was his fourth one in thirty years, and if I knew him, he had all the old ones stored away in the attic at the cottage. So I had Toník give it to him. Josef used to make fun of me whenever he saw me with his briefcase, saying a briefcase in a woman's hands was like a gun with the safety off. Not that it bothered me, but if Josef joked about something that meant it also irritated him, and I didn't need any problems right now, since I needed to get everyone back to Prague, where I could take care of them, because I knew I couldn't leave Aunt Anna out of my sight for more than three days before the poor thing started to waste away. All I really wanted to do was cry. And I couldn't even do that. When I told Toník, he said he had put something in the thermos of coffee I drank to calm my nerves, to help me make it through, he said, and when I asked how come he drank it too, he said it was awful what Maximilian had done to them, especially getting the little one involved. When he said that, coffee or no coffee, pills or no pills, I burst into tears like an ordinary helpless woman, which at that moment was exactly what I was.

My daughter had lost a baby I didn't even know existed, and Kryštof had lost a little brother or sister without even knowing it. I managed to get them all to Prague. Josef changed the lock on the apartment so Maximilian couldn't get in, then went knocking on all the tenants' doors to ask them to replace their locks, and I reported my son-in-law to the police. Josef, meanwhile, stayed with Alice in our old apartment, and little Kryštof seemed quite happy to have him there, although after a few days he started asking why Daddy had hurt Mommy so much, and I wrote a letter to the priest who married them to tell him what Maximilian had done and to warn him that if he dared come anywhere near my daughter I would kill him with my own two hands, but he just wrote back something about God and forgiveness and how it wasn't his place to judge the sins of God's children, which according to him was everyone under the sun. What else should I have expected from a priest who'd never had a child, I realized afterwards. I had to write him, though, since Maximilian had disappeared off the face of the earth. He wasn't at work or at his friends' or anywhere else, but I had a feeling, based on what little I was able to get out of Alice, that he had another woman somewhere. Every afternoon I went to the hospital to see Alice and to the apartment to see Kryštof and Josef and brought them all lunch, and as quietly and unobtrusively as I could, I paid close attention to my husband and discovered the poor thing could barely hear at all anymore without that little device in his ear. Toník went to visit too, but it was such a deathly atmosphere there I probably would have fallen apart if Toník hadn't prescribed me some pills. Finally one day Aunt Anna noticed that I was going out regularly and said she wanted to come along and, besides, I needed to get some sleep. I didn't object. She wanted to go, so I took her with me. It was a hassle dragging her from one side of Prague to the other, what with all the buses and trams, but we did it. As soon as we got there she started chatting away with Josef, she, who couldn't even remember the name of the person she had just spoken to. The batteries were running low in Josef's device, and Kryštof couldn't stop laughing listening to the two of them, confused about who they were talking to and what they were saying. When Josef realized Aunt Anna was calling him a different name every minute, he thought it was funny too, and then she started to laugh as well, and afterwards, when we got home and she heard the clock in the living room chime, she said, "I've spent ages looking for that thing. You should've told me it was there," and then, "Next week let's all go to the zoo. They're bringing in a new elephant. That child of yours will love it." I told her Alice was too big for that sort of thing now, but she said she meant Kryštof, so instead of trying to explain I just nodded my head.

After a long time passed without my hearing any word about

what was going on with my bastard son-in-law, I went to the police, but they told me the case had been dropped. When I asked why, the officer looked at his papers and said, "Your daughter was here and she said to stop the whole thing." I got angry and said they had two doctor's reports or assessments, or whatever they were called, and I didn't agree, but the policeman said I wasn't there when it happened, and besides it was none of my business, since I wasn't even a witness, and my daughter, who was a direct participant—he actually said that: *participant*, which means he believed she had been beaten—didn't want to testify. So then I got really angry and said, "So, what, was he supposed to cripple or kill her? Isn't it enough that the lousy creep gave her a miscarriage?" The officer gave me a sad look. "It's always hard with cases of domestic violence, ma'am," he said. He looked around a moment, pulled out a glass, filled it with water from the tap, put it in front of me, and said he understood me, but he didn't understand at all, so I realized I'd better leave. When I talked to Alice about it that evening, she said it wouldn't fix anything anyway. "Do you really want me to have my son's dad locked up?" she asked. I didn't answer and left to go see Aunt Anna, who looked at me and said, "Květa, if you're not careful, you're going to turn completely gray." The fact that she didn't mix up my name caught me totally off guard. In fact I was so bowled over I burst into tears again later that night as I was flipping through an old album of black-and-white photographs, trying to figure out who was who in our unhappy family.

I thought I was going to see Josef more often during the six months he was in Prague, especially after Alice came home from the hospital. Actually, I didn't think it, I wished it. But he went back to the cottage in Lhotka in the spring. When he was here in Prague, in our old apartment with Alice and Kryštof, I suddenly realized that I still loved him. It was different now than thirty years ago, obviously. We weren't going to concerts together anymore, and he avoided me. Every so often I went out to Lhotka to visit Alice and Kryštof. After the disaster with Maximilian, Josef had stopped objecting, so I could do that now. He put up with me. I scoured Prague in search of batteries for his hearing aid and left them on the shelf above his collection of gramophone records. He didn't say anything, but when his ran out, he took them. I know—I counted them. And one day I caught him in the act of some poorly hidden affection. I had gone mushrooming out in the woods with Kryštof and it started raining, so I wrapped him in my raincoat, but I got soaked to the bone. When we got back and I sat down in the kitchen next to the stove, Josef brought me a towel and made me some grog. I didn't even want to drink it. I just wanted to save it. Then he brought me two aspirin, and I took one, but the other tablet I still have tucked away in a small inlaid box that Josef bought me on vacation once, ages ago, and now it's my secret sentimental aspirin.

(2)

Květa couldn't persuade her daughter to have Maximilian's assault investigated, so that, as Květa said, they would put him away where he'd be out of decent people's hair. In return for Alice's not pressing charges, Maximilian agreed to an immediate divorce. Josef lived at the cottage in Lhotka and sometimes Květa would drive out there to spend the weekend with Alice and Kryštof. Once, she arrived unannounced, on her own and full of hope, only to have Josef declare before she even made it past the entryway that he urgently needed to go to Prague. She spent two days at the cottage by herself, feeling so profoundly alone that she vowed never to do that again. She didn't try to find out whether Josef was telling the truth. It was irrelevant. Going through old clothes in the closets. Throwing away old newspapers and magazines. Finding old strawflowers, which every year Josef forgot to replace with new ones, in the most inappropriate parts of the house. Doing all this enclosed her in a secluded shell of silence and concentrated solitude. The only walk she permitted herself was a trip to the garden restaurant and the cemetery, and even that she didn't do until after the last train from Prague had arrived, so she could be sure Josef wouldn't show up any sooner than the next morning. He didn't show up at all. She walked up and down the one long street in Lhotka several times, greeting the neighbors and then returning to the cottage.

It wasn't easy going back to an empty house, especially knowing that the person she had come to see had left it because of her.

As Kryštof got older, Josef became more adventurous, taking him on trips to see steeplechases, castles, greyhound races, flooded quarries, twice by train to the Baltic Sea in Poland, once to the Adriatic Sea in Yugoslavia, the Markéta motorcycle speedway in the Břevnov section of Prague, hockey games, soccer, and all the while carefully monitoring Kryštof's movie theater attendance to make sure he saw at least one Western a week, which Kryštof then had to recount to him in its entirety. But what gave him the greatest pleasure were the trips they took together. Josef became an expert in timetables, with a meticulousness unique to him. He created his own system of symbols and abbreviations for train station pubs and restaurants, which he jotted down in his notebook. Even the tiniest snack bar received a detailed evaluation, along with its frankfurters, sausages, kielbasas, and various types of potato salad. There was one thing Josef was adamant about: children, unlike adults, needed to eat regularly. At the same time, however, he also believed that Kryštof should be able to eat what he liked, not what his mother and grandmother thought was good for him. In the event that they ever happened to travel the same route twice, they knew exactly where to find a meal—they knew which place had tolerable potato salad and which place it would cause stomach cramps, so it was better to go with the kielbasa or meatloaf instead—thereby eliminating the need to waste precious time buying groceries. In summer they slept in youth hostels; in winter, being at the whim of the weather, they traveled less often. School was no problem for Kryštof. Josef imbued him with so much knowledge of math, chemistry, and physics that he didn't even realize he was learning most of the time. Occasionally it irritated Alice that her son spent more time at the cottage than at home, and she never did understand what he loved so much about being in that poorly heated house. When Kryštof was nine, Josef decided he deserved his own room. When he was eleven, Josef decided the one he had was too small and he needed to build him a new one in the attic. The two of them completed the job in under four months. When Kryštof was thirteen, Josef's only regular contact with Prague came in the mediated form of his grandson taking a bundle of dirty laundry from Lhotka to Prague with him every week and bringing it back clean, ironed, mended, and patched. It gave Alice the feeling she knew what was going on with her son and her father. It wasn't entirely true, since sometimes they went on long trips that she had no idea about. They once spent a whole week in Slovakia without her knowing it. They stayed with a friend of Josef's who had written to him that a bear had been spotted walking around the village and if they came they might get lucky and see it. The bear didn't show its face all week, but they did see a lynx, which was enough to satisfy them. Kryštof had a relatively large number of absences from school, but given that he was generally a good student and that his grandfather attended parent-teacher meetings, there was no reason for concern.

Nineteen eighty-nine saw Josef in the hospital. He had been feeling tired, then a little confused, and all of a sudden the left side of his mouth stopped obeying him. When he woke up a few days later, he discovered he'd had a stroke. As a result, it took at least another year before he realized that the government of the country had changed. Kryštof, meanwhile, found himself a girlfriend who sometimes stayed over with him in Lhotka. When Josef came home from the hospital, he discovered he didn't need to take his laundry to Prague anymore, since Kryštof and Libuše had bought a washing machine. At first the sudden interruption of laundry packages back and forth from Lhotka to Prague took Alice by surprise, and then she found out her father had had a stroke. She gave her son, who now stood several inches taller than her, a long talking-to, to which he coolly responded by saying that Grandpa just didn't feel like telling anyone.

Aunt Anna was so captivated by the Velvet Revolution, which happened that year, that she broke off her preparations for death and for the first time in years went to an eye doctor for stronger glasses. After that, she started reading the newspapers again, listening to television and radio programs, and reveling in the endless supply of new magazines that had suddenly appeared. In order to make sure her aunt received the pension increase she was entitled to that year, Květa had to obtain new documents for her, and to her astonishment she discovered that in fact Aunt Anna wasn't her aunt at all. She spent a few days trying to decide how to tell her, and when she finally did, her aunt just waved her hand and said that according to the latest research everyone on Earth was related to each other, and the whole human race most likely came from Africa. Either present-day Ethiopia or Mozambique, she wasn't sure. When Květa asked how she knew that, her aunt replied that she should be less concerned with herself and pay more attention to the world around her, and it was about time she got herself a proper man. When Květa said she had been married nearly her whole adult life, her aunt just raised her eyebrows and said she certainly hoped to be introduced to her husband someday. Although she couldn't walk as well as before, ever since November 1989 Aunt Anna had been faring better and better. Květa watched with amazement as her aunt became well informed on global affairs, and if every now and then she couldn't remember someone's name, she agilely came up with a nickname to replace it. For example, she had started calling the president the scooter king. *King* because he lived in the castle, *scooter* because he had revealed in an interview that he used a scooter to wheel down the castle's lengthy corridors so he could get as quickly as possible from one office to another. Květa could hardly find fault with her aunt's choice of nickname, since it had a certain logic to it and it accurately described the bearer's features, as he appeared to Aunt Anna at least, if not to the world. Little Kryštof saw his father only once or twice a year, when Maximilian would turn up unexpectedly and unannounced. The meetings were more to satisfy his own conscience than out of any interest in his son's present, past, or future.

One day in March 1991, Aunt Anna received a letter in a yellow envelope that was slightly more elongated than the state-approved standard. The stamp had a little queen with a crown on her head and the postmark said *London*. She thought it over a minute, then remembered that she had some relatives who had gone overseas to work before the invasion in '68. They had had some children while they were there, who had never been back to the Czech lands. Reading the letter she gathered that their son was planning to come to Prague, though she promptly forgot his name and from that point on referred to him only as the cousin. The letter said he would be arriving sometime in the next few days but didn't need anything from Aunt Anna, so she didn't understand why they had bothered to send the letter. "Everyone needs something," she insisted. "Everyone! You need your man back, even though you won't talk about it in front of me. You keep it a secret from me, and damned if you aren't ashamed of it too!"

14

THE COUSIN'S ARRIVAL—A LETTER—
CONVERSATION WITH JOSEF

(1)

The cousin flew into Prague's Ruzyně Airport equipped with perfect Czech and a detailed knowledge of Czech and East European history. It was his second visit to the city. He didn't remember the first, which had been fifteen years earlier, when he was ten, and consisted of a single-day stopover in Prague on the way from Helsinki to Vienna with his mother, who had traveled to many countries around the world in her life, in search of landscapes that were typically Czech, in particular ones that reminded her of the Elbe Lowlands region where she had grown up. On their arrival in Prague she was immediately informed that she, being an emigrant, had the wrong visa and that of course no one there could issue her the one needed for a longer stay. So, to the officials' displeasure, they spent one night in a hotel, since the airplane that was to take her and her child back to where she belonged—that is, back to the capitalist West—had no more flights scheduled that day. All the cousin remembered about the visit was what his mother told him later on. The airport in Prague was more or less interchangeable with any other. It had no particular atmosphere of its own, the sole attempt at ambience being the same decorative flowers arranged in the same parts of the same-looking check-in areas in the same portable planters by the same glass doors of the arrival and departure halls. His mother had told him that a distant relative of his aunt would be waiting for him at the airport, a lady by the name of Květa. They had sent a photograph of Jiří in a letter to Aunt Anna in advance.

For people in England, *Jiří* was a strange name and nobody there could pronounce it correctly. Whenever he tried to teach someone the proper pronunciation, it took forever, with pathetic results. At best, they managed to say *Jírží*. Ever since he was little this had caused him problems, which was why he preferred *George*, which was the English translation. Now, for the first time in his life, he was about to spend some time in a country where everyone would be able to pronounce his name correctly and everyone understood Czech, that mysterious language that in London only his mother, father, and sister knew, plus the few people who gathered at the Czech club every once in a while. Life behind the former Iron Curtain promised to be a great adventure.

The plane to Prague was of Russian make, old and creaky, and Jiří had the distinct feeling the rivets holding together the sheets of the fuselage were experiencing material fatigue. When they flew over the border, the captain announced that they had flown over the border. As they made the approach to Prague, the flight attendant pointed out Karlštejn Castle on the right-hand side of the plane. Jiří gave his neighbor an apologetic smile and leaned across him to look out the window. From this height, it looked even more photogenic than on the postcards. A passage from the tourist guides suddenly came to Jiří's mind: established in 1348 as a place of safekeeping for the crown jewels by Charles IV, King of Bohemia dash Holy Roman Emperor, known to the Czechs as *otec vlasti*, "father of the nation," which was something between a title and a sign of respect. Impressive.

As the plane entered turbulence it began to shake and buck. Jiří regretted having eaten lunch instead of following the example of the Czech passengers and ordering beer or some other alcoholic beverage. The plane landed. It was drizzling rain. A bus drove across the runway to pick them up, and carried them to the terminal. They waited until a representative of the airline appeared, opened a door, and told them to have their passports ready. He said everything twice, in Czech and English. He made two mistakes in English, but his accent was better than the one of the airline representative in Paris, where Jiří had been on his last trip, and unlike his French counterpart, at least the Czech was trying to make himself understood. Jiří took it as a good sign.

In the room next door were two glass booths with policemen sitting inside them. The passengers formed two lines and approached the booths one at a time, laying their passports down on the counter. The policemen's uniforms were dark green with red shoulderboards. No smiles. They looked strict, serious, funereal. Jiří's turn came and he handed the policeman his Czech passport. Of course it was written there that he had been born in London, so the officer carefully inspected every page, weighing it in his hand, then looked up at Jiří. Jiří gave him an encouraging smile. At the airport in Paris, everyone smiled. In Rome, Düsseldorf, even Israel, they smiled. Not in Prague. In fact the look on the policeman's face gave Jiří the feeling that he had done something wrong, so he stopped smiling in case the officer misinterpreted it. After thumbing through the passport one last time, the policeman turned to the personal information page. "Born in London," he said. Jiří wrinkled his brow to indicate he didn't understand whether it was a question or a statement. "Hmmm," the officer said. He picked up his rubber stamp and applied it to Jiří's passport with no change in expression. It dawned on Jiří that this man never smiled at anyone. Evidently his uniform didn't give him much opportunity. Its forest green was too much of a constraint. He might as well have been waiting for an armored transport carrier to surface from a trench camouflaged in branches so he could hop on board and go barreling down the runway to defend the country's national interest. He tossed Jiří's passport onto the counter with contempt and called out: "Neeeeext!"

It wasn't a very encouraging beginning, Jiří thought. It had been more than two years since the Velvet Revolution, but apparently the news hadn't reached the airport yet. But so what, Jiří thought. It's my first time in Eastern Europe, I can't complain. He quickly corrected himself. I mustn't say "Eastern." Mum and dad were always a bit touchy when it came to that. "Central" is better. Yes, that's it. Central! Central Europe!

He picked up his suitcase and duffel bag from the baggage claim and walked out to the main hall. About thirty people stood waiting for passengers from the London flight, five or so holding signs. None of them had his name on it. Květa probably hadn't arrived yet, Jiří thought. He scanned the hall one more time, then went to change some money. He bought a can of Coca-Cola, sat down on a bench, opened the can, and took a sip. After ten minutes or so, the cluster of people waiting had dispersed. A gray-haired woman of about sixty stepped up to him: "Are you Jiří by any chance?"

Jiří looked her up and down. She had on a three-quarter-length coat with a fur collar that in England would have had its owner ostracized for cruelty to animals. Jiří tried to reassure himself that it was fake.

"Yes. Yes, I am. Jiří Nováček," he said.

"I'm Květa Černá. I think I'm your aunt." She went out of her way to pronounce every word carefully. He was a foreigner, after all.

"*Dobrý den,*" said Jiří.

"*Dobrý den,*" said Květa, bending over to shake his hand. A reconnaissance of the cuffs on her sleeves revealed that they were fur as well. Glancing into her eyes as he shook her hand, he realized he had never seen eyes like hers before. Emeralds are green, aren't they? Jiří thought. Having never actually seen an emerald before, he wasn't sure.

Květa gestured toward the door, and he followed her out with his bags. They came to the bus stop and she began to explain how they would get to where they were going. Jiří listened attentively, and when she mentioned Vinohrady and Jan Masaryk Street, his ears perked up. "Wasn't he that minister they killed?" he asked.

"Why yes, how did you know that?" Květa replied with evident delight. Jiří blushed and sensed she could see it on his face. Attempting to wipe it away as quickly as possible, he said:

"I didn't know people grew grapes in Prague."

"Grapes?" said Květa. "Oh, you mean Vinohrady. Yes, it does mean vineyards, but it's just the name of a neighborhood."

"I understand," he said, smiling. "But I know you grow wine somewhere in the Czech lands. My mother told me. Somewhere along the Elbe?"

"Yes," Květa said, losing interest in the conversation. "Yes, all over the place. Moravia too, and Mělník, and by the way did I tell you that you'll be staying with my daughter in Vinohrady?"

"Oh," said Jiří.

"Yes, my daughter."

"With your daughter in the vineyards where they don't grow wine," Jiří said. Květa didn't answer. It was close to four P.M., the time when she normally had at least a small cup of coffee, and she was really starting to feel it. When they got to the apartment, Alice put Jiří in the room that belonged to her son, Kryštof, who hadn't slept there in two years. After Jiří had been introduced to Alice and unpacked his bags, the three of them went to see Aunt Anna.

As they entered the apartment, Jiří noticed several smells simultaneously. The first was the fragrance of plants from the garden, wafting in the open window. Next were the faint odor of floating dust particles and a barely perceptible scent of urine. When they walked into the living room, he saw a petite woman with the wrinkled face of a turtle, wrapped in blankets and sitting in a tall armchair. She must have been at least ninety years old. Her white strands of hair stood out against the brown fabric of the headrest. Moving extremely slowly, she removed the layers of blankets one by one, beckoning to Jiří with a wrinkled hand indicating that he was to advance. He had been granted an audience.

"So you're little Jiří," Aunt Anna said, seizing the open letter from the dressing table with her right hand while clutching her glasses with the other. "How are your parents? I hope they're well. They ought to be, with a son like you!" Jiří took a deep breath. "I'm sure they must be glad they have a son," Aunt Anna went on.

"I have a sister, too," Jiří broke in, giving everyone a cheerful smile.

"No use having a daughter," Aunt Anna said. "Look at me. I didn't have any children, but I certainly wouldn't have wanted a daughter. Look at us here," she said. "Three women. Three! You know men don't have it easy, and they don't get to have any fun in life." Ever so slowly raising an index finger, she added, "They don't live to be as old either. Men, poor devils."

"Where did you hear that one, Auntie?" Alice asked, listening with half an ear as she helped Květa prepare dinner.

"Everybody knows that! Don't tell me you never heard it," said Aunt Anna. "They die six or seven years younger."

The doorbell rang. Květa ran off and a moment later came back into the room with a slightly balding man twirling a pair of large black glasses in his hand.

"This is Mr. . . ."

"Verner," the man said.

"Mr. Verner here says you invited him to dinner, Auntie. Is that right?" Květa asked awkwardly.

"Oh, nice to see you, Karel," Aunt Anna said.

"Will your friend be eating with us?" Alice asked Aunt Anna while her mother stood behind the man's back shrugging and rolling her eyes.

Aunt Anna ignored her question, tugging on the gentleman caller's jacket sleeve. "Have a seat, Karel. Sit down, sit. Now you're not going to believe it, but this young man here is the son of Eva and . . . God, what is the name of that husband of hers?"

"My father's name is Jiří, same as me," Jiří said.

"We haven't met," Květa interjected. "My name's Černá and this is my daughter Alice."

"Verner," said the man. "Pleased to meet you."

"Now stop that, Květa, and get dinner ready. Jiří here must be hungry after such a long journey. Aren't I right?"

"I could eat a little something," Jiří said.

"Do you hear that, Karel? You hear how beautifully he speaks Czech?"

"Oh, yes, very nice, very nice," said Mr. Verner.

"You know, I was thinking, Karel. You're in insurance still," Aunt Anna said.

"I haven't been at the insurance company for a long time now. I stopped working there before the revolution."

"So where are you now?"

"I'm at that bank. I told you that. We talked about it."

"Ah, the bank, well, that wouldn't be too bad either. Maybe you could find something there for our boy here, Jiří. Some kind of employment."

"Oh, thank you but that won't be necessary," Jiří said.

"You be quiet. You don't know how things work here," Aunt Anna said. She looked at Mr. Verner. "Just like his mother, isn't he? Just like Eva, especially the mouth, don't you think, Karel?"

"I'm really sorry. Here we are talking about you . . . as if you weren't even here," Mr. Verner apologized.

"Never mind," Jiří said.

"At my age," Aunt Anna said, "and I'm going to be ninety-five, Karel. At my age I don't have time for courtesies anymore. You know."

She gave Jiří a sharp stare and lifted her arm, indicating that he should leap from his seat and support her as she rose from the chair. And so he did. Aunt Anna rewarded him with a fleeting smile and patted him on the arm that she was using to prop herself up. "Karel, please, could you hand me that cane over there . . . that one, that's right."

Mr. Verner handed her the cane, and leaning one arm on it and the other on Jiří, she made her way into the next room for dinner. Jiří struggled to adjust his strides to Aunt Anna's tiny footsteps as Verner walked behind them, watching attentively lest the slightest shudder of need ripple through her fragile body. In that way, step by step, the three of them proceeded to the table where dinner would soon be served.

At dinner Jiří was pleased to discover that his intellectual labors to decipher the complicated scheme of his family, which in its intricacies surpassed even the filigree fabrics of the ancient Venetian masters, had paid off, and he was beginning to understand who he was actually related to. However, just as he thought he was starting to grasp where one thread ended and the next one began, he found himself once again hopelessly perplexed by the tangled logic of family relationships. Aunt Anna, Květa, Mr. Verner, it made no difference who said what, it all sounded the same—for instance, Aunt Anna sketching out one of the clan's adjacent lines: "But then after the putsch in forty-eight he got remarried in Germany. Then her sister moved from Canada to Vienna and had another child there with her second husband, and her sister, she lives here in Vysočina, so she wasn't allowed to go to college. Then her daughter, who can't be much older than your Kryštof, Alice, she went and married a distant cousin of hers from Opava, and that's about it."

Jiří was beginning to realize that historical dates weren't enough for him to gain a full understanding of the Czech world. He didn't let it discourage him, but he did conclude that it was going to require a substantially greater degree of energy and ingenuity than he had initially estimated.

(2)

Date: whenever, second day in Prague

Hi sis,

I'm writing like I promised. I hope I have the right address so it reaches you without going halfway around the world before finding its way back to London where it sits for three months, like last time, when I was in Rome. Just for the record, I talked to Mum and Dad. There was a bit of confusion, since they called the hotel but I had canceled the reservation and the staff there didn't give them the number I left. Then Dad got the bright idea of calling Aunt Anna, but either she couldn't hear or she forgot. She's practically a hundred years old and she looks like a sharp-eyed little turtle. Anyway, they tracked me down eventually; she probably gave them the number for Alice, who's Aunt Květa's daughter. It isn't easy working out who's who, and I still have no idea which ones are actually our relatives. The airport was the usual thoughtless affair. All the flowers are dry and the streets are untidy. Rubbish spilling out of the bins and fag ends all over the place. On the other hand they've got this funny apparatus they call a *tramvaj*. That's tramway to you, sis. I don't think they realize it's an Americanism and that they're actually little electric trains. They run precisely on time. An odd contrast with the filthy streets. Then they also have the *metro* here. It's excellent, truly excellent. I'm sure you'd love it—it's the answer to all your crazy sci-fi dreams. It runs perfectly and inside it's spotless, unlike the streets, almost like Germany, but the design is the thing. If you can imagine, the stations look like the inside of a spaceship from one of those old sci-fi TV series, the ones you and Mum and Geoffrey love so much—Buck Rogers and Star Trek and all that. Just picture aluminum foil in all different colors with geometric patterns stamped into it, hemispheres and dimples and such. I don't know how they came up with it. Brilliant. As Dad would say in Czech: *k sežrání*. And as if that weren't enough, the rest of it's covered in marble. I kid you not. Either artificial stone or marble, like some kind of outer space mausoleum. I just love it!! But you're better off not telling people here what you think. They're a bit on the sensitive side. You'd just love it. So those are my first travel notes. Say hi to Geoffrey, and give Mum a call or she'll start cursing you again. And don't even think about mentioning what happened in Paris.

George

P.S. I hope you noticed how great my Czech is! Eh

(3)

Mr. Verner always carried thick black glasses with him, though he rarely put them on. Most of the time he shifted them back and forth from one hand to the other, sometimes opening one temple or the other, as if lost in thought and focusing on the moment when he would put them on; sometimes he would rest one of the temples on his upper lip, but Jiří, whom he never referred to as anything but *Cousin*, had never seen him wear them. Mr. Verner possessed a corpulent frame of medium height. His cousin, despite being only a few inches taller, at twenty-six was bound to have his slender figure viewed as much more elegant and graceful, bringing him the superficial sympathy that makes life so much easier for its recipients without their realizing it. Mr. Verner had white hair, cropped closely on the sides around his ears and temples. The rest of his head was bald and covered in dark-tanned skin. He had a habit of breathing deeply in and out, as if in the middle of some strenuous physical exercise. He wore his tie loose and was always in a rush. It wasn't clear where to or why, but one day when the cousin asked, he bit down forcefully on one of the temples of his glasses and gave it some thought. Detecting no trace of irony in the cousin's question and believing him to have asked out of genuine interest, he decided to give him an answer. "Every official, Cousin," Mr. Verner said, "is like a limited train. More precisely, like something between a limited and an express. An express draws too much attention to itself, while a limited is more important than most other trains, but not so noticeable. Haste is the base speed for an official. You have to make everyone else think you have not more work than you can manage, since that could be used against you, but more than anticipated based on the administrative agenda, legislation, and client demand." The cousin wracked his brain over the sentence for a while. He knew all the words, yet the meaning still eluded him. He shook his head from side to side. "If it looks like you can't keep up with the work, you could be deemed incompetent, do you understand?" The cousin nodded. "Whereas if it's evident from your behavior that your superiors are giving you perhaps not unreasonable but let's say poorly thought-out instructions, which are unnecessarily complicating your life, then you've won." The cousin nodded again, trying to grasp what implications this information could have for him. He had been employed at the bank for a week now, but had yet to understand what his job would entail. His supervisor, one Mr. Dostál, had given him direct instructions to make arrangements for the furnishing of three offices. Jiří had gone back to ask him several times what the offices would be used for, but from his answer it was clear even he didn't know. All that Dostál told him was it was possible the offices might be for them, so he should make sure they were quality furnishings. That was roughly two days' work, then Jiří had nothing to do again. For lunch every day they went to a restaurant that was just under ten minutes' walk away, where Mr. Verner would meet him and Mr. Dostál. The pudgy Mr. Verner would always sweat during the soup. He consumed it quickly, with a certain doggedness, then, pulling a white or light blue handkerchief from his pocket, he would wipe the dewy sweat from his face, at which point he turned visibly calmer, becoming an affable companion. The cousin lived with Alice, who took him out to the cottage in Lhotka several times so he had a chance to meet her father, Josef, and her son, Kryštof. Alice had assumed the cousin and Kryštof would become friends, if for no other reason than that they were both roughly the same age, but Kryštof devoted most of his time to the fair-haired Libuše with a devotion she had never seen in him before, and spent most of the interim playing checkers with his grandfather. Josef was an old man. At first Jiří didn't even realize he was in a relationship with Květa, since she looked a good ten years younger than she actually was. She looked about sixty, whereas her husband, despite being seventy-six, looked to be nearly eighty-five. When Jiří looked at Josef, he saw a tall, thin old man, who sometimes walked with a severe limp on his left leg. It was hard to answer when Josef asked him what was new in England, even though it was a question he got often. It seemed as if no matter what he said, the questioner was satisfied. When Josef asked how he liked it in the Czech lands, Jiří replied that he hadn't been anywhere in the Czech lands yet except Prague, but Prague was probably even more beautiful than Venice or Jerusalem, which he knew intimately and which up until that point he had considered the most beautiful in the world. His answer seemed to give Josef a shot of energy, as he suddenly began trying to convince Jiří that he was wrong, despite having never seen either Venice or Jerusalem with his own eyes. He rubbed his palms together, making a sound like rustling leaves, and propped his right foot on a wooden swivel stool that had originally belonged to a piano.

"We love Prague very much, too much. It just isn't right. All my life, apart from the ten years I spent locked up in the mines, that is, I was a structural engineer in Prague. I know the subsoil of all of Central Bohemia. I know the methods for laying foundations and the foundations of almost every building in Prague. I used to know the geological survey maps by heart, although now that I'm retired, I'm even forgetting some of the things I thought I'd never forget." It wasn't at all clear that either Josef or Jiří had any interest in what the other one thought, or that either one of them was even trying to communicate. But Josef had the idea stuck in his head, so he kept going.

"You know, every time I come to Prague I feel like I'm in a museum. The year before last, when I was in the hospital, I was lying in bed just steps away from the Faust House. We're just peppered with history here." Kryštof, who was outside in the garden, dismantling and cleaning the lawnmower, overheard a few words of the conversation through the open window. He came into the house, went to the kitchen, made two pint glasses of soda from the raspberries Libuše had picked, and carried them in to Josef and his mother's cousin. The cousin was just about to leave the room, but when Kryštof set the glass in front of him, he picked it up, took a sip, and sat back down again. "Grandpa doesn't talk much," Kryštof said. "In fact it's pretty rare, but every now and then he chats up a storm, don't you, Grandpa?" Kryštof said, handing a glass to Josef. Josef just looked at the soda, nodded his thanks, and went back to his thoughts. He was thinking what a big city the capital was, a museum, disgustingly big and disgustingly ugly. As disgusting as a collection of stuffed animal carcasses. But he didn't see any need to say so to their young relative from abroad. I wonder just how much he knows about Prague, Josef thought. Out loud he said, "Once you get to know Prague a little more, we can have a chat about it." Then he turned himself to his drink, every so often picking up the glass and running it over his right cheek, then his left. He still couldn't feel the left side of his face as well as the right. Like the way he felt after getting anesthesia at the dentist. He wondered why he no longer found the city enchanting. Maybe beauty was just a matter of a few recurring patterns. Maybe it was all just applied geometry. A few shapes over and over again. What was architecture other than applied geometry? Triangles. Spheres. Helixes. What else was the whole virus of Baroque? That wasn't it, though. What was it? he thought. Maybe it was the fact that nothing had been developed in more than a hundred years. "Maybe that's it," he said, turning to the cousin. "It's preserved, like canned food. The whole thing's conserved to death!"

"Prague, you mean? You mean Prague is too well preserved?" the cousin asked.

"Did you know there's the skeleton of a whale in the National Museum on Wenceslas Square? Don't ask me what it has to do with the Czech nation's moral or intellectual values, but imagine you lived inside that skeleton. Every day you would wake up and walk through those ornate halls filled with stuffed marmots, weasels, and hedgehogs that have to be sprayed with naphthalene so they don't get infested with moths. That's what Prague is like. Dead and lifeless. Just a bunch of slicked-up carcasses for the tourists to sink their teeth into like hyenas swarming over a hunk of dead meat. Just one great big putrefying tourist attraction. The new bosses don't give a second thought to the people who actually live there. They don't even pretend to care about them anymore. Next thing you know they'll put a glass roof over Old Town Square and Wenceslas Square. It's only a matter of time. Technically it's no problem, I could figure it out in three days. Then they'll seal it off, reserve half for tourists and make the other half into some tacky museum. If you lie down with a museum, you get up with a museum. What else do we expect? We're getting what we deserve."

It worried Kryštof to hear his grandpa talk like that. His rambling speeches, leading from nowhere to nowhere, combined with the fact that his ability to play checkers had greatly declined since his stroke, were disturbing. Before he went to the hospital, their victories and defeats had been balanced roughly one-to-one, whereas now his grandpa lost all the time. Not only that, but he had begun using unusual turns of phrase that he previously denounced as imprecise and suitable only for opera librettos, where, as he put it, they had their place. In the past he had always expressed himself in simple, pragmatic terms, speaking clearly and precisely. Now his precision was gone. The one thing that gave Kryštof some reassurance was that in the past few weeks his grandpa had seemed happier and had begun to do a little tidying up at home in Lhotka. Maybe at last he was starting to get a little better.

15

THE CARP LETTER

Dear Sara,

I've decided to write you a letter describing my past few days. Yesterday I returned from a course outside of Prague where the bank sent me for several days, and after lugging home my bags full of presents, I decided to go get something to eat. It was freezing out—cracking cold, as they say here, though I've yet to figure out what the "cracking" actually means. In any case I'm told it has nothing to do with hitting anyone or anything. That's just FYI, in case you're interested, since the Czech we speak at home is a bit different from the Czech they speak here, and seeing as you're my older sister I thought you might want to know. At any rate, I was on my way to get a bite to eat when I saw some men standing out on the street in leather aprons. I didn't see any girls or women, so I assume it's always men, but they had on these long leather aprons, dripping with dirty water. Up until yesterday I thought the locals were quite friendly and rather civilized. At least that's how they seemed. But the ritual I witnessed yesterday really took me by surprise. It must have been sometime during the night, they lined the street with these big barrels of water with fish inside. They call the barrels "kegs" here, the same as the ones for beer. I don't think they put fish in their beer, but after yesterday I'm not so sure about anything anymore. What threw me most, though, wasn't the fact that they had fish in the vats, or that they managed to set them all up in a single day. It's that they kill them—that's right, they're killing them as I write this, right out there in the street, on the corner—right on the spot. The men in the aprons have a set of knives lined up next to them on the table, and a net that looks like a shoddy, oversized snowshoe. Using the net, they scoop the fish out of the water onto the table, and drop a cloth on top of it and hold it down so it can't slip away. Then they kill the fish with a blow to the neck. Usually it starts flopping around from side to side, since even with its little brain it has a hunch what's in store. There isn't any sound at all. It's completely quiet, except for the water sloshing. I wonder if they would still do the killing out in public if the fish could make noise. If the city was filled with wet, gasping moans and choking and screaming. As it is, the only sound you hear is sloshing water. After the men in aprons deliver the death blow, they hold the fish in place and with a move too quick for me to follow, they slice open its belly and remove the warm, steaming guts. A few times I had a feeling the fish was still alive then, seeing as it was still moving. But when I asked about it, I was assured that by that point the fish are already dead. When they slice open the belly, everything gets covered in blood. Nobody seems in the least bit bothered. Gallbladder, intestines, heart, they throw it all away, along with the rest of the internal organs. I'm sorry I didn't get too detailed a view of that part, Sara. Even so, I almost threw up several times. I had gone out to get something to eat, but you probably won't be surprised to hear I didn't end up getting anything. Actually, that's an understatement. For two days I couldn't eat at all, given that I was passing vats full of fish every day. I tried to avoid the execution sites. But then the weather turned cold and puddles of water and fish blood froze on the pavement. After a few days I was finally able to control my gag reflex and I even managed to get a little something down, so I started thinking about it again. I believe this type of behavior is called a custom. I'm no expert, thank God, but I'm fairly sure it can't be classified as mass hysteria. Number one, it isn't a group activity. Each person buys his or her fish individually. Number two, nobody shows any signs of heightened emotion. And number three, the locals claim they've been engaging in this activity for several hundred years now. I have no way of verifying this, so I remain somewhat skeptical. Nevertheless they enjoy the ritual, and pass it along to their children. It gives them satisfaction and makes them happy. One article I read said some of them take the fish home and put it in their bathtub, so their children can play with it. Then they take the fish, still alive, and set it free in the river. That's the good news. The bad news is, another article I read said a lot of them take the fish home and kill it themselves. I don't know whether they don the same ritual clothing: the long leather apron, the tall waterproof boots, and the special cap or hat, which also seems to be part of the professional fish killer's outfit. My guess is the cap also helps protect them from the cold. I didn't dare ask my native friends about it, though, since they already suspect that as half-foreigners we don't share their beliefs, so they tend to be rather careful about what they say when I'm around. Still, they all agree this is the way to celebrate the holiday of peace, joy, and good cheer: Christmas.

Bye for now,
George

16

ALICE AT HER FATHER'S—THE DISPLAY CASE—ATTEMPT AT RECONCILIATION

(1)

Alice took a train to Lhotka that was supposed to arrive Friday afternoon at one thirty-seven, but due to a track closure, rail service was replaced by special buses for part of the route. There were two buses and not all of the train passengers fit onto them. This resulted in several heated arguments between the passengers and the dispatcher, who adamantly insisted that the whole business had basically nothing to do with him. After twenty minutes of waiting, another bus finally showed up to carry the passengers who didn't fit on the first two. Alice arrived two hours later than she had planned. She wouldn't have seen Kryštof and Libuše in any case, since they had left already that morning, but the loss of time annoyed her. On her way to the cottage from the station, she stopped at the drugstore and bought several brands of powerful cleaning fluid in plastic bottles of various shapes and colors. Failing to recognize the woman who rang up her sale, Alice concluded that she must not be from Lhotka. While paying she was surprised to discover that the cashier had a foreign accent. What kind of person came to seek her fortune in Lhotka? Alice wondered. In a city, sure, even a town, but out here in a village? She came to the cottage, walked through the garden, and finding the door unlocked, went inside. Her father wasn't there. She set the bags down in the entryway, took off her coat, and went outside. She found her father in the shed in back of the house. The door was ajar, and he was shifting a wooden workbench with a vise attached to it toward the window.

"Hi, Dad," Alice said. He didn't hear her. She repeated her greeting, but he went on sliding the workbench across the floor of unplaned boards. She stood watching until finally he managed to get it directly beneath the window. He bent down over it, laying his head to the benchtop and looking up through the open window. She couldn't figure out why. She walked up to him and gently gripped him by the arm. Startled, he wheeled around and said, a little more loudly than necessary, "Howdy, daughter."

"Hi, Dad," she said, kissing him on the cheek.

"Wait," said Josef. "Wait here a minute," he ordered her, and ran off to the house. "Now I can hear you," he said when he returned.

"That's good," said Alice.

"Yes sir, it's a fine little device," Josef said. "Have a look." He took it out of his ear, laid it in his palm, and raised it to her face.

"Hmm," said Alice.

"You see," he said, still speaking a little too loud.

"I see," said Alice. "Tiny, huh?" Her father held it up in front of her eyes a moment longer, then carefully placed it back in his ear.

"Really tiny, and lightweight," her father said. "It isn't uncomfortable at all, you know. Being that it's so light."

"That's great," said Alice.

"Well, you know. That's progress for you. No stopping it," her father said with a grin. He wrapped his right arm around her shoulders and they walked toward the house. "Kryštof says you've been overdoing it on the job, so I'm supposed to keep an eye on you and make sure you don't do any work."

"I see," said Alice. "Well, I guess that's about right."

"Well, you won't get to see much of him. He just left today on vacation with that blonde of his."

"At least I'll get to see you!" Alice said, clutching her father under the arm.

Alice spent two weeks at the cottage in Lhotka, during which she discovered that her father was still surprisingly strong, though occasionally, especially when he was tired at night, he limped on his left leg. He asked after her cousin and Aunt Anna, and when she asked him about Libuše, he grimaced: "Just please don't treat her like a mother-in-law, Ali." The way he looked when he said it, like a big hissing tomcat, all of a sudden she realized he was defending Libuše. She asked how much they knew about her, without any awareness that she was acting the same way her mother did when she found out Alice's relationship with Maximilian was starting to get serious. Josef said it wasn't entirely clear who her father was, and her mother was nothing much either. "The main thing," he concluded, "is not to get mixed up in it. The last three days the poor girl's been cleaning like a madwoman. She didn't say anything, but it was obvious it was for your sake. She doesn't care about me—she's used to me by now—and, well, you know Kryštof, he couldn't care less."

Alice could tell, of course, in the first three and a quarter seconds after she set foot in the door that somebody had been cleaning. Within the next few seconds, both the strengths and weaknesses of her likely future daughter-in-law were obvious to Alice from her achievements and deficiencies in the cleaning department. Deep down inside Alice knew the way her son's girlfriend cleaned shouldn't be the decisive criterion in his choice of partner, yet she couldn't tear her thoughts away from the sloppily cleaned windows on the second floor and the unwiped dust on top of the wardrobe in her father's room, which she had examined while he spent the afternoon in the shed. She didn't realize it, but she had been irritated by her phone conversation with Kryštof in which he'd told her it would probably be a good idea for someone to spend the two weeks with Grandpa while they were away on vacation, since he had the feeling something wasn't quite right, even though all the test results from the doctor came back fine. It took two days for her to realize how irritated she was, watching with disapproval as her father made his coffee too strong and observing herself as she began to hector him with pointless sermons. He stared at her a moment in amazement, saying nothing, making no attempt to argue, and then, when she was done, he said: "Kryštof was right, as usual. Just calm down and try to relax, Ali. You need it." Then he calmly went back to drinking his overly strong coffee and building some kind of display case out in the shed. That afternoon it dawned on her how she was behaving. Her father was more relaxed than she was. The next morning she noticed he had begun shaving with an electric razor, which surprised her, given how much he had always hated them. When she asked him about it, he said that even he was fallible and that every day he realized how much he was selling out to the present. The real reason, however—that he didn't want her to see the way his hands shook when he shaved—he kept to himself. After a few days Alice calmed down a bit and adapted to his daily routine. In the morning, around seven, he got up and went out to the shed to work. At eleven he stopped, walked out to the mailbox to pick up the newspaper, and went to wash up in the bathroom. Depending on the weather, he would sit and read the paper on the bench out in the garden or take it inside to the kitchen with him. At first Alice tried to have lunch ready around noon, but on Tuesday her father said that from now on they would walk to the pub in the village together for lunch. When she objected that her food was healthier, he dismissed her with a wave of the hand. "I guarantee I'm going to die absolutely healthy, and besides, I want to take you out and show you off a bit." When the weather was nice they sat at one of the tables outside, underneath the boughs of the chestnut trees. Every now and then her father would exchange greetings with someone, and Alice had no recollection of at least half the people he said hello to. She also realized at one point that to call the house her father lived in a cottage was actually inappropriate, given that over the past more than twenty years he had been there he had made it into a proper home. Sometimes their conversation meandered from Alice's childhood memories to stories from Josef's time in prison. At others, especially when it touched on Libuše, whom Josef stubbornly insisted on referring to as the blonde, their conversation went nowhere. Even once Alice accepted that Libuše was a balanced, capable girl, she wasn't entirely able to let go of her concerns. As Josef thoughtfully studied her face, she studied him right back, saying: "I know there's nothing I can do. I'm just a little scared, that's all." Then her father would remind her how happy he and her mother had been when she introduced Maximilian to them. How impressed they had been. "And we know how he turned out, don't we, Ali? Speaking of which, what's going on with him, anyway?" Ever since he had stopped having to pay alimony, nobody knew. Once Kryštof became an adult, Maximilian stopped seeing him. Sometimes Alice would also talk about how she never entirely understood what went on between her father and her son. She only knew that each of them always stuck up for the other. She also finally had the chance to tell her father off for making Kryštof wait to tell her and Květa that he'd had a stroke. "It's simple, Ali," said Josef. "He gave me what I could never have with you. He made up for it all. When I came back from prison, you know, you were almost a grown-up woman."

"Really?" Alice said. "That never occurred to me. I mean, how old could I have been? Ten? Eleven?"

"That's not the point," Josef said with a wave of the hand. "The point is you were almost all grown up. I'm really sorry I couldn't be with you more when you were little. It's all my fault. When you have a child, you should just keep your mouth shut and stay in line." Alice argued back that she had always respected him for his courage and bravery and that he had made her proud. "Pride?" Josef said. "What use is that?" At the end of the week the temperature dropped, so he moved indoors from the shed to the house, where he continued work on his display case. It also meant that they spent a few hours more together each day. At the end of the week a visitor came from Brno to see Josef, a grizzled man who looked to be around fifty years of age. It was the journalist who had written the articles about political prisoners before the Russians invaded. Alice's father had forgotten to tell her he was coming and only remembered half an hour before that he was supposed to meet him at the train station in Lhotka. She managed to persuade him to change his pants at least, though she failed to convince him that a flannel work shirt wasn't the most appropriate attire for receiving visitors. That day, for a change, Josef allowed Alice to make lunch. When the journalist arrived, he ate with them, and then the two men closed themselves up in Josef's room.

The journalist had changed. First of all, he wasn't a journalist anymore. He had moved back home after spending years in exile and now worked for an organization that helped people like Josef. Josef had exchanged a few letters with him and at his request had visited the office in Prague that was looking into his arrest, imprisonment, and conviction. The man had put on weight over the years. He had gray hair and crow's feet around his eyes. He didn't look at all like the young man who had come to see Josef more than twenty years ago. Asked why he was still doing basically the same thing, the man said nearly half his relatives had met the same fate as Josef. "Why didn't you tell me that then?" Josef asked.

"I guess I was a little embarrassed," the man replied.

"Embarrassed?"

"Yes. Not for my relatives, but that I might not be objective enough. Or, as they say now, impartial."

"So where were you all this time?" Josef asked, and the man hesitantly told him about all the foreign countries he had been in. When he left, Alice could see that her father was in a good mood.

"Now I can finish that display case. Maybe they'll finally do an investigation, and then once the whole thing's under way, I can bring it to your mother—my wife—in Prague," he said in a meaningful voice. Alice knew she hadn't misheard, but she felt the need to act as if he hadn't said anything.

"What are you saying, Dad!" she said after a moment's delay. "What are you talking about?" Her father gave her a brief, casual glance, almost as if he hadn't heard. "You and Mom broke up more than twenty years ago." Her father looked at her again.

"In fact it's been twenty-five years, three months, and seventeen days. Assuming you mean the length of time we haven't been living together."

"You've been keeping track?"

"Well, I'm not entirely sure, since after the time I spent in the hospital, you know—I was unconscious for a few days, so I have to check the calendar every now and then. I get mixed up."

"So you've kept track this whole time?" Alice repeated.

"I've kept track all my life. I'm an engineer. I'm used to it from work," Josef said. He looked at Alice, who stared back at him, nodding her head the way she always had, ever since she was a little girl, when something intrigued or surprised her, or she was trying to make sense of something.

"Twenty-five years, three months, and seventeen days," Alice said. Her father turned to walk away.

"How do you know, Dad? How do you know that Mom will take anything from you? How in God's name do you know, when for all those years you treated her so . . . so dismissively, with such contempt. How do you know? How in the hell do you even dare!"

By the time Josef sat down in the chair, all his ideas, strength, energy, and authority had drained out of him, leaving only a numb, sick old man.

"Well, sweetie," he said, "the truth is . . . the truth is . . . I . . . I don't know anything, I really don't. I can only hope that she'll . . . eh-hem . . . somehow . . . forgive my behavior. That's it . . . that's all I've got."

"That she'll forgive you?"

"I can only hope, sweetie. It's all I can do."

"All right," Alice said.

"It's just a display case."

"Just a display case, right," she said, nodding with clenched lips. "Yes, just a display case." As she repeated his words, she was glad she had nothing important she needed to do that day, since she was sure she would have made a mess of anything that required even a drop of concentration. In her memories she had looked back more than once into the maze of her parents' curious relationship. A bizarre maze littered with traps and taboos, with insidious snares and pitfalls.

"So you won't tell her about the display case?" Alice's father asked.

"Tell her?"

"I'd kind of like it to be a surprise, you know. Can you keep it a secret?"

"I don't know, Dad. I don't know," Alice said.

"You don't know, sweetie?"

"I don't know, Dad."

The whole time Alice was in Lhotka, her father spent repairing an old wooden display case from the turn of the twentieth century, as 1900 came waltzing in, adorned in Art Nouveau. Kryštof had bought it once upon a time to store his tools in. But then, together, he and Josef had built a long wooden shelf that was a much better place for storing his pliers, screwdrivers, saws, hammers, screws, and nails. The display case stood on four legs, more than four feet in height. The case itself was three feet tall and roughly twenty inches deep. Inside, it boasted a sophisticated system of wooden brackets for holding shelves in place at variable heights just a few inches apart. After it had stood for years, dirty, old, broken, and hobbled in a corner of the shed, Josef found a new use for it. During the cleaning he undertook when he came home from the hospital, he had opened up a few old boxes containing objects that he and Květa used to collect. Some potsherds excavated near Olomouc. A handful of Celtic agates. Some clam and mussel shells, two Czech groschen, four pieces of moldavite, one trilobite, a large specimen of rose quartz, some garnets from Kozákov, pebbles from Bojkovice, a bronze ax, and several miniature copies of seal casts from India. They had accumulated the items as a couple before Alice was born, when the two of them used to go on trips and scour antique shops. Their value was doubtful. Combined, they probably weren't worth any more than the scattered memories they evoked, but the unused display case, Josef decided, was exactly the thing to show them off to maximum effect, and so he set out to repair it. First he burned off the old varnish, then he sealed it, sanded it, restained it, impregnated it with wax, polished it, had the windows cut, installed them, cleaned and repaired the lock, mounted a large photocopy with images of cuneiform on the inner back wall, dusted and cleaned the objects, arranged them on the three glass levels of the display case, then packed the objects back up in the boxes, dismantled the case, and began to pack and prepare it for the trip to Prague. All of this he did piecemeal over a period of several weeks, as if trying to make the job last. Alice witnessed only the final procedures, impregnating the wood with wax and polishing. Her father was worried about the polishing and asked Alice several times what she thought of it. But she didn't give it much thought. She liked the way it looked, and when her father asked for the umpteenth time what she thought, she just said she didn't know. "Nobody knows," he replied, "but you're the only one I can use to judge whether or not your mother will like it." "It could use some varnish," she said finally, recognizing how important it was to him. "I would give it some varnish, but leave it for now. Once you get it to Prague, I'll find some discreet way to ask Mom about it." Her father didn't say anything, but he seemed satisfied.

By the time Kryštof and Libuše came back from their two-week vacation, the display case was repaired, dismantled, and ready for transport. It took another few days for Josef to make up his mind where to put it. In the end he decided it should go in Alice's apartment, since, as he discovered, Květa had been complaining there was too much old junk at Aunt Anna's. When Alice told her mother that Josef was planning to move an Art Nouveau display case with their old souvenirs into her apartment, Aunt Anna said:

"That Josef of yours, my dear Květa, is starting to lose his marbles. You have to look to the future, not the past. Both of you act like you were still living twenty years ago. A pair of funny old fish. Don't look at me like that! Why don't you do something about it?"

(3)

It was, of course, sheer coincidence that one morning, at exactly a quarter past nine, Josef turned up with Kryštof at his daughter's apartment in Vinohrady. He had a knapsack on his back, and together the two were carrying an incredibly long, ridiculous bag containing all the parts of the display case. Kryštof helped Josef unpack everything and said he would see him that evening. Before he could leave, though, Josef suggested for the umpteenth time that he really ought to walk around and look at a few town halls first before deciding whether to hold the wedding in Prague or Kostelec, which was the capital of the district that Lhotka belonged to. It was the first time Alice had heard anyone mention a wedding, and she wasn't sure if it was just a dumb joke or the clumsy way the two men closest to her had decided to break the news to her that Kryštof was getting married. Once Kryštof left, she began asking questions, and Josef told her he had been trying to talk Kryštof into holding the wedding in Prague for two months now. He added that he didn't like to visit the city and, in fact, enjoyed it less and less, but he couldn't deny that it offered a comparatively large selection of town halls. Kryštof, however, steadfastly refused. "Do you realize you've made a villager out of him?" Alice said. Josef found that amusing, and when he was done laughing he replied that he wasn't doing it for Kryštof's sake, but for the sake of the blonde, as he still referred to Libuše. When Alice informed him that Květa was coming to lunch at noon, he looked at his watch and retorted that last time it had taken him one hour and forty-seven minutes to assemble the display case, including the time he spent looking for the Phillips screwdriver, which Kryštof had borrowed and forgotten to return to its place in the tray. Seeing as it was already nearly a quarter to ten, Josef got to work.

"Does your mother and my wife still show up a half hour before she's invited?" he asked.

"Not anymore, Dad," Alice said. "Not for a while now. She usually comes only ten or fifteen minutes early now, but she still complains that everyone else is late and she's the only one who's punctual."

"So she's getting older, too," Josef said, and he began pulling his tools out of the knapsack. When at exactly half past eleven, the door opened and Květa walked into the apartment, the display case had been assembled for fifteen minutes already. Josef looked at his wristwatch, thinking about the fact that his wife had always showed up a half hour early, and that some things never change, and that he still knew his wife better than their daughter did. As Květa stepped into the room from the entryway, Josef rose from his chair and Alice realized she hadn't seen him that nervous in a very long time.

"Hello, Květuš," he said.

"Hi, Josífek," Květa said. She approached him somewhat stiffly and offered her hand, which Josef shook. Then all of a sudden they hastily embraced, hurriedly kissed, and swiftly stepped away from each other again. They're both nervous, Alice thought. She said hello to her mother and the three of them went together to look at the display case, which Josef had set up in Alice's room. As they stepped through the door, Květa took in the view of the wooden Art Nouveau case with its three aquamarine glass shelves. On the middle shelf were the clay potsherds, the Celtic agates and rose quartz were on top, and the trilobite was all the way on the bottom of the case, with the pebbles from Bojkovice on one side, the bronze ax on the other, and behind them the copies of the seal casts from Mohenjo-daro in present-day Pakistan. On the level above, the bottom shelf, were the garnets from Kozákov.

"So you found the agates?" Květa said. "And those must be the pebbles from Bojkovice," she said, obviously pleased.

"Precisely," Josef said with a satisfied air. "It was all there in those two boxes I rediscovered."

"Uh-huh," Květa said, studying the other objects. "You know, Ali, we bought these before you were born." She reached out her hand and touched the display case. "Those weren't even deciphered yet back then, were they, Josef?" she said, pointing to the cast of a small elongated seal depicting a one-horned ox with several mysterious letters above it. The cast of another seal showed a boat with an oarsman.

"What was it, Josef, that we read in that book? Three steps . . . No! With three steps Vishnu measured the entire universe. Something like that, wasn't it?" Květa said. "Have they deciphered it yet?"

"I don't think so," Josef said. "It takes time, you know. It isn't that easy."

"Now come and have lunch or it'll be cold. Come on! You can look at it afterwards," Alice said. "I still haven't looked myself." She went and sat down at the table.

"So what is that there in the back, Josífek?" Květa said during the soup.

"That's cuneiform," Josef said. "You know that."

"Oh, you're right. We went to those lectures at the library together, didn't we?"

"What library?" Alice asked.

"The City Library," Květa said. "Actually, Josífek, I'm curious where you dug up those pebbles from Bojkovice. I'd really like to know."

"It was all there in that box."

"I could have sworn I took them to Aunt Anna's. Back then, when you moved out."

"So what's so special about those pebbles?" Alice asked.

"It's a long story," said Květa.

"So you aren't going to tell me? Is that it? I have a right, don't I, Dad?"

"Well," Josef said, "it was a long time ago."

"Some other time, Alice, some other time. It's a long story," Květa said. As Alice cleared away the soup bowls and set the plates of roast pork down on the table, she couldn't help but notice her father looking out the window with a vaguely optimistic expression and her mother smiling slightly.

"So, Mom, did you hear that Kryštof and Libuše are going to get married?" Alice asked in an attempt to end the silence, interrupted only by the clatter of cutlery, the pouring of beer into glasses, and her parents' dopey smiles. The question served to stimulate the conversation for a while, but once everyone had finished eating, Květa got up and began to put on her coat.

"Where are you going, Mom?" Alice asked, picking up on her father's brooding look. "Why don't you stay a while?"

"Oh, I'm just going out for the pastries," Květa said. "I stopped in before I came here, but they weren't fresh. I can tell! The lady told me to come back after noon, when they bring in the fresh ones."

Květa left and Josef went out to the balcony for a smoke. When Alice went to tell him his coffee was ready, she could see he was restless, tapping his ashes into a pot of blooming red geraniums, so she went and stood beside him, gave him an encouraging look, and when he finished his second cigarette, they went inside together.

"It's a good thing you finally got around to it, Dad," she said. Josef looked at her, then at the display case, then back to her.

"Well . . . What was it supposed to do? Lie there forever? Here at least it will go to use."

"You mean you might come visit Mom?" Josef gave no reply. "I think she'd be pretty happy to see you every once in a while."

Josef cleared his throat. "You didn't by any chance ask if she prefers it polished, or whether she'd rather have it painted with lacquer?"

"I didn't ask yet," Alice said. "I haven't had a chance."

"It's not actually that important, it's just . . ."

"I'll ask. I'll figure out some discreet way, all right?" Alice said.

"You think she liked it?" her father asked.

"What can I say? You saw her, right?"

"Well . . . I guess so."

"Sure, she did."

"Really?"

"Of course."

"What about you, Alice," Josef said, wrinkling his brow. "Do you think it's silly?" Alice shook her head. "So what are you going to do now, if Kryštof goes and marries that blonde?"

"It doesn't change a thing, really," Alice said. "They're living with you anyway, and they'll probably stay there, no?"

"Well, I hope so."

"I don't think I'm going to get him to Prague. I've already tried that before."

"He's too well brought up," Josef laughed. "That's why he'll stay with me," he added with mischievous glee.

"So actually nothing's going to change," Alice said.

"No? I guess you're right. So what are you going to do?"

"You know, Dad, I had sort of a feeling that you knew . . . about the wedding . . . and actually now that Kryštof's with Libuše, I don't know why, but sometimes I remember back to what it was like when I was little."

"Don't worry about them. They can handle it," Josef said.

"Oh, I'm not," Alice said.

"So what do you remember?" Josef said.

"Well, all sorts of things. Usually at night, when I can't fall asleep . . . the other day I was remembering Grandma."

"But you couldn't have any memory of her, Ali. She died when you were four or five."

"So?"

"It just seems unlikely."

"Well, I remember her . . . and the way Mom always used to wear long skirts. Long skirts and blouses with long dark sleeves."

"I tell you, the things women remember. I can't even remember what sweater I got for Christmas last year. It's awful," Josef said.

"That never was your strong point, Dad. But I remember everything. I remember how when Grandma died, Mom wore a long dark dress for weeks afterward. I even remember she had a rash or something."

"A rash?" Josef said.

"Or something like that. I saw her in the bath a few times and her skin was all red."

"From what?"

"The rash."

"What did it look like?"

"Oh, I don't know, these sort of little red scars. Or was it eczema? I don't really know."

Just then they heard the keys in the door and Květa stepped into the entryway holding two cardboard trays wrapped in paper. She walked straight into the room where Alice and Josef were talking.

"Well, they came," Květa said. "I had to wait a while, but they're definitely fresh. Here you go. And don't get up, since you're having such a nice talk," she said. She laid the trays on the table and went into the kitchen for plates. Josef stared shyly down at the table. Květa came back with plates and spoons, unwrapped the two bundles of pastries, and served them onto the plates.

"We were just reminiscing, Mom," Alice said.

"Oh, what about?" Květa said.

"Well, Dad here doesn't believe that I remember Grandma," Alice said.

"Oh, you must have been awfully little," Květa said, putting a plate in front of each of them. She sat upright and put her hands on her hips. "You couldn't have been older than five when she died—and you remember?"

"I remember how sometimes she used to give me a bath, and I remember that long black or dark blue dress you used to wear all the time after her funeral."

"Dark blue dress," Květa repeated. "I honestly don't remember."

"Yeah, you had a rash or hives, remember?"

"No, I don't," said Květa.

"Yeah and when Dad came back, it went away. Remember now?"

"I don't remember anything like that!"

"Well, I think it was some kind of nervous reaction, because it went away as soon as Dad came home," Alice said. She took a bite of her pastry. Her father sat holding the plate of cake, staring at it dumbfounded. Suddenly he heaved a sigh. It sounded like he couldn't breathe. Only after the second time and the third did Alice and her mother turn to look and see him staring at the plate, tears streaming from his eyes. It was amazing, just two or three breaths in and out and his face had turned soaking wet. He sobbed, unable to catch his breath no matter how much air he took into his lungs. Tears streamed down his cheeks and chin, shaven specially for the occasion, and dripped onto the floor and the carpet and his mirror-polished shoes.

"What's going on?" Alice said. "Did I say something wrong? I've always loved Grandma."

"Alice, please, just be quiet already!" her mother said, raising her voice. Her father began to rise from his chair, wheezing and gasping for air. He reached into his pants pocket, pulled out his handkerchief, and wiped half of his face dry. His right leg, independently of the rest of his body, tried several times to take a step. Květa dropped her plate, leaned across the table, and grabbed his hand. As Josef slowly sank back into his chair, Alice saw that he was in danger of toppling backward over the headrest and hitting his head on the ground, so she caught hold of him and together with her mother slowly lowered him into the chair. With one hand her mother unbuttoned his shirt, while with the other she attempted to keep his slumping body upright.

"Josífek, my God. Josífek, forgive me, forgive me," Květa said under her breath, breaking into tears.

"What did I say, Mom?" Alice asked, massaging her father's temples.

"Will you please be quiet, Alice! Just shut up! Not another word!" Květa shouted. Her tears smeared her understated makeup across her white blouse, producing a remarkable map of her body. The two women lifted Josef from his chair and laid him on the ground. Alice ran to the kitchen to call an ambulance while her mother sat on the carpet beside him, cradling his head in her lap. Every second or two she leaned her face down to his mouth to check whether he was breathing regularly, breaking into fits of dry sobs as she stroked his hair and repeated his name over and over.

When Alice walked back into the room and saw her mother stroking her father's face, it was obvious he wasn't breathing. "Mom, Mom," she said, pressing her shoulder against her, "Daddy's dead, look . . ."

Květa went on holding Josef's head in her hands until the doorbell rang and two men in white coats came in. They said something and Alice said something back. One of them bent over Josef's body and the other gestured to Alice and Květa that they should go into the next room. From the kitchen, out of the corner of her eye, Alice saw the man stand up from her father and turn his head to the other man to indicate there was nothing else they could do. She burst into tears. Her mother gave her a hug. One of the men from the ambulance thrust a form into her hand, said good-bye, and they left.

The two women remained sitting in the kitchen, snuggled closely together. The mother stroked her daughter's hair, her tears now dried while her daughter's tears were just beginning to do their work. Exiting her tear ducts, they emerged on the slope of her nose, streaking down across the valley of her sunken cheekbones before landing, reunited, in the dampness of her handkerchief. Květa unconsciously ran her left hand over her chest, as if trying to remove the makeup from her blouse, the makeup that was supposed to make her beautiful, desirable, and attractive to her husband, who, unwittingly and against her will, in spite of everything time had thrown in their path, in spite of history, in spite of her body's surprising desires, in spite of their separation and the irritating, annoying, unrelenting buzz of stinging memories, she had never stopped loving all her life.

17
LETTER ABOUT A THIEF

Hi sis,

Yesterday I finally got a proper job. You won't believe what I'm going to do. At the bank where I work, Mr. Verner told me they want me to write up comments and recommendations for the head of the investment division. Let me explain. In 1991 there was an exhibition in Prague. Judging from the stacks of papers and boxes of newspaper clippings they gave me, it's obvious people had great expectations for it. It was called the Universal Czechoslovak Exhibition, or something like that. I don't know what they exhibited, and it's not even important from the bank's point of view. What's important is that it resulted in a debt of several hundred million crowns. You read that right. It's not a mistake. Close to a billion crowns in debt. And now that Czechoslovakia has divided like a cell into two even smaller countries, nobody wants to pay it, which means the bank where I work is stuck with it around its neck, as they say here. And they gave me the job of writing up a history of the exhibition and other ones like it and proposing a creative solution to the problem for the media. Not a financial solution, mind you — I wouldn't even know how, since I don't know the first thing about finance — but a creative solution. I didn't know exactly what that was supposed to mean, so I asked Mr. Verner and he said they probably had in mind for me to compare it to similar exhibitions, and explained that the 1991 exhibition was held in honor of another exhibition that took place on exactly the same site in 1891. Can you imagine? A hundred years before! And supposedly *that* exhibition was held in honor of some other exhibition that took place a hundred years before *that*, in 1791. Can you imagine? Mozart was still alive back then. Anyway, that's my job. So I started right in on it. Mr. Verner said that if I didn't know which way to go (meaning "what to do"), I should use history. They're big on that here, history. Mr. Verner said I could use history to get out of anything. So I've got a feeling over the next few weeks I'll be spending many hours engrossed in the study of local history.

Otherwise, if you can believe it, Mr. Černý died. He was the husband of Aunt Květa and the father of Alice, who I've been staying with. Alice and I went to see him a couple of times. He said some strange things about Prague. I think he liked the city but he didn't like what was going on there. By that I mean what most people call globalization, though it's really Americanization. I don't think they're too clear on that here. Anyway, he came to visit the flat I've been staying in with his grandson and they installed quite a nice display case with a collection of some sort of stones, and after that, from what I understand, they had lunch and then he just died. Alice called an ambulance, but even though they came right away it was too late. I didn't want to ask about it. I just know what Alice told me. The whole week, on and off, I heard crying on the other side of the wall. But there's actually something else I wanted to write you about. This week Mr. Verner said he was going away on a business trip to Vienna and asked if I could do him a favor by going to a pub and giving his phone number to a friend who he described to me in detail. I asked why he didn't just call him, but he said he didn't have his number. When I asked how long they'd known each other, he said more than twenty years. So I went to the pub—actually it was a garden restaurant adjoining a small football stadium—and it turned out to be closed. So I waited around until then I noticed an older man with a gray crewcut standing off to the side. I realized that must be the man I was waiting for, so I went over and asked if his name was Karel. He said yes, so I gave him the number. Then he invited me for a beer, but I declined, since the way they drink in this country is really out of control, and I wasn't in the mood for any boozy Slavic brotherhood. When Mr. Verner got back, I asked him about it and he said that he and Karel had known each other since August 21, 1968. After I'd handed off the phone number, I walked down from Náměstí Míru to Václavské Náměstí to buy dad a birthday present, and there was a small rally of skin-heads and neo-Nazis going on, and the police were standing across the street from them, filming it. There was nobody else commemo-rating it, apart from that. It wasn't till a week later that I realized that day was the reason why Mum and Dad stayed in the UK. They call the UK England here—the Scots and Irish wouldn't be too happy if they found out. Anyway, Mr. Verner told me that night in 1968 he was home alone and went to bed about ten o'clock but couldn't get to sleep. He had a feeling there was somebody walking round the flat. So he woke up, put on the light, read something a while, then fell back asleep and the next thing he knew he had the feeling someone was shaking him. So he woke up and saw a man standing over him in coveralls, shaking him politely and saying, "Sir, wake up and don't be afraid." Before it dawned on him, he heard the man, who was a bit older, apologizing and pointing out the window. "What are you doing here?" Mr. Verner said, and then all of a sudden he heard trac-tors going down the street. A bunch of tractors at five in the morning? How can that be? he thought. So he went and looked out the window and saw a line of tanks driving down the street, and the windowpanes were rattling like crazy and everything was shaking from the noise. Turned out the tanks were Russian and there were soldiers sitting on top of them in green uniforms holding machine guns. "What's going on," Mr. Verner said, "and what are you doing here?" But the man just kept on apologizing: "I'm a thief, Mr. Verner. I came to rob you and I'm really sorry I woke you up, but this is the third column of tanks now, so I decided I'd better wake you, since this looks like either war or the Russians are attacking us. I put back everything I took and left it on the table in the next room and I suggest you call your parents and your wife. I hope you aren't angry, but I saw your lovely photographs of them, and I also saw you have a phone in the hall, so please give them a call, since either way, whether it's war or occupation . . . Well, anyway, I'm off, and once again I apologize, but I truly and honestly wasn't expecting anything like this." So Verner said he took the man by the hand and said, "For Christ's sake, man, don't go out there. They might shoot you or something." But the thief still wanted to go, since he was afraid Verner was going to call the police. But after the next column of tanks rolled by, they both realized that the police weren't working that morning anyway, and the thief took the liberty of asking if he could make a call. So he made the call and then when he came back into the living room he started crying. "My sister lives by the border with Poland and she says they're up there too. We're being attacked, Mr. Verner." So Verner said, "At least tell me your name so I know what to call you. You can't go anywhere now anyway." So the man introduced himself as Karel, and Verner said: "Well, Karel, take whatever you need. I can't take it with me to the grave." And Karel said, "I can't. I don't need it now." So Verner said: "Did you find the cash?" And Karel said: "Of course I did. Everyone always puts it in a cup on the second shelf in the cupboard. I put it back, though." "Take at least half," Mr. Verner said. "I can't," said Karel, so Verner went and forced him to take half the money. Then, after the tanks had passed, he walked him out to the intersection and they helped set up some makeshift barricades. But then Karel said he had to go since his wife might be worried. So if you can believe it, they stood there on the intersection and gave each other a hug, and Verner said: "Take care of yourself, Karel. Human life doesn't mean a thing to those Russians." And Karel said, "If we survive," since he was afraid it was going to turn out like the massacre in Hungary twelve years before, "if we survive, meet me at the pub Na Růžku one year from today and I'll give you your money back. I'm a little hard up right now. Remember: Na Růžku. It's halfway between you and me." And ever since then, they meet at the pub every year on August 21st. I asked Mr. Verner how come he didn't know Karel's name and address, and he told me, "Cousin, life has taught me to respect privacy. Karel has never told me his address or last name and I've never asked. The fact that we've been meeting once a year for over twenty years to share a drink or two is more important to me than prying into his private life. Sometimes one of us can't make it. It's happened three times or so, and when it does, the one who can't make it sends a messenger so the other one will know he's all right. There you have it. And six months ago they changed my number and I'm not in the phone book, so this year I sent you, Cousin."

That's all for today, sis. *Ahoj*, George.

18

LOVE LETTER IN CUNEIFORM

Jiří came home from work to find the old, restored display case in the living room, the window wide open, and several official forms on the sideboard in the kitchen. It wasn't until he went to his room and took off one of his shoes that he heard Alice sobbing on the other side of the wall. He put his shoe back on and went out into the entryway. But Alice knew the sounds of her nest better than her thoughtful relative, and before he had made up his mind whether to knock or not, she opened the door to her room, her face dried, swollen, and makeup-free, in a black skirt with her hair pulled tightly back from her forehead. Jiří learned from her that Josef had died. But before she closed the door to her room behind her again, so she could devote herself to her grief in peace, she told him his dinner was on the stove, all he had to do was strike a match and reheat it. The Slavic insistence on regular meals surprised Jiří. There were times he even found it moving. Not that he always liked the food placed in front of him, but there was something touching about the emphasis on maintaining regular eating habits.

Earlier, when Květa came home with Alice, the sound of the door slamming had woken Aunt Anna. She opened her eyes. A slight quiver ran through her as she sat in the chair, and as Alice and Květa entered the room, she looked them over alertly, and said in a weary voice, edged with anger: "All right, girls, tell me who died." Instead of answering, Květa just swallowed her tears, and Alice nodded a few times, then said:

"Daddy, Aunt Anna. My daddy."

"Good God," said Aunt Anna. "But you're all so young compared to me." She sighed and slowly began unrolling the blankets she was wrapped in, then even more slowly rose from her chair. Alice and Květa rushed toward her as they realized she was planning to stand.

"Sit, auntie, please," said Květa, choking slightly on her words. "Just sit right there and don't try to go anywhere."

"But, girls," Aunt Anna said, "today it's my turn to wait on you."

"Please, you'll fall," said Alice.

"All right," said her aunt. "Then I'll just sit down at the table and you two can tell me all about how it happened."

Instead of describing the final moments of Josef's life, their tenderhearted recollections blasted off like a rocket of overlapping and unfolding memories, then soared across the expanse of years and watershed moments like a light biplane. Květa sobbing, Alice swallowing her tears, each of them with both hands clutching one of Aunt Anna's wrinkled, shriveled, mottled hands.

The next day the two women left for Lhotka, where Kryštof and Libuše had begun preparations for the funeral. After a few awkward moments, they agreed that Josef would have his funeral in Prague but be buried in Lhotka. Libuše stayed out of the nerve-racking debate, interrupted every other minute by a loud swallowing of tears. Květa and Alice wanted Josef in a cemetery in Prague, whereas Kryštof favored Lhotka. Eventually they reached an agreement, although she couldn't fail to notice Kryštof quietly repeating to himself: "Compromise, dirty compromise." The reason for the visit to Lhotka was that Květa wanted to pick out some nice clothes for Josef to wear in the coffin. It wasn't until they got to Lhotka that she realized he was wearing his best clothes in Prague. Before they left, Alice and Květa took a few trinkets from Josef's room to remember him by. The next morning Kryštof went up to the attic, where the wrapping paper and boxes for Christmas gifts were stored. He picked out the nicest box, brushed off the dust, and carried it down to Josef's room. There he took a few phonograph records that he remembered from their covers as being his grandfather's favorites, put them in the box, closed it up, and took it back to his room. That evening, when Libuše came home from work, she lifted the lid off the festive box, looked inside, and saw it was full of old records. She asked Kryštof about it, and he said they were his grandfather's favorites.

"He always used to look through them, even when he couldn't hear them with his ears anymore," he said.

"Are you going to listen to them?" she asked.

"No, I'm not into music, but this way at least I'll have a piece of Grandpa nearby," he said.

In Lhotka, Kryštof gave his grandfather's address book to his mother, and Alice began the preparations for the funeral. Květa helped her out here and there, and for the first time in her life she was forced to realize that her strength was diminishing. It was all she could do to have the obituary printed. The printer's was located on a street in the hospital district, near Karlovo Náměstí, that was home to several health care facilities. As Květa entered the office, a man in a beige sweater came out of the next room to greet her, introducing himself and inviting her to have a seat. Květa sat down and the man placed two huge folders on the table in front of her stuffed with quotations and sample layouts of funeral announcements. Palm leaves, ferns, roses, hyacinths, several crowns of thorns and more or less stylized crosses, the variety of symbols seemed endless. It made Květa's head spin.

"I know it's a lot," the man said, noticing her hesitation. "There's no rush. May I offer you some coffee or tea?"

Květa shook her head. The man stood up. "Take your time, Mrs. Černá. Choose whatever you like. I'll be sitting right in the next room. Just let me know when you're done. My door's open if you need anything."

Květa sat going through the funerary symbols a while, then got up and walked around the room a few times. She noticed some sounds from outside and looked into the next room. The man she had spoken to had stepped out for a moment. At the back of his office was a set of glass doors through which she could see some machines working rapidly. It looked somewhat like a loom. A printer, Květa thought.

Oh, of course, the printer. Josef would have liked that. Engines, motors, machines, he was into that type of thing. Finally she decided on the quotation "He has not died but lives on in our memories." She added "husband, father, grandfather," and called in the man who was operating the printer, who checked the whole thing over with her one more time in detail, and then at last she could go. Before she reached home on the tram, she realized again that she was losing strength. I wonder what it could be, she thought. She didn't know, but one thing she was sure of was it wasn't just the aging of her body, brain, and muscles. Yes! she suddenly realized. A lack of hope! That's it! Which isn't at all encouraging and can't be cured, she added to herself after another moment's thought.

Three weeks after the funeral, Květa came home to find a bulky registered letter in a reinforced envelope that Aunt Anna had had to sign for, since at nine A.M., when it arrived, Květa had been out buying groceries. Aunt Anna forgot about it, so the letter had lain hidden beneath her sweater until the next day, when she uncovered it again while rearranging her things. She put on her glasses and saw the large state seal and the tricolor of the national flag. The state seal was stamped in gold. Funny I didn't notice that yesterday, Aunt Anna thought as she handed the letter to Květa. "This came yesterday," she said.

"You hobbled all the way to the door for it, Auntie?" said Květa in a chiding tone. "You know I would have come and gotten it. You could have fallen."

"Oh, please. I took it slow. All this fuss over one letter," Aunt Anna snapped, evidently pleased.

"So the mailwoman waited for you?"

"You see the letter, don't you? So I guess so. Besides, whenever I hear the bell I just shout that I'm coming but slowly so she'd better wait. And she does. What else can she do?" said Aunt Anna. Then she pokily shuffled her way out to the mailbox in the hall, where her daily ration of two newspapers was awaiting her.

Květa studied the envelope. It seemed a shame to tear it. She took a pair of scissors and slit it open. Inside was a letter on heavy handcrafted paper embossed with a watermark of the state seal and a wreath of linden leaves. Before Květa could finish reading it, Aunt Anna was back with the newspapers. She spread them out on the table and carefully studied the front page. The front page was the best: it had the biggest headlines. Thanks to modernization, the pictures on the front page were printed in color now, which made it easier for her to get an overview. That was the type of progress that seemed truly useful.

"Imagine that, Auntie. Assuming, that is, I've understood it correctly. I'll have to read it through one more time, and I think I'd better give Alice and Kryštof a call." Aunt Anna fixed her with a look of disgruntlement, having just begun to read an article about a team of researchers who had completed their mapping of the sugar beet genome and claimed that one of its genes was identical to that of humans. She was a little taken aback by the news and didn't know what to think. Whenever she didn't know what to think about an article, she circled it in thick red pencil and reread it in the afternoon, by which time she had usually formed a basic opinion. Aunt Anna gave up her disgruntled look, having noticed that Květa wasn't reacting to it.

"Well, what is it?" she said.

"Imagine that. They've given Josef a medal."

"A medal?" Aunt Anna asked.

"A medal," Květa repeated.

"What for?"

"Bravery."

"Bravery?"

"They say here," Květa said, "that they're recommending he be decorated for bravery demonstrated during the time of his incarceration, when he risked his own life several times to help his fellow prisoners, and for standing up to totalitarian despotism."

Aunt Anna calmly removed her glasses, set them down on the newspapers, and said, after a moment, into the silence: "Well, those nincompoops were sure in a hurry. He's resting in God's truth now."

"They say," Květa said, "that it would be a posthumous decoration. Here: 'in memoriam,' dash, 'for bravery, awarded posthumously.' If I accept, I'm to contact them in the manner most suitable to me."

"In the what?" Aunt Anna echoed. "What in heaven's name do they mean by that?"

"Don't worry, Anna. I understand."

"So when are they sending it?" Aunt Anna asked.

"I don't think they are."

"No?"

"No."

"Then how are you going to get it?"

"I guess I'll have to go there. No, wait, they say if I accept it on his behalf, that either I can go, or a designated individual, since I'm his widow, can go in my place. They say daughter, grandson, or family friend."

"Family friend, hmm?" Aunt Anna said. "And where to?"

"The castle, Anna. The castle in Prague."

"Oh, I see. So that what's-his-name would give it to you? You know who I mean." But Květa was still a little bit thrown by the whole thing, so she wasn't giving Aunt Anna her full attention, even though, as usual, her aunt was struggling fiercely for it.

"Oh, what do you call him, I can't remember now. You know, the scooter king."

"Yes, that's the one," said Květa. All of a sudden she couldn't remember anything at all, she was so moved by the fact that they were giving Josef a medal for what he used to mention, only occasionally and evasively, as playing boy scout.

Autumn was approaching at a rapid clip. The national holiday, commemorating the founding of Czechoslovakia at the end of World War I, and All Souls' Day were as usual both in the same week, but Květa had never paid much attention to it before, until this year, now that Josef had died. She drove out to the cemetery in Lhotka three times a week, and when Kryštof found out that his grandmother was going to the cemetery and didn't even bother to stop in and say hello, he gave her a scolding, put a set of keys in her hand, and demanded she come by their place for dinner or tea at least every once in a while. The cemetery in Lhotka was on a slope at the bottom of a hill. At the top of the hill was the church, and when most of the leaves fell off, after the first brief and as usual unexpected cold snaps, Květa took pleasure in raking them off of not only Josef's grave, but the surrounding ones as well. Sometimes she would make the walk up the hill to the church, sit down on the low stone wall, and stare out at the gently rolling autumn landscape. Occasionally a few tardily flocking birds would appear that she hadn't managed to identify yet, and the more visits she paid to Josef's cemetery the less surprised she was that he had left Prague and moved here. It wasn't until Kryštof pointed out that the date of his grandfather's posthumous decoration was nearing that Květa looked at the calendar and realized she had promised Mrs. Langmajerová, who was in charge of the cemetery, that she would be there that day instead of her. A repairman would be coming to fix the pump that supplied the whole cemetery with water. They tried to talk her out of it, but Květa made up her mind to stay in Lhotka and sent Alice to accept the medal in her place. When her daughter came home with the medal, Květa put it, and the box it came in, in the display case that Josef and Kryštof had brought to Prague. Everyone had expected Květa to be happy about the honor, but she acted as though it meant nothing to her. Sometimes she would absentmindedly stroke Kryštof on the back. Sometimes she would praise Libuše and her grandson for the way they took care of the house, but she always felt most at home with her memories.

On St. Cecilia's Day, in late November, she sat down on a bench in the cemetery and didn't wake up until after dark. She was chilled to the bone, and the stars spread across the sky looked magnificent, even if she didn't know a single one of their names. She walked straight to the train from the cemetery, and when she got home she felt even sicker than she had initially thought. Even tea with rum and onion juice squeezed into it, Aunt Anna's recipe that had carried her father through the trenches on the Italian front in World War I, didn't help. When the local doctor came and examined her, she immediately ordered Květa to be taken to the hospital with pneumonia. Alice took over caring for Aunt Anna, dividing her time between work, the hospital, and her aunt. Aunt Anna was saddened, not because she didn't trust medical science—in fact just the opposite, it was one of the things in which her faith had gradually grown—but because she could glimpse a hint of resignation and weariness in Květa's eyes. Nothing can top the experience of a nearly hundred-year-old woman, she liked to say, although what she never added was that many of her friends had also had eyes full of resignation and weariness a few months before she had seen them for the last time. Everyone would like to be able to see into the future, she reflected. Or at least nearly everyone. But if the poor souls only knew what awaited them, some of them might wish they hadn't. She was feeling lonely, so when cousin Jiří was given a car for work and offered to bring her over for dinner every other day, nobody was as grateful for it as she was. If she'd learned anything in all her years it was that nothing fends off death more effectively than the foolishness and reckless optimism of youth. And so several times a week the cousin came and picked her up in his car. Eventually he got used to her excruciating slowness, and it pleased her to no end having a bright red car parked in front of her building. One day after dinner, when Jiří was out of hearing, Aunt Anna boasted to Alice that she had discovered the last remnants of vanity in her dotage. After all those years spent nowhere but inside her apartment and in and around the neighborhood park, she was amazed at how the city had changed. New buildings. Repaired facades. So many cars and renamed streets. Eventually those rides became the highlight of her week. "You know, the strange thing is, Ali," she said one day, "I noticed that your cousin inflames even me, an old lady, with lust. Of course not in any way that you would understand. You're still too young for that."

"So what is it like, Aunt Anna?" Alice asked.

"Well, for one thing, I stopped taking those pills the doctor gave me to help with my breathing. Whenever that boy is around I breathe fine. And I don't seem to need them the rest of the time either, so I just keep them stored in a drawer for when he goes back to England. Now I don't want you to think it's him. I mean, it is, because he's a

young man. Men are a basic part of life. No woman should be without one, remember that."

The conversation was starting to remind Alice a little too much
of her aunt's favorite topic, and as her mind raced, wondering how to
change the subject, all of a sudden Jiří materialized out of nowhere.
"So what about you, Aunt Anna. Did you ever have a man?"

Aunt Anna turned her wrinkled face to him, and to both his and
Alice's surprise she slowly broke into a wide smile. "Well, of course
I had one, my dear boy. His name was Bedřich and he had the most
beautiful mustache in the world. I'm sure you would laugh if you saw
him now, but in those days it was the fashion. It's been a good forty
years since he passed away."

Finally Aunt Anna had a chance to look at the collection in the
display case as well. She had a small frame and couldn't stand too
long, so she asked Jiří to take the items out, so she could look at them
under the lamp after dinner, before he drove her home. The first one
that captured her attention was the medal. "They did a very nice job
with it. Really very nice," she commented after thoroughly examining
it under a magnifying glass. Jiří realized it had been a long time since
he had seen anyone study an object like that. Aunt Anna and her slow
movements existed in a different time zone. One in which the careful examination of things and people still brought satisfaction. As she
inspected the medal, she leaned against the backrest of the chair in a
way that suggested she was thinking. She studied the moldavites and
delicate Celtic agates. She was intrigued by the copies of castings of
Indian seals, remarking that she had seen the animal depicted on one
of them during a trip to Poland in 1934. "I believe they call it a bison.
I don't know what it would be doing in India," she said, emphasizing
her astonishment. One by one she scrutinized each item. Unlike Josef
and Květa, who had collected the objects years ago, Aunt Anna was
more interested in the future than in the past, and her attentive inspection was actually intended as a way of showing respect for Alice.
Finally Jiří took out the two big sheets of paper pinned to the wooden
rear wall of the case. As he handed them to Aunt Anna, she made a
critical face at the arrowlike designs pointing in all directions. "How

this fits in is a mystery to me." She paused a moment, then added: "The nice thing is the drawing is big enough that I don't need a magnifying glass, like I do for those stones or the medal, but on the other hand we don't even know whether it's right side up or not. It could be upside down and I wouldn't know the difference." She examined the two sheets covered with wedge-shaped marks until dinnertime. When Jiří drove her home that night, Aunt Anna said to him on the stairs: "I think Josef left behind a surprise for us." Jiří's thoughts had veered off in an entirely different direction, so it took him a moment to reorient. "What kind of surprise?" he asked.

"I'm not exactly sure," Aunt Anna replied, "but I noticed he sketched the marks in pencil first and then inked them in afterward. So if Josef put that much work into it, I figure it might mean something."

"So Mr. Černý did that?" Jiří asked.

"Oh, I'm positive. His signature is there, and on the other side it says something about a surprise and Květa. I can't remember anymore what."

"I'll take a look at it with you next week," Jiří said. They had reached their destination, and he had to keep running back downstairs to switch on the light, which was perfectly timed to keep going out whenever they reached the middle of the staircase.

"Good-night, my boy," Aunt Anna said when she finally reached her door. "Drive safely, and by the way, do you have a girlfriend?"

"Well, I might still have one," he said.

"Might? Do you know or don't you?"

"She's in Paris."

"Paris? Well, you might as well not have one then. Either she's here, or you're there, or you find somebody here. I know what I'm talking about, boy," she said, wagging her cane at him and shuffling through the door.

It wasn't until Alice ran into her father's friend Dr. Lukavský in her mother's room at the hospital that she realized she was worried about her mother and didn't like the way she had been acting. "She always used to put on makeup, at the very least she drew in her eyebrows, and now, Uncle, now? What's wrong with her? She hardly even talks. She just spends all her time remembering," Alice said, unconsciously taking advantage of running into Antonín to give vent to all her fears. He gave her an answer intended to reassure her, although in spite of his medical education he didn't understand the reason for Květa's illness, which had started out as ordinary pneumonia. She was veiled in the violet scent of resignation, and he refused to think of her as a patient. He had ordered himself not to, and he intended to carry out his order.

The next Monday after dinner, Jiří remembered what Aunt Anna had said to him about the paper pictures with the wedge-shaped marks. He took them out of the display case and laid them in front of her under the harsh light of the table lamp. Aunt Anna spun the sheets of paper around, nodded to Jiří, and without looking up, said: "As long as I've got you here, my boy, I don't need my glasses or a magnifying glass. Come closer and read it to me."

Jiří pulled up his chair, lifted one of the sheets, and examined the marks. Written in neat, tiny letters it said: *To Květa from Josef.* On the next line beneath it was written: *Dear Květa, as you know, our anniversary is coming up soon. So I got the idea of expressing what I feel for you in this way. For your eyes only. The truth is I hope what I have to say on these two pages makes you happy. Just a little surprise from me. Josef.*

Jiří finished reading the text and Aunt Anna waited a moment to hear what came next. But that was it.

"That's all there is," said Jiří.

"That's it? Nothing else?" she asked.

"No, that's it," said Jiří.

After he'd driven Aunt Anna home, Jiří asked Alice if she knew anything about the sheets of paper inscribed with cuneiform, and he showed her the other side with the rows of tiny neat script. "That's my father's writing all right," said Alice, "but I couldn't say what he meant by it." After a few days Jiří convinced Alice to go out to Lhotka and see whether Josef had left a letter there for Květa. Alice didn't pay it too much attention at first, but then, reasoning that it might make her mother happy, she gave Kryštof a call. She learned that he and Libuše had already readied Josef's room for Květa, and he had given it a fresh coat of paint, which it badly needed. Kryštof said they hadn't thrown away any of Josef's things, especially not his papers, and that he'd take a look, but neither he nor Libuše had come across any letter. A few days later Kryštof stopped by the hospital to visit Květa and told Alice there wasn't any letter among Josef's things.

Jiří, who had to pass through the room with the display case in it in order to get to his bedroom, suddenly got an idea and decided to share it with Alice. "I have a feeling," he said. "I think I figured it out." He went on, holding the two pieces of paper in his hand. "I believe the letter is right here in front of our eyes. Only it's written in a foreign language, in cuneiform." Alice was amused. Kryštof would have never dreamed up something like that, she thought. "Fine, and . . . ?" she said, drifting off into awkward silence.

"Maybe you should go show it to Aunt Květa?" Jiří said.

"You know, Jiří," Alice said, "things weren't exactly ideal between my mom and dad, and with her in the hospital . . . I'm not so sure it would be good to ask her about it right now. She's got enough to deal with as is. Though it's true I had the feeling they'd been getting closer again."

Jiří studied Alice a moment, then said, "What does that mean, getting closer?"

"Closer, you know, like loving each other. But whatever, I'll bring it to my mom tomorrow."

The next day at the hospital, she showed her mother what Jiří and Aunt Anna had discovered, and asked what she thought of it. "Your dad—well, your dad was born the same day they announced they had deciphered the Hittite language. And when we were young we used to go on dates to lectures by Professor Hrozný, the man who cracked the code," Květa said. That was as far as she wanted to go. The only one who seemed haunted by the two sheets of images was Jiří. One day, when Alice came home, he said: "I've got it, Alice, I've got it. I figured it out and tomorrow we're going to have it deciphered, or translated, rather." Alice already knew what he was talking about. "You know what, Jiří? I've got a lot on my plate right now. Why don't you go by yourself?"

And so, resigned yet filled with a sense of adventure that can be experienced only in Eastern Europe, the next day Jiří knocked on a door with a plaque that read: *Dr. Jakub Hájek, Office Hours Tuesday and Thursday 15.00–17.00.* Beneath it, added in hand, was: *Office hours are not intended for tutoring before exams.* A few students paced back and forth in front of the door, waiting their turn. Jiří's turn came at four thirty. He knocked on the door. "Come in," he heard, and entered. A thin man stood on the other side of the desk, his face covered with a full graying beard. "Hello," said Jiří.

"Hello," said Professor Hájek. He studied his guest a moment. "What can I do for you?"

Jiří introduced himself and said: "I have a favor to ask, Professor. I have a text that I need translated."

"Where are you from? How come I've never seen you before?"

"I already have my degree, though it's in economic history, which is nowhere near as interesting a field as yours," Jiří said. "The reason I'm here is, we found this thing at home and we don't know what it says, and I believe it was written by one of my relatives who recently passed away, to his wife, who's now in the hospital. Although . . . maybe the whole thing is nonsense, but would you mind taking a look?"

"Did this relative of yours study in our department?" Professor Hájek asked.

"I don't think so," Jiří said. "I mean, definitely not. He was a civil engineer. It's just I was told that they met here—that is, he and his wife—at Professor Hrozný's lectures, but I'm not exactly sure."

"But that must have been . . ."

"My aunt is a little over seventy," Jiří said.

"All right then, let's have a look."

Jiří pulled the plastic folder from his briefcase containing the papers and handed it across the desk. Professor Hájek studied the papers a while and Jiří had the impression he was actually reading.

After about ten minutes, the professor removed his glasses, opened a drawer, took out a tissue, and wiped his glasses a few times, looking embarrassed.

"Eh-hehm," he said, clearing his throat. "It is in fact a letter, and if I may say so, of a personal," he cleared his throat again, "a very personal nature. I would go so far as to call it a love letter, so to speak . . . though of course, that's not for me to say." After another pause he said: "Do you have a pen and paper?"

"Of course," Jiří said, taking out a ballpoint and a scrap of paper.

"That won't be enough. Here, sit down," said the professor, pointing to an empty desk. Jiří sat down and the professor placed several sheets of blank lined paper in front of him. "I'll dictate," he said. He paused, then added, "You know, there are a few mistakes. In particular, repeated errors in the perfective and the active and passive voice. On the other hand, in a very inspiring way he has created several neologisms for which Hittite has no words, and there is also some interesting vocabulary of non-Hittite origin. I suggest that I quietly correct the errors and translate the other words into Czech as the author most likely intended. Do you agree?"

"Please," said Jiří. "Ready when you are."

Professor Hájek began to read, slowly and distinctly:

Dear Květa,

with great delay I have realized that I still love you. That is why I must tell you: I still love you! My shyness and lack of common sense, together with the pain inflicted on me by the news of your long-ago relationship with Hynek, have resulted in this constant searing pain becoming entangled with a feeling of humiliation. As a result I have tried to deny and erase my love for you. Yet I have found that I am not capable of it. In fact I must admit that I have never been capable of it, though I consciously attempted with all my might to do so many times. At first when I left you I tried to forget you, and I hated you several times a day. Yet my hatred was knottily intertwined with my enduring love for you. Every day for many years I tried to forget you. But then I would see you somewhere and once again I would bitterly realize that my hatred for you was gone and I had to try slowly to rebuild it. They were bitter moments, full of despair and the unrealized dream of forever erasing you from my life. So it went, day after day. But then, just when I thought I had succeeded and that, at least in my mind, you had ceased to exist, I would once again be reminded of you by Alice. As she matured, her voice became increasingly similar to yours. One day, years ago, when my hearing was still good, I asked her to go find out how much it would cost to buy a new vise in Prague that I needed for my workshop in Lhotka. A few days later she called and when I picked up the receiver I heard you. She didn't say, "Hi, Dad," the way she usually did, but just spit out a confused list of prices for different items, and instead of her again I heard you. I hung up with my heart pounding so hard that I didn't think I would survive the day. My dream of banishing you from my head and my heart for the rest of my life had run aground. No matter how I tried, I found that all my intentions fell to pieces like the Tower of Babylon. The well-hewn granite blocks of my pain were not capable of holding together that terrible edifice. It took a long time for me to discover that the reason for my failure was not lack of hatred, but the excess of love I never stopped feeling for you. I am sure all these things will seem self-evident to you, Květa. But I was truly unaware of them. I never much concerned myself with my feelings or yours. Both of us have had to pay for this unfortunate negligence. I can only say that I apologize to you and that I regret it. I am an old fool who in his understanding of your feelings and his own does not reach even to the constellation of freckles covering your right ankle. But I must admit that when I realized my memories of you caused love rather than hate, I felt like an inventor or an explorer who had discovered new lands. Really! I'm not exaggerating! Forgive me and my foolish metaphors, but I think I felt the way my childhood hero James Watt must have felt when his improved steam engine began to work at full capacity. I don't know how to explain it any less foolishly. For that matter I'm not a poet and I am well aware that my attempt at an apology and an explanation of my love only goes to show that my foolishness and folly have grown in direct proportion to my increasing years. My love still exists. It exists to this day, and to this day it grows stronger. Once upon a time I was sheepish and bewitched! As bound to happen to anyone gazing into your eyes.

My dearest, I am now trying to overcome my conceitedness, my hollow pride, which instead deserves to be called vainglory, and after many futile attempts I have managed to forgive you. It was not easy, it was hard work. Brick by brick I dismantled the grand edifice, which only got in the way of everything and was entirely useless. I came to know the feeling that the workers must have had dismantling the remains of the unfinished Tower of Babel. My strenuous work, however, was redeemed with relief. I would hate ever again to undertake such a foolish, clumsy, and nonsensical comparison, but in my lungs I could smell the melting and the perfume of budding shoots. I will spare you all the worthless feelings which I encountered along the way. I can tell you about them later, and if you permit us to see each other at least every now and again, then perhaps we may also have some time left for that. There is but one thing I wish to ask of you: Please forgive me my complacency and conceitedness, and forgive me the pain I have caused you. I beg of you!

Though I remain convinced that time is a fixed physical quantity and I am aware that a second is merely one eighty-six-thousandth of the mean solar day, I confess, Květa, that I waver in my faith. For my senses betray me more every day, and the days fly by incessantly like a herd of stampeding colts. I fear I won't have the chance to tell you of my lasting love. Nearly everything in life has taken less work than to admit this to you. Thus it occurred to me what a letter might look like in the language of the Hittites and their cuneiform script. I was driven to this folly by the memory of our first meeting, our first dates. This is the one thing I know I don't have to explain to you.

Josef

When Jiří came home, he removed the translation of the letter from his briefcase as dictated to him by Professor Hájek, who had also added a few explanatory notes. Looking at his transcript of the translation, Jiří realized Alice wouldn't be able to read his writing, and rewrote it in cursive, then returned the two original sheets of paper to the display case. Alice came home from work, the two of them had supper, and when they were done, Jiří gave her the translation to read. She washed her hands with soap, dried them, and carefully laid the letter on the table. When she had finished reading it, she read Professor Hájek's notes, asked Jiří to explain what a neologism was, said she would take the letter home to show her mother the next day, and thanked him. Jiří wrote a letter about it to his sister, explaining that it felt like stepping onto an elevator carrying two passionate lovers who had something so important to tell each other that they ignored the other people getting on and off at each floor, who meanwhile did their best not to notice the lovers' glances and caresses, maintaining a neutral, noncommittal smile as the elevator traveled up the shaft. But he couldn't shake the feeling that it was inappropriate. He repeated to himself that honestly nobody, including him, could have known what was contained in the letter, but the feeling that he had peeked behind the screen into a bathroom where, naked and scarred, troubled, aging, and abused, love and illusions sat in the bathtub washing each other, made him very uncomfortable. It was reassuring to him that Alice's response to the letter was far less emotional. Also she told him that if he wanted he could go with her to the hospital to see her mother the next day and explain to her exactly how the whole thing had happened and what the translator had told him. Jiří agreed and they both went to bed.

They arrived at the hospital the next morning a few minutes before eight. They climbed the stairs to the third floor and proceeded to make their way down the corridor with the vaulted ceiling to Květa's room. Alice stopped a moment, smiled uncertainly, and pulled the translation out of her handbag. She glanced at it, then hurried to catch up with Jiří, who was now a few steps ahead. As they passed an open office, a nurse inside called out to them, and rushed past

Jiří to Alice as if he were invisible. "Mrs. Černá, Mrs. Černá!" Alice stopped and looked back. "I assume you didn't get the message?" she said. Alice shook her head and shot a quick glance at Jiří. The look on his face was neutral, as always when he was worried. He really is half English, Alice thought to herself as the nurse opened the door and they stepped into her office. Inside, a woman sitting behind a desk in a white coat told her that her mother had passed away at five thirty that morning. Only when Alice clenched her lips did Jiří realize how much she resembled Květa. Alice's eyes wandered over a large photograph of a mountain valley behind the woman's back. Later Alice realized that the calendar was two years old. "I'm so sorry, Mrs. Černá," said the woman behind the desk.

"I think," Alice said, "I have to go home now." The woman behind the desk said she just had to take the personal belongings her mother had had with her. She handed Alice a ballpoint pen and pointed to the space on the form where she was supposed to sign. Then she opened a large envelope containing several rings, a watch, a gold chain, an ID card, a wallet, a small journal, and an envelope with seventy-six crowns and a few hellers. Alice wasn't in the mood to check anything and with an air of irritation signed to acknowledge receipt of the items. Jiří told the woman he would take care of the rest. She said that if they wanted to see the body of the deceased, they would have to call in advance, and handed Jiří a small card with a phone number and address on it. She said the body of the deceased was now at the address on the card. Alice stood, turned around, and left without saying good-bye. Jiří, realizing she was irritated, got up and followed her out. After they walked a few yards, the door to the office behind them opened again and the nurse who had led them in before came running out. "Mrs. Černá," she called, "Mrs. Černá!" She caught up to Alice and handed her the paper with the translation of Josef's letter. "You dropped this," she said breathlessly. Alice took it, folded it into her handbag, and thanked the nurse. As they walked down the stairs, she looked at Jiří, pulled out the letter, and said, "Damn fools, why couldn't they have told each other all this years ago? Old fools, both of them! Crazy fools. Why couldn't they just talk? They were still in love. Why did my dad have to make it some complicated thing with a bunch of stupid secret writing? And my mom, too! Her too, Jiří!" She started to cry. "What were they playing around for like that? My crazy, stupid parents. Why did they have to do that? Christ on crutches, couldn't they have just talked?" The nurse who handed her the letter watched from a distance. Jiří looked back at her several times, but as they walked down the stairs he lost sight of her. "I guess they did the best they could," said Jiří, who was sad himself, since he felt sorry for Květa. He felt sorry, even though he had known her only briefly, and at that as a slightly arrogant, always elegantly dressed, but mostly impatient elderly lady. Alice waved her hand. "Those were different times, of course. I realize that, but he still loved her, and she loved him, so what were they doing, the crazy fools?" She stopped and looked at Jiří: "You think I wanted a pair of crackpot heroes for parents? God, no. That's not what I wanted. I wanted normal parents who could be together and get along, more or less, but oh, no, not them. And now Mom goes and dies. They both piss me off. Now with this they've pissed me off for good. The both of them!"

They walked out the hospital door and headed home. Alice told Jiří not to hail a taxi, she preferred to walk. There were tears running down her cheeks, and some people turned to look at them in the street. Alice didn't lean on Jiří for support, walking straight ahead, bolt upright. She was moving fast, but every few blocks she would suddenly stop, breathing frantically or digging through her handbag for a handkerchief. Jiří wanted to duck in somewhere and buy her tissues, but he was afraid he would lose her. He didn't know his way around Prague that well yet. One minute she was giving him a little smile through her tears, the next she didn't even seem to notice he was there. She was sobbing so loudly that some of the people waiting at the tram stop turned to look, assuming Jiří to be the cause. Even though he knew he had no reason to feel that way, he was embarrassed. He reassured himself with the thought, You wanted adventure, now you have it.

The funeral was a few days after Three Kings' Day, and although it had been a tame winter up to then, a few days before the ceremony a genuine East European winter set in. It isn't history or politics or philosophy that divides Eastern Europe from Western, Jiří mused. It's much simpler than that. What it boils down to is what kind of winter they have. The difference between London and Prague was more than thirty-five degrees. It was so cold everyone assumed that Aunt Anna would stay at home and they would have to go to the funeral without her, but she'd made up her mind to go, and her decision was final. Jiří drove her to the crematorium, pulled into a parking space, and slowly helped her out of the car. The snow had been shoveled, but there were a few tongues of ice on the sidewalk here and there, which Aunt Anna, with Jiří holding her by the shoulders, carefully picked her way around. There were about twenty guests at the funeral. Kryštof, Libuše, Alice, Jiří, and Aunt Anna sat in the first row. After a short speech, the ceremony came to an end. The music stopped, the coffin rolled backstage on its bier, and the mourners approached to offer their condolences. Jiří stood between Alice and her aunt, and Alice was the only one who could convince Aunt Anna to sit. "Everybody's dying, I'm the only one left," she complained. "And now, on top of everything else, you're stuck with me."

A few days later, Alice made an appointment with her uncle Antonín. After an exchange of pleasantries and memories, she plucked up the courage to ask, "You must know, Uncle. What was the story between my mom and her lover, anyway?"

"You're sure you want to hear?" Antonín asked.

"Yes, I'm sure. I want to know what really happened."

"Well," Antonín began, and he proceeded to tell Alice the story of the three friends. A story so clichéd it was almost embarrassing. Alice listened in amazement, shaking her head in disbelief and interrupting every now and then to ask a question. Before ending, Antonín said: "You know, it's the most natural reaction there is. When somebody attacks someone, when they hurt them, when somebody has power over someone, the person who's the victim tries to get along with their attacker. When you're afraid for your loved ones—and your mother really was afraid for you and Josef—sometimes it happens that the victim establishes a relationship with the attacker. Sometimes they even fall in love. It may be irrational but it happens. It's a reaction to help prevent more aggression on the part of the attacker. It's been described and researched, and maybe some of the therapies that help people will eventually even make their way here to this country. But people like your mom have had to live with it all their lives. And the eroticization of pain is just one of many things that go along with it."

"Well, that's all well and good," Alice said, "but the problem is it can be used as an excuse for anything. Plus there's also the fact that she knew him before she married my dad."

"We're a small country," Antonín said. "Everyone here will always know everyone else, more or less. In fact, maybe that's what makes it worse."

"Right, and as for her . . . shall we say temporary erotic preferences, nobody cares about that anymore. But she didn't have to make my dad suffer."

"I'm not so sure you should blame her for that."

"But I'm really angry at her," said Alice. "I'm furious."

"How come?" Antonín asked.

"Because she died second. If Dad had died second, I'd probably be just as mad at him."

Antonín shrugged. "Remember that pastry chef who made the cake for your wedding?"

"How could I not?" Alice said. "It's the only one I've had so far and it wasn't the kind of cake you forget."

"I ran into him recently. If you can believe it, he told me he made up the whole thing."

"What whole thing?" Alice said.

"These stories he made me suffer through. He made them all up."

"How come?" Alice asked.

"Now that's a story," Antonín said. "We ran into each other on Charles Square and stood there for about two hours while he explained. I've got an address for him somewhere. Anyway, if you can believe it, he was with his wife, the one who so mysteriously disappeared. She lived for years somewhere in Germany, or maybe Austria. Salzburg, I think."

"Salzburg?" said Alice.

"I think that was it. I'm not positive. Anyway, right after the revolution, Christmas of eighty-nine, she came back to him."

"Uh-huh," said Alice, her thoughts now clearly elsewhere.

"Listen, as long as you're here," Antonín said, "you think that cousin of yours could translate something into English for me?"

"Sure," said Alice. "Why not? He doesn't know his way around here too well, but he likes meeting new people. He'd be glad to get to know you. I'll set it up, don't worry. What is it you need?"

"A colleague of mine from London is going to be coming here in about a month. Sort of half private, half for a little conference I'm putting together. Actually, I don't even know how he found out. We weren't expecting anyone nonlocal. In return, maybe I could take your cousin somewhere outside of Prague. Like Český Krumlov, say. Give the kid a little look around the country."

"That'd be great, Uncle, that'd be nice. I'll let him know," Alice said.

19

WOLF THEOLOGY

The two men sat in the hotel room. It was raining outside. Jiří busied himself straightening something on the bed, every now and then glancing out the window.

"It's not going to stop," he said after a while.

"I guess not," Antonín said.

"So the theater's out then."

"Looks that way."

"We could go to Mass," Jiří said, watching as his companion tapped the tip of a ballpoint pen on the nightstand next to the bed.

"I haven't gone to church in years."

"How come?" asked Jiří. Without waiting for an answer he added: "Supposedly this church, can't remember what it's called, but supposedly it's originally from the thirteenth century."

"I don't believe in God," Antonín said, "and I couldn't care less what century the church is from." There was a moment of silence. Jiří noticed that Antonín had stopped tapping the pen on the nightstand.

"But how come? How come you don't believe? Does it have anything to do with your being a doctor?"

"No, why would it? Although actually . . . no. It's got nothing to do with it."

"I don't know if it's appropriate." Jiří paused. "Appropriate to ask, I mean." He turned around on the bed so he could look his companion in the face.

"Well, it's not a particularly emotional matter for me. And besides, it's been a long time since I stopped believing. Now I believe that I don't believe."

"I don't mean to pry. I just wondered," said Jiří.

"So should we go get some food?"

"All right," said Jiří. "But actually I always thought faith could be a help to doctors."

"What kind of opening gambit is that?" asked the doctor. "Is that supposed to help get us through the rain?"

"What's a gambit?"

"Oh, nothing, you chess virgin, you," Antonín said. He stepped up to the open window and closed it part of the way. He took a bottle of brandy from his briefcase, a glass from out of the case, and gestured to Jiří to help himself. "You're right, faith does help. Assuming you have it, that is."

"So does it help you, or has it ever?"

"Yes, of course, certainly. When I had it, it helped. I could really use a smoke."

"Smoking isn't allowed in here, but it doesn't bother me," said Jiří. "We can leave the window open when we go."

"I was planning to have one on the way to the theater, and during it too. Since the theater's outside, I'm sure you can smoke there. I've been looking forward to lighting up in the theater all day. I assume the local thespians won't be too exciting."

"Mmm," said Jiří. "You can have a smoke at dinner. I don't mind."

"Shall we go then?"

"You know, I'm actually not that hungry yet. But we can go now, if you want to smoke on the way."

"That's all right, I can wait. If I can't practice faith anymore, at least I can practice willpower." Jiří didn't respond, staring into the rainy street out the window.

"If you want to light up," he said, "I can open the window a little more."

"No, that's fine," said Antonín, slipping his pen into his shirt pocket.

"What is it like to lose faith?" asked Jiří. "Does it happen all at once, or is it . . ."

"A gradual process, is that what you mean?"

"I'm not quite sure how to put it," said Jiří. "Do you know what I mean?"

"The year before I graduated, I was on an internship in Slovakia and I asked for a placement there. It wasn't even that hard. Nobody was too eager to go there."

"What's a placement?" Jiří asked.

"In the old days, under communism, that was a decision by the authorities about where you would work. I also considered Ostrava, but I liked nature, so instead I went out to the tip of Slovakia. I knew the area a little, so I applied and I was accepted."

"I guess we're not going to that church then, are we?" Jiří said.

Antonín shook his head. "I always thought God was slightly benevolent."

"What do you mean, *slightly?*"

"You know . . . our family was Catholic for many generations. And when you're Catholic that long, you believe the same thing as your parents and grandparents. You believe that God is infinitely merciful, but only slightly benevolent."

"I thought you said you didn't believe anymore?"

"Let's go have dinner," Antonín said, putting on a cardigan vest.

"So what was it like out there?" asked Jiří.

"I still remember there was a little blackboard next to the gatehouse in front of the hospital entrance. You know, like at school—only it never had anything written on it. One day I asked the gatekeeper why it was there and he said in case of emergency. 'What kind of emergency?' I asked. 'The kind that are unpredictable,' he said. 'The ones that no one expects.' I don't remember anyone ever writing anything on it. I would always stop when I came to it and light a cigarette, which lasted exactly as long as it took me to make my sleepy walk to the unit every morning."

"It's stopped raining. Shall we go?"

"Let's."

"So how did you lose your faith?" Jiří asked.

"I'm pretty long-winded, huh?"

"That's not what I meant."

"It's all right, I am long-winded . . . When you believe the way I did and you come from a family where it's tradition and tradition is something you don't really talk about, it's easy to believe in a luke-warm way. At least it was for me. But I think it's safe to say that it was the same for my parents. My mother was kind of a snob about it, un-like my father. I'd say his faith was more condescending."

"So what happened?"

"What happened was I fell in love. I fell in love and didn't even know it."

"How can you fall in love and not know it?"

"When you start asking questions like that, you're in serious dan-ger of having the same thing happen to you. I would advise that . . . never mind, sorry. *I would advise* and *I'm important* are both clear signs of poorly managed old age."

It stopped raining.

"After a few weeks working there, I saw Klára for the first time, in the garden on the hospital grounds. I didn't know her name yet, I only found that out later, but I saw two women sitting on a bench: one on the elderly side; the other one, next to her, a tall blonde with long, flowing hair. These days she'd probably have a career as a model for one of those magazines my daughter reads. But that didn't exist back then. She sat straight, almost perfectly still. Then all of a sudden she turned and looked me right in the eye. I felt it in my gut. Blue-gray eyes and blonde hair down to her waist. She was so gorgeous my cigarette almost fell out of my mouth. Gorgeous and loaded with sedatives. It was like she was made of rubber. Walk, eat, and sleep, that was all she did. I asked a colleague about her one time and he said that she was in shock, but he didn't know how long it would last. That was the last time I asked."

"Why don't we go to dinner? You can tell me the rest on the way."

"You're right," Antonín said, and they went out into the street. The historical city center was crowded with restaurants.

"What are you in the mood for?"

"How about fish?" said Jiří.

"There's a restaurant by the river, but I doubt the fish come from the Vltava."

The restaurant was half empty. They chose a table and sat down. Antonín laid his cigarettes next to the ashtray. They looked through the menu and ordered their meals.

"So did you fall in love with that blonde?" Jiří asked after a while in silence, starting in on his soup.

"Yes. I was in love with Klára, and with the nature all around. I knew I was in love with nature, fortunately. I adored it. I walked all over the place. Thick, green forests. Dense woods. Dark, wet, lush greenery, with headstones all over the hills."

"Headstones?" Jiří asked, slurping from the bowl as he tipped it toward him and spooned the last drops of liquid into his mouth.

Antonín glanced around distractedly, following Jiří's maneuvers out of the corner of his eye. "That corner of the country was as charming as it was deserted. It was deserted right up till the end of the war. You couldn't even tell that there had been a war there. I knew it, of course, the same way I knew that in 1882 Koch published his first work on TB. But that's it. Just information. When I walked through the villages in the countryside, though, I discovered that the locals never went into the forest—they just walked along the edge. At first I thought it was because they were so close to the border with the Soviet Union, nowadays it's Ukraine. Then one day, equipped with a good tourist map, I asked how to get to the next valley, and a woman in a village told me there was a path over the hills, but the last time she had taken it was on a march two or three years after the war. By the time I got there, it had been more than ten years since the war."

"So how did they get from one valley to the other?"

"The regular way, by bus."

"But why didn't they take the path?"

"Well, one, it was harder, and two, because of the smell."

"What smell?"

"The war had passed through even that remote region. I realized that the Germans had dug in there, in the mountains, gorges, and passes, dead set on not letting the Red Army pass. Apparently they call that a retreat to fallback position. Also, as one of my colleagues from there explained, there was no way around it. What with the mountains and all. So there had been fighting there. Even the smallest patch of land was full of steel. And fallen soldiers, too. The woman in the village told me the stench in the woods was so bad for years after the war that they just stopped going there. There were thousands of buried soldiers."

"Mm," Jiří said. "I don't think I want that fish anymore."

"Sorry, I wasn't thinking."

"I thought you were going to tell me about faith and all that."

"Ach. I apologize. I didn't realize where it would take me. Memories, you know? It's been a lot of years."

"I don't think I want that fish anymore," Jiří said again.

"So order something else."

"I really am interested, you know. It's just that I missed breakfast."

"Oh, I understand. But you have to eat something. Otherwise your sugar will drop."

"So then you met up with her later?"

"I went to consult with a colleague about something one day, and the conversation somehow ended up turning to Klára."

"So what did he tell you?"

"People there are closer to each other, and I think nature is also closer to them. Have you ever seen a wolf? I mean in nature, not just a picture or on TV."

"Once. At the zoo. Why?"

"My colleague told me what had happened to her. She came from a nearby village, good family, had just finished high school in the district capital. The principal was going to recommend her for college in Bratislava, on the other side of the country, all the way down in the south. Having a college degree doesn't mean that much anymore, but back then, you know, if you were an ordinary person from a little village, where war blew through once every hundred years and then everyone just forgot about you for the next hundred, it meant a lot. Apparently Klára and her fiancé had been talking about getting married, and that winter they went to a party. Some people say they had a falling-out, that she and her boyfriend had a fight. But I also heard that Klára and her cousin cooked the whole thing up in advance, and then again other people say Klára got mad at her boyfriend for dancing with one of her relatives more than was appropriate."

"I'm going to switch to the *svíčková*," Jiří said. "How about you?"

"I think I'll stick with the fish."

"So how did that woman or girl end up in the hospital?"

"The girl — she was still a girl at the time. Though as I said, people didn't remember too well what actually happened between Klára and her fiancé. To make a long story short, Klára left the party sometime around midnight. The village she lived in was a few miles away. It was winter, which out there always meant snow. Snow and cold. Bitter cold. People here can't even imagine. Anyway, sometime after she left, her fiancé found out, so he left too, and went after her. But they never made it home. As midnight came and went, Klára's mother began to get worried. The only phone in the village belonged to the chairman of the Unified Peasant Cooperative. When Klára's mother woke him up, he called the pub where the dance was being held, but all they could tell him was that Klára and her fiancé had both already left. Their families and friends organized a search party with the border guards, the forest workers, and the gamekeeper. The soldiers brought machine guns, the workers took blowtorches. Nothing else works on wolves. The only thing they fear is fire. The two groups started down the path, one on each side. In each group there were a few border guards with machine guns and a few men with blowtorches and shotguns. Along the way one of the groups got attacked by a wolf pack in the dark. They fended them off with the blowtorches, spraying flames at them, but the longer the flames, the faster the fuel ran out. Everyone stuck together, and the soldiers went through several rounds of ammunition, firing blindly into the dark. It's hard to hit a pack of wolves circling you in the dark. There's always the risk you'll shoot another man. Flames shed light, but also shadows. Not to mention the confusion, which a pack of wolves knows how to take advantage of. They found Klára up in a tree, clinging to a branch. The bark of the trunk was shredded bare. Her boyfriend, or what was left of him, was under her, at the bottom. Two men climbed up to try to get her down, but she just kept going higher and higher. She wasn't even screaming, they said. Just grunting. Her knuckles were swollen from the cold and from gripping onto the branches for so long. Her fingernails were torn off. They had to tie her up once they brought her down. She couldn't tell the difference between people and animals anymore. They made a makeshift stretcher out of branches and tied her onto it. The blowtorches were running low on fuel, so they had to run all the way to the nearest village. When it got light, a section of the border guards returned, more heavily armed, along with the workers and the gamekeeper to collect the remains of Klára's fiancé, but they found nothing. The wolves had beaten them to it. Later, the boy's family held a symbolic funeral, burying just a few bloody rags in place of his body. So that girl, that was Klára."

Jiří set his fork down next to his knife on the plate, wiped his mouth with a napkin, and slid his plate to the edge of the table. Along the way it bumped into the pepper shaker, but he caught it before it could tip over. He picked the plate back up with both hands and slowly set it down at the edge of the table. For a while, neither of them said anything.

"Want some coffee?" Antonín said finally, breaking the silence.

"If I drank alcohol, I'd have a shot, but I guess coffee will have to do."

"You don't drink at all?" Antonín said.

"Oh, normally I do, but not today."

"Why not?"

"It's a fast day today."

"That didn't even occur to me, you know? Everyone thinks that God wears their colors. I'm a Sparta supporter, and I couldn't stand the thought that God might root for, say, Slavia. When I still believed, I just assumed God was Catholic. It didn't seem strange to me. But once I found out what I just told you, I stopped believing. It put a crack in my faith."

"The devil's main job, after all, is to break our faith," Jiří said.

"Oh, of course, but from what I've read of Ignatius of Loyola, I thought the devil disguised himself as things that were seductive and inviting. Things and situations where it wouldn't even cross our minds to think about God. And I'm telling you straight out, don't try to pull the Book of Job on me."

"So why do you think it happened?"

"I couldn't come up with a reason, that's the problem. Not a one. God let it happen and just left them there. I thought about it a lot, but couldn't come up with an answer. My God had ceased to be benevolent, even slightly, and instead was infinitely merciless."

"Sometimes we don't understand the ways of God's providence."

"Wrong! We nearly never understand! Trying to reconcile Tertullian of Carthage with Origen the eunuch is a hell of a job, my friend."

"*Credo quia absurdum*, 'I believe because it is meaningless,' that was Tertullian," Jiří replied. "*Credo ut intelligam*, 'I believe so that I may understand,' was Saint Anselm of Canterbury, not Origen."

"Really? I can't keep track anymore," Antonín said. "Is that right?" he asked, but didn't wait for an answer. "'And the son of God died; it is believable because it is foolish. And buried, he rose from the dead; it is certain because it is impossible'?"

"Yes: *Credo quia absurdum*."

"But literally what it means is, 'I believe because it is absurd.' That's what I'm saying. I was stripped of faith by my God. Absurdly stripped of my absurd belief."

"Maybe the way you've been thinking about it is wrong."

"What else can it be except wrong . . . and imperfect? Given that we're only human."

"Well, of course, but . . ."

"In the end, after her life went on, I had to admit your uncle was right."

"Who?"

"Josef."

"What has he got to do with religion?"

"Not very much, but he did give me some advice back then."

"The last time I talked to him he was old, incoherent, and didn't look well."

"Back then we were young. Josef was a different man. He had charm and sparkle, up until he went to prison, and then . . . then things changed him."

"What advice did he give you?"

"Apart from his own work, he was also interested in logic in those days."

"And?"

"And the combinations that he used to beat me at chess. He was a master of rook endings, but I suppose you know nothing about that?"

"No," Jiří said, laughing. "I really don't."

"There was a beauty to his rook endings, a beauty with steel-blue logic. They were memorable defeats. My most beautiful." Antonín paused. The conversations at the surrounding tables had died down, and outside, in the street, another downpour had begun.

"So what did he have to do with logic?"

"It was a hobby of his . . . and back then he gave me some advice, and he was right. He told me not to look at the problem from a personal perspective but from the standpoint of infinitary logic. Which even God trembles before, as he used to say."

"So what was his advice?"

"He advised me to break the problem down into simple, logical steps. Like moves on a chessboard."

"You can't play chess with God. That's true blasphemy."

"I thought I would offend you sooner or later."

"Explain!"

"One of God's qualities is His infinite kindness, correct?"

"Of course, that goes without saying."

"What Josef explained to me back then was that, theological loopholes and silly equivocations about the incomprehensible ways of God's providence aside, there are only a certain number of possible alternatives."

"And what alternatives are those?"

"Josef sketched it out for me something like this. The most important characteristics of God are: one, omnipotence; two, omni-science; three, omnipresence; and four, infinite kindness and love. I'm leaving out the less important ones, which even you Christians can't agree on among yourselves. The question is, If infinite kindness is one of God's attributes, how do you explain all the crap and misery in this world? Josef counted them all off on his fingers for me. One, the first alternative is your benevolent Catholic God doesn't see, which is why He does nothing about it, but this contradicts your good Catholic belief in his omnipresence. Two, He isn't capable of distinguishing good from bad, in which case maybe he should have stayed in paradise along with the bedbugs, the brontosaurs, and that snake, poor thing. This second alternative is ruled out, since your good Catholic God, in all his greatness, is omnipresent, and as we already noted, point four also applies, that is, infinite kindness and love. That means there's nothing we can do about it, since as you pointed out to me, God is also all-powerful. The third alternative is that there is a God: He exists, sees everything, is omnipotent, and likes what He sees. In which case this omnipotent, omnipresent being can't also be infinitely good. Otherwise it would do something about all the crap and such that goes on in the world. If anything does exist that is om-nipotent and omnipresent, it can't be God if it leaves everything the way it is. In which case that being, from a strictly logical point of view, has to be—the devil. The next-to-last alternative implies that this at least more or less possible, hypothetical Catholic God sees everything and doesn't like it, but can't do anything about it. Which would mean he's in the same situation as both of us. The bottom line being, there's a fifth alternative."

"Which is?"

"He doesn't exist."

"Doesn't exist?"

"That's right."

"But, but . . . that's a cheap argument."

"Cheap perhaps, but undeniably logical."

"But surely you can't reduce God to some shaky logical argument?"

"Whenever you ask about something truly basic, like how God created the universe or where God lives or is, people who believe always say you're asking the wrong question and that your arguments aren't deep enough. Even if I asked a simple question, like how come there aren't any brontosaurs on Noah's Ark in the Bible, they would all say I'm asking the wrong thing."

"I'm not saying I know the answers, I'm just trying to ask."

"Then you're better off than most."

There was the sound of a cat meowing from outside. The rain had stopped. The cat began meowing louder, only now it seemed to be coming from the kitchen. Antonín ordered two coffees and for himself a large cognac. He gave Jiří an apologetic look. "Fasting." He lit a cigarette and sucked in the smoke, repeating the action several times. Inhale, exhale. Jiří shifted uncomfortably in his seat. He probably didn't want to disturb Antonín. Again: inhale, exhale. After another moment or two, Antonín said:

"That cat meowing, I suppose that was from the river. At any rate let's hope," he added. "Let's hope it isn't in the kitchen."

"It was probably attracted by the smell of fish."

"Probably," Antonín said.

"It wouldn't be the only one."

"Probably not," said Antonín. Just then, there was a sound of shattering glass in the kitchen and the guests in the restaurant fell silent. The waiter at the bar flashed an embarrassed grin, uncertain whether to go see what happened or pretend everything was all right. After a moment or two, he decided not to go anywhere. There was the sound of quick steps from the kitchen and agitated voices.

"It must be like opium for cats," Jiří said.

His companion stared out the window at the wet cobblestones on the street.

"What's like opium for cats?" he asked.

"The fish."

"Fish are like opium?"

"I'm saying for cats it's like opium."

"Uh-huh," Antonín said. Along with most of the other guests, he was listening to the voices arguing in the kitchen. Another voice had joined in. The waiter had given up trying to pretend and was now listening with unconcealed interest. Suddenly a new sound erupted from the jumble, like a long, narrowly modulated meow.

"So it is in the kitchen."

"What is?" Jiří asked.

"The cat," Antonín said. "That doesn't bode well for their hygienic practices."

"Well, as I was saying," Jiří said, "it's like opium for them."

The kitchen door flew open and two men, one in a T-shirt and corduroys, the other in a suit, burst into the dining room. The man in the T-shirt was shouting at the man in the suit. Meanwhile they were both trying to catch a bird that was zigzagging back and forth between them, meowing nonstop.

"It's a peacock," Antonín said, but before Jiří could reply, the peacock disappeared under a table at the other end of the dining room and the guests nervously sprang from their seats.

"You're the one who wanted it for brains and tongue," shouted the man in the suit.

"No, I didn't. It just escaped from the castle and came over here."

"The castle, right. I'll give you the castle," the man in the suit shouted, shaking his fist. "If you harm so much as a feather on him, not only are you gonna pay, but I'm gonna knock your teeth in." Suddenly there was a squeal and the peacock shot out from under the table, through the legs of the guests and its pursuers. Whether guided by animal instinct or operating purely at random, it headed for the glass front door, which at that very moment a middle-aged man was opening for his female companion, who on seeing the bird sprang back with a startled shriek. The peacock let out a wail and dashed out into the streets of the Renaissance city. The man in the T-shirt glanced back at the woman as he ran out the door, shouting: "Are you stupid? You know how much that bird's worth?" and went chasing after the peacock. The man in the suit paused to offer a grimace of apology, then joined in the chase, shouting at the man in the T-shirt:

"It's a coincidence, Mirek! Just a coincidence!" A group of guests at the two long tables in the corner of the restaurant applauded and belted out some sort of cry three times.

"They must be foreigners," said Antonín.

"I'm a foreigner too," said Jiří. "Sort of."

"No, you're not. You speak Czech."

"Oh, right," said Jiří. "I didn't think of that."

The waiter looked as if he were about to deliver a long speech, but then instead just asked if anyone wanted to settle their check. Jiří said: "I thought it was a cat, that whole time, till I saw it."

"Me too," said Antonín.

"Talk about out of thin air."

"Right, exactly, but let's not even talk about what plans they might have had for it in the kitchen."

"Plans? In the kitchen?"

"Yeah."

"No, I agree, let's not." After a pause, Jiří went on. "So tell me, how did things end up with, you know, what's her name, Klára?"

"Klára?" Antonín said. "How did things end up with Klára?"

"How did you finally meet her?"

"Well, sometimes she was better, sometimes worse. Eventually she started going under on us. Her depressions were very deep."

"I'm not surprised," said Jiří, "after what she went through."

"Of course, and then she underwent shocks, electroshock treatment."

"There was nothing else you could do?"

"There was—leucotomy—but that's even worse."

"What's that?"

"The term by which most laypeople know it is lobotomy. The separation of the frontal lobes from the rest of the brain."

"My God, that's barbaric."

"It's an irreversible operation."

"It's barbaric."

"Seeing as you're a layperson, I'm not going to discuss it with you, but the whole principle of treatment is based on the degree of knowledge available or accessible to us at any given moment."

"Does that apply to logic, too?"

"I don't know."

"Didn't that seem strange to you, just cutting up somebody's brain?"

"It wasn't just cutting up a brain."

"But afterwards the people weren't themselves anymore."

"They were, to some extent, and we hoped it was the better part, the part that wasn't harmful."

"To some extent?"

"Yes, though it's true sometimes we couldn't say if it was more or less."

"Didn't you care?"

"Of course we cared."

"Then how could you do it?"

"We were trying to help the patients. We just wanted to help."

"It never occurred to you that you might be harming them?"

"Without a little harm there wouldn't be any medicine."

"A little harm. You call that a little harm?"

"Don't pick apart my words."

"You're the one who said it."

"It was used only in extreme cases."

"Could you still have fallen in love with her after that?"

"You seem pretty worked up all of a sudden."

"Could you still have loved her after that?"

"One thing at a time."

"Well, could you?"

"One thing at a time, please, if you don't mind. I don't know. How could I? And besides, in the end we didn't do it."

"Not to her, you didn't."

"Of course it was performed on other patients, and at the time I was trying to focus on other things."

"So you never had any doubts?"

"Of course I did. But I also believed. Not because it was absurd, but so I could understand. I tried to understand, and I did. At least back then I thought I did. I thought we were all in God's hands, to some extent."

"You don't think so anymore?"

"Not after what happened to Klára."

"It sounds like a very hard decision, but nature isn't God. Maybe it's more like He allowed it."

"Where is God's will in all this? Where is suffering? When hunger drives the wolves out of the forest . . . and man is a wolf to man? And when our loving God is a wolf?"

"Our?"

"Of course *our*. There's no point trying to get out of it, even if you don't believe. A loving God goes only where He belongs."

"Where he belongs?"

"If he stayed in a hotel, I would definitely give him a worse room than Koch."

"Who's Koch?"

"Robert Koch. He's no longer with us, but back in his day, he worked on TB. But I've wandered off topic again. What I wanted to say was, electrotherapy worked for depression, but we weren't prepared for the side effects."

"Side effects?"

"At first we didn't understand. One of the nurses actually figured it out before any of us."

"Figured out what?"

"Klára started getting visitors. More and more. Then one day the chief physician called me in and told me what he'd discovered. The number of visitors always increased whenever she had electrotherapy."

"Electrotherapy?"

"Every visitor had to sign in to the register on the unit, and when the chief physician looked at the register and Klára's chart, it lined up. He pinned it on the head nurse. At first she tried to wriggle out of it, but in the end she told the truth. Klára was telling fortunes."

"Fortunes? What do you mean?"

"She was predicting the future."

"Predicting the future?"

"Yes. Klára was predicting the future."

"What? How?"

"In fact, ever since she had begun getting electroshock, for two or three days after, she would complain that her head hurt and she couldn't get out of bed. There was nothing strange about that in itself, but then one day the head nurse's son was supposed to travel to Košice, and she said to someone in front of Klára that she wished her son would leave already, so she could finally get some proper cleaning done at home. At which point Klára interjected that her son wasn't going anywhere and she would be glad for it, too. The head nurse remembered her words. A few days later, two local trains crashed into each other. Nothing too serious, but they brought in a few of the injured to our hospital. The head nurse was on pins and needles, since her son was supposed to have been on one of the trains. He wasn't on the list of injured and the police didn't have him on the list of passengers. At noon he turned up at the hospital to see his mother. It turned out he had just overslept. He didn't even know about the accident. In a rare show of emotion, the head nurse threw her arms around his neck. But she remembered what Klára had said, and the next day she asked her how she had known, but Klára didn't remember. It was like it had been erased from her memory. The head nurse mentioned it to the other nurses, and word spread. That also explained the unusual rise in requests to work on the unit on certain days. They just started asking her questions."

"About what?"

"Everything. One of the nurses wanted to know whether she and her husband were going to get the money his parents had promised them. Another wanted to know whether their adoption would come through. Another asked about her inheritance."

"So . . . what were the results?"

"She was right about all of them."

"Really?"

"Really. Usually her state would only last a day or two after the shocks, then it would stop. She could take one, two, three questions at most, then she'd be exhausted, fall asleep, and it wouldn't work after that."

"What did you do about it?"

"Do? We wanted to study it somehow, since the electrotherapy was helping. She wasn't in danger anymore of needing a leucotomy."

"I still find the whole thing barbaric."

"Please, I've had patients who were so depressed, sometimes even suicidal, that they got down on their knees and begged me for the treatment."

"I don't doubt your goodwill, or the expertise of your diagnosis. I'm just saying the practices in your day strike me as barbaric."

"I will never cease to admire the untainted purity of youth, along with the purity of dilettantism and the purity of the Immaculate Conception."

"*Credo quia absurdum!* Absurd, please, absurd . . . meaningless, meaning without any apparent reason, but meaningless isn't barbaric!"

"Of course, *credo quia absurdum* was also a help to me back then."

"And . . ."

"Back then, yes . . . And then the secretary of the local Communist Party heard about Klára's abilities."

". . . ?"

"First he held a hearing in the chief physician's office. The chief physician was pretty surly, but he stood up for his patients. So the secretary called the hospital director onto the carpet, and the director sent the chief physician away for a long fellowship at a research institute where he had been rejected several times before, and while he was away, installed a man who was indebted to him as acting unit head."

"How come the rest of you didn't put up a fight?"

"I was pretty good friends with the attending physician, so I knew he had done absolutely everything he could. In the end the secretary ordered them to increase the number of shocks to boost her ability to prophesize, and my friend refused."

"What happened?"

"He was temporarily transferred to another unit that had a shortage of doctors."

"They could do that?"

"They can always do almost anything. You know what Tacitus wrote: *Rara temporum felicitas, ubi sentire quae velis, et quae sentias dicere licet.*"

"What does that mean?" Jiří asked.

"It means: 'Rare are the happy times when you can think what you want and say what you think.' We were just too close to the Russian border."

"That's a funny . . ."

"Excuse?" Jiří shrugged. "Maybe you're right and we were just making excuses because we were scared. But anyway, meanwhile Klára's . . . fame, I guess is the best way to put it, spread through the nursing staff and people started paying her respect."

"How do you mean?"

"I noticed the nurses who worked on her unit started getting little gifts from people. Klára started getting gifts too, and flowers, lots of flowers, which she in turn gave to the other patients. They also started showing not exactly respect toward her parents, but something like it. I've never encountered anything like it, before or since."

"Sounds like mass hysteria."

"That occurred to us too. But . . ."

"But what?"

"There were the results. Before the Communist secretary had a chance to interfere, we ran a few tests on Klára."

"What kind of tests?"

"Her attending physician, the chief physician, and I each came up with a question that we posed to her. Then we wrote down her answers and put them all in a safe."

"What were the questions?"

"The chief physician asked what type of degree his son would receive. Martin, her attending physician, asked who would fill the vacant position on our unit, and as for me, I asked when my sister would get married."

"And . . . ?"

"She said the chief physician's son wouldn't graduate, which was strange, since he was an excellent student, but then it turned out he was having a relationship with a woman that his father, the chief physician, didn't approve of, so the son left home, dropped out of college, and never returned to his studies. As for the position on our unit, it went to an excellent doctor from the next district over, who had gotten divorced and needed a job that came with an apartment. There was no surprise there, since he was clearly the best candidate. Well, and what she said about my sister also turned out to be true."

"And after that?"

"Once they sent the chief physician away to do research and transferred Martin, her doctor, I didn't have access to Klára anymore. They had brought me in because they thought I could be useful, but without them around, there was nothing for me to do. And her new attending physician made that crystal clear to me."

"But you must have done something."

"Yes, but I didn't like it. It looked like they were starting to give her drugs that made her condition worse, and nobody knew exactly what was going on. I also heard she was starting to have epileptic seizures. Friends and relatives of all the influential Communists were streaming in and out of there, and it was obvious they were asking her about their future. She would wake up afterward and not remember a thing. For them it was perfect, but from a long-term point of view it was clearly harmful to her health."

"So what did you do?"

"One day I waited for her down in the park. I sat next to her for a long time, wondering how to begin. I didn't want to dig a hole to fill a hole. I didn't want to cause her any more trauma. So I just started in to the best of my conscience, being as neutral as I could. Or what I thought was neutral. I started by asking the name of some of the flowers in the flower beds. She answered. It wasn't until I was sitting next to her like that, close enough to touch, that I realized for the first time how beautiful she was. At that moment I felt all the familiar symptoms that indicate not a myocardial infarction, but unfortunately that incurable emotional affliction against which no vaccine has yet been found."

"And what about her?"

"Well, I was sitting there on the bench next to her and all of a sudden she said: 'Why? Why all this?' And it dawned on me that she understood what I was thinking and feeling. It wasn't clear to me yet, but apparently it was to her. Because a moment later, she added: 'It isn't going to work. Forget it, Doctor.' 'What?' I asked. 'Is it really that bad?' she said. 'My God, why do people act like that? Haven't I had enough already?' Then she got up and walked away. I tried to get her out of the hospital. I tried to get them to stop the electrotherapy, but it was no use. Finally I went to see the Communist secretary. I thought he would throw me out as soon as I walked through the door, but he didn't. He listened to me a while, asked me some questions, then told me he would look into it. I was surprised. Two days later the director of the hospital called me in and yelled at me for about half an hour, saying if I was going to complain to the Party secretary, my up-and-coming career wouldn't last for long, he would see to that personally. Then, still screaming at the top of his lungs, he told me Klára had been released, so I could do whatever I wanted with her. When he finished screaming, he asked in an offhand way whether the secretary had asked any questions about pavilion seven. 'No, he didn't,' I replied. I was happy. The next day Klára was released, and a few weeks later I persuaded her to start again somewhere else, and found something for her in Bratislava through some people I knew. When the unit head returned from his research residency and I told him what had happened, he said: 'Do you know what's going on in Seven?' I started to tell him what I knew from the hospital's internal documents, but he cut me off. 'That's the official version.' 'Is there some other version?' I asked. 'No, just that one,' he said, and shrugged. As he was making his rounds the next day, he stopped me on the staircase, looked around to make sure that we were alone, and said: 'Don't ask anyone what's going on in Seven. There are terrible things going on there. They bring people in and . . . and . . . do terrible things to them. I think they were afraid that Klára was going to stir something up with all those quaint symptoms of hers, so they let her go. That's how come the director was asking you about Seven.' 'So what's going on over there?' I couldn't help myself. 'Don't ask anyone,' he repeated. 'It's terrible what's going on. None of us would want to end up in there. They've got the whole thing under wraps, the secretary, the director, all of them.' I continued to see Klára off and on for a few more years, but then I realized that seeing me kept reminding her of what had happened in the woods. So I banned myself from having any more contact with her. I had to. It was best for her."

"I thought it was true love."

"True? I never knew one truer. The fact that we never shared a room together or exchanged bodily fluids was insignificant."

"And then what? What happened after that?"

"Nothing. A few years later I married my wife. And we've been together ever since."

"And her? Klára?"

"I think I've had more cognac than advisable. But I'll find my way back to the hotel. I just might need to lean on you a little."

"But what about Klára?"

"I've already said more than I should have. They're about to close up and we need to pay."

20

LAST LETTER, REPORT ON AN EXHIBITION
AND A FEW BROKEN CHAIRS

Hi sis,

In your last letter you asked about my impression of Czechs and Bohemia, and if I would think about it before I came back to London. So I've thought about it and here's what I've come up with, but keep in mind this is "for your eyes only," or as they say here, *přísně tajné* ("strictly secret"). Being part Czech ourselves, I reckon we're closer to them than any other foreigners, though on the other hand it may also mean I'm a bit biased toward them. But the Czechs are strange creatures. The idea of "being Czech" basically boils down to being a small people with a common history and historical experience who, on top of that, speak Czech. For example, they're shockingly cold. Definitely colder than Brits. It's virtually unthinkable for anyone in Prague or Hodonín to crack a smile on the street. And the way salespeople and waiters act is really something to see. They're rude and crude, and sometimes even swear at customers!! I didn't believe it when I read it in the guidebooks, but it's worse than you can imagine. You go to buy something, potatoes, for instance, and you pretty much have to expect the salesman's going to yell at you. Can you imagine? Brilliant! Worth a trip, don't you think? Another thing that's even better is even though they act like that, they have this amazingly deep-seated idea that they're one of the most educated, most cultured nations in the world. You've really got to hand it to them! First of all, they don't even pay their teachers — that is, they pay them about as well as teachers in Albania. Secondly, they spend less money on culture per capita than Russia. As a result, about four times more tourists go to Budapest each year than Prague, even though Prague's much more beautiful. But the Czechs just assume they don't have to tell anyone, since everyone already knows. I guess you could say they consider themselves the navel of the world. They haven't realized yet that that's what leads to all the racism and discrimination against minorities, and it's only going to get worse. The bottom line is, facts and information hardly mean anything here. I'd almost say it's the country's hallmark. If the facts don't agree with them, then too bad for the facts. They also seem to consider themselves cynics, though that's probably due to the rapid transition from communism to capitalism. As Oscar Wilde said, a cynic is a man who knows the price of everything and the value of nothing. You know what I mean. Like everyone else in Eastern Europe (except the Poles), people here are very shy and reserved in public. They also tend to assume that anyone who's depressed must be a wise and deep thinker. I can go into it more some other time, but basically they believe that anyone who talks about death or the universe must be really important, even though in most cases the poor guy probably just needs a shrink. People here also have a strange attitude toward psychology and philosophy. If you can imagine, more students want to study psychology at university here than any other field. Amazing. Supposedly it's been that way for several generations now. I wonder, have you ever heard of any major school of thought in Czech psychology? It's kind of like, Name the three most famous Belgians. Anyway. It's probably because Czechs are the biggest atheists in Europe, and therefore the world. It has to come out somehow. It's also unbelievable with philosophy. Yesterday I read the obituary of a film director from Scandinavia in one of the local papers. It mentioned Plato twice and Aristotle once, but nothing about who the director studied with or who he influenced, none of that. Can you name three major Czech philosophers? Navel gazing again. Masaryk maybe? But what he did was more like what we call sociology today. As for the lack of religion, there's sort of a natural plebeianism here. I've noticed, for instance, that nobody dresses up at all for Christmas or birthdays. You would never see a woman put on a nice dress and a man put on a suit for a family dinner at home, there's no such thing here. Sometimes they walk around in tracksuits at home, even if they don't play any sports! At first I saw it as just a really appealing casualness, but then I realized that, apart from festive occasions like a holiday meal at home, nobody ever wears a suit or any nice clothes at all. There are all kinds of things they don't do that people just do normally everywhere else in Europe. But now for the positives: It's really great talking to people once you get to know them. They've got a terrific black sense of humor and a wonderful attitude toward old people. When an old person gets on the bus or the tram and there aren't any seats free, someone always gets up so they can sit down. It's totally normal. I've also noticed that family is really, really important, almost as much as in Italy, even if at first glance nobody would ever think to compare the two countries. People our age are pretty much the same as people under thirty in England or Holland or anywhere else. In private, they're incredibly warm and will tell you all about their lives, even the most intimate details, over a cup of coffee. In other words, something no Brit would ever do. In that sense they're extremely open. It isn't easy to get your bearings here, but every day I learn something new. Under the right conditions, the Czechs can be a bit like the Germans, but that's one thing you absolutely cannot say to them. It's like telling someone in England they need a bath. Even if you're right, they would probably take it as a tremendous insult. But they're much more like the Germans than any other neighboring country. The Czechs have a special relationship to them: it's like they admire them and are repelled by them at the same time. In that way I guess they're probably the same as the rest of Europe. They also have special manners here about what to say and what not to say so the other person doesn't "lose face." Dad used to do it sometimes, even though it didn't make any sense at home. Say somebody in the building leaves his junk out in the hallway and it's getting in everyone's way. I say: Why don't you tell him to move it? And they say, no, as long as they can squeeze by it's OK, even though it gets on their nerves and they obviously mind. Sometimes I feel like I'm in a samurai movie, set in medieval Japan. The etiquette's so complicated and plotted out to the last detail. But younger people don't bother with it too much anymore. So, in a nutshell, that's my answer to your questions before I leave Prague. The rest is from my work for the bank, which I wrote you about last time. I collected the documents, but my boss Karel was the one who put the whole thing together. Happy reading.

George

P. S. It doesn't make much sense to me, but write me what you think.

Signature of conformity: Head of Department Karel Verner
Documents prepared by: Jiří Novák
Status: Confidential

Re: Notes on the history of trade fairs in the Czech lands, which may suggest some solutions to problems caused by debt remaining from the Universal Czechoslovak Exhibition of 1991.

The first industrial exhibition ever was organized by the Society for the Promotion of Arts, Manufactures, and Commerce in 1756 and 1757 in London. Primacy of place in the rest of Europe after that belongs to Prague, where the first exhibition was held in 1791 on the premises of the present-day Karolinum, on the occasion of the coronation of Leopold II as king of Bohemia. This exhibition was not yet called an exhibition in the true sense of the word, but rather a *Collection of Goods*. It may be worth recalling that the Austrian composer W. A. Mozart was commissioned by the Estates of Bohemia to compose an opera for the occasion. He managed this feat in 18 days' time, and titled the work *La clemenza di Tito*.

The Prague Jubilee Exhibition of 1891, organized in honor of its modest predecessor of 1791, was an undertaking on an entirely different scale. The Jubilee Exhibition was divided into 27 groups with a total of 6,348 prizes awarded to exhibitors. From a financial standpoint, which is the primary area of concern to our bank, it is of significance to note that although there were

2,432,356 paying visitors in attendance for the 1891 Jubilee Exhibition, and the original budget was 1,132,000 guldens, the actual outlay was 1,606,522 guldens. As illustrated by these brief statistics, expenditures were thus nearly half a million guldens higher than originally planned, to be precise 474,522 guldens, a historic experience which the organizers of the Universal Czechoslovak Exhibition of 1991 would have done well to be aware of.

I further consider it necessary to clarify certain ideas that served to guide the exhibition. For example, the central palace was designated the *Czech Temple of Labor*. Statues representing *agriculture* and *industry* stood vigilant watch over the exhibition, of which the famous Czech poet J. Neruda wrote that it served "to stave off all manner of moral and material misery, to [assert] the equal right of all to the greatest achievements of the human spirit, to rally the various tribes of the human race toward an ardent campaign for the prosperity, welfare, and well-being of all humanity." As we see, this excerpt expresses in artistic language the passionate enthusiasm that inspired, albeit for other reasons, the Universal Exhibition in 1991. Compared with the exhibition of 1791, however, no artist comparable to W. A. Mozart was involved in 1991.

Thirty-one years after the (1891) Jubilee Exhibition, the Prague Sample Fairs were launched, in 1920, on the same site in Prague, Stromovka Park. The first Prague Sample Fair was opened on September 12, 1920, at nine o'clock A.M. in the Industrial Palace on the same site (Stromovka). The opening speech was delivered by then Mayor of Prague Dr. Baxa, followed by an address by Prime Minister Tusar. It should be noted that his government handed in its resignation the next day, and therefore it was his last official speech as premier. The Prague Sample Fairs were intended to allow wholesalers to purchase goods from manufacturers before the spring and fall business seasons. The aim was to ensure that goods did not remain unsold in warehouses, so fairs were held in March and September. The fairs served their purpose for many years, and were very successful commercially, up until the economic crisis. The largest attendance at a Prague Sample Fair was in fall 1929, with roughly 560,000 visitors. Several years prior to that, in 1925, however, construction began on the famous Trade Fair Palace, which now houses the National Gallery. The building was supposed to be completed in fall 1927. The original plan was for four buildings, one for 40 million crowns, two for 50 million, and one for 26 million. Altogether, then, it was planned that the cost of all four buildings would be around 166 million crowns, but when other costs were factored in, the total rose to 190 million crowns. Then, however, the costs for the first building more than doubled, so work on the other three buildings failed to proceed. The sales crisis following World War I resulted in financial crisis for the Prague Sample Fairs, which the organizers attempted to solve by sending a train to the Balkans, where they hoped to acquire new customers. The man they put in charge of the train, Mr. Kamil Vrána, was a relative of the trade fair director. From October to December the train traveled across Slovakia and Subcarparthian Rus, through territory at that time belonging to Romania and Bulgaria. Stops, coordinated with promotional events at the trade fair in Prague, were made in the following towns: Oradea, Cluj, Timişoara, Craiova, Bucharest, Rusçuk, Varna, Stara Zagora, Sofia, Galacs, and Iaşi. The campaign's success, however, was difficult to evaluate and there was no attempt to repeat it. During the economic crisis of the thirties, the directors of the fairs did what they could to promote them. In 1929, for example, the Prague Sample Fairs participated in the selection of Miss Czechoslovakia, while the Trade Fair Palace hosted concerts as well as an exhibition of tsarist treasures.

During World War II, in 1941, the buildings of the trade fair grounds were occupied by the Geheime Staatspolizei — Staatspolizeistelle Prag, aka the Gestapo. Later, the Zentralstelle für jüdische Auswanderung, or Central Office for Jewish Emigration, took over several pavilions. Prague's Jewish inhabitants were sent from this site to their death in the concentration camps. Only one document survives documenting this history, referring to a few dozen discarded chairs "broken by Jews." In 1942, Nazi Propaganda Minister Joseph Goebbels issued an order canceling all trade fairs on the territory of the German Reich. After the war, the Prague Sample Fairs were restored for a short period. The last one was opened on May 19, 1951, by then Prime Minister Antonín Zápotocký. Reportedly 122 special trains arrived in Prague with 208 shock workers. After that, the fairs were abolished.

The brief history we have assembled here demonstrates that there is but one conclusion we can draw from the past: the future, again, will be difficult. It seems the only thing we can be sure of is that it will be just as unpredictable as the past. If then our bank and our system of society are to exist in more or less approximately the same form as we know them today, it is in our opinion very likely that another "jubilee/universal" exhibition will take place in 2091. Certainly there will be societal pressures not to break with three hundred years of tradition. Therefore we would recommend transferring the debts from the 1991 exhibition to a special account established with an eye to a future exhibition in 2091. Given the national character of the three exhibitions in 1791, 1891, and 1991, with the latter linked to the fairgrounds in Stromovka, it can be more or less inferred that any potential future exhibition in 2091 will be held on the same site, i.e., in Stromovka. We therefore propose monitoring all activity in the area up until 2091, since based on our projections, political-commercial activity should increase proportionately as the date approaches. This will give our institution a head start on our competitors and, we hope, allow us to recover our bad debts, albeit with some delay. Our only wish is that the fairgrounds serve as a place of normal business activity and that no portion of the Czech population be deported anywhere in the future. This is unfortunately one of the potential outcomes in our detailed forecast. This potential negative scenario, however, falls outside the framework of analysis of our department and our financial house. In any case, were any negative signals to appear pointing in this direction, our banking house would most likely relocate to some other democratic country and give up on this region of Central Europe.

21

SUKTHANKAR

The last few messages concerning the three-day conference that Dr. Antonín Lukavský was helping to organize reached him too late. His colleague Dr. Kadlecová, who was co-organizing it with him, had insisted on sending him all the messages by electronic mail. Dr. Lukavský was proud of the fact that he had learned to use e-mail at an age when most people retired, but the day before yesterday, when the computer network administrator had begun explaining to him in intricate detail why his computer was working great again, but great in a slightly different way, he got fed up with the whole thing and as a result he didn't read her message about their colleague from England until now, on the way to the airport, where he was going to pick him up. His name threw Antonín for a loop. Unconsciously he had been expecting an English name, but the name under Basic Information said "Dr. V. S. Sukthankar." That didn't strike him as even slightly English. Indian maybe? He read on. Under Position it said "Consultant." That's something like chief physician here, Antonín translated in his head. Under Age it said "35." Pretty young for a chief physician, Antonín thought. You wouldn't see that here. Nobody under forty would ever be approved, although on the other hand times were changing, even if slowly. Dr. Lukavský got off the bus at the airport and entered the arrivals hall, where he sat down on a bench and quickly wrote in capital letters on the other side of the paper he had used to print the e-mail: DR. SUKTHANKAR. Then, paper in hand, he went and joined the usual cluster of people waiting for the passengers to exit the plane. A few minutes later, the passengers from the London flight began streaming by. He counted around thirty, and not one of them responded to his sign. It must have been only half full, Antonín concluded, looking around. Not only weren't there many passengers, so he couldn't have overlooked him, but he didn't see anyone who looked even remotely Indian. Just what I needed, Antonín thought. Here I am drowning in work and he misses the plane. Now I'll have to drag myself out here again later. Lucky for me I'm retired and only work quarter-time. I'll just take next week off and make up for all the hours of sleep I lost. Still. Antonín wasn't pleased. He walked around the arrivals hall a little while longer, then headed back outside. He waited for the next bus and rode back to his office. He had just brewed a cup of his favorite linden tea when the telephone rang. It was Dr. Kadlecová on the other end, telling him Dr. Sukthankar had just called from the airport. He'd had some problems with customs and was just leaving now for the pensione they had booked for him. The news didn't improve Antonín's mood, but he agreed to pick Dr. Sukthankar up at the pensione at five P.M.

A few minutes after five, Antonín entered a narrow entryway with a reception desk on one side and a few high-backed armchairs on the other. An unobtrusive man lifted himself from one of them and introduced himself in English as Dr. Sukthankar. Antonín had been expecting to have problems with his English, so he was pleased to discover that he understood every word. Dr. Sukthankar's pronunciation was textbook English. In fact the only thing conspicuous about him was his thick blue-black hair. He expressed the usual request of every foreigner to take a walk around Prague, and since that was exactly what Antonín had expected, he readily took on the role of guide. By the time they reached the Old Town, he had learned that Dr. Sukthankar had been detained at the airport, subjected to a thorough search, had his suitcase and ID taken away, and had been locked in a room with no windows for nearly half an hour. Before Antonín could compose the questions he wanted to ask in comprehensible English, Dr. Sukthankar beat him to the punch:

"What is *seekin?*"

"*Co to je síkn?*" Antonín translated the question for himself. "I don't know," he said in English. He thought a moment, then said, "There's no such word in our language."

"Aaah," said Dr. Sukthankar. "I obviously must have misunderstood. It was some word the policemen kept saying to each other."

"Would you mind repeating it?" asked Antonín.

The two men stopped walking and Dr. Sukthankar very diligently tried to reproduce the sounds of this unfamiliar language: "*Sikkin. Seekin. Skahn.*" Antonín listened, shaking his head. "*Sink. Skahn. Skaahn.*"

Suddenly it came to him. "Do you think maybe *tsikahn*?"

"Oh, yes," said Dr. Sukthankar. "That's it!"

"Now I understand," Antonín said.

"If it's something very rude, please don't tell me," Dr. Sukthankar said, seeing the look of hesitation on Antonín's face.

"*Cikán* means 'Roma' in Czech," Antonín said after a moment.

"So that's why I was detained?" said Dr. Sukthankar. "Because I look like a Roma?"

"It seems that was the reason."

"I've read a little about your country in the papers, but I haven't paid too much attention. I trust it isn't against the law to be a Roma here?" Dr. Sukthankar said with a laugh.

"I'm going to file a complaint," Antonín said. "You were officially invited to attend our scientific conference." Sukthankar noticed his grizzled old colleague was turning red in the face.

"Oh no," he said quickly, "don't do that. I'm just here on a little trip because I had a patient from here a few years ago, and I'd like to take a look round Hungary and Austria as well. I'm used to it. It's just bureaucratic harassment."

There was an awkward silence, broken only by a passing tram.

"Would you mind showing me how to get to Wenceslas Square? I've heard so much about it," said Dr. Sukthankar after a while. They both realized he was only saying it to break the awkward silence, which had rapidly expanded to take on a variety of ornate and unanticipated meanings.

"Of course, I can take you," Antonín said. "After that, we can sit down somewhere for a while, have a cup of coffee, and I'll tell you about our conference, which starts tomorrow."

"That would be very kind of you," Dr. Sukthankar said.

Once his guest had taken a look around the square, Antonín found a café in one of the side streets, and they sat down and finally had a chance for real conversation. Dr. Sukthankar was a psychiatrist as well as a psychologist, and ran a psychiatric unit in a hospital in northwest London. The purpose of his trip was tourism. He declared this fact several times, with obvious pleasure. "All year long I plunge into the depths of my patients' souls, but on holidays I always make time to relax, to be totally superficial and commit myself to a wholly consumerist view of the world."

Antonín couldn't tell if his colleague was being ironic or not, since he didn't feel as at home in English, so just to be on the safe side, instead of laughing he asked: "So by the way, what should I call you? I have the feeling I'm not quite pronouncing your name correctly."

"Just call me Vish," Dr. Sukthankar said. "That's short for Vishnu."

"Vishnu, Vishnu, Vishnu," Antonín repeated. "That's the name of a god, isn't it?"

"Yes," said Dr. Sukthankar. "My parents are Hindu and so am I." He noticed that Antonín was paying close attention, so he went on. "In our religion, Vishnu is the god who created the universe in three steps."

"It's a completely different tradition than in Europe," Antonín said. "Completely different. Here in Europe, we give people names of saints, not gods."

"I was born in England, just outside London in the county of Surrey, and went to Catholic school as a child," said Dr. Sukthankar. "I'm British and European with Indian ancestry."

"Oh, of course, of course," Antonín said. The conversation was turning in a direction he wasn't sure he wanted to go.

"So what was it that actually brought you here to see us, then?" Antonín asked.

"A few years ago I had a patient from the Czech Republic," Dr. Sukthankar said. "He had been living in England a long time, he wasn't allowed to go back, and he missed Prague terribly. He always said it was the most beautiful city in the world, so I decided I needed to come have a look."

"So how do you like it so far?" Antonín said.

"Beautiful. Truly beautiful," Dr. Sukthankar said. "So beautiful there are moments when it reminds me of places in India."

"Is that right?" Antonín said, using the most reserved tone of voice he could muster.

Dr. Sukthankar spent one full day at the conference and the rest of his four-day visit in Prague playing the perfect tourist. He saw Prague Castle, Charles Bridge, Kampa Park, Old Town Square, sampled the beer, took in a few bookstores, and spent half a day in the University Library. On the eve of his departure to Vienna, Dr. Lukavský invited him out to dinner. As long as he had even a smidgen of energy left, he knew he had to keep up his foreign contacts at all costs. He asked again how Dr. Sukthankar had enjoyed his short stay.

"You know," his English colleague replied, "that Czechoslovak patient of mine I told you about had a recurring dream: He dreamed he went down to the underworld and when he came to the gates he saw a giant man riding a giant bull. The man came to a sudden stop and the bull reared up, but the man kept control of him and said to my patient, 'Eat these leftovers from my bull. Eat them, just as your father once did.' My patient, we'll call him Max, hesitated a moment, but then did as the giant asked. He passed through the gates into the underworld and came to a large square, like one of the squares in Prague, he said, with ordinary people walking up and down the sidewalks. He stopped a moment to get his bearings and suddenly saw a homeless man running toward him. The strange thing was, one second he was invisible, the next he was not. He ran into Max at one of the moments when he was invisible, and before Max could figure out what had happened he was gone. Then he discovered that the strange homeless man had taken his letter of safe conduct, stating his name and the purpose of his journey to the underworld, which meant he might not be able to get back. Nervous now, Max continued to make his way through the underworld, wandering off course and getting lost several times. He didn't know which way to turn. After walking down several streets he found himself in a large garden on a tract behind a palace. There were two women there weaving fabric on a loom. One with black thread, the other with white. Nearby he saw a huge wheel being turned by four girls. The wheel had three hundred and sixty-five spokes and there was a man standing spread-legged in the middle who looked like the man on the bull Max had seen in front of the gates. Only this man was a little younger and smiled at Max. Finally Max found a way leading out of the city, and once he was outside the walls he saw a small lake with water lilies on it. He plucked one of them, and when he finally reached home he asked his father about what he had seen, and his father said: 'Those two women were weaving the present, which will become the history of the future. The man in the middle is the Guardian of Truth and Lies, who sees to it that they remain separate. The wheel is obviously a representation of the year with its three hundred and sixty-five days, and the four girls are the four seasons. The leftovers from the giant bull that you ate were the elixir of immortality, which is what saved your life in the underworld after the stepbrother of the Guardian of Truth and Lies, whose name is the Defender of Myth and Illusion, stole your letter of safe conduct.' And that's it," Dr. Sukthankar concluded.

Antonín squirmed in his seat a moment or two, then said: "Obviously, if we analyze the dream using Jung with a slight Adlerian modification, then, . . ." He paused, noticing Dr. Sukthankar gently shaking his head.

"I'm afraid that's not it. In fact my patient's dream was nearly identical to a story from the Mahabharata. An epic poem, you might call it sort of an Indian *Odyssey*, though about fifteen times longer. I discovered the story yesterday in a catalogue on a computer at one of the libraries recommended to me by your colleague Dr. Kadlecová. The librarian was even kind enough to translate a portion of it into English for me. So that's most likely where my patient got it from. A book. And then years later, it turned up in a dream."

"So no such thing as mystery then?"

"None."

"I believe that's what they call globalization, no?" Antonín said.

"I suppose," said Sukthankar.

"Oh, you know what? You'll definitely know the answer to this. Why is the lotus flower so important in India?"

Dr. Sukthankar thought a moment, then said: "I think because it symbolizes purity and beauty. It grows out of mud, but no mud ever sticks to it."

"All right then," said Antonín. "So, how have you liked it here?"

"Beautiful city," said Sukthankar. "Gorgeous, in fact. And those statues on the bridge . . . the Charles Bridge, it's called?"

"Yes," said Antonín, "Charles, although most of the statues, maybe all of them, are of saints, you know. Christian saints. So what do you think about Christianity, anyway?"

"I don't know," said Sukthankar. "I may have told you, but I went to Catholic school as a child."

"Right, so what do you think? I mean, as someone who belongs to two cultures."

"I don't have any opinion on that," Sukthankar said. "Although the founder of modern India, Gandhi, when asked what he thought of Christianity, said he thought it would be a good idea."

"I see," said Antonín. "Well, as I said, our history isn't exactly rosy or optimistic. It's got all sorts of shadows and cobwebs."

"That doesn't surprise me," said Sukthankar. "A city this beautiful couldn't have risen up out of nothing."

"Like your lotus flower," Antonín said in amusement.

"Yes, like the lotus," Dr. Sukthankar said with a smile. "My grandfather in India used to end ceremonies by saying, 'The wheel of being rolls through this world, without beginning and without end. It rolls through this world, causing creation and extinction. The wheel of being rolls and rolls on, without beginning and without end.'"

"Now that's globalization," said Antonín.

"In a sense," said the doctor. "In a sense."

22

A RUN THROUGH THE WOODS

A thought emerges in Josef's mind as he runs: the world is divided in two. Top and bottom. Left and right. Moving and still. The part of the world that's old, as old as the world itself, and the younger part, with blood, veins and arteries, brains. The world is split from top to bottom into worlds of green and red. The world of insects and animals, the bloody human world, and then the green world, roots sunken firmly in the ground. The world of grasses, trees, herbs, the world of saps, resins, and juices . . . and all of it the world of landscapes that preceded the world of unreliable insect and human muscles pumping blood—hearts.

But whichever way Josef turned, left or right, this world was out of order. Either the world itself had been castrated, or the mirror of deeds had been turned around to the point that the meaning of natural was in question. It couldn't be, it was impossible, Josef reflected. It was absolutely to the core, to the bone impossible for nature, here, somewhere between the forty-ninth and fiftieth parallels north of the equator and the thirteenth and fourteenth meridians east of the Greenwich Observatory, to be so heterogeneous that the world truly didn't make the slightest sense at all anymore. How could the worlds of sap and blood be so interstitched, interlaced, implanted into each other that two giraffes, one rhinoceros, and three spiny anteaters were roaming around free at this latitude and longitude? It couldn't be. Why, just a few months ago the whole place had been covered in snow. What was going on with the world? Was it out of joint, or had it just sprained an ankle that could be set back at least more or less in place with the help of some vinegar and splints? Josef turned, rotated, made a move that resulted in his left foot crashing down on a branch that splintered more out of dryness than because of his weight. He sprang up again, startled by clouds of dust and spores, sparkling pridefully in the afternoon sun as they floated up to the level of his anxious eyes from the lowlands of semiwithered moss. His body made nearly a complete clockwise pirouette, swaying as he looked back in the direction he had come from. One of the giraffes was staring right at him. He'd never realized before how big and beautiful the eyes were on an average-height giraffe, and shouting, "It can't be!" and "Fifty degrees north of the equator!" and "In the Czech lands? The Czech lands!" and "My God, in the Czech lands!" he abruptly shot off again in the opposite direction from the one the two giraffes and three spiny anteaters had come from. The rhino was either still far behind him or had wandered off in a different direction.

It was a Wednesday morning, still hot. The year: 1945. The place: somewhere southeast of Plzeň.

Josef ran, fleeing, stumbling. Leaping over stumps without even trying to dodge the branches. He was a man in flight. But his strength hadn't abandoned him. He didn't know how long it would hold out, and he was afraid to look back. Animals, wild animals, in the middle of Bohemia. He would have smiled if he'd had the energy: southeast of Plzeň wasn't the middle of Bohemia. The sweat poured off of him, he knew he couldn't keep running for long. The forest floor was starting to slope slightly downward; he had already fallen several times, somersaulting downhill, but he suddenly stopped to listen. First he heard the stream, then saw it. Sprinting over, he knelt down and splashed water on his face. Then he plunged his whole head in and drank. Every so often he lifted his head to take another look around, but he kept on drinking. Once he had drunk his fill, he stood up and listened carefully, scanning the area, but there was no sign of the animals. If they were chasing him, or even if they just happened to be coming his way, they would be here in a couple of minutes. He waited to see whether they appeared at the top of the slope. He was being careful now not to step on anything. Nothing but silence, sunlight falling down between the trees, and stirred-up dust. All of a sudden he realized he had been holding his breath the whole time. He leaned against a tree and took a deep breath. Arched his back and raised his head to look into the treetops. For a moment he didn't realize what he was seeing, what he was looking at. By the time he did he was back on the run. A tiny little monkey with disproportionately large eyes and long fingers stared back at him from the tree. I've never seen such a thing, Josef thought. Once again he was a man in flight.

After a while running, he began to detect the slightest trace of a path. He sensed it more with his legs than with his relentlessly darting eyes. There were fewer and fewer sticks, dry pine needles, and broken branches. His legs were getting more agile despite the trembles of fatigue running through them. Now his head, too, began to sense the gentleness of a trail unfolding before him. He huddled close to the ground. Pressed his head into the dust of needles and rusty bark. Scanned for shapes with his frightened eyes. Trying to bring them into focus and burn them into his brain. Gradually, a path appeared. His eye caught it as it measured the angles, drawing the scale and discerning the shapes. A small, nearly invisible trail tracing a route through the hot dust. The only thing that had made seeing it possible, though, was the fact that his head was pressed firmly against the needles, the temporal bone of his skull providing a solid base for his eye, allowing the ants it crushed to death to deliver one final bite to the large animal that went by a human name. Josef stood up. His body, driven like a pointer dog by fatigue, had lost its coordination. He shot off like a spring energized by joy. Joy! Joy! With a strength not so long ago forgotten and scared to death. He leaped up somewhat higher than necessary, his legs starting to run before they touched the ground. Taking hold while he was still in the air. Digging in now as his body landed, swaying on impact, recalibrating. Now fully synchronized, the camshaft took off in the direction of the path. After a few more minutes, the path became visible to the naked eye. After a few more breaths, the end of the forest was also in view. After a few more blinks of the eye, a dirt road spread out before him. Josef set out along it. Running at first, till fatigue declared itself, then downshifting to a trot. Next, alternating between a walk and a trot, scanning the surroundings, then finally just walking as fast as he could. As fast as his strength would permit, though it had left him a long time ago. He went on like that for at least an hour. It was impossible to say how long. Amid the exhaustion, and with weakness in reach, even Josef couldn't tell whether time was passing faster or slower. He tried to estimate how much distance he had covered. To no avail. He realized with some unease that it couldn't have been more than an hour since his encounter with the two giraffes, the rhino, and the anteaters. And then, as was bound to happen sooner or later, he saw the half-demolished building. A farmstead. Josef reckoned there had to be a village close by, but couldn't see it. The road ran alongside the building and continued on. It suddenly struck him how quiet it was. He wasn't in the woods anymore, but out in the open. Not a soul around, with the forest back in the distance behind him, an occasional gust of wind rustling the pines. He entered the farmyard, or what was left of it. An elongated structure. Stables on one side, barn on the other, well right nearby. The last side of the rectangle was formed by the sticks of what had once been a fence. Probably whitewashed with lime. No sound of animals. He walked into the yard. He had an urge to call out. Actually, he just had an urge to let someone know he was there. But he didn't even want that, actually. He just had the urge to wash up, have something to drink, think about what had happened to him, and also, pee in peace. He walked a few times across the farmyard, back and forth. Peeked into the barn and the stable. Listened, didn't hear any people or animals, nothing. He leaned against the well and realized how hard he was breathing, no, not breathing, puffing like a freight train. He looked into the well, took the bucket and threw it down. Noticed the rope on the bucket had snapped and been retied. But just then someone or something grabbed him by the legs, and before he knew what was happening, he was flying down headfirst. Without realizing it he screamed. Screamed with whatever air was still left in his lungs in spite of the shock. Screamed, roared, shrieked, squawked, squealed. He flew a long time, hundreds of thousands of years, until his whole body jerked to a stop and he was left hanging. In total darkness. His left foot was tangled in the rope from the bucket.

His hands were scraped bloody from trying to grab the walls of the well. A twitch ran through his body as he hung, head down. Again and again he tried to haul himself up with his two bloodied hands, and once he'd roared the last remains of air from his lungs, he gasped for breath and tried to look up toward the light. He did, and up above, where just a few breaths in and out ago the cerulean canvas of the sun-bewitched sky had stretched, there was now . . . space. The small black circle of the mouth of the well filled with stars. Where there should have been sky-blue heaven, now there was a night sky. As his muddled brain ceaselessly arranged and rearranged the stars into constellations, he wondered which spectrum of visible light the well was screening out and just how deep he actually was. Even the skin from his hands he had left behind on the rocks lining the well was starting to hurt now. He had just about had enough.

He wondered what he had done to deserve this, until it dawned on him that merit had nothing to do with the situation he was in. His left leg was falling asleep and the blood was rolling in and out of his head like surf. His heart was pounding so hard he thought the sound must be carrying up to the mouth of the well. It felt as if his veins were going to burst they were stretched so tight, and the blood was going to start squirting out of his body, filling the well and drowning him. He would choke to death, croak, perish in his own blood. No, easy now. Easy. Whoever or whatever it was, he said to himself, he had to get himself out of there. Slowly he attempted to lift the upper part of his torso. It was hard going. He had a feeling there was someone or something up there watching, so he tried to be quiet. Quiet as a mouse, so whatever it was up there would forget about him and not come and drown him. He kept trying to pull himself up again, then falling down again, hanging. And again. Slowly. Another try. No go. Again. Slowly. One more time. Almost. No. Again. And . . . quiet. Grab hold. Try again. One more time . . . Got it. No, yes. Slowly, don't breathe. Just a little more. A little bit. A little bit more. Careful. Careful. Almost there. A little more. Made it. I made it. Yes, yes, yes . . . I'm there. Got it, holding on. Josef slowly pulled himself up. First he grabbed hold with the middle finger of his left hand. Pulled himself up. Grabbed hold of the rope and swung. Virgin Mary Mother of God and the Seven Mercies, no! He wanted to scream, but kept quiet. He waited for the rope to stop swinging, then grabbed hold with the other hand. Little by little he pulled himself up. Didn't even breathe. Tried not to breathe. Tried not to be. The rope started to sway again. No! He wanted to yell, but didn't dare. Now he had his head up to the level of his ankles, he could prop himself up with his hands. He could feel the blood pulsing in his hands and his rope-choked leg. He swallowed hard, breathing softly. It worked. His leg was back where it belonged. Feet below, head above. Josef held the rope a while, thinking, not in words, but in screams inside the walls of his skull: It wants to kill me! It wants to kill me! Something wants to kill me. Something or someone. It threw me down the well. Careful now. It wants to kill me. Gotta get up. Caaareful, Josef, caaareful. He was climbing higher and higher, but just to make sure, he let go of the rope and wedged himself in between the walls. Feet and hands. Slowly, yes, very slowly, clawing his way up. At first all he could see was stars in the black circle of the well's mouth. But the higher he climbed, the brighter the sky became. Until at last the stars melted away and the blackness dissolved into a desolate powder-blue sky. He was halfway up the well when suddenly it went black again. He looked up and saw an outline. Nothing more than an outline. Nothing more, nothing less. Then he heard a roar roaring at him: "Not enough for you, you bastard? Wanna crawl outta there, huh? You piece of shit, you just wait!" "Jesus Christ," Josef said out loud now. "They really want to kill me," and he began clawing and scraping his way up even harder. Before it went black again, he could feel pebbles dropping into his hair. He tried to squeeze as close as he could to the wall as a boulder went flying past. "Nooooo!" shouted Josef. "Please, nooo. I didn't do anything to you, leave me alone. Let me climb out. I didn't do anything. Please just let me climb out!" Josef screamed. Now he could clearly make out the outlines of a human shadow. The shadow stopped moving and a voice called down, "Who the hell are you?" "I can explain everything," Josef shouted. "I didn't do anything, I've done nothing!" After a while the voice called down again, "Say thrushes." Josef didn't understand, but he shouted up anyway, "Thrushes!"

"No, no," the voice said. "Say three thousand three hundred thirty-three thrushes thrashing and so on . . . If you know the rest, then say it, so I know you aren't German."

"Three thousand three hundred and thirty-three thrushes thrashing through three thousand three hundred and thirty-three thorny thickets."

"And what're thrushes?" said the voice from above.

"What are thrushes?" said Josef. "They're little birds that eat worms and insects, and they're known for their melodic songs."

"All right then. All right," said the voice from above. "You can come up, but slow. Nice and slow, got it?" After a moment's hesitation the voice added, "You can climb up that rope." Josef didn't trust him, so he just gripped the rope while he edged his way up with his legs spread against the walls of the shaft.

"Now," said the voice from above, "one more time, tell me three hundred and thirty-three."

"Yes, sir!" Josef bellowed. "Three thousand three hundred and thirty-three thrushes thrashing through three thousand three hundred and thirty-three thorny thickets!" Over and over and over until he reached the top of the shaft. As the lip of the well came within reach, Josef's heart was pumping all his blood into his ears. He couldn't hear anything but his own boiling blood. Nothing but blood. He tried to be alert and on guard, but by that point it was beyond him. He stuck out his head and rolled his body over the lip of the well. He dropped on the ground and took a quick look around. A tall old man walked slowly toward him, holding a double-barreled rifle aimed at Josef's stomach. He had gray hair and glasses, and a tiny little monkey sitting on his shoulder, like the one Josef had seen in the forest that set off his panic attack. The monkey had great big red childlike eyes, and its fingers were unbelievably long. It licked the index finger on one hand while with the other it gripped the old man's neck. It looked at Josef. Josef looked at the rifle, then at the monkey. The old man held the gun and looked at Josef.

"So you're Czech," the old man said.

"'Course I am, what else would I be?" said Josef. The old man studied him warily. The monkey went on licking its finger.

"I've seen that before!" Josef blurted.

"What?" the old man asked.

"That," Josef said, pointing to the monkey. "I saw that monkey."

"It's an ape, not a monkey," the old man said. "What are you doin' here?"

"I was mushroom hunting," Josef said.

"What would you be doin' that for?" the old man asked. "There's a war on and it's May!"

"Well, not really, but I was walking around. Do you want to kill me?"

"No," replied the old man.

"Then why did you throw me down the well?"

"I thought you were one of them."

"Who?" Josef said.

"You know, them," said the old man.

"I have no idea who you're talking about," said Josef.

"You know, them," said the old man. "Those runaway soldiers wanderin' around, tryin' to get to the Americans. Had some problems with 'em in the next village over."

"But I'm Czech, sir."

"Well, all right, I know that now," the old man said.

"So why do you want to kill me?" Josef shouted.

"I don't want to kill you."

"Then why are you pointing that rifle at me?" Josef shouted again.

"Don't worry about it. Doesn't shoot anyway," the old man said, "and quit shoutin' and come inside." As he turned around and walked toward the building with his rifle, the monkey on his shoulder turned and stared back at Josef with its enormous eyes.

"C'mon in!" the old man shouted to Josef.

"I'll be right there, thank you," said Josef. He quickly turned and dashed toward the fence, unbuttoning his fly as he ran. He let loose before he even came to a stop. Hearing the sound of Josef urinating, the old man stopped on the steps, turned, and looked at him. The monkey on his shoulder also turned to look. The old man shook his head in disgust, waited for Josef to button his fly and come into the house, gestured to a chair, and Josef sat down.

"Forgive me, boy," the old man said. "I thought you were one of those soldiers, you know." Josef shook his head. "There was shootin' in the woods yesterday and day before." Josef shook his head again. "We was watchin' you, ever since you came runnin' out of the woods. Me and him," the old man said, nodding to the monkey. "He don't miss a thing," he said. "As soon as something starts to happen, he gets nervous."

"How did he get here?" Josef said, swallowing several times. "I mean it's impossible. I saw giraffes in the woods—two giraffes, a rhinoceros, and three spiny anteaters. We aren't in Africa."

The old man cracked a smile. "So that's why you were all green and runnin' like that. That's how come," the old man gave a laugh.

"And that thing there was looking at me in the woods," Josef pointed to the monkey.

"Now hold on there, boy. That ain't no thing. That's Hank."

"Hank?" said Josef. "Yep, Hank," the old man said. "And if you saw more than one of 'em out in the forest, that was his lady."

"His lady?" Josef said. "But how did they get here? How did that happen?"

"You're not from around here, are you?" the old man asked.

"No, but how did they get here?" Josef said.

"Cause if you was from around here, you'd know the Count had a collection of animals up at the castle. Like his own private zoo."

"Zoo?" Josef said. "That's right, zoo," the old man repeated. "When he was young, he went all over the world studyin' animals, and every year he'd have a few of 'em brought back home."

"So but how did they end up in the woods?" Josef asked.

"Beats me. But the folks in the next village over say the Count must be dead, since he never would have let 'em go. The whole war he always made sure they got fed somehow. Said a man can take care of himself, but not a giraffe in the Czech lands."

"So what all did he have? What kind of animals?"

"Well, one time he had a lion, but he passed away before the war," the old man said.

Josef hemmed and hawed a moment. "So how am I going to get back to my family? My mother and father and Květa must be out of their minds with fear, but I'm not going back through those woods."

"Well then, I s'pose you'll have to stay here," the old man said. "Till it blows over. You're just lucky you landed on giraffes and rhinos. Least they don't carry guns." The man got up and put a tin can on the stove. When the water started to boil, he poured it over some chicory, and handed the mug to Josef. Josef took a sip.

"Should I go?" Josef asked after a while.

"Well, no one's askin' you to stay. On the other hand, there's not much place to go. We were scared, too," the old man said. "Me and Hank."

Josef didn't know how to answer, so he just grunted and nodded. As he finished his chicory coffee, he realized it was the best he'd had all war, since 1939. He was about to thank the old man but got distracted by the monkey sitting on the table watching him. It took a few steps toward him, flared its nostrils, and snorted in and out, sniffing him from a distance.

"Go on, shoo," Josef growled.

The old man looked in the monkey's direction. "You don't smell too good to him either, you know." He paused, then added, "S'pose I oughta get you some bandages, make sure that don't get infected."

"Mm," Josef said. The old man went into the next room. There was the sound of tearing, then he came back holding a soft cloth with a large wet spot that smelled sweetly of alcohol. He nodded to Josef and Josef laid his hands on the table. He winced as the old man began to clean the abrasions, but the smell was comforting.

"Is that silk?" he asked as little by little the cloth took on the color of his drying blood. The old man straightened up and gave Josef a look.

"Clean it yourself. I got other things I have to do. Clean it and get the hell out. No one invited you here!" He hissed out the corner of his mouth at the monkey, who climbed up on his shoulder, then took his rifle and went into the next room.

When Josef was done cleaning his wounds, he folded up the silk cloth, now brown with the oxidizing blood, and laid it on the table. He sat a moment, waiting. Then he got up and knocked on the door to the room the old man had disappeared into. The door opened and the old man came out holding his rifle.

"Well," Josef said. "I guess I'll be going."

"All righty," the old man replied. "I'll show you the way." They walked out the door. "If you don't want to go back through the woods, just take this road here till you come to the village, then from there there's a road into town."

"Thank you," Josef said.

"So what's your name, anyway?" asked the old man.

"Josef, and you?"

"Mine don't matter, old man like me." He took a deep breath and went on: "If you want the train, though I doubt it's runnin', you'll have to go to the next village. It's a bit of a hike, but they got a telephone and a telegraph, so you can let your family know."

"Thank you," said Josef, eyeing the rifle the old man kept clenched in his hand the whole time.

"Not at all, Josef. Not at all."

"Well, I'll be going then," said Josef.

"All right, then go," said the old man.

Josef took to the road heading away from the woods, as the old man had described, walking faster and faster, till he was moving at a light trot. He turned around to look back a few times and saw the old man standing at the fence, leaning on it with one arm while in the other he held the rifle. A few minutes later, he heard a shot ring out behind him. His heart stopped and he wheeled around. In the distance he saw the silhouette of the old man, aiming his rifle into the low-hanging clouds, and sensed more than saw the faint haze of smoke rising out of the barrel. Josef didn't bother to see what came next, breaking into a run. Some time later he came to the village. A dusty road and flowers in the windows. He saw the fork in the road before he reached the square. At the first building he knocked on the door.

"*Dobrý den*," he said as it opened. "Good day."

"*Grüß Gott*," said the woman, who looked to be about fifty, lifting her eyes from her sewing. Josef switched to German, explaining that he needed to get to a telegraph or telephone. The woman took him to her neighbors next door. After a brief conversation, they told him which road to take and said, as far as they could tell, most of the German soldiers in the area had surrendered to the Americans. Before he left, Josef decided to ask about the old man. He left out the part about him throwing him down the well.

"Oh, that's old Mann," they said. "He used to work in the zoo. Took care of the animals. Supposedly even took some of them home."

For a few years after that still, people reported hearing strange sounds and voices in the woods. The war came to an end, and without telling the animals the Great Powers drew an imaginary dividing line through the woods. Liberated against their will by U.S. shrapnel and a panicked zookeeper, the animals were now in the Soviet sphere of influence. A few months after the war, there was still talk of snakes as thick around as a grown man's thigh, of exotic monkeys, large and small, leaping from branch to branch, of giraffes and rhinoceroses, but no one knew exactly what was true and what was fantasy. People also said some starving Russian soldiers devised a plan to hunt them down, but when their commanding officer found out, he turned purple with rage, called the unit to attention, and started screaming at them that no matter how great a victory the Red Army had achieved under the command of Josef Vissarionovich Stalin, it didn't give anyone carte blanche for unlimited carousing, and he urged them to remember that the military penal code was still in force. Apparently, the Russian officer's show of outrage on that improvised roll call square southeast of Plzeň gave the animals the gift of another few months, perhaps even years, of life. The fact remains, however, that after several harsh winters the gripping descriptions of wondrous creatures ceased to occur. There was peace, at long last. Peace and quiet.

When Josef got to the station, it was clear the trains weren't running. Nobody knew when they would be, and as the dispatcher pointed out, even if they were running, it wouldn't be wise to take them, since there was an army using them now, and the army using them now probably wouldn't be using them for long. The telegraph and telephone weren't working. He recommended to Josef that he stay in the village. Then Josef got an idea. He would go back through the woods. He had been sorting things out in his head along the way, and as he spoke to the dispatcher he realized he was actually glad the trains weren't running, the wires weren't transmitting, and he had to stay where he was. He didn't know why at first. But then he realized he was glad because he didn't feel any fear anymore, he was no longer terrified. His blood wasn't pounding through his veins like a hunted animal. The moment the dispatcher had said his fill, he got the idea to go back. He bought some food in the village, ate, and headed back the same way he had come, only now he avoided the places where he might be seen by any of the people he had spoken to before. He felt no need to talk to them and didn't know how he would be able to explain in his broken German why now he wanted to go back through the forest he had fled from just a few hours earlier. So he went back. He stayed off the roads, since there was still a risk he might run into soldiers, but he tried to stay in sight of them, as he had before. He skirted the village, forded the stream, and had to backtrack several times because he got confused, but eventually he figured out the right direction, and found the path he had taken. He knew the return trip wouldn't take as long. As he came in view of the lone farmstead where he had met the old man, he discreetly took a wide arc around it, listening closely. Not a sound. As he walked past, he stopped to look several times. But there was no sign of the old man and even when the wind let up he didn't hear a thing. Finally Josef came to the woods. He felt safe here. Now that he knew where the animals had come from, the only thing that upset him was he couldn't remember if spiny anteaters were African or Australian. Walking through the woods, he had to backtrack several times, but after a while he found the path he had run down before. He slowed down, looking around him. Every now and then he would stop, look, and listen, soaking up the smells and sounds. Now he longed to see the animals that had terrified him before, to balance out the fear and dread with his new-found excitement. The animals, however, were nowhere to be seen. Except for the wind and his footsteps, except for the rustling leaves and the thumping of his heart, the woods were silent. Josef decided to change his approach. He thought deep and hard, trying to free himself of emotion. The question is, he said to himself, where are they? Meanwhile he realized he knew next to nothing about the animals. I don't even know what they eat. I don't know what they eat at home, in their own environment, never mind here in the for them exotic territory southeast of Plzeň. I wonder what they think about being here? After a while he realized he wasn't going to figure out where the animals were hiding, but what irked him the most was not knowing what they ate. Then he got thirsty. He vaguely remembered where he had been when he came across the stream on his first trip through the forest. So he rotated the image in his memory 3.142 radians, which is the same as one hundred and eighty degrees, and found his way there unerringly within a few minutes. He rinsed off his face, had a drink, and suddenly realized that every animal, wherever it's from, has to drink eventually. They get thirsty just like me, he thought. I can't believe I didn't think of that before. He set out along the streambed and, little by little, as he got closer to the city, the stream changed into a brook. He followed the brook all the way to a factory at the start of the suburbs, but didn't see a single animal apart from two red squirrels. The city was in the midst of an uproarious celebration. An advance unit of the U.S. Army had arrived in Plzeň. All the chewing gum had been handed out, and no one, except for his fiancée, Květa, had even noticed Josef was missing. He also found out that several smaller German units had surrendered after a violent shootout in the woods outside of town. At first he didn't think anything of it, but later he realized his father, who came to spend his summers here and knew almost everyone in town, was talking about the same woods Josef had passed through twice that day. He also heard that during the shoot-out the private zoo near the castle had been peppered with bullets and some of the animals had probably been caught in the crossfire between the advancing Americans, the retreating Germans, and the Russians closing in on them. He kept the whole adventure to himself for quite some time, but eventually he confided in Květa, who made a quick trip out there with his parents in the summer. She got upset and told him he was crazy, did he realize what could have happened to him? Josef didn't pay much attention to her reaction. He was still mainly disappointed that he hadn't seen any animals on the way back. The fact that he had probably crossed the front line twice in one day wasn't what stuck in his memory. Then Květa told him that as soon as everything settled down, they could finally get married as they had promised each other at the start of the war. As usual, Květa realized that she couldn't get too angry with him, or rather that there was no point, since it wouldn't do any good anyway. When a few days later they announced their intention to their parents, Květa's mother, a former deputy chief of the regional Sokol organization, a patriotic gymnastics club, recovered from the surprise to deliver a lengthy improvised speech, in which she emphasized that the two of them were young, in love and full of energy, which was not a particularly revelatory statement, that thank God they had all been lucky enough to survive the war, which was true, and that after the second war her generation had been through, Europe and the rest of the world had obviously learned their lesson, a claim which was boldly optimistic.

"You have a happy life ahead of you, children," said Josef's future mother-in-law. "The fact that the war has come to an end in our country, and that the American and Russian armies have come together here and defeated fascism, means that all our problems will soon be solved. You have a truly beautiful life ahead of you. Mankind has always been able to learn from its experience. Two wars in twenty years, why, that's absurd. It can't happen again. Children, you have a happy life ahead of you."

Květa's mother was rather moved by her short speech, but she noticed Josef whispering something to her daughter. Květa quietly laughed. She had eyes only for him, as they say, and it was obvious neither one of them had been listening to her at all.

AUTHOR'S NOTE

The quotation from Macrobius in the epigraph is a description of the three-headed creature at the feet of the sun god Serapis in the temple in Alexandria, from *Saturnalia*, Book I, Chapter XX, fifth century A.D.

The Bertrand Russell quotation comes from his introduction to Wittgenstein's *Tractatus Logico-Philosophicus*.

In Chapter 20, I draw on the excellent book by Miroslav Moutvic, *Pražské vzorkové veletrhy 1920–1951*. I wish to thank him here.

T. Z.

In 1999 Tomáš Zmeškal, a high school English teacher, began writing his first novel, *Milostný dopis klínovým písmem* (*Love Letter in Cuneiform*). He completed it in 2003 and spent years trying, without success, to find a publisher. Finally a friend brought it to Viktor Stoilov, founder of Torst, the most important Czech literary press to spring up after communism crumbled in 1989, and in 2008 Zmeškal's debut appeared to near-universal acclaim. It finished second in the Prague newspaper *Lidové noviny*'s Book of the Year survey of authors, editors, publishers, and critics; was shortlisted for the Magnesia Litera Award for Prose; and won both the Josef Škvorecký Prize and the European Union Prize for Literature. The novel sold more than ten thousand copies in its first three months in print and is now in a second edition—in a country of ten million people, that makes it a best-seller.

Love Letter in Cuneiform spans (although not in chronological order) the twentieth century's latter half in Czechoslovakia, from the end of World War II and the Communist Party's seizure of power in 1948 to the Party's downfall in 1989 and the years immediately following. Where is the line between sanity and insanity? Are there limits to human love? Is there God? These are a few of the lightweight questions Zmeškal explores in his novel. At its core it could be called a family saga: the story of Josef Černý, a structural engineer who ends up a political prisoner (what for we never learn: "The reason is irrelevant now," as Černý drily notes); his wife, Květa; their daughter, Alice; her husband, Maximilian; and Alice and Maximilian's son, Kryštof. Also figuring in the plot are Jiří/George, the cousin from

London, and the psychiatrist Antonín (aka Toník or Tonda) Lukavský, a family friend who serves as a linchpin to Marek Svoboda, a delusional pastry chef whose visions, scattered across three chapters, detour into the realms of philosophy, theology, and literary theory, with an excursion or two into fantastical versions of history, and a chilling foreshadowing of the surveillance-plagued society that we inhabit today. The other significant character, Hynek Jánský, isn't a family member but a close friend of both Josef's and Květa's who tears their marriage apart over the course of the most emotionally disturbing scenes in the novel.

What follows is a brief sketch of where *Love Letter in Cuneiform* fits, and doesn't fit, into the context of Czech literature. My observations come from the point of view of a translator rather than a scholar, meaning they are intended more as a suggestion of which directions to look in, which corners to peer around, than as any kind of authoritative or critical interpretation.

Most Czech reviewers sought, in their assessments of the novel, to compare Zmeškal to other successful Czech authors who have cropped up in the decades since the Velvet Revolution: Jáchym Topol, Petra Hůlová, Emil Hakl, Martin Ryšavý, Radka Denemarková, and the half-dozen or so others most often chosen to represent the "post-1989" generation at literary events, both at home and abroad. These reviews focused on the fact that Zmeškal was a new author, a "new voice" (though, at age forty-two, he couldn't rightly be called young), and that while most of *Love Letter* takes place under communism, the novel plays out in the realm of personal relationships, with history and politics as an underpinning or backdrop rather than the subject matter as such—a hallmark of post-Velvet writing, distinguishing it from the "evergreens" of late-twentieth-century Czech fiction, especially those best known in English: Milan Kundera, Ivan Klíma, Josef Škvorecký, and (to some degree) Bohumil Hrabal. Yet a few of the book's reviewers dug a little deeper, as well as farther afield, and my own feeling is that this is where the most fertile ground is to be found for contextualizing Zmeškal and his first novel. Among the Czech writers compared to Zmeškal, Jiří Gruša makes the most sense to me. Certainly there are at least surface parallels between *Love Letter* and Gruša's most famous novel, *Dotazník aneb Modlitba za jedno město a přítele* (1975; translated by Peter Kussi into English in 1982 as *The Questionnaire, or, Prayer for a Town and a Friend*), described by one Czech critic as having a "Kafkaesque labyrinthine quality and an Orwellian eeriness." Moreover, *Love Letter* shares with *The Questionnaire* a reveling in science, religion, mythology, and the surprising ways in which they overlap and intermingle. Another Czech author fascinated by the connections between science and spirituality is Martin Vopěnka, a former astrophysicist whose *Pátý rozměr* (2009; slated for publication in Hana Sklenková's English translation as *The Fifth Dimension* in 2015) includes a reflection on the relationship of meditation to black holes. Looking outside the Czech realm, how can anyone today use the word *labyrinthine* in association with literature and not instantly think of Borges? Apart from *Love Letter*'s nonlinear narrative structure (and the "forking paths" of the garden in the opening of Chapter 6), it also exhibits some Borgesian mythogenic blending of fact and fiction: as in, for example, Chapter 11, "Second Vision of Immortality," with its ingenious reimagining of the world-famous astronomical clock on Prague's Old Town Square as a time machine involving particle accelerators and decelerators (the latter a Zmeškal invention, which he found out actually existed six months after the novel was published). Finally, one author I have not seen mentioned in any Czech review: Philip K. Dick. Although on its surface the world of Zmeškal's first novel may bear little resemblance to any Dickesque reality, underneath it's roiling with more than enough paranoia and slippery identity to fill the pages of any Dick fiction.

Zmeškal was born in Prague in 1966 to a Czech mother, Anna Zmeškalová, and a Congolese father, Joseph Lukoki, making him the first "Afro-Czech" writer, as he refers to himself. His mother came from a village called Běleč, near the city of Kladno, famous as the birthplace of Czech heavy industry, with coal mining dating back to the mid-eighteenth century and iron production to the mid-nineteenth. His mother studied several foreign languages (English,

German, Spanish, French) and had a knack for them, but worked much of her life in dull office jobs dealing with foreign trade. His father was an intellectual, a student of economics, who traveled thirty-seven hundred miles overland from Léopoldville, capital of the Belgian Congo, to Conakry, in Guinea, then another thirty-two hundred miles in the air to the capital of the Czechoslovak Socialist Republic, in November 1959, under an assumed name, to win support for the soon-to-be independent Republic of Congo.

The only reason I know these facts is that Zmeškal revealed them in his third book, *Sokrates na rovníku: Rodinné reportáže* (Socrates at the equator: Family reportages), a work of literary nonfiction published in 2013. Previously, Zmeškal had shared details of his personal background only in dribs and drabs, sprinkled across interviews. (The sole reference to his African heritage in *Love Letter*, in fact— more of a nod, really—is the character Václav, who appears in Chapter 6: "'This is my brother doctor, friends,' said the pastry chef. 'And these are my friends, doctor. This is Václav,' he said, pointing to a brown-skinned African man of average height eyeing the doctor suspiciously.") In *Socrates*, however, Zmeškal recounts the years that he spent trying to track down his "prodigal father," who left Zmeškal's mother and Czechoslovakia in the late sixties, and of meeting his extended family in Congo for the first time.

As a child, Zmeškal said in an interview with *Naše rodina* in 2010, he "was always scrawling something." Still, as a teenager he ended up at a technical high school for civil engineering rather than at a *gymnázium*, studying liberal arts. "My friends saw me writing all the time and said I should go study Czech and Czech literature, but when I asked about it, I was told in no uncertain terms that I would have to join the [Socialist] Youth Union, or even the Party. And I didn't want to do that."

While Zmeškal for the most part chose to leave his personal life out of his debut, his second novel, *Životopis černobílého jehněte* (2009; Biography of a black-and-white lamb), which he wrote in 2005 and 2006, while still seeking a publisher for *Milostný dopis klínovým písmem*, contains several chapters he describes as "inspired by personal experience," though, he insisted in an interview with Radio Prague in 2012, "the main line is not autobiographical." Again the story takes place under communism, again it centers on a family, but this time the main characters are twins, Václav and Lucie, born to a Czech mother and an African father. The difficulties they face growing up black in a near-lily-white society are drawn directly from Zmeškal's own experience. In one episode of *Životopis*, for instance, a military orchestra rejects Václav because of his skin color. As Zmeškal told *Reflex* in 2010, "I auditioned for that orchestra as an amateur clarinetist, and I passed, but in the end they didn't take me because the *politruk* [Communist Party overseer] got his hands on a photo of me. It was clearly due to my origin." Still, the novel's main concern is not racism per se, but the crushing conformism that permeated every aspect of life in 1980s Czechoslovakia.

In 1987, at the age of twenty-one, Zmeškal received a permit from the authorities to leave Czechoslovakia and travel to London to marry his English girlfriend, whom he had met in Prague. Two years later, the Iron Curtain fell and the East bloc dissolved. Zmeškal's homeland was no longer a Soviet satellite. Yet he decided to stay in London, studying English language and literature at King's College, then teaching English himself and delivering the English mail. Over the next eleven years, he traveled back to Prague repeatedly, at one point remaining for a year before returning to London. Finally, in 1998, he made up his mind to resettle in his native city. As he told Radio Prague in 2012, "I'm a city person. I love the countryside, but the city is where I want to be, because I love art and culture and I love meeting people, and Prague is definitely my home, for sure." Since then he has worked as a lecturer in English literature at Charles University, as well as a translator and interpreter. He is currently employed as a high school English teacher, as well as offering private lessons in creative writing, and is at work on a third novel.

It was a genuine pleasure to find my way through the maze of Zmeškal's *Love Letter*, and I hope to be able to translate another one of his books before long.

Alex Zucker

Tomáš Zmeškal was born in Prague to a Czech mother and a Congolese father. In 1987 he left Czechoslovakia to live in London, where he studied English language and literature at King's College, University of London. He returned to Prague after the collapse of communism, in the 1990s, and since then has worked mainly as a writer, a university and high school teacher of the English language and contemporary English and American literature, and a teacher of creative writing. He has published two novels, one work of literary nonfiction, radio plays, and short stories. His works have been translated into nine languages. He is active in the Czech PEN Club and is a cofounder of the Czech Writers Association. Apart from writing, he paints. His debut novel, *Milostný dopis klínovým písmem* (*Love Letter in Cuneiform*), won the Josef Škvorecký Prize and the European Union Prize for Literature. His second novel, *Životopis černobílého jehněte* (Biography of a black-and-white lamb), was shortlisted for the Josef Škvorecký Prize. His most recent book, *Sokrates na rovníku: Rodinné reportáže* (Socrates at the equator: Family reportages), is a work of literary nonfiction about his search for his father.

Alex Zucker has translated novels by Jáchym Topol, Petra Hůlová, Patrik Ouředník, and Heda Margolius Kovály. From 1990 to 1995 he lived in Prague, working for the Czechoslovak News Agency and *Prognosis*, the country's first English-language newspaper. In 2014 he was commissioned to create new subtitles for *Closely Watched Trains*, the 1966 Czechoslovak New Wave classic based on the Bohumil Hrabal novella. His essay "O Pioneer! Michael Henry Heim and the Politics of Czech Literature in English Translation" appeared in *The Man Between: Michael Henry Heim and a Life in Translation* (Open Letter). In addition to his translation work, he coedited the volume *Reconstructing Atrocity Prevention* (Cambridge University Press). Among the honors he has received are an English PEN Writing in Translation Award, an NEA Literature Fellowship, and the ALTA National Translation Award. He currently serves as cochair of the PEN America Translation Committee.